RAVANA

Book 2

Jacquelyn Bishop

Ebook ISBN : 978-1-80623-705-0

Paperback ISBN : 978-1-80623-706-7

Table of Contents

PROLOGUE

Snow fell in fine, swirling veils over the black stone walls of Ravana, softening the edges of a place built more for power than comfort. Inside its walls, the bitter winds howled through the corridors like wolves at the door, but no one dared to speak above a whisper unless summoned. Not in the house of Laird Kenneth Ruthven.

He was young—no more than five and twenty—but already feared as a man without mercy. The castle had grown colder since his marriage to Meg, the sweet lass with starlight in her eyes and quiet strength in her spine. No longer. That light had been bruised, beaten, broken. And on this night, even the New Year Mass could not reach the stones of Ravana.

Richard Buchanan lay in the darkened bed, his breath curling in the frozen air. Steward to the laird, husband to Meg's dear friend Moira—and yet, at this moment, lost to everything but the ache of his heart. He should not have come. But when Meg had slipped into the courtyard, he could no more have resisted than stopped the tide.

She came through the falling snow, cloak drawn tight, her face pale beneath the flickering torchlight. He saw the bruise at her temple. His hands curled into fists.

They did not speak at first. The wind carried every word too easily in this cursed place. But when he stepped forward and wrapped his plaid around her shoulders, their eyes met—and the rest of the world fell away. One kiss. Just one, stolen like breath in the cold, before sense returned.

"I must go," she whispered.

"I know."

He pulled free the silver and sapphire brooch that bore his family crest and pinned it to the plaid. "For warmth," he said. But they both knew it was more than that.

5

They did not hear the bootsteps crunching in the snow behind them.

From the shadows, Bram watched with narrowed eyes. When they parted, he stepped forward and plucked the abandoned plaid from the ground.

By the time Meg returned to her chambers, Laird Kenneth was already waiting.

There were no words. No accusations. Only his fists, his belt, and then worse.

* * *

Richard slept fitfully, unaware of the evil already done.

But in the Great Hall, Bram delivered the plaid into the laird's hands.

And Kenneth Ruthven smiled.

The room was dark. The dying embers of the fire cast a red glow as Richard lay in bed, staring at the shadows as they moved across the walls in a demonic dance. He tried to relax so that he could drift off, but despair enveloped him like the darkness of the night. Kenneth's sneering, hectoring voice haunted him. The crushing weight of his failure oppressed him. *I am a fool,* he berated himself. *Nothing but a blind, stupid fool.* He had sworn to protect Meggie from Kenneth. What had ever made him think that he could? He could not bear to think what had happened when he had left them alone in the laird's room.

Moira sighed beside him, snuggling into the hollow of his shoulder. He could hear her breathing in the slow, even rhythm of sleep, and looked down upon her sleeping form. Her head rested so trustingly against his shoulder, and he breathed in the faint scent of her. And now he had placed her, and their unborn child, in danger as well. A fresh wave of misery and guilt threatened to engulf him, but he fought it off. *I must not allow this desperation to get the better of me. I must find a way to protect them all.* He thought of Meg, alone at Ken's cruel hands, and he was filled with anger, and a new determination to dig deeper within himself. Somehow, he would help her. His arm tightened protectively around Moira. Somehow, he would safeguard and shield them, to his last breath, if need be.
* * * *

Richard struggled to awaken from the nightmare. His heart drummed against his ribs in a frantic, aching tattoo. He gasped for air. A bead of sweat trickled from his hairline, and he quickly wiped it away as he came to the realization that it had only been a dream. The night had been full of dark, disturbing dreams. They all highlighted Moira or Meg in mortal danger, and him trying futilely to rescue them. Each time he hastened to save them, his efforts went all wrong. He could not seem to run, or he would trip, or lose his way. Or he would reach them, only to discover that he'd been tricked, and there was nothing but a child's rag doll, and Kenneth laughing derisively at him.

The overwhelming sense of helplessness pressed down upon him like a physical weight, and stayed with him long after the dreams had passed.

* * * *

The new vicar, the right Reverend Edmund Corrie by name, arrived at the castle and was settled in Father William's old quarters. He was young and enthusiastic, and immediately assumed his duties there. He began instructing the castle and the village populace in the Protestant faith, but he could see that it was not going to be an easy road for him.

Father William was tended to in his new quarters near the kitchen by the maids, and visited daily by Richard. He said Mass in his tiny room every morning in the predawn hours, attended by trusted servants, loyal knights and their ladies. Neither Kenneth, nor the new chaplain saw, heard, nor suspected.

* * * *

A messenger arrived a few days after the new year had begun with a letter for Meg from Gladstone Castle. Meg was sitting at her dresser while Eleanor braided her hair when the knock came.

"Enter," she called.

The servant stepped inside and put the missive into Meggie's outstretched hand. Meg recognized the writing immediately.

"Thank ye, Aggie," she said. "Is the messenger who brought this letter still about?"

"Nay, m'lady, the laird sent him away immediately."

"Oh," Meggie sighed disappointedly. "Och, well, then, ye may go, Aggie."

She curtsied and left the room.

Moira, who was sitting in the alcove by the window, embroidering tiny animals on a baby's gown, looked up. "Who is the letter from?" she asked.

" 'Tis from my mother," Meg answered eagerly. As she hastily tore open the seal and began to read aloud:

December 30, 1564

My Dearest Daughter,

I write this letter in the hopes that it finds ye and Moira happy and in good health.
We had a pleasant Twelve Christmas Days. Winter has set in, and all the fields are snowed under. It has been very cold, but we are all well and warm within the castle.

Gilly, our dear child, and your beloved cousin, has been married to Sir Thomas Munro earlier this month. The wedding was planned hastily, and held in the chapel here at Gladstone Castle. We did our best for her, poor child. We ken that she had hoped for someone younger, but we ken that Sir Thomas will be good to her, and hope that she will be happy.

Even though we are many here at Gladstone, our home seems empty now without my three girls. May God be good to you in this coming new year. Your father and brother sends their love.

Mother

Meg sat silently at her dresser by the fire, confused by her mother's message. *What is this?* she wondered. *Gilly married, and so quickly? And to Sir Thomas Munro, Father's best friend? He is so much older than Gilly! What has sanctioned this turn of events?*

"What d'ye make of it?" Meggie queried, looking up from the letter toward Moira. "Och, what is it?" she cried suddenly, at Moira's stricken expression. For when Meg had begun to read the words, Moira had felt her body turn cold.

Her face flushed a deep scarlet when Meg turned to her, then drained of all color. Meg jumped up and ran to kneel beside her. Moira looked as if she were about to faint, and pressed her palm protectively over her middle, as if to shield the child from what she knew. She took a deep breath to calm herself. She could guess why Gilly had been so hastily married. The very thought sent chills through her. She had, after all, told her that she had spent the night of Meg's wedding with

9

Richard. Moira closed her eyes. *No!* She willed it not to be so, even as her heart squeezed with the knowledge of the truth.

"Is it the baby? Are ye ill?" Meg asked, looking worriedly into her face.

Moira rested her eyes on the parchment Meg still clutched in her hand. Anger, mixed with resentment prickled up her spine, and the desire to snatch the paper away, to crumple it and throw it into the fire, nearly mastered her. But caution prevailed. Barely able to hide her trembling, she cleared her throat. "I'm all right...'tis nothing." Her mouth was dry, and her voice sounded little more than a croak. "Some water..."

Meg hurried to the ewer of water on the table, and poured her a cup. "Here," she said, handing it to her. Moira drank it slowly, giving herself time to recover sufficiently. " 'Tis nothing," she repeated.

Meg was not so sure. She bit her lip, and exchanged a worried glance with Eleanor. She decided not to press the issue, for fear of upsetting Moira even more. Instead, she asked quietly, "what d'ye think of my mother's news?"

" 'Tis a surprise, indeed," Moira answered dully, staring at the floor. "I-I think I will go down to the kitchen and have some peppermint tea." She rose from her chair.

"All right, then," Meg said. "D'ye wish me to ring for it? They can bring it to ye here."

"Och, nay," Moira told her, wishing only to get away from Meg's probing eyes and worried expression.

* * * *

Moira hurried down the stairs and into the kitchen, which was abustle with life. Cook boys, scullions and various underlings rushed through the hot, humid air, rattling pans, stirring stews, slaving over potatoes and vegetables. In the dimly lit pantry alcove, a washer woman splashed water around the floor with a mop.

Mrs. Campbell stood before the long table, watching two girls knead the bread. Beyond that, Bram was leaning against a huge, sweating stone colonnade, talking with Leah, his wife. He looked up when Moira entered the room.

"Mistress Campbell," she asked. "May I have some peppermint tea? My stomach seems a bit upset this morning."

Mrs. Campbell nodded to one of the underlings who promptly fetched it for her. She took the warm drink gratefully, and went back into the Hall, sipping the soothing brew as she walked.

Bram followed her, but stopped in the doorway. "M'lady?" he called softly. He stood, holding his hat with both hands, twisting it around.

She turned toward him. "Aye?" she asked, her face upturned in question. "What is it, Bram?"

When she said his name, his arms prickled and his knees went weak. Her voice sounded lyrical to his ears, it flowed as gently as a stream through his mind, yet its eroding effect upon him was devastating, washing away every thought but one. He wanted her. But he knew that he could never have her. Their stations were too far apart. And, of course, they were married to others. And that thought brought him back to Richard. Richard, who did not deserve her. He could feel the anger against him rise like bile in the back of his throat. *How I hate him!*

"Bram?" Moira said softly, tilting her head toward him. "Did ye have something ye wanted to say to me?"

Her gentle voice called him back from his thoughts, and he swallowed back the bitterness in his voice. His eyes looked upon her with genuine compassion, and he took a few steps toward her. "M'lady, I am afraid that I have some distressing news for ye."

"Aye?" she whispered uneasily.

She is so beautiful, Bram thought, *I canna allow Richard to hurt her.* He took a deep breath and pulled himself erect. "I have seen yer husband in the garden with another." The cup slipped from her hands and shattered on the stone floor. She felt as if someone had poured icy water down her back. "I-I dinna understand..." she stammered, shaken. His ferret eyes held her motionless, like a small bird in the shadow of a great hawk.

"It was Hogmany. When he left the dance. He met her in the garden. I followed them. He gave her his plaid. I saw them kiss."

Moira blanched. "Who?" she breathed.

"The lady of the castle."

"Nay! I dinna believe ye! Ye dinna ken what ye are saying!" she protested, rebuking him with a quivering voice. She shook her head stubbornly, refusing to look at him. But deep inside, she knew that it only confirmed what she had already suspected.

" 'Tis true, m'lady," he answered. "Ask him, if ye can trust him not to lie to ye." He lowered his eyes and bowed. "I dinna wish to cause ye pain. I only thought that ye should know."

"I-I…" her voice faltered, and her lips trembled.

Bram could see the hurt in her eyes, and the lines of his face grew bitter and hard. *Damn Richard to Hell!* How he ached to be the one to give her comfort. "I am sorry--"

She gave a small gesture to quiet him. There was silence in the room, except for the crackle of the roaring fire, and the sound of his words ringing in her ears. Moira raised one hand to her temple and rubbed it, as if a headache were beginning there. "Ye must excuse me," she said, the words choking in her throat. "I am not feeling verra well." And she turned toward the stairs.

* * * *

Her thoughts ran unchecked, Bram's words echoing through her head, as she ran blindly toward the shelter of her room. *Richard and Meg, Richard and Meg, her husband and her mistress…her friend…*

She rounded the corridor and saw Meg coming out of her chamber, and stopped short beside her own door. Moira did not say the things that she was thinking, but only glared at her with stifled resentment.

"Are ye all right, Moira?" Meg asked, her voice full of concern at the expression on her face. She reached out to her, but Moira pulled away from her touch.

"Leave me alone," Moira said, her voice unsteady. "And stay away from Richard, too. He is my husband, not yers. I've seen the way ye look at him. He belongs to me, and I willna have ye come between us!"

With that, she pulled the latch and stepped inside, slamming the door behind her. Then she leaned back, bracing herself against the door, as the hated tears began to fall. She buried her face in her hands and wept, as her knees bent and she slid slowly to the floor.

Meg stood alone in the corridor. She listened to Moira's pitiful sobs, and wondered what had caused such an outburst. Mary's words came back to her once again: "Ye must have the courage to live with things the way they are." Oh, but she was trying! Hadn't she sent Richard away that night in the garden? And he had gone, knowing that it was the right thing to do. *Didn't that count for something? What could have upset Moira so?*

* * * *

Moira had wept after closing herself into the safety and privacy of her own room...but not for long. She stood and pulled herself together. She fussed nervously about the room during the afternoon, dry-eyed, and waited for Richard, her mind full of what Bram had told her. Her doubts swirled around her in an endless eddy, and she reminded herself of the reason that Richard had married her. Not because he was in love with her, but so that she could stay with Meggie. He had said as much. And she had accepted, knowing then the place that she held in his heart. And what had that gesture brought to any of them? She felt further removed from Meg than if she had remained at Gladstone. She longed to speak with someone, to share her feelings, her confusion. Obviously, she could not talk to Meg. Should she confide in Mary, her sister-in-law? Did she really want anyone else to know? If she told Mary, perhaps she would only succeed in driving a wedge between all of them: herself and Mary, herself and Richard, Richard and Mary...no, the complications ran too deep, turning her stomach into knots.

Finally, she heard the latch lift, and turned toward it, as Richard stepped inside. Immediately he sensed her mood, and knew that something was wrong.

"Moira? What is it, mo cridhe?"

"Where have ye been?" she demanded sharply.

13

He looked at her curiously. "I've just come from doing the castle logs. Why? What ails ye?"

Her expression was reproachful. "Are ye sure that ye havena been with Meggie?" she asked, knowing how childish the words sounded. Her voice quavered, despite her attempt to sound calm, and she could feel the tears burning behind her eyes. But she refused to give into them. She did not want to cry! She closed her fingers in the voluminous skirts of her gown to keep from grabbing Richard by his shirt and shaking him with all her might.

He was shocked by her outburst. "Of course not," he told her. "Who has told ye such a thing? Come, this canna be good for the child." He reached down and tugged her wrist until she released her grip on her gown, then took her by the hand. But she bent her head and looked away from him, barricading her mind against the tenderness in his voice.

She pulled her hand away from his and stepped back, glaring at him with open suspicion. "Bram told me that he saw the two of ye together in the garden the night of the New Year's Eve dance. He said ye gave her yer plaid...and that ye kissed her. Is it true?"

Bram! Now he knew who had watched them in the garden. But he could only look at Moira, unable to think of a suitable reply. He felt a pang, a deep and reproachful hurt in his heart at the expression she turned on him. He opened his mouth several times as he searched for the right words.

She stared at him, waiting, while he hesitated. She could tell from the look on his face that he couldn't decide what to say. Her rage slowly broke through the numbness, and she flared at him accusingly. "Have ye nothing to say in yer own defense? Is that what happened to yer plaid that night? And the brooch? Ye gave them to her? What else happened?"

He glanced away from her reproachful eyes, as a tinge of red crept up from his throat to his cheeks. "Nothing. Nothing happened. There is naught between us." His voice sounded empty and hollow to him.

"Tell me the truth, Richard, whatever it is. That should be the easiest answer to come by."

" 'Tis true, I did talk with her in the garden that night. I saw her leave the Hall, and she looked so distressed. I was concerned. She was crying when I found her. I merely tried to comfort her. We did nothing. It was verra cold that night. D'ye remember? I wrapped my plaid around her shoulders because she was shivering. I left her there--" *With her heart breaking, and mine as well,* he thought bitterly. "I came back inside. D'ye not remember?" He shook his head. "I dinna ken what happened to my plaid after that," he added offhandedly, and knew his words must sound lame. "Please, Moira, ye must believe me. Dinna fret yerself, for the sake of our babe. I love ye, lass."

The truth? Perhaps--but all of it? She weighed the sound of his voice, his expression, and the fact that he didn't meet her gaze, and came to her own conclusions. "Do ye?" she asked him, a lick of sarcasm in her voice. She felt as hollow as a dead tree. "What of the kiss?"

The words hung in the air between them, sharp and cutting as a razor's edge.

Richard's heart pounded painfully in his chest. His lungs burned for air, and he suddenly realized that he was holding his breath. He did not want to lie to her, but he did not wish to hurt her, either. He drew a hesitant breath. "I merely tried to comfort her, as a father would a child." The pain he saw in her eyes made him feel sick inside. "Please, Moira, forgive me." The gaze he bent on her was serious and steady. "I promise ye, Moira, I will never be untrue to ye."

She glared back at him without saying a word. Did she believe him? Could she trust him? In her heart a cold wind began to blow, and it frightened her. She turned away from him suddenly, her shoulders slumping.

Tentatively Richard came up behind her. She didn't move, even when he slipped his arms about her. He could feel her tremble against him. Gently, he rested his cheek against her hair.

"I'm sorry, a leannan," he murmured into her ear. "Please forgive me."

She turned then, and wrapped her arms tightly about him, resting her head against his chest. She could hear his heart beat steadily against her cheek, and her trembling eased a bit. What choice did she have?

* * * *

Richard and Moira reached an uneasy silence that day. They behaved as usual, but there lingered in the air a vague sense of injury and constraint. Things were not yet healed between them. She had forgiven him, but their words still hung in the air in memory, not to be easily forgotten.

Richard finally chose to confront Bram about his part in it. He made his way across the courtyard to the stables, and found Bram in the paddock, exercising the horses.

"MacKenzie!" he called, leaning over the fence rail. "I'll have a word with ye."

"What d'ye want, Buchanan? I'm busy," he said, without turning around.

"Give over to the lads. I'll speak with ye now."

Bram turned, acutely aware of the tone of his voice. "Jasper," he said to the man beside him. "Take over."

Reluctantly he walked toward Richard. "Aye?" he said.

They stood facing each other from the opposite sides of the fence. "Perhaps we could talk somewhere more private?" Richard asked.

Bram set his face grimly, and gestured inside, leading him into the tack room. It was empty, save for the table and the tack. He smiled affably enough, but Richard could see the small lines of ruthlessness around his mouth, and the touch of arrogance in the set of his shoulders. "All right, here we are. Why dinna ye tell me what this is about?" Bram looked him over disapprovingly.

"I hear ye've been talking with my wife," Richard began. "Seems ye've been spying on me."

A sudden gleam came into Bram's ferret eyes. "Aye, I suppose ye could call it that. I only told her what I ken she had a right to know."

"I'll thank ye to keep out of my business, and keep to yer own. Stay away from my wife."

The line of Bram's mouth tightened, and a deep crease at the corner grew deeper, but he didn't say anything. A small muscle jumped on the side of his neck. Finally, he replied insolently, "And what if I choose not to?"

Richard seized him by the shirt, twisting his hands into the material, yanking him towards him, and shaking him slightly. "I ought to run ye through, ye insolent bastard!" he said through clenched teeth. "D'ye ken the harm ye've done?" His face was flushed with fury and he breathed deeply, inhaling the scent of Bram's sweat.

"The harm *I've* done?" Bram shouted back, the blood rising to his face. "It was *ye* who did the harm! Ye should take yer own advice, and stay away from her ladyship, before ye find yerself on the wrong end of the laird's sword!" he spat at him.

Richard shook him again, this time in earnest. Bram's head jerked violently, and his teeth clacked together, making him bite his tongue.

"Get yer damned hands off me!" Bram shouted, struggling to escape his grip. "Let go!"

Slowly, Richard's hands relaxed. He pushed him back a pace, panting with emotion. Bram was right. He himself had caused the problem. That bit of babble had reached home. He stared at him, and his eyes narrowed for a moment, debating what to do next.

Bram's lips twitched. "Are ye quite finished, yer lordship?" His voice was cold. "Ye should curb that temper of yers."

Richard did not reply, but only snorted briefly as they stood glaring at each other. He did, at last, break the silence.

"If ye ever speak to my wife again," he warned him, his words slow and deliberate, "I will kill ye." He gazed at him levelly. "Watch yer back." With that, he turned on his heel and walked down the corridor, without a backward glance.

"Watch yer own," Bram replied under his breath as he watched him go.

* * * *

The work on the castle lands had resumed once again after the Christmas holidays. They were, however, marked with special ceremonies. On Plow Monday, the first Monday after Epiphany, the sixth of January, also known as the feast of the Magi, a plow race was held, beginning at sunrise, amongst the men of the village who plowed part of the castle's pasture which was to be cultivated for the coming year. Each man tried to draw a furrow in as many different strips as he could. The ridges that he marked he would sow for the laird that year, and glean the remaining grain for his family.

Another custom was Fool's Plow, which the youth of the town joined in. A group of young plowmen hauled a plow through the village, asking for pennies from door to door. Their leader, a dark lad, dressed as an old woman whom they called Bessie, wore a bullock's tail under his gown. Another youth accompanied them, wearing a fox's skin as a hood, and another, dressed as a fool, carried a stack and a bladder. Children skipped merrily along with them, and in the evening, they held a bonfire in the village square.

Little real plowing was done until Candlemas, February the second. It was a holiday, formerly known as "The Feast of the Purification of the Virgin," which the villagers had always celebrated with a procession, carrying candles. But since the laird had returned from court and forbidden all Catholic observances, they merely changed the name and carried on as before.

* * * *

Meanwhile, letters from court arrived in a steady stream. Kenneth's uncle, Lord Patrick, was incensed by the way things were going in Edinburgh.

Darnley had arrived at Wemyss Castle on Valentine's Day. The queen had been immediately taken with him, and welcomed him into her favored circle of friends and attendants who shared her informal musical evenings, suppers, and card parties. They would sit together in the evenings in the queen's private chambers, where Darnley played the lute, and he and Riccio sang before the fire. "The queen was caught up in his snare," Lord Patrick insisted vehemently. "Darnley is with her always, he has become her lap dog. He is a long lad, beardless and lady-faced. The Lords have had much speculation as to what Elizabeth could have been thinking, allowing him to come north. He is Catholic, but it is obvious that he is not a zealous one. The majority of the Lords seem to dismiss him as a lightweight. All but the queen's brother, James, Maitland, and myself, that is. Darnley has dined with Lord James, and attended one of Master Knox's sermons with him, which implies that, Catholic though he might be, he has some idea of political strategies. His pretty face and pretty manners mask something more dangerous, I fear. The cardinal of Lorraine calls him 'an agreeable nincompoop.' But such characters have a way of becoming a threat when thrust into serious situations. He is headstrong and ambitious. He has always been spoken of as a possible husband for the queen, but very low on the list. I fear the worst."

And the litany of countless intrigues did not stop there. It was also clear how Lord Patrick felt about Riccio, the queen's little Italian secretary. The Lords of the Congregation had sent Melville to inform the queen that the people of Scotland did not like or trust Riccio. "They are using that deadly word 'spy' to describe him, but the queen does not listen to her counsel, and continues to favor him, as she does Darnley."

Each letter seemed to enrage Kenneth more. He would closet himself with Richard for hours at a time when one arrived, and when they would emerge, Richard would always seem worried. The laird obviously sided with his uncle and the Lords of the Congregation against the queen, and Richard had no idea where it would all lead. He only knew that it did not bode well.

Then one day, late in February, a messenger from the queen arrived. He was taken immediately to Lord Ruthven, who was with Richard, discussing the accounts ledger from the month of January, each column neatly tallied to the last farthing. The messenger was told to deliver the missive personally to the laird, who thanked him.

Kenneth did not recognize the writing upon the scroll, but he did indeed know the messenger. He anxiously broke open the heavy seal. As he read, a smile brightened his handsome face. It was an invitation to the wedding of Mary Livingston, one of the queen's ladies-in-waiting, to Lord John Sempill. It was to be held at Holyrood, on Shrove Tuesday, March 6, 1565.

The laird was ecstatic to be counted among the wedding guests.

"My wife and I have been invited to court for a wedding!" he said, clapping Richard on the back. "We will take but a small retinue with us for safety, while ye and Rees and the others will stay behind to guard Ravana." He began to plan the trip. "We will leave a few days early, so as to have a few days visit with my uncle and cousin." He laughed. "Och, 'twill be grand!"

Richard was not so sure how grand it was to become a part of the clashing elements at court. He stifled the sense of dread that griped him by the throat. There was a faint flicker of unease in his blue eyes. "I believe it is wise for me to remain here," he agreed. "My wife is with child, and I dinna think the journey would do her any good. Besides, it is time for the work in the fields to begin in earnest now. I was away for yer marriage in the autumn, and I fell so far behind in the accounts."

At the mention of the child, Kenneth's expression grew dark, and he surveyed him coldly. "We will begin our travels shortly. Go now and prepare for it." He waved his hand in dismissal.
* * * *

Richard knelt before the fire in his chamber, adding kindling to the flames as Moira entered, and sat down heavily upon their bed. "Och, I am so weary."

"Long day in the solar with the other ladies, mo cridhe?" Richard said with a smile, as he rose and came to sit beside her. He began to rub the small of her back, and she sighed blissfully.

"Och, that feels good. I should like to forget supper and just rest here."

"So would I, a leannan, but I have work to do. Kenneth and Meg have been invited to a wedding at Court. I must prepare for their departure." He looked back at his wife. "Ye look a bit pale, mo cridhe. Mayhap ye should lie down."

He stood as she brought her legs up on the bed and laid back. She settled her head comfortably on the pillow and closed her eyes.

Richard poured some water from the ewer into the basin on the bedside table and sluiced his hand in it, then smoothed his fingers over Moira's cheeks.

"Better, my love?"

She opened her eyes and smiled up at him.

"Aye."

A tiny fluttering sensation in her abdomen startled her. "What was that?" she gasped, placing her hands lightly over her stomach in wonderment.

Richard raised a questioning eyebrow, and cupped his hand over the small round swell of her belly protectively. "Did it hurt ye?" he asked.

A slow, knowing smile lit her face. "Nay," she said, as a series of quick movements rippled inside her. She giggled, her lethargy vanished. " 'Tis life I am feeling."

* * * *

Kenneth and Meg set out early on the last day of February with their small retinue. The journey to Edinburgh would be slow, as it had been a bleak and exceptionally cold winter, and the snow still lay upon the ground.

But Kenneth looked forward to his trip to court. They arrived safely the next day and were welcomed heartily into his uncle's home where they visited for a few days before the wedding.

After the wedding there were three days of masqueing, feasting and hunting at Hollyrood Palace and grounds, the celebrations came to an end. Kenneth said his good-byes to his uncle and cousin, hoping to return to court again soon. Then he, Meg and their small entourage made their way back to Ravana.

CHAPTER THIRTY-FIVE

There would be no Lenten Season this year. Not the way they were used to keeping it, anyway, with the cross and holy images of the castle and parish church shrouded in purple veils. On Palm Sunday, the parishioners would not carry the familiar yew twigs in procession, following the Host and Cross to the Kirk yard. On Good Friday, the Cross would not be unveiled and set upon the steps of the altar, and the fragrant smoke of incense would not be burned while the congregation came forward to reverently kiss it, kneeling and bowing low. The Host would not be "buried" then, in a special Easter sepulcher in the wall of the castle chapel or village church, surrounded with candles. All the familiar ceremony was gone. They would not extinguish the candles and fires on Easter Eve, a new fire ceremonially kindled as the great Pascal candle was lit during an all-night vigil in the church. There would be no ceremonial opening of the church sepulcher, and the Cross and Host carried to the altar. Ravana was now a Protestant household. Edmund Corrie was doing his best to see to that. Easter would no longer be a day of exchanges, like Christmas, between Laird and tenants. In the past, the tenants had brought baskets of eggs, and received a celebratory feast. The week following would no longer be celebrated with games and tilting at the quintain.

The long weeks of fasting, which coincided with the slack season when provisions were running out, had always been brought to close by the Easter cycle, celebrated with the famous eggs, rediscovered with pleasure after the long fast. But now the eggs, the hallowed bread, the green boughs of Palm Sunday, and all the other marks of celebration were gone. Outwardly, anyway. Father William continued to observe the Lenten season in his small rooms off the kitchen, joined there by the faithful of Ravana.

Laird Kenneth spent his days hunting and hawking with his falcon, Juno. And he spent his nights visiting the town's public houses for his drunken midnight carousing.

Word from court of Lord Darnley's illness, and Mary's growing fondness of him, reached Ravana. Darnley had first suffered with a bout of the ague, to be swiftly followed by the measles, and nearly left the world. It was said that the queen cared for him in the sickroom herself. The Lords of the Congregation had found the whole situation insufferable.

* * * *

Meanwhile, life at Ravana proceeded along normally. The blossoms of the Spring intermingled with the grasses of the green of the meadow, nodding among the new, thin blades, luring a profusion of colorful butterflies, skipping and flitting in the warming air.

One afternoon after dinner, the women retired to the solar with their needlework, threads, and frames, as was their usual custom. They settled themselves in their semicircle around the fire, and the pleasant hum of conversation filled the room. Gabriel soon joined them with his lute. He sat upon his stool near the fire, and began to strum and sing softly, accompanying them with his melodies, his music soothing and calm.

While the others worked diligently, Eleanor tried to sew, but she didn't seem to be able to keep her mind on what she was doing. Dinner had seemed tasteless to her. Now she sat trying to concentrate on her embroidery, but her eyes were tired, and she was having trouble focusing. Everything in the pattern reminded her of Gwyllyn. She jabbed her needle in and out of the cloth, but the orangey-red thread that she pulled through the panel called to mind the color of his hair, and the green silk that twined into vines and leaves, the color of his eyes. She had thought of him many times during these last few days. She closed her eyes and felt him with her once again.

"Eleanor? Eleanor? Are ye all right?"

"Hmmm?" she asked, startled out of her reverie. "Och, aye, m'lady, I am fine."

She busied herself with her embroidery once again, but it took all of her effort just to pull the needle through the thick canvas. This lethargy, this weakness, made her feel very strange. She tried to concentrate on Gabriel's silky strains, but suddenly felt a sharp twinge in her lower abdomen. It came and went swiftly. But a few minutes later another came, and this one rippled across her belly, taking its

23

time before it too disappeared. Before Gabriel had finished the last verse of the song, which he had begun at her first stab of pain, a third one had come. It seemed to begin in her lower back and radiate to her lower abdomen. She moaned. This time she knew. It was a labor pain.

Gabriel stopped playing and looked up. Mary also heard the soft moan and looked up from her sewing. Eleanor was clutching her embroidery hoop tightly, her eyes wide. Everyone knew immediately what was happening. The birth pains were starting.

Mary was already at her side. "Come," she said gently, taking her arm.

"No," Eleanor whispered, a look of panic on her face. She dropped her sewing and clutched at her belly as if expecting to discover something. Just then she felt the pressure building again. "The baby…he's coming…"

"Aye," Moira smiled.

"See if ye can stand up," Mary told her. "We must get ye to bed." She pulled Eleanor's arm around her neck and wrapped her own arm about her waist to support her. Her legs felt surprisingly boneless. Before she had taken very many steps, there was a sudden gush of fluid as her water broke.

"Och, no," Eleanor wailed.

"Och, now dinna ye worry," Meg told her soothingly. "Let's just get ye to yer own chamber where ye can lie down and rest."

Meg put a supportive hand beneath her elbow and helped her to stay on her feet and walk slowly across the room. They managed to get her to bed and settled her as comfortably as they could.

She waited, holding her breath for the next pain. Pain that she must face alone, now that Gwyllyn wasn't here. No, not entirely alone. She had Mary, Moira, and even her mistress, the lady of the castle with her. Suddenly, all the debilitating languor disappeared, and she knew there was only one thing she wanted, and cared about passionately. Gwyllyn's child. By the saints, she wanted this babe! She'd suffered for it already, what did the pain matter, when she'd be able to hold the child in her arms at the end of it? Much heartened, she settled back against the pillows to rest until the next spasm came.

Meg and Moira folded the linens and placed them under Eleanor's hips as the pains came and went. Copper pans clinked together as they were made ready to heat the water.

It seemed to Eleanor, in those brief moments when she could think clearly, that climbing into her bed had somehow caused her labor to speed up. The pains continued, strong and vigorous, and ever more frequently. Her face contorted with the pain, and she held her breath, making little noise as she writhed with their ebb and flow.

Perspiration broke out over her forehead and upper lip as another pain filled her body. Meg sat beside the bed, timing the contractions and speaking soothingly to her, trying to keep her calm. "Breathe, Eleanor, ye mustn't hold yer breath with the pains. Breathe."

She held her hand, and put cool cloths on her head, drenched in lavender scented water, to help cool her body and face. Moira and Meg took turns massaging her lower back when she complained about the pressure she felt there. The birth process continued relentlessly, and she became completely absorbed in her part in it. Meg encouraged her to relax between the contractions, but it became increasingly difficult as the pains became more frequent. She labored on through the evening.

Moira lit the candles in the chamber as the light began to fade, but kept the light low, to give the room a restful atmosphere. Then she came to sit by Eleanor's side with Meg. She placed her hand over Eleanor's abdomen and felt it draw up and grow hard beneath her touch.

" 'Tis happening again," Eleanor whimpered, as the sensation of pain came again, wiping all other thoughts from her mind. She clutched at Moira in agony. She was beginning to feel that it would never end.

"Yer doing beautifully," Moira reassured her. "And just think, each pain brings ye closer to holding yer babe in yer arms. Think how far ye've come."

Eleanor smiled and nodded as Moira squeezed her hand reassuringly. Exhausted, sleep overcame her between contractions.

The contractions came on top of one another, and she began to feel nauseous, and alternate between feeling chilled and very warm. Her legs felt crampy and cold, and she began to tremble. She felt overwhelmed, discouraged and afraid. "I canna do this any longer," she panted.

"Och, 'tis nearly over," Meg told her, taking her hand, and hoping that she was right. "We will help ye. Ye are not alone."

The pain began to grow once again inside her. "I feel like I need to bear down with the pain," she groaned.

"Aye, ye can push now. 'Tis time," Mary told her.

Eleanor felt relieved, knowing the ordeal would soon be over, and pushed with all her strength. She let out a long, agonizing yell as the baby pushed through her. Mary could see the baby's head crown.

"That's it," Mary told her. "Just breathe now. Relax."

But as the baby's head and shoulders gradually began to emerge, Mary could see that the cord was looped around its neck. She deftly hooked her finger under it, and gently worked it over the baby's head. When the head had been delivered, she gently stroked the nose downward, the neck and under the chin upward, to help expel any excess fluid. But the baby's eyes were closed, and it did not breathe, cry or respond, as Mary rotated and guided the second shoulder free. The quiet was shattering. Eleanor gave a scream of anguish.

"No, oh God! No! My baby!" she sobbed, panicked. Meg held her and stroked her hair as they stared helplessly at Mary.

Mary quickly placed the baby on Eleanor's abdomen and began to massage its little chest, willing the breath into its tiny lungs. No response. Its tiny blue body lay inert on top of its mother.

Mary picked the baby up by its heels, still attached to its mother by the cord, and held the baby upside down. She began patting it vigorously on the back. Eleanor lay on the bed, sobbing, distraught, watching, while Meg and Moira both tried to calm her. But she would not be comforted.

Desperate, Mary hit the baby hard on the back. A plug of mucous flew out and suddenly it began coughed, gasped, and began to breathe. And then along with Eleanor's cries of joy, they could hear the baby's indignant wails.

"The Blessed Virgin be praised!" Eleanor laughed through her tears, as the baby cried out loudly, and Mary placed the baby in her arms.

"Ye have a son."

"His name is Gwyllyn," Eleanor said, cuddling him close to her, caressing his tiny hands.

Mary clamped and cut the umbilical cord, using cumin to seal it, while Moira took the baby and gave him a brisk, stimulating rubdown, then wrapped him in a blanket. Meg cleaned Eleanor and helped her into a fresh gown, and changed the soiled linens underneath her.

Moira put the infant to his mother's breast, as the tears spilled down Eleanor's cheeks. His lusty cries turned to contented gurgles as he began to suckle. Despite all the times she'd imagined this moment, used it to sustain her through all the long, difficult months, she hadn't realized how deeply she would feel its intensity. She looked up at the women with relief and gratitude. "Thank ye, Mary. Ye saved him…ye brought him back to me…thank ye all."

The baby's complexion was fair, and he had big, blue eyes like his mother, and a faint fuzz of copper colored hair upon his head.

Meg was deeply moved by the experience. It had been an amazing and enlightening time, and she recalled the look of triumph on Mary's face as she coaxed the reluctant baby into life. Her gaze focused once again upon Eleanor, and she couldn't tear her eyes away from the warm scene of mother and child. They were truly miraculous as they lay there, with Eleanor resting her cheek against the soft fuzzy head crooning soft endearments.

Moira leaned down and cupped the small downy head in her palm, eager to hold her own child in her arms, yet a little reluctant to endure what she knew she must to gain such a prize.

* * * *

Later that night, as Eleanor sat in the big bed, her child cuddled to her breast, she sighed and leaned her head back against the pillows and watched the hearth flames dance. She was lulled by the gentle smacking noises the baby made as he nursed contentedly, mesmerized by the flickering fire into a dreamy euphoria. She heard a familiar, heavy booted step in the corridor. The sound stopped just outside the door. There was the click of the latch, and the door swing open on its hinge. She closed her eyes, breathing in the well-known and well-loved scent. The footsteps continued across the floor, and the chair beside the bed creaked. She did not feel alone anymore, but warm and happy. An overwhelming sense of peace enveloped her.

"We have a son," she whispered.

CHAPTER THIRTY-SIX

Summer began with May Day celebrations, jousting and the faire. May was the month with the first blossoms on the trees and hedgerows. May was also a time for love-play, a time when the moral taboos were relaxed. On the eve of May Day, the village youths went out to the forest, which approached to within a mile of town, to cut branches, which they placed before the doors and windows of the houses where there were marriageable girls. Before daybreak, the young people of the village joined in "bringing in the May", venturing into the woods to cut wildflowers, greenery and hawthorn boughs.

The first day of May dawned blissfully warm and brilliant. The sun beamed down from a canopy of deep, tranquil blue, and filmy clouds floated on high. It looked like the cold and rains had finally come to an end. Crimson poppies amid a vivid array of wildflowers blanketed the green, swept with the warm May breezes. Bees hummed from flower to flower, while colorful butterflies flitted playfully between the blossoms. Along the muddy banks of Ravana's moat, the daisies danced in the gentle wind, while a family of swans swam gracefully by.

On the edge of the woods, colorful tents and bright pavilions had sprung up all over the green where the faire was held and the lists had been built. The large meadow was arrayed in the finest green grass, and fringed on one side with a forest of huge budding oak trees, tipped with fresh, tender green.

The lists were oblong, made of wood, with linen cloth draperies and a large wooden stand with rows of benches that stood on either side for the spectators on this occasion. Decorated with shields and paintings, pennons and banners of red, black and yellow above the tents, along the lists, and over the red and black canopy erected to shade the ladies and their attendants from the bright sunlight.

The openings for the entries of the combatants was at either end of the lists, wide enough to admit two horsemen riding abreast. There was a herald stationed at each opening, attended by three trumpeteers, and a strong body of men-at-arms for maintaining order, and to see that rules of the tournament were obeyed.

Just beyond the southern entrance to the lists were the tents containing refreshments of every kind for the spectators and combatants alike. Behind the tents, cooks toiled to roast fat sheep and huge oxen. The mouthwatering aroma of roasting meats, freshly baked breads, and pies stuffed with pork and raisins, filled the air.

Nearby, pints of ale were set out to tempt the coins from the thirsty crowd. There were also farriers, armorers, and other attendants, ready to offer their services, whenever they might be needed.

Colorful booths with bright pennants flying dotted the south green by early morning. Merchants hawking their wares, offering every manner of wondrous thing, along with the jesters, jugglers and palmers wandered the grounds. People milled about, ladies dressed in beautiful gowns, escorted by gentlemen in elaborately trimmed tunics, strolled through the maze of tents, peddlers and soothsayers. Musicians and wandering troubadours roamed the green, singing their songs of chivalry, while young boys teased and chased girls, darting in and out of the crowds. Paupers begged for alms, and soldiers speedily found acquaintances, as they made their way through the miscellaneous assemblage.

Meg, dressed in a soft yellow beribboned gown, made her way through the crowds and vendors, amid the gaiety and color, with Moira and Mary. Eleanor, who had only delivered two weeks earlier, had stayed back in her rooms at Ravana, happily attending to young Gwyllyn.

"Look ye, Mary!" Meggie giggled, pointing to a merchant with a cartful of gloves. "There's a red pair, sure to match yer dress!"

The women stopped to inspect the beautifully embroidered merchandise. They were all the colors of the rainbow, made of silks and leather, with many different designs sewn into the fabric. Meg picked up the red silk pair that had caught her eye and held them out to Mary, who took the gloves from her and sniffed delicately. "Roses," she said with a smile. Then she slipped her hand inside, turning it this way and that to look at them. They were embroidered with tiny white silk butterflies at the wrist.

"How does it look?" she asked the others, stepping back and holding her gloved hand against her bodice. She wore a red satin gown, her bodice embroidered with floral designs.

"Och, 'tis a perfect match!" Moira told her.

"Aye," Meg intoned with an emphatic nod.

Mary shook her head, with a twinkle in her eye. "Och, and 'tis what Rees deserves, insisting that I wear red. I shall spend the money that he gave me to buy him a new silver bridle." She laughed, knowing it was exactly what he expected her to do. She reached into the purse that hung at her waist and pulled out a gold coin.

They continued on through the maze of vendors set up near the tourney grounds. There were polished wooden and ivory combs, copper kettles and spoons, bronze knives and spices from faraway lands, boots made with fine leather with embroidery on the toes, and beautiful gems of rubies, emeralds, and pearls. They stopped to laugh at a puppet show, admire the goldsmith's wares, and to examine the religious objects that were offered by a man with a big tray suspended by a leather strap around his neck.

One merchant's booth was filled with beautiful bolts of cloth, shiny brass needles, and bright ribbons of every color. They lingered, asking him to show them all his wares. He gladly pulled down all his fabrics so that they could feel the softness of them.

Meg held up a particularly large bolt of lilac brocade, draping an end across Moira's shoulder. Now, near seven months pregnant, her gowns were quite voluminous and loose, to accommodate her ever growing stomach. "It looks like there might be enough fabric here for ye to make yerself a new dress," she teased.

"Psha!" Moira answered with a playful swipe, though her eyes did linger over the material.

"Buy it," Mary told her. "Richard will not mind."

"I will," Moira said enthusiastically, her eyes sparkling. "And I shall make a new dress to wear after the babe is born, to dazzle him with." She laughed, already planning the style, and looking over the laces and worsted ribbons the vendor proffered temptingly, to go along with the material. Moira fingered a spool of delicate lace. It would certainly be a demure touch to a low décolletage.

Mary read her thoughts. "How much for the lace?" she asked.

"A shilling a length, m'lady," he answered.

"So dear!" she exclaimed, outraged. "Come, sister, surely there are other goods that will take yer fancy."

"Ye'll not find anything finer in Edinburgh itself. My wares come directly to me from France and Italy," he returned defensively.

Mary frowned, watching the smile fade from Moira's face as she turned reluctantly away.

"She'll give ye one shilling for the fabric and the laces," Mary bargained. "Not a farthing more."

"Madame, ye wound me!"

They began to barter back and forth, and finally settled on a price, while Moira eagerly chose the thread, laces and caddis ribbon she wanted, then paid the man, happily tucking her purchases under her arm.

"Madame," called a peddler behind them.

They turned to see a man standing beside his pushcart, and joined the other ladies who were crowding about the cart, softly cooing over his merchandise. His cart was full of children's toys, and they begged him to demonstrate each one.

The peddler was a young man with a flashing smile, dark hair, and tanned skin, and eyes as black as coal. He bowed low, his plaid nearly touching the grass.

"An honor, m'lady," he said, and picked up a multicolored top. Placing its pointed tip on the edge of his cart, he set it spinning. "What think ye of this?"

The crowd of women let out a collective, "Ahhh!"

"This would be a nice gift for Eleanor's baby," Meg said, picking it up as it began to wobble.

"Aye," Mary said. "In a year or so. If ye want something now, perhaps one of these rattles." She reached into a pile of small toys and came out with a brightly colored noisemaker, small enough to be held in a baby's hand.

"Of course," Meg said. "I'll have this one."

"A farthing, m'lady," the peddler said, as she pulled out her coin.

"Have ye come from Edinburgh?" Mary asked the vendor as he quickly popped the coin into his purse.

"I came from Glasgow, Madame, and lately from Crieff." He lowered his voice to a whisper. "I dared not stay there, though, not one day, for sickness had broken out."

"The sweating sickness?" Mary asked anxiously, as the icy chill of dread prickled up her spine. The sweating sickness had come to Ravana ten years ago and nearly wiped out the population of both castle and village. The old laird and his wife had succumbed, leaving Kenneth the new master. He had been away in France at the time, studying, and therefore had been spared. She and Richard had both sickened with the disease, but had been young and strong enough to recover, as had Rees, Gwyllyn and a few others. Their own parents had not been so lucky.

"Nay, Madame, but just as bad. 'Tis the plague."

"Plague! In Crieff?"

"Aye. There were ten deaths that day, I was told, if I may believe the innkeeper where I stopped for ale. I saw the telltale red ringed swellings among a few of the people I met on the streets, and hurried away as fast as I could."

"Sweet Savior," Mary groaned.

"I left town as soon as I could, and I've told everyone I've seen traveling in that direction of the news."

"Aye," she said worriedly. "'Tis good of ye to pass along the news." although her mind was on far darker thoughts, she continued examining his goods. It was disturbing to think that the plague was less than a day's journey away.

CHAPTER THIRTY-SEVEN

By ten o'clock the meadow was crowded with horsemen and people on foot, hurrying to the tournament, and shortly thereafter the grand flourish of trumpets announced that the tourney was soon to begin. The spectators thronged forward to take their places in the galleries, but not without the usual quarrels concerning the good seats.

Meg, Mary, and Moira found their place in the gallery, spread with tapestries and carpets, and fitted with cushions for the comfort of the noble ladies and gentlemen who were expected to attend the tournament. A narrow space between the galleries and lists accommodated the landowners, burghers and their families, the clerics and all those of the class considered to be the lower gentry. The remaining multitude arranged themselves upon the higher ground that surrounded the lists, or perched themselves upon the branches of the stout oak trees that surrounded the meadow. The procession would be held in midmorning, and all the knights would ride their splendid horses before the stands to greet the onlookers.

Gradually the galleries became filled with knights, nobles, and beautiful ladies colorfully arrayed with richly tinted mantles and gowns of the gayest shades. The silken dresses of the ladies were weighed down with jewelry and furs.

A scuffle broke out below where Meg, Moira, and Mary were seated, when two men began to argue over the last available seat in the gallery. It began with shouting, elevated to pushing and shoving, then quickly escalated into a fight. The men-at-arms dispatched them with brief ceremony with the shaft of one's battle axe and the pummel of the other's sword.

The lists now presented a most splendid spectacle. The sloping galleries were crowded with all that was noble, great, wealthy and beautiful in Midlothian, and the contrast of the various dresses of the spectators made the view as colorful as it was rich, while the interior and lower space, filled with the burgesses and yeomen, formed, in their plainer attire, a dark boarder around the circle of brilliant embroidery, relieving, and at the same time, setting off its splendor.

There was a great display among both spectators and the elaborately clad participants. Even the squires appeared in different costumes as the day wore on.

Young men eager for action, full of knightly aspiration and desirous to prove their skill against the challengers, rode their spirited horses back and forth to make them ready for the joust. Others passed their time in shooting with bows and arrows, hurling lances, tossing heavy stones and rocks, or playing dice and a variety of other games, invigorated by the food and drink they consumed. Young girls watched them from the barricades, the air charged with passionate excitement by their flirtatious behavior.

Earlier that morning, the men had drawn lots to determine who rode in which group of sets, and who was to ride against whom. They bantered back and forth, boasting of the feats they would perform, mocking each other's claims. Rees and Richard were chosen to ride in the first group of sets, and Moira chewed her lip nervously. She had never seen a tourney on such a grand scale.

"Mary," she whispered apprehensively, "are ye certain Richard will be safe?"

Mary smiled at her with an attempt at a confidence she did not feel. She had always hated the tournaments on May Day. "Of course he will be. Dinna fash yerself. He has trained for this sort of thing for many years. Both he and Rees are skilled jousters."

Indeed, tournaments were a highly skilled and often dangerous sport. The knights who entered the competition had had long years of apprenticeship. The manipulation of a powerful thoroughbred horse and a heavy lance, complicated by the restrictive movement and limited vision imposed by the armor, was a skill acquired only with many hours of patient practice at the quintain and the ring. She had watched them train often. She twisted her red scarf into a tight knot, recalling the skirmishes and fearsome accidents of the last tournament.

Moira watched her fidget anxiously. Arching her brow, she asked, "And ye dinna worry for Rees?"

"Nay, of course not," she answered, moving restlessly as she knotted her scarf again. "Why do ye ask?"

"Och, no reason," Moira said, pulling the mangled red silk from her hands.

Startled, Mary looked up at her and grinned sheepishly.

Suddenly the trumpets signaled the start, and a young lad dressed in Ruthven livery strode to the center of the list and began to call for all the brave knights within the sound of his voice to come together to do battle, and be judged according to their skill and prowess. Then he began to cry the rules of the tournament.

The contestants were divided into two teams. The mounted jousters were to run at each other, wooden lances tucked under their right arms, and try to break their lances against each other. Points were accorded to each man according to where he struck his opponent's body, the number of lances broken, the number of courses each man ran, the number of times a man was struck, and whether the lances were broken or not. The winner would receive a large emerald on a golden chain for his prize.

When the herald finished his proclamation, he began to shout, "Largesse! Largesse!"

That was the signal for the crowd to rain down gold and silver pieces from the galleries to the seats below. Meg, Moira and Mary took their coins and threw them out, the gold and silver twinkling in the sunlight to the flourishing sounds of many horns. The townspeople bent to gather what they could, while a yeoman called out, "Honor and glory to all the brave knights!"

When the acclamations ceased the herald withdrew from the lists, while another flourish of trumpets sounded. The knights rode by twos onto the field, with Lord Ruthven riding in the front. The glittering procession of participants into the lists was impressive as the knights presented themselves to the spectators, riding in long lines of gaily colored pageantry before the stands, their pages walking beside them in matching livery. It was a beautiful sight, to see so many gallant champions mounted so bravely and armed so richly, marching ready and prepared for an encounter so formidable, seated on their war saddles like so many pillars of iron. When viewed from the galleries they presented the appearance of a sea of waving plumage, intermixed with glistening helmets and tall lances. Their armor was lavishly trimmed with fur or fringed with gold and jewels. They wore richly embroidered garments, elaborate silks decorated with brooches and pendants, diamonds and pearls. Ostrich feather plumes, or models of bears and fowl decorated the knight's helmets. Lances were painted with beautiful designs of blues and reds, or else dipped in silver or gold that flashed in the sunlight. The field was completely covered with luxurious and elaborate arms.

Kenneth was in the lead, his large horse prancing. He was resplendent in a beautiful surcoat of red, lavishly embroidered with black and gold down the facings and around the hem. It covered most of the mail shirt except the V at the breast, and this of the very latest fashion. Rare and costly, it was made of heavy rings of metal linked together, rather than sewn into leather strips. Even his gloves had plates of metal sewn to the backs to protect his hands. His helmet was brand new undented steel, polished to a high sheen, crowned by an image of Venus, topped with a red ostrich plume. His open faceplate displayed his expression of insolence, mingled with a reckless and haughty indifference, his disposition confident in the superiority of his birth and wealth.

He caracoled a half turn to the left, laughing loudly and boldly, eyeing the beauties who adorned the lofty galleries. The splendor and richness of his costly garments, together with the grace with which he managed his horse, were enough to merit a clamorous applause. He joyously caracoled around the lists, ending in a high courbette, his horse poised on his haunches and pawing the air, before rejoining the others.

Moira spotted Richard, resplendent in green silk and velvet vestments over his armor, an emerald plume on the crest of his silver helmet, astride his magnificent large gray charger. Thunder was dressed also in silver and green, prancing and gleaming, the sun glinting off his silver trappings and green silks. The sight of them took her breath away, and her blood stirred as she watched her husband proudly.

The men circled the field, restraining their fiery steeds, and compelling them to move slowly, exhibiting their paces together with grace and dexterity. The riders reined to a stop in the center. Each man was then called forward to receive his token of affection from his chosen lady in the audience.

Kenneth was the first to be summoned. Meg leaned forward, but to her surprise and embarrassment he passed her by, and instead paraded before a group of admiring ladies. He stopped in front of a whore from the village, and lowered his lance to her, his expression openly lascivious. The crowd fell silent. Meg looked first to Moira, then to Mary on her other side, but there could be no doubt what he meant. A murmur ran through the crowd. She threw a quick look at Kenneth, but could see only his fierce helmet. *Was it common for a man to spurn his wife in such a fashion?* she wondered, and she flushed scarlet.

The whore pulled her stocking provocatively from her leg and leaned over the railing, her breasts seductively revealed. She tied it meaningfully to the point of his lance. He grinned at her, then rode away.

Meg felt a mixture of anger, embarrassment and confusion. Kenneth's public rebuff had humiliated her. Although his total disregard for what was proper should not have surprised her. How like him, after all.

When Richard rode forward and pointed his lance toward Moira, his armor glinting and sparkling in the sun, she was filled with pride. She could see that he was thoroughly enjoying himself, and with a smile, she thrust her green silk scarf forward and knotted it about the lance. Richard gave her a broad wink, then lifted the long lance in a salute as he turned his horse skillfully, guiding Thunder with his heel and his knees.

Moira's heart raced with excitement. To her surprise, she found the atmosphere of the joust to be a sensual experience. It combined the spectacular with all the excitement of a dangerous and skillful sport, as well as attendant hero worship. Added to this was the element of idealism the ladies who watched from the stands were there to inspire, as well as admire, to strengthen their knight's courage by their presence. As she watched her husband join the other knights, the smile that curved her lips was for Richard alone.

From the place where the groomsmen waited, Bram's eyes searched the crowd. He saw Richard offer his lance to Moira, and watched as she laughingly tied her scarf to its shaft. With a groan, he spat angrily in the dirt.

Each knight was recognized and called forward to receive their token to carry into battle from their wives and sweethearts. Mary presented her red scarf to Rees as he lowered his lance to her. When she had finished tying the bedraggled favor to it, he placed his hand over his heart and grinned cheekily at her. She laughed and blew him a kiss.

When each man had taken his turn, the crier called out again. Meg's eyes followed Kenneth as he kneed his horse forward, and led the procession off the field. With the eyes of the immense crowd upon them, they all retreated to the extremities of the lists, where they remained drawn up in a line, awaiting the signal of encounter with the same ardor as their steeds, which, by neighing and pawing the ground, showed their impatience. As yet, the knights held their long lances upright, their bright points gleaming in the sun, and the streamers with which they were decorated fluttering over the plumage of the helmets. Thus, they remained while the marshals of the field surveyed their ranks with the utmost exactness.

Sitting astride his powerful mottled gray horse, Richard came to the front of the rank when the herald called him to the list for the first joust. He snapped his visor shut and latched it, ready for his first round. His opponent was a man from Glasgow who wore armor decorated with a sun. He rode a large white charger draped with yellow trappings.

A low wall of wooden planks had been built before the stands with barriers along the sides, and a low fence down the center to prevent the knights from actually colliding with each other.

Richard urged Thunder to the head of the list and evaluated his adversary. The man's horse was young and skittish, ill-trained for the joust. But the man seemed full of confidence.

The crier shouted the ready command, and both men lowered their lances horizontally along the sides of their horses' necks. Thunder flicked his ears back and tossed his mane with a snort, pawing the ground in eagerness. The crier waved his banner to the flourish of clarions and trumpets, and Richard leaned forward, digging his heels in and sending his horse into the opening head-on charge at full gallop. He steadily aimed his lance at his rival's shield, his mind intent on winning the set.

But his opponent's horse, which was young and headstrong, reared and plunged in the course of his career, disturbing his rider's aim. Richard declined to take the advantage which the accident had afforded him. He raised his lance, and passing his antagonist without touching him, wheeled his horse and rode back again to his own end of the lists, offering the man the chance of a second encounter.

This time they met almost in the center of the lists, and he felt the well-remembered bone jarring impact as his lance collided with its target, the full weight of man and horse behind the blow. The other man's lance skittered off his shield. A cheer went up at the first loud thwack! of lance hitting steel. Richard's lance shattered with such force that the pieces flew high in the air, to the wild cheers of the crowd. Even so, as his horse galloped past, he still heard the thud as his opponent hit the ground.

The crowd cheered loudly for Richard's accurate aim and firm seat, as he reined in and slowed Thunder's speed, circling the lists to calm him.

The man from Glasgow rose to his feet with the help of his squire, pulling his helmet from his head. Richard was relieved to see that the man was not injured, but his expression was angry. He had come all the way from Glasgow with high hopes, and already, he had been disqualified.

Thunder cantered to the far end of the list, where Richard's page was waiting with a fresh lance. Already his mind was on his next opponent. The crier waved the banner for the start of second set, and the two men rode toward each other on thundering hooves. Their lances struck their objectives with a staggering jolt, and Richard's rival reeled in his saddle. With each pass that was made the cheers grew louder.

"He is wonderful," Moira breathed with admiration. "And the people like him."

"Aye," Mary agreed, her voice full of pride for her brother.

One by one the little skirmishes were fought, as they contrived to unhorse their opponents in a kaleidoscope of different postures, from the dramatic downfall of both knights and their horses amid shattering spears, to the formal politeness of an encounter in which the jousters missed each other completely. The vanquished retired to their tents and pavilions to remove their armor, have their wounds attended and down huge mugs of ale.

Rees, riding toward his first opponent, had to move aside as the other man's lance struck his saddle, but at the same time his own lance broke, giving a clear solid hit to the other man's body. The man rolled on the ground, grasping his hands full of dirt at every turn.

If at all possible, it was best to maneuver so that your opponent's lance struck your saddle or your horse, for demerits were given then.

Richard stood to one side and watched Rees and his next opponent run at each other. They were both excellent fighters, and he could see that unless one of them had luck on his side, the match would be a draw. On the third run, Rees had broken his third lance against his opponent, just as his opponent had broken his third lance against Rees, both splintering their lances without advantage on either side.

Richard waved the page away and took water and a fresh lance to Rees.

"He allows the tip of his lance to tilt upwards, and I believe that he is closing his eyes just before the hit," Richard said to Rees while he drank. "When he approaches along the tilt, keep yer body square on him, and when ye are about to strike, turn yer head toward him as

41

much as ye can, in order to see him directly, and not through the corner of the visor. Try lifting yer lance a bit under yer arm, and if ye were to swing in to yer left, I think ye might take him."

Rees grinned, then lowered his faceplate. "I will do my best," he said, adjusting the lance that Richard handed him under his arm.

It was the only run in which Rees 'lance broke, but his opponents did not. Instead of bearing his lance point fair against Rees ' shield, he swerved so much from the direct line as to skitter his weapon across his person, thus giving Rees the higher score.

The shouts of the multitude, together with the acclamations of their heralds, and the clangor of the trumpets, announced the triumph of the victors and the defeat of the vanquished. The former retreated to their pavilions with honor, and the latter, gathering themselves up as best they could, withdrew from the lists in disgrace and rejection.

The barriers opened at the end of the field, and Kenneth paced into the lists on his charger, draped in red and black silks, wearing his polished armor that glinted in the sun's rays. His shield, a heavy frame of wood covered with hide hardened almost to the consistency of steel, bound and bossed with metal, was painted with the Ruthven crest, a ram's head. As he passed through the lists, he gracefully saluted the crowd and lowered his lance to them. The dexterity and grace with which he managed his steed caused a shout from the crowd to go up. Then he reined his horse backward through the lists, until he reached the northern extremity, in expectation of his antagonist. This feat of horsemanship again attracted the applause of the multitude. The Laird was about to ride against his first opponent.

When the two champions stood opposed to each other at the two extremities of the lists, the public expectation was strained to the highest pitch. The trumpets had no sooner given the signal than the champions vanished from their posts with the speed of lightning. Kenneth's heavy horse thundered down the field, and he kept his body tilted forward, his lance low, the whore's stocking whipping in the wind. The opposing knight spurred against him, his horse carrying him at a furious pace. They closed in the center of the lists with the shock of a thunderbolt, and when Kenneth struck him on the shield protecting his breastplate, the blow was so hard that the man fairly lifted out of his saddle and hit the ground, landing with a crash of armor. He left him rolling on the field under a cloud of dust, and spurred on.

"He is good," Meg said under her breath.

The next comer took the lance his squire handed him once he was mounted. He nodded his readiness, and Kenneth slammed his faceguard down. When the herald blew his trumpet, he thundered forward, horse and rider in perfect coordination. The lances shivered up to the very grasp, resulting in a spectacular splintering, and it seemed at the moment that both knights had fallen, for the shock had made each horse recoil backwards upon his haunches. The skillful riders recovered their steeds by use of the bridle and spur, and having glared at each other for an instant with eyes that seemed to flash fire through the bars of their visors, each made a demivolte, leaping with a half turn, the forelegs of the horses raised, and retired to the ends of the lists, received a fresh lance from the attendants.

A loud shout from the spectators, waving of scarves and handkerchiefs, and general acclamations, attested to the interest by the spectators in this encounter. But no sooner had the knights resumed their stations, then the clamor of applause was hushed into silence. It seemed now that the multitude was afraid even to breathe.

A few minutes pause having been allowed that the combatants and their horses might recover their breath, the trumpets once again sounded the onset. The champions sprung from their stations a second time and closed in the center of the lists with the same speed, same dexterity and the same violence as before. The ranks shuddered on both sides, and from the clash there arose a loud din, with another great cracking of lances.

But on the third pass, his adversary aimed at the center of Kenneth's shield and struck it so fair and forcibly that his spear went into shivers, and Kenneth reeled in his saddle. The opponent broke his lance against Kenneth, and managed to dodge the laird's lance. A point scored for the opponent.

Stung with madness, both at his disgrace and the acclamations with which it was hailed by the spectators, Kenneth returned to his station. Without alighting from his horse, he called for a cup of wine. Opening the lower part of his helmet, he quaffed it, casting a resentful glance at his antagonist. He then threw his cup to the ground, his eyes blazing, and he slammed his faceplate down as he took his place at the end of the lists.

The trumpet sounded and the herald called the signal words, "Laissez aller!" Kenneth lowered his lance, and dashed his spurs into the flanks of his horse. In this encounter, he charged his opponent as he would charge a man on a battlefield. He was out for blood. He sat firmly in his saddle, leaned forward, held his lance in his gauntleted hand, and charged at full speed, directing his lance toward his opponent's shield. As the two parties rushed upon each other at full gallop, he changed his aim almost at the point of encounter. He addressed it to the helmet, a mark more difficult to hit, but which, if attained, rendered the shock more terrible. Part of his success was due to his own physical strength, and part due to the immense power of his horse, as he bore down on the knight who rode against him. They met in the middle of the lists with a shock. Fair and true, he hit his opponent on the visor. He struck him so forcefully on the casque that the laces on the helmet broke, and he was knocked from his horse, arcing rather gracefully over the steed's rump, to be trampled under the hooves of his own horse. Blood gushed from his nose and mouth, and he was quickly dragged to safety by his pages, unconscious and covered with mud.

Opponent after opponent went down, and the crowd roared louder and louder at each fall, both amazed, and marveling at his skill. It seemed anyone who pitted himself against such competition must pay a high price.

Between jousts, the heralds addressed the ladies and pointed out to the audience how the knights risked life and limb to win their favor. "Love of ladies! Splintering of lances! Stand forth, gallant knights, fair eyes look upon yer deeds!"

Kenneth watched the other jousters from the sidelines, learning their skills and weaknesses. Lances broke and shields were holed, hauberks torn, saddles emptied as riders tumbled, while their horses sweat and lathered. All drew their swords on those who clattered to the ground. Some rushed up to accept their surrender, others to their defense. At midday one of his pages brought a bowl of meat and fruit, but he waved the boy away. He wanted no food to weight him down and satiate his appetite for battle. He stood and paced between bouts and did not speak to those around him. He kept his battle lust high and gave no thought to exhaustion. The heavy-boned tiredness would come later.

Four times he met an adversary on the lists, and each time he rode away the victor.

Rees also fared well on the lists, but even so, Mary held her breath at each pass, afraid that he might be harmed. He rode well, wielding his lance with ease, and conducting himself nimbly against his competition. But eventually he was felled by a man more lucky than skillful, when his stirrup broke. Mary leaped to her feet and pressed her hands to her mouth, but Rees got to his feet without help, and left the lists with good grace, saluting his opponent.

There were few serious injuries and no fatalities. Several knights had been unhorsed, and many unhelmed, and a good number of spears broken. A few men had been injured badly enough to require stitching or care from the barbers who waited in a nearby tent, and one man had gotten his foot caught in the stirrup when he fell, and broken his leg, but by all standards the tournament of May Day was considered a success.

The victors drew lots to determine opponents, and as time passed the same men returned again and again to the lists. As the tournament drew to a close it came down to three men--Richard, Kenneth and a highly skilled knight from Inverness who kept himself by attending tournaments throughout Scotland and England.

The three remaining men came together at the northern end of the lists to draw lots. Richard was pitted against the man from Inverness.

Bram had stood at one end of the lists watching the jousts all day, as he cared for the horses of Ravana between each run. He could see that Richard and his opponent were well matched, as the trumpets sounded and the two men took their places at opposite ends of the field.

Lackland stood near him, watching the set. He noticed the unsettling glare fixed on Bram's face and clapped him on the back. "Who is it ye watch wi 'such a black scowl on yer face? Surely 'tis not Richard ye wish to see downed."

Bram spit in the dirt. "I should like to see his guts spilled on the ground," he said with feeling. Lackland blinked uneasily at the tone in his voice and backed away, to join another group of onlookers from the stables of Ravana. It was then that Bram decided to loosen and cut half way through the cinch on Richard's saddle, hoping that it would slide, and snap at just the right moment, causing him to fall…or perhaps, worse…A slow smile spread over his face and his beady, ferret eyes did not waver from the man he considered to be his enemy.

He waited impatiently for his chance. When Richard had broken three lances against his opponent, and the opponent had broken his third lance against Richard, they brought their horses in for a rest. Richard dismounted and gave Thunder over to Bram. He was breathing hard as he dropped his shield to shake his arm after a particularly hard counterblow. He flexed his hand to relieve its numbness. He pulled off his helmet then, pushing his hair back from his eyes, and wiping his sweat streaked face. Nodding his thanks to the page, he welcomed a cool drink.

After a short refreshment, he took his horse from Bram, mounted and accepted his lance from his squire.

He rode his horse into position, and on the signal, he lowered his lance. At the trumpet's fanfare, he pressed his heels down firmly in the stirrups, and spurred his horse forward. Squeezing his legs tightly against Thunder's body, he allowed his body to go with the rhythm of movement of the horse, with a single goal. His adversary also pounded forward, shrieking madly, his lance directed straight at Richard's breast.

Everything happened so fast. Suddenly, just before they made contact, Richard's saddled shifted slightly. Too late to parry the thrust, he felt the lance skitter across his shield and slam into his shoulder, slicing through the mail with surprising ease. The spectators in the stands rose with a single gasp. Mary yelled in surprise, Moira clapped both hands over her mouth to stifle her scream. Meg's heart pounded fearfully.

The shock of pain was immediate and excruciating as it coursed through his arm, and his lance failed to meet his opponent. Thunder stumbled as he reeled in the saddle, and tried to keep himself erect. The horse reared, and the saddle slid off, taking Richard with it, the splintered lance sticking out of his shoulder. He hit the ground with a bone-jarring thud, his teeth clicking painfully together, his helmet cutting into his forehead. Warm blood ran into his left eye. Gasping and tasting dirt, he quickly extricated himself from his stirrups. He sprang to his feet in readiness, his breath coming in painful gasps, his shoulder throbbing. He drew his sword, waving it in defiance.

His opponent sprung from his steed, and also unsheathed the sword at his side. He swung his sword in a wide downward arch, sending it crashing down with all his might, nearly felling Richard with a massive blow. Richard quickly deflected the attack with his shield, but the punishing shock of the blow on his wounded arm sent him down on one knee. He could feel warm blood oozing down his right arm, wet and sticky. His adversary wielded his sword at him again, but Richard pivoted left and spun out of his way.

He regained his feet, and with his sword swinging, Richard dove back in and attacked his opponent. In no time at all, the exhilaration of battle drove everything else from his mind. He did not believe that he had ever faced such unholy zeal in an adversary. The man from Inverness struck back at him with all his force, and their swords met with a metallic crash of steal, as Richard blocked the blow. The clash of their blades drew sparks, as metal struck against metal. The noise echoed in their ears, drowning out the crowd's cheers of approval, who were obviously enjoying the show.

But the battle was quickly exhausting every ounce of Richard's strength and concentration. He managed to block each deadly blow that the man from Inverness rained down on him, but the throbbing pain in his injured shoulder intensified with each jarring impact. Each time their weapons clashed together, the man gave a shout of laughter mixed with curses and seemed to redouble his efforts. It was without a doubt the hardest Richard had ever had to work to protect himself. This man bested all his previous opponents for sheer blood lust. He fought without fear, clearly taking pleasure in every touch of their blades. Richard had to think quickly and clearly as the man's blade arced down on him once again. In a single smooth movement, he managed to duck under the swing, then parry with a clash of steel. But his opponent twisted back and hooked his foot around Richard's ankle, sending him sprawling on the ground. As he fell backward, his adversary's sword continued downward, slicing his thigh neatly to the bone. He heard from faraway the sound of Moira's scream.

"Yield ye," the knight from Inverness said, standing over him and holding his sword point against his chest.

The fight was over. The man from Inverness had won. Amidst the cheering, he reached down and hauled Richard to his feet, then shoved him backward so that he wouldn't think the action to be an act of kindness. Richard's squire was there to help him limp off the field.

Moira had managed to hold herself back until now. She had risen with the crowd when he was struck, and her heart still pounded with fear. She had clung to Mary and Meg throughout the sword fight, barely breathing, her eyes full of terror. Her stomach clenched tightly, the babe kicked and squirmed inside her, reacting to her anxiety. But now, the tension released, she pulled away from them, and headed toward the barber's tent, with Mary on her heels.

Meg stayed where she was. Though she longed to follow them, she knew that it was not her place. Tears burned behind her eyes. Her heart tugged at her to run after them, to see for herself that he was all right.

* * * *

Kenneth turned his horse in readiness to finish the fight with the man from Inverness, his battle lust high. At the signal, they plunged forward. The knights hurled toward each other. With a clash of lance and steel, the man from Inverness gave a cry and fell backwards. With a violent thrust, Kenneth had disabled the last man.

Kenneth let his horse slow to a trot, then circled, to see the man sitting dazed in the mud. The pages quickly hauled their master out of the way.

The crowd's roar of approval for the laird's victory was deafening, for winning the joust carried with it immense prestige. Drawing deep breaths into his lungs, he galloped around the lists, his broken lance upended in victory, the whore's stocking flying from the handle where he had tied it.

The heralds called out, "Our generous Laird Ruthven burns with courage, prowess, and boldness!"

As he rode passed the canopy on his way back to his tent, the other men crowded around his horse and lifted him off, carrying him from the lists in triumph upon their shoulders. Amid the cheering, he shouted back to the whore in the stands, "I claim ye as my prize! Come and be my fair damsel this night!"

* * * *

Richard's page helped him to pull off his helmet and unlace his mail hood. He looked down to find several inches of splintered lance lodged in his shoulder between the breastplate and arm encasement. The blood ran down the armor in thin streams. He filled his burning lungs, as he pushed back the hood with his left hand. His face and hair were soaked with sweat and blood, and he wiped it away with his hand. The page hurriedly unbuckled the armor that encased his upper body, and helped Richard to ease out of it. The padded shirt beneath was soaked with blood, his hauberk ripped.

Rees was suddenly there beside him. "Well done!" he said, laying his hand on Richard's uninjured shoulder.

Richard blinked up at him. "Pull it out," he told him.

The squire stepped back, not wanting to be a part of it. Rees glanced around. "Let the surgeon do it."

"Do it now!" he hissed through clenched teeth, his face a mask of shock and pain.

Rees took a deep breath and set his jaw as he took hold of the lance and pulled with all his might. The lance came free.

Exquisite pain tore through Richard, and brought him to the edge of fainting. His knees buckled and he nearly went down in the dirt again, but Rees quickly slipped Richard's sound arm around his own shoulder. "Next time keep yer shield up," he suggested with a sidelong glance, as he led him toward the barber's tent. Through worried eyes, he noted how pale he was. His lips were parted in a grimace of pain and effort as he sucked in hissing breaths between clenched teeth. Rees gave him a strengthening smile, and his eyes lit with humor as he pointed down to Richard's wounded thigh. "Ye still have all yer bits and pieces, I trust," he said with a cheeky grin.

The expression in his mischievous brown eyes made Richard snort. "Aye, I do, the important ones, at least. Dinna make me laugh, ye wee gomerel. It hurts me," he said.

They entered the barber's tent, and Rees gently eased him down upon the first available cot. He closed his eyes with a sigh.

Moira and Mary fought their way through the crowd and arrived a moment later. Moira's eyes brimmed with tears and she ran to her husband. "Och, Richard," she breathed.

At the sound of her voice, he opened his eyes. He managed a reassuring smile when he saw her anxious face, and reached up with his left hand to caress her cheek. "I'm not dead, mo cridhe. Dinna look so frightened."

"Yer bleeding," she told him unnecessarily, her voice faltering. She pulled her square handkerchief from her sleeve and began to wipe the blood away from his eye. Her hand trembled. His fingers lightly squeezed her arm in gentle reassurance.

A dark stain ran the length of his right arm, the blood glistening bright against the dull iron of his mail sleeve and smeared along his side. Mary reached for his right hand. It was icy, wet and smeared with blood.

"Rees, help me with this hauberk," she said, taking control of the situation. Together they drew it off. Mary leaned forward and peered at Richard's shoulder. So much blood had soaked into the sleeve, she could not see how badly he was hurt. The sleeve clung to his arm all the way to the wrist.

"Ye promised ye wouldna get hurt, ye great lummox," Mary scolded, as she pulled her knife from the purse at her waist. She caught hold of the loose fabric at his throat. "And now ye've gone and ruined yer padded shirt. Never mind. I'll do it."

"Ye'll do what?" he asked, eyeing her knife.

She lifted an eyebrow as she tightened her grip on his shirt. "Dinna ye trust me, little brother?"

"Should I, now that I'm at yer mercy?" His lips parted in a pained smile.

She poked the blade into the material, and sliced open the bloodied sleeve. He endured her gentle probing without comment. The sight weakened Moira, and made her stomach seethe.

"Get me a linen, or something to staunch this blood." Mary barked the order, and Rees handed her some thick pads of cloth. She held one to her brother's shoulder, applying direct pressure with the palm of her hand, and told Moira to do the same on his wounded leg. He grimaced and tried not to flinch.

The barber next to them finished his work and turned toward Richard. Mary saw that his hands and clothes were bloody as he placed his basin of water and sewing implements on the cot beside Richard. She wrinkled her nose as she noticed the telltale pink tinge to the water, and his bloodied instruments. As he reached for a probing tool, Mary batted his hands away in a huff.

"Wash yer hands before ye touch him," she commanded sharply. "And bring fresh water to cleanse his wounds. Ye will wash those instruments as well."

"But m'lady--" the man opened his mouth to argue.

"Do as I say!" she snapped back at him and he turned away, exasperated and muttering under his breath.

* * * *

Unable to hold herself back any longer, fear and worry overcame Meg's sense of duty, and she hurried toward the barber's tent. She had to see for herself that Richard was all right.

She raised the flap and glanced around, concern flooding her face. The brightness of the outside contrasted with the darkness inside the tent, temporarily blinding her. As her eyes adjusted to the semidarkness she found him.

"Richard!" she gasped, rushing to his side and reaching out to touch him. "Och, Richard, are ye hurt badly?" There was a softness to her voice that implied deeper feelings than she meant to express.

Shock and pain threw Richard off his guard, and his expression betrayed the intensity of his feelings, which, at other times, his prudence, at least, concealed. He tried to lift himself from the cot. It was everything he could do to keep from enfolding her in his arms when she reached out to him. But he managed to check the almost irresistible impulse. The blood that he had lost did not prevent a flush from crossing his cheek, knowing that he had unconsciously betrayed his deep feelings for her, and the awkward attempt he made to conceal it only made him feel more foolish.

Moira saw the emotion with which Richard gazed at Meg, and it only served to remind her that the love which she felt for him was not mutual. Jealousy seared her, and the gentleness left her eyes. She turned on Meg, her eyes blazing. "Get out!" she hissed. "He is my husband. Ye do not belong here. Go, join the feasting at the castle, and leave us to tend our own."

Meg slowly raised her eyes to Moira's face, and saw the depths of her feeling. She knew that she was right, but her heart ached to stay and help. Her eyes darted uncomfortably from one face to another. They all looked back at her in awkward silence. Richard glanced away, ashamed.

"A-aye," she whispered, backing away and blinking back her tears. She attempted to smile with uncooperative lips. She looked back at Richard. "I-I am relieved--to see that ye..." her voice faltered and broke.

By now Richard had exchanged his tender gaze for an appropriate one, filled with no deeper feeling than that which expressed a grateful sense of courtesy for her concern. His answering voice was a hasty and hesitant attempt at the tone of calm friendship.

Mary listened to the exchange of words and watched Meg's hurried departure uneasily, as she cut Richard's legging from the deep gash in his thigh. She yanked the material away a bit rougher than she intended to do in her frustration. He hissed in pain and raised himself upon the cot, but said nothing to her. Mary bit her lip guiltily. "Is duilich leam, brathair," she murmured. *I am sorry, brother.*

He nodded.

The barber returned with fresh water and clean instruments, muttering to himself. He began to wash away the crimson stains. Mary couldn't bear the way Richard winced under the barber's rough and hurried ministrations, so she dismissed him in a fury.

Moira blanched when the cuts appeared as Mary cleansed the wounds, and felt as if she might faint. The whirling spots began to dance before her eyes, and the air felt close and stifling suddenly, but instead of giving into it, she took Richard's hand and met his eyes. He could see the genuine concern she was feeling. "I'll be all right, mo cridhe. This is no' my first wound."

"Aye, well it may be yer last if ye dinna hold still now," Mary told him curtly as she gathered the needles, thread, and leather strap for her work. "This is going to hurt, Clot-heid," she said in gentler tones.

He glanced at her needles, then looked up at her. "Aye, no doubt it will, wi 'ye to do the job."

She straightened and put her hands on her hips. "Shall I call back the barber?" He frowned and she smiled at him. "No, I thought not."

Richard's page appeared at that moment with a goblet of red wine. He took it gratefully and downed it in one draft, then handed the empty goblet back to boy.

"Here, bite down on this," Mary said, offering him the leather strap. He took it and placed it between his teeth, shifting it back and forth between his teeth for a more comfortable grip.

"Moira, I shall need yer help to cut and tie the thread for me." And Mary began her instructions. Richard watched Moira's face as she glanced over at him nervously. He clenched his teeth down on the strap and made a face at her. She giggled and pushed his head back down upon the cot.

With a nod from Mary, Rees grasped Richard's right wrist firmly so that he could not jerk away reflexively when the needle went in. Richard took a deep breath and set his teeth hard into the leather strap.

Mary used the special technique that their mother had shown her, while Moira cut the thread and handed her the second needle with the threaded loops prepared. While Mary set the second stitch, Moira tied another loop, and the process was repeated again. Other than the sheen of sweat that broke out on his brow, he laid upon the cot silent and motionless, his mouth set in a tight, rigid line. Moira could not bring herself to watch, so she turned away and kept busy with the thread.

"Are ye all right?" Mary asked her brother, when she was nearly done stitching his shoulder wound.

"Aye," he answered, his teeth clenched tightly on the leather strap. "But can ye no' hurry and get it over with?"

He gasped when she started sewing up the deep gash in his thigh, and perspiration beaded on his upper lip, but he did not utter another sound.

When she was done, she bound the wounds with strips of white linen, tying them securely. His wounds were deep, but unless they became infected or he was seized by the mysterious and greatly feared stiffening sickness, he should heal well.

He rolled his shoulder gingerly, trying to loosen the tension, and wiggled his fingers. "Everything still seems to be in working order," he said.

"Did ye ever doubt it?" Mary asked, raising a stern eyebrow. "Now, can ye stand?"

Rees hooked Richard's sound arm over his shoulders and helped him to his feet, supporting his weight when he would have staggered, and they all started back toward the castle.

Outside of the barber's tent, musicians struck up a lively air as the procession started back to the castle with songs along the way. The banquet would be starting soon, and after supper there would be plays and diversions, as well as dancing and singing.

The signs and sounds of a tumultuous throng of men lately crowded together in one place, and agitated by the same passing events, were now exchanged for the distant hum of voices, forming their own conjectures, of the different groups dispersing in all directions, and these speedily died away into silence. No other voices were heard, save the voices of the menials who stripped the galleries of their cushions and tapestries, and wrangled amongst themselves for the half empty bottles of wine and relics of refreshment which had been served round for the spectators.

Richard was glad that he could skip the banquet and sleep the rest of the evening. His right shoulder and leg were an agony of fire, and he didn't think he cared to joust again soon.

* * * *

After several days of hunting and feasting, feats of archery, bear-baiting and other popular amusements, the tourney would be over. The knights, their ladies and their servants would go back to their homes, leaving the south slope of Ravana a trampled field of dirt and litter. Several men would be dispatched with two nags to clean up the mess. In time the grass would return, and Ravana would once again be surrounded by an apron of green.

CHAPTER THIRTY-EIGHT

Moira did not join in any of the festivities after they had gotten Richard to bed. She was too worried about his wounds. He did not care for all the fuss, and she could see that he was not going to be an easy patient.

When they had gotten him up to the room, he promptly collapsed upon his bed and closed his eyes, the grooves around his mouth etched deeply with pain. His wounds throbbed wretchedly, endlessly, and his head fairly reeled with it. Conscious thought had become difficult, and he only wanted to sleep. He felt he had never wanted it more in his life.

Moira began wrestling with his boots. He opened his eyes a slit. "What are ye about now, woman?"

"I'm trying to undress ye for bed, so ye can rest more comfortably. Yer a bloody mess," she told him. "Yer clothes are getting blood everywhere. If ye'll just cooperate, it will be easier for us both."

"Just leave me be, Moira." His voice was weary, the pain intense.

"Brother, are ye daft?" Rees chided. "Ye ken ye never refuse a lass when she wants to help ye take yer clothes off--Ooof!" he grunted when Mary gouged him in the ribs with her elbow.

"Not now, Rees!" Mary admonished, and grabbed for his ear, but he laughed and ducked just out of her grasp, grabbing her wrist and holding it firmly. He brought it to his lips and kissed her knuckles.

Richard heaved a sigh and gestured impatiently. He struggled to raise himself as Mary pulled her husband out the door. Moira manhandled Richard out of his boots and leggings with some difficulty. Then she gently daubed the cut above his eye. The sodden cloth stung, and he sucked in a hissing breath between clenched teeth. The necessary torture of the ministrations of the last couple of hours had left him irritable, and his body pleaded for rest. Demanded it. But he hadn't the strength anymore to argue. So he allowed her to finish cleaning the dried blood away without another word. At long last, she drew the blankets up over him. Exhaustion overtook him and he fell asleep quickly.

She pulled a chair up beside their big canopied bed, and wilted into it with a sigh. The sounds of war cries, the clash of battle and the moans of the injured echoed in her mind, sending a chill down her spine. She was shaken, and watched his every breath while he slept, relieved to hear it come in an even rhythm. After a while, convinced that he would be all right, for the time being at least, she took up her sewing. The room steadily darkened.

* * * *

Down in the Great Hall, there was much feasting and merriment. Laird Kenneth celebrated his victory with wild abandon and much drinking and dancing. He kept the whore by his side all night, as Betsy MacCallum watched jealously from the kitchen, anger coursing through her veins.

The strains of music and raucous voices drifted up through the castle corridors to the rooms upstairs. Meg retired to her rooms after the banquet, complaining that she did not feel well, and lay down upon her bed, fully clothed, listening to the wild laughter and debauchery below.

A young squire came in to light the fire. Moira put her embroidery aside and leaned over to check her husband. He was still breathing easily, and seemed to be resting. She ran her hand lovingly over his hair, then tucked the blankets more securely around him.

Tiptoeing across the room so as not to disturb him, she lit the candles and drew open the curtains to the fragile moonlight. Then she returned to sit by the side of the bed, watching his face while he slept. His lashes fanned out against his cheek, and sleep eased the weary edge the pain had caused. He moaned softly, and she pressed her palm to his brow, feeling for fever, then brushed back the curling wisps of hair from the cut above his eye.

Mary and Rees came in to check on him and found him sleeping peacefully, so they left, but Moira would not leave his side. She pulled out her beads and began telling them.

A short time later he began to stir. "Moira," he said, his voice hardly above a whisper.

"Aye, a leannan, I am here." She leaned over him, touching his hand gently, feeling for the dreaded fever. His fingers curled around to hold hers, cool and flexible.

"Is the banquet still going on?" he asked. "Or are they dancing? I believe I hear the strains of music. Dinna ye wish to join in the fun?"

"Och, nay, mo cridh, I dinna wish to leave ye. Dinna talk. Try to sleep." She put her lips to his forehead. Thankfully, his skin was cool, his pulse strong and steady.

"I am not fevered." He smiled a little, recognizing the purpose behind her gestures. "I am tired and sore and hungry. I could eat, if ye could but put a pillow behind me."

That was wonderful, she thought with a relieved smile. *It was a good sign*. She called a servant and sent down for some food. Then she propped him up with pillows.

Soon the rattle of dishes outside the chamber door announced the arrival of a servant bearing a tray. Moira took it from the girl and set it down on the table beside the bed. Hot, savory steam rose from the bowl of stew, and when she handed it to him, he ate with appetite, then set the bowl aside. Then she poured him a cup of wine. He drank it thirstily, then leaned back against his pillows and closed his eyes.

"Will ye lie down again?"

"Not yet," he said, although his voice sounded tired. "Movement is too painful."

He heard her sigh and opened an eye, to see her frowning at him. "I will soon."

She was silent for a while, sitting with her hands in her lap.

"I am all right, Moira," he told her with a smile. But it was a pain filled smile, she could see. "Ye need na' sit and watch me. I willna turn into a pumpkin, I promise ye. Go back to yer needle or yer beads."

There was a knock at the heavy oak door. Moira started to rise and answer, thinking it was the servant, come back for the tray. But before she could get there, Mary and Rees lifted the latch and entered.

Mary had a tankard in one hand and a bowl in the other, clean linens draped over her arm.

"What's all this, then?" Richard asked, surprised and suspicious at once.

"We heard ye were awake. I have concocted a salve and poultice for yer wounds, and an infusion for ye to drink." Mary handed him the tankard. "Drink this."

"God's bones," he sighed as he took the cup from her hand. "Dinna ye do enough to me back at the barber's tent?" He peered doubtfully into the tankard, wrinkling his nose at the smell. "What is it?"

" 'Tis an infusion of Echinacea and Goldenseal root."

He swallowed some and choked abruptly, gasping at its potency. The tankard twitched in his hand, nearly spilling. "It tastes foul!" he wheezed, coughing to clear his throat as he struggled to find his voice. "Ye've nearly strangled me!"

"Then perhaps it will be effective against yer dull wit that got ye into this predicament," she countered, with a look of affectionate mockery. "Drink it while I see to yer bandages."

"What have ye got in that bowl?"

" 'Tis a paste of bear's breech and myrrh. God bless me, ye ask a lot of questions. Be still now, and let me tend ye."

Richard protested mildly, but allowed her to undo the bandage at his shoulder. She carefully untied the linen bandage and removed the cloth, to inspect the deep, red wound. Then she dipped a thin slat of wood into the white paste and drawing a generous dollop, smoothed it thickly over the stitches. He grimaced a bit at her ministrations, but when she applied the poultice, he let out a yell. He jerked straight up, causing the poultice to fall upon the bed before she could secure it.

"Holy Mother of God, Mary, that burns like hell!"

"Why, Richard, ye call upon the Blessed Virgin? Dinna let the Reverend Edmund Corrie hear ye say it," she smiled, raising a mischievous eyebrow. She pushed him back against the pillows and pressed the poultice back to his shoulder.

He glared at her and hissed, "Ye dinna tell me it was going to burn the flesh off my bones!"

"Nonsense, 'tis doing nothing of the sort. Dinna carry on so, my bonny wee cockerel, or I'll quit doctoring ye, and then where will ye be?"

She frowned and took a gentle swipe at his head in response to his hopeful expression.

"Drink yer medicine, there's a good lad," she told him, ignoring his resigned sigh. She pulled a clean bandage from her sleeve and rebound his arm with several layers of linen that crossed his chest, then tied it in place over his shoulder. She looked over at him and nodded at the tankard. "Drink it, ye addle-pated slack wit!"

Reluctantly he obliged her, and managed slowly to choke down most of the bitter brew, as she yanked the covers down to repeat the whole process on his leg. He struggled uncomfortably through her doctoring.

"And while ye deal with that, brother," Rees said with a rueful nod toward his wife, "I have a bit of news for ye."

"And what is that?" Richard asked, casting a final dark look his sister's way. She smiled up at him angelically.

"I ken the reason yer saddle slipped off yer horse."

His curiosity piqued. "Aye?"

"I fear ye were sabotaged. Someone cut more than halfway through yer cinch."

"What!" Moira cried. "Someone deliberately--"

"Who d'ye think it was?" Richard's face was grim.

"I questioned some of the grooms. Lackland told me he thought it might be Bram."

"Bram always did have a spite on ye," Mary said.

"Aye," Richard agreed with a sigh. "Ow!" he exclaimed loudly as Mary secured the poultice to his leg. He scowled at her.

"Och, pish-tosh," she told him, without stopping her work to glance up at him.

When the ordeal was finally over, she pulled the covers back up over him. He glared at her from over the rim of the tankard as he drained it.

"There's a good laddie," she said encouragingly. She bent over and kissed him on the forehead, then ruffled her hand over his unruly curls. "Clot-heid," he said affectionately. "I'll look in on ye in the morning."

As she left, Richard shook his head with a sigh, and sank back against the pillows.

* * * *

The candles guttered out as a faint light broached the sky to the east. The room was dim with the early pink light of dawn. Morning was on its way. Moira rose from her chair, where she had been embroidering about the neck of their baby's tiny gown. Richard had been sleeping for some time, moaning softly with every exhaled breath. She stepped very quietly to the bedside, not wishing to wake him if he still slept, but he opened his eyes a slit when she came near. He winced as his body tingled to life.

"Do ye wish a drink, mo cridh?"

He swallowed thickly and licked his lips. A persistent dryness parched his mouth and he nodded his head against the pillows.

She fetched him water and raised his head, placing an arm beneath his back, pressing the edge of the cup against his lips, while he roused himself and drank thirstily. She could feel the heat of his neck against her arm, and fear began to mount, unbidden, inside her. When his thirst was quenched, she set the cup aside, and pressed her hand briefly against his forehead. The fever was starting.

Her hand felt cool against his skin. He could feel the heat of his body at her touch, and he saw the fear of it in her eyes. He ran his tongue over his dry lips and tried to give her a reassuring smile. Her lips began to tremble, and he reached up to touch her face, attempting to turn her fear aside.

"Have ye slept this night?" he asked.

"Aye, certainly," she lied. "Ye must not talk now, Richard."

He rolled his head on the pillow with a sigh and let his eyelids fall shut again. His shoulder and thigh felt hot and swollen and full of fire. His head throbbed, his muscles ached from the jarring his body had taken the day before when lance met steel in the skirmishes he had fought, and his joints ached from the fever. Every part of him ached, throbbed, burned, or stung with its own unique degree of exquisite pain. He moaned, obviously restless and uncomfortable, and tried to shift himself more comfortably. He moved his hips a little, edging his left elbow under himself, and tried to lever himself up. The chills came upon him then, sending a white-hot pain through his injured leg, that magnified his misery and made him groan.

"Are ye all right, Richard?" Moira asked, frightened, not knowing what to do. Tears glittered on her lashes, and her heart was wrung to see the expression of agony on his face.

"I'll do," he told her between clenched teeth. He closed his eyes tightly, but he could not stop shaking. He dug his fingernails hard into his palms and clenched his jaw until it hurt, his joints rigid, as he stifled a moan.

"Shall I call Mary? Ye are getting feverish." She took his burning hand and held it against her cheek. There was no doubt about it. His fever was climbing alarmingly.

"No!" he groaned irritably, pulling his hand away from her as he struggled against the shaking. "I said I'll d-do. I dinna n-need my s-s-sister here to fuss over me with her b-burning poultices and vile elixirs." He set his teeth hard in his lower lip.

Moira bit her lip worriedly as she pressed a cool damp cloth to his forehead. "I only thought she could ease yer suffering."

"I'm all right," he moaned as the shivering began to slow, then finally subside. He slumped, exhausted, against the pillows and closed his eyes, breathing heavily.

"I will call for some food for yer breakfast, then," she said tentatively.

"I am not hungry."

"Ye must eat to keep up yer strength."

He rolled his head on the pillows. "Moira, please..." He opened his eyes and saw the pained look on her face. He sighed resignedly. "Och, verra well, then."

She called for a page to bring some soup, and tried to settle him comfortably. "I can prop ye up with pillows the way I did last night."

"Aye," he sighed, his voice still edgy with pain. "That'll do."

She shifted him and fluffed his pillows, bracing his back with their feathery support. He held his breath, trying not to gasp with the movement. He did not want to upset her more by giving into the pain. He set his teeth and helped her to pull himself erect. Waves of dizziness almost overcame him, and he bent his head and waited for the feeling to pass.

A soft rap at the door announced Aggie, with a cup of thick chicken broth and egg yolk custard for breakfast. Moira opened the door to her, and the savory aroma wafted in the air as Aggie placed her tray on the bedside table.

"Och, sir, ye look like yer horse rolled over ye! How d'ye feel?" she asked, handing him the broth.

"I feel...much worse than that," he told her as he raised the cup awkwardly to his lips with his left hand. "I feel as if Ravana toppled and fell on me." She smiled and he nodded acknowledgement to her. "Thank ye for the soup, Aggie."

"Aye, sir." She bobbed a curtsey and left the room.

Another knock. Moira and Richard exchanged glances. Who now?

"'Tis Mary," a voice from the corridor called. "I've come to see to yer wounds."

Richard made a sound of annoyance in his throat as Moira gratefully flew to the door to let her inside. She bore an ominous looking tray covered with a few jars, a large bowl, some strips of linen, and another tankard.

Richard watched her grimly as he set his bowl of broth aside. He licked his lips in irritation. "I ken ye did enough damage to me last night with yer needle, poultice and elixir. Ye nearly put me under. Did ye come back to finish it?" His voice was curt and agitated.

"Aye, ye great lummox," she said good humoredly. "Now let me tend ye." She set the tray down and busied herself with the medications and fresh bandages. "A bit frachetty this morning, are ye?"

"Go away, Mary, and leave me to rest in peace."

He turned away from Moira when she urged him to eat more. She could feel the tension mounting in the air as brother and sister glared at each other.

"Rest in peace now, is it?" Mary said, her voice heavy with sarcasm. "Is that what ye'll be wanting us to put on yer tombstone? Mayhaps 'Rest In Peace, Ye Stubborn Numpty 'since yer too stubborn and too proud to let us care for ye properly," she sneered. "Is that it?"

He scowled at her. "I dinna have any intention of dying on ye, ye stiff-necked, spiteful wench!" A spasm of coughing descended upon him then, awakening the sleeping demon in his leg. He groaned, shoving his left fist hard against his mouth, to stifle the sound. As the waves of pain subsided, he raised himself, his eyes blazing at her. "I'm not done yet, Mary, no matter what ye may think!"

Moira watched their exchange of angry words with mounting dread. She attempted to fluff the pillows behind him. "Let me help ye lie down. Ye must rest. Save yer strength for healing."

"For Christ's sake, Moira," he snapped at her. "I am not sleepy! Will the two of ye no' leave me alone? I am not a child, to be watched and coddled and told what to do! Why d'ye treat me like one? Stop fussing over me! I dinna want to be poked at anymore!" he said sharply. He rubbed his hand against his temple to still the pounding there, and grimaced with pain. His hand trembled. "Och, my head aches like the verra devil! Women, dinna fret me! It only makes me feel worse!"

Moira burst into tears. Mary cast a thoroughly disgusted glance at her brother and pressed her lips together with unfamiliar restraint. The muscles in her face tightened and she could feel herself shaking with the effort to contain her anger. Her eyes narrowed warningly.

He looked uneasily from one face to the other. He felt strangely light-headed, and there was a dreamy edge to his vision. His rubbed his hand over his face.

"Och, Moira, please forgive me. I am sorry. Dinna weep. My head aches, my arm and leg hurt like hell, and I feel strange. I will rest. I will do whatever ye wish," he said contritely. "But without the two of ye gawking at me and fretting every time I feel a twinge," he added.

"God bless me, if I ever saw such a contrary great fool of a man!" Mary said as she put her arms around Moira's shoulders.

" 'Tis all right, Mary," Moira said. "I am only a little tired, so tears come easily."

Mary looked at her. Weariness did lay heavy upon her, dulling the brightness of her eyes, and etching shadows beneath them. Clearly, she hadn't slept the night before.

She sighed. "All right then, Moira. I'll leave ye alone with this hardheaded thimble wit," she said with a nod toward her brother. She gathered up her tray of bandages. "I'll leave the elixir. See if ye can get the clot-heid to drink it." And with that, she was gone.

Moira watched the door close behind her, then turned to Richard. "Ye shouldna have made her angry. She only wanted to help ye."

Richard snorted. "She'll be back, I've no doubt. She canna keep from torturing me for long." He sighed as he raked his fingers through his tumbled mop of hair.

Moira picked up the tankard and held it out to him.

"Put that down. I willna drink the foul stuff."

She took a deep breath and set it aside. "Would ye like for me to read to ye, then, since ye canna sleep?" Moira offered.

"Nay," he told her. "Ye should rest yerself." He looked at her with a sheepish grin. "I've no reason to growl at ye. Will ye forgive me?"

She bent and kissed his cheek. "Aye." She gestured toward the bowl of broth. "Would ye like some more soup?"

He shook his head wearily. "I've no appetite. If I take anymore--" he was interrupted by a harsh burst of coughing, "--I fear I shall be sick," he finished weakly. He felt nauseous and lightheaded, and only wanted to close his eyes and sleep.

Moira sat down beside him and smoothed back the tumbled curls from his forehead. He smiled up at her, then closed his eyes, sighing under her hand. She didn't like the look of him. His cheeks and brow were flushed, and lightly sheened with dampness, his lips were dry and cracking from the fever, and his eyes were smudged underneath with tiredness. His skin felt hot to her touch.

Coherent thought was becoming almost impossible for him, and he was remotely surprised at the rapidity his fever was increasing and his strength decreasing. Even his teeth felt strange, and there was a sick buzzing inside his head. The world was far too bright, he thought, wishing that Moira would pull the drapes and block the sunlight. It gave him a feeling of vertigo, and he began to shiver.

"I am verra cold," he husked, as great shudders wracked his body, and a darkness deeper than night began to take him down.

Moira went to the chest at the foot of the bed and pulled out a blanket. "Ye must lie down now, love, and try to rest," she said. It was as if she were speaking to him from the top of a deep well into which he was falling, and then he knew only darkness and silence.
* * * *

Sleep did not drift upon him peacefully, but grabbed him with rough hands, pulling him deeply into the darkness of an exhausted sleep. He descended heavily into a foggy world where the only landmarks were pain: his throbbing shoulder, the deep burning of his leg, where time was unknown to him. A low moan escaped him, and a slight frown creased his brow, but his eyes did not flicker. Moira sat by the bed, watching him sleep. A warm tear rose unbidden from her eye and fell onto his cheek. He gave a slight twitch, but did not wake. Moira sniffed, and looked down at his strong, square hand, corded with tendons and veins as it lay still and unresponsive on the blanket.

66

How dearly she loved his long, sensitive fingers as she laced them in her own and hung over him, caressing his hand lovingly, sobbing softly and wetting it with her tears.

A harsh voice from the door drew a terrified gasp. "Is he dead?"

"Och!" Moira cried. "Ye gave me a fright. Thank God 'tis only ye, m'lady. No, he is not dead, but the fever is beginning."

Meg hung at the door hesitantly. "I knocked, but ye dinna answer."

Moira smiled. "I dinna hear it. Please, step inside, and keep me company. I fear what is to come." She sniffed, and the hated tears coursed down her cheeks. She pressed her hands to her face.

Meg's heart went out to her. She hurried to her and knelt beside her, holding her as her body was wracked with sobs.

"Och, now, Moira, he'll be all right," she crooned softly, rocking gently, her arms a comfort. She held her until her sobs began to still. Meg smiled at her with a false assurance that twisted in the pit of her stomach.

They sat together near the fire in the huge hearth, sewing baskets near at hand, to pass the time while he slept. Nerves stretched taut, stomach knotted, Meg attempted to play the calm and unaffected lady that Moira needed her to be--a role she could barely sustain. Despite her best efforts to distract her attention, thoughts assailed her--frightening thoughts--and waves of uncertainty had her fidgeting at every sound.

Hours later, he began to stir. His eyes fluttered, and he uttered a thick moan as he tried to raise himself.

"Och, nay, mo cridh," Moira said softly, gently pushing him back down on the bed. "Ye'll open yer stitches." He felt hot beneath her hand.

He opened his eyes and saw, through fevered mists, the anxious face of his wife. Grinning demons with red eyes floated in her hair. He put out his hand to ward off the phantoms.

"Begone, devils!" he cried out weakly, looking at her with haunted, feverish eyes. "Away from me!" His breath whistled out softly, and he raised his hand to cross himself with the holy sign, but his hand fell limp.

"Delirium," Moira said grimly, then turned to Meg. "Quickly, ye must fetch his sister."

Meg darted out the door.

Soon she was back with Mary, who went quickly to her brother's side. Rees followed on her heels.

They found Richard heavy-lidded and groggy. His face was ashen and his chest rose and fell rapidly. Mary could hear his chest rattling, and cared very little for the sound of it. His skin burned beneath her touch, dry and parched, fiery with heat. When she untied his bandages, the source of the fever was plain. She found the flesh a puffy mass with a foul smelling yellow-green ooze forming along the edges of his wounds, and sticking to the strips of linen. She could see the ominous faint beginnings of red streaks that would eventually lead to his heart and kill him. Panic made her own heart beat faster, her palms suddenly wet.

"Sweet Savior," she whispered, gingerly touching the swelling flesh. He winced when she touched it, and resumed his mumbling gibberish, twitching his head from side to side and shivering with a violent chill. "How long has he been like this?" she whispered, laying a practiced hand on his armpit and groin. No hint of a relieving sweat.

"He just now woke like this."

Rees reached for the jug of water at the bedside, poured a cup, and handed it to Mary. Together they lifted Richard's shoulders, and Mary pressed the cup to his lips, but he would have none of it.

The fever continued to mount for three days. The red lines of infection became more pronounced as they marched over his shoulder and up his leg. Chills continued to whip through his body. For five more days he burned and raged at those who attended him. His sleep was not easy. He twisted and muttered incoherently to himself, chasing his own phantoms. Images of blows dealt and received, of horses rushing upon each other, of shouts and clashing arms, and all the heady turmoil of a confused fight flashed in his fevered mind. His wounds festered, and day after day he raved deliriously at the sounds in his feverish head.

During the days of his struggle Moira, Mary, Rees, and Meg tended him, feeding him and nursing his wounds. Mary used all the skills she had learned, trying desperately to save her brother, spending hours concocting salves and ointments made from agrimony, calendula, marigold, and plantain, using the leaves, flowers and stems, chopped finely and mixed with lard; poultices of linseed oil and violets to draw the poisons, and elixirs to speed the healing. She carefully cleansed his wounds, and applied compresses of balsam and vinegar alternately with rosemary and thyme. She boiled herbs and white willow bark to make infusions to reduce his fever and ease his pain, and forced them between his parched lips.

She boiled twigs of rosemary plants and used the water to wash him after fits of sweating during his fever, and changed his clothes and bedding. Upon the bedside table she put a small metal cup filled with lavender scented oil into a heavily embossed iron base, and placed a candle under it. The scent was meant to soothe his mind and body.

He drifted in and out of feverish sleep, coughing weakly, his chest full of rales. They plied him with teas made from chamomile, Goldenseal, peppermint, rose hips, and yarrow. They soaked cloths in warm water and lemon juice, and wrapped them around his leg as a compress. A dry cloth was placed on top, woolen leg wrappings put on over this every half hour. But there was no improvement.

The days passed one into another. Meg and Moira became close friends again. They each drew comfort and strength from one another in their shared grief, grateful for each other's company. They prayed together fervently, or sat in companionable silence by the fire after a long day when they were too tired for anything else.

* * * *

Moira slowly raised herself from the bent position of changing the linens on the bed. She resisted the urge to rub her lower back, for she knew that if Mary caught her at it again, she'd nag her to leave off her care and make her rest. Not that the thought didn't hold a certain

69

appeal, if truth be told, for her body ached from weariness. But she could not bring herself to leave Richard's side.

Mary scowled at her, then drew a chair close to the bed and pointed to it. "Ye sit there. 'twill be more comfortable for ye."

Moira looked surprised.

"Did ye ken I wouldna notice how ye've been rubbing yer back? Sit," she commanded.

"Och, and ye've become a tyrant," Moira said gratefully, pleased that she had not sent her away as she had everyone else. She sighed tiredly, and placed her hands on both arms of the chair to ease herself into it, for the babe made her feel heavy.

Mary glanced grimly at her brother. An ominous green pallor touched the edge of his jaw. The first faint traceries of infection had appeared on Richard's torso in a network of twisted red lines. The infection would reach his heart soon, no doubt. A chill ran down her spine as that knowledge sliced deeply into her heart like a knife. She looked sadly back at Moira, and laid a hand upon her arm.

"Rest yerself, sister. I am going to fetch Father William. I fear there is nothing else we can do."

The despair in her voice filled Moira with a long-dreaded horror. Her hand went suddenly to her throat, clutching it as though her breath were being strangled from her body. Her eyes were sharp with understanding. "No," she murmured, shaking her head against the knowledge. Hot tears gathered behind her eyes and spilled down her cheeks. "No…"

* * * *

Mary left her brother's room and found Kenneth in the corridor. He had just stepped from his room, and was dressed to go hawking.

"Kenneth," she called, putting her hand upon his arm to detain him. He turned toward her impatiently. "What is it?" he growled.

" 'Tis Richard. He is verra ill. I fear he may be dying." She looked into his eyes, hoping to see a sign of concern or compassion. Instead, something cold, intense, and remorseless glared back at her.

"What is it ye wish me to do about it? I have neither the time nor the inclination to visit a sick room, this day or any other. I am on my way to the mews." He bowed to her. "I bid a good day to ye, Madame."

He turned and continued down the hall, but she stood her ground. "I believe he needs the Sacrament of Extreme Unction, m'lord," she persisted. "The Last Rites."

He stopped in his tracks. "Ye ken the papish ways are forbidden here," he told her without turning around to face her. Then he walked on.

A stirring and a soft sigh sounded from behind her. Mary turned and gasped. Betsy MacCallum stood in the Laird's half opened door, her bodice torn, her skirt askew. But what caught Mary's eyes was the large purple bruise on her cheek and the cut above her lip, as she peered sadly after him.

* * * *

Left alone for her mind to mull over the situation, the frightening thoughts churned, until Moira began to feel ill. *Don't follow that path*, she cautioned herself. She felt it was her duty to maintain a brave front, to show confidence in God's mercy and Mary's healing abilities. But such a pretense was now beyond her strength. She looked at Richard in dull despair. He had not opened his eyes in lucidity for days, and he had stopped squeezing her hand in reassurance. She blinked back the tears that stung behind her eyes. She'd done all she could, and she wondered why it wasn't enough. All she could seem to do now was to tremble and fight back the tears. She was so tired--not simply with physical weariness but emotional as well. Since the beginning of her pregnancy, her emotions had grown excitable and uncertain. This last week it seemed that she could not make it through an entire day without weeping. Her stomach clenched with fear, and the baby began to kick and squirm, perhaps in reaction to her tension. Taking several deep breaths, she willed herself to be calm and consider what she should do. She stroked her stomach to soothe the babe--and distract herself-- and tried not to imagine the worst. What would she do if Richard died? But matters of life and death were in God's hands, not her own. Her heart wrenched. Surely a loving God would not take Richard from her? She closed her eyes and repeated a Pater Noster, and crossed herself.

* * * *

There was a quiet stirring in the corridor. The door opened and Father William, Mary, Rees, and Meg stepped inside. Father William was dressed in a long cloak, a hat slouched down over his face to hide his features. He carried in his hands a small box. As he entered, he walked over to Moira and took her hand in his.

"Peace be with ye, my child," he said in a soft, kindly voice. "Do not be afraid. I have come to anoint yer husband with the Holy Sacrament, to absolve his sins and commend his soul to God."

A wretched sob tore from Moira's throat and her hand tightened on the old priest's hand. Meg put her arms about her, whispering soothing words, feeling her own heart breaking in two. Mary and Rees set about quietly lighting candles at the head and foot of the bed, while Father William opened his box and laid out the covered chalice that held the consecrated Eucharist, and the vials of holy water and anointing oil. He draped the white vestments across both forearms, took his prayer book in his hands, and began to chant the Latin rites. His tone was soothing, the soft murmurings peaceful. Then he took the vials of blessed water and oil, each in turn, and anointed Richard's body with the Sign of the Cross. He ended with a Pater Noster, which they all joined in on, the whispered "Amen" echoing in their ears.

* * * *

Mary continued to pour over her books of healing in desperation, with Rees by her side, doing what he could to encourage her. Moira and Meg sat by the fire staring at each other in silence, listening for any change.

The hours drew on. Dinner was brought up. Mary refused to eat, but continued her studies. Rees ate with no appetite, but out of habit. Meg thought her food looked revolting, but managed to put it into her mouth and chew it, then swallow it, though she thought it tasted like paste. Moira could not even manage that. Distractedly, she pushed her food around her plate until it mashed together in the center into a very disagreeable lump. Then she rose and went again to look at her husband. Tentatively she reached out, and her fingers grazed the partially healed gash above his eye. He moaned a stream of slurred phrases and then fell silent. Her hand dropped away and she fetched a deep sigh.

The sight brought an ache to Meg's throat. "Moira, ye must eat, for the baby's sake. Ye are weary. I fear ye have not rested well these last days."

"And ye have?" she smiled wanly.

She went to sit beside the fire, and picked up her sewing, but her hands lay still on the embroidery frame before her.

Meg stifled a yawn and slumped in her chair, propping her elbows on the arm rest, her chin on her fist. Soon her eyes drifted closed, and her head began to droop, her fist sliding up her cheek. Her head jerked up, and she struggled to sit up straighter in the chair. She smiled sheepishly at Moira, who smiled back.

" 'Tis all right," Moira told her. "Sleep, if ye can."

Meg shook her head, both in disagreement and wonder. Sheer will alone must be giving her the strength to last, Meg thought. She stood up and went to the basin of water, and splashed her face.

"I will watch with ye," she said, sitting before the fire once again. But before long, she propped her head up with her hands again. And soon her head began to slip down again. And this time there was no stopping it. She leaned over the arm of the chair, cradling her head in her arms, her breath coming in the even rhythm of sleep. Moira let her rest and continued her vigil alone.

* * * *

Someone was shaking her. She tried to burrow deeper into the dream. She didn't want to wake up now. But the hand was persistent and would not stop shaking. Her dream became misty and then dispersed as the smell of the wood fire in the hearth overcame her senses. She opened her eyes.

It was Moira. She looked frightened and her eyes were wet with tears.

"What is it?" Meg asked. *Is he dead?* she wondered fearfully, too scared to say the words. She glanced furtively at Richard. Rees stood at the foot of the bed watching Mary, who stood over her brother mutely, gazing down at him, a look of despair on her face. He had cast off his blankets and the firelight gleamed in his open eyes. He babbled incoherently, the misery in his voice making the hairs on their arms stand on end.

Meg put her arms around Moira and felt her trembling.

Richard's babblings ceased, and Meg looked over Moira's shoulder at him.

Mary took a deep breath, dashing away a tear from her eye. She leaned down near her brother's ear. "Ye listen to me, Richard Buchanan, ye stubborn thickwit!" she said, her voice shaking with emotion. "Ye willna die on me, Clot-Heid! D'ye hear me? By all that is holy, I'll not let ye!" She turned abruptly toward her husband. "Rees, bring three of your strongest men here now." Her breath came fast, with a new determination. "M'lady, I must ask ye to leave, and take Moira with ye."

Struck dumb by her tone of command, everyone obeyed. Mary sent down for buckets of fresh water and gathered her scissors, knife, needles and medicines. She set the water to boiling in the hearth and when Rees had brought his men, ordered the four of them to sit on Richard to hold him still while she opened his stitches and slit his wounds to the bone, and washed them thoroughly with boiling water. Richard struggled and yelled against the pain until he fell unconscious once again. Then she restitched his injuries and drew the blankets back over him. As a last resort, she sent down to the kitchen for old bread and cheese, green with mold.

CHAPTER THIRTY-NINE

The world still lay wrapped in darkness when Richard floated into a foggy consciousness. *Am I dead?* he wondered.

No, death would not bring this wracking, shuddering heat and cold. He shrank from waking. He had hovered on the edge of it before, each time driven back into peaceful oblivion by the pain. But this time it was different. He could feel her presence, smell her scent, the scent of lavender. It beckoned to him, and he could not resist the lure of it. He tried to open his eyes, but they would not cooperate. He willed his mouth to form words, but the only sound that emerged was a groan. *That is all right,* he thought. *It is not seemly to call out another woman's name other than my wife's.* A cool, soothing cloth daubed his face and forehead, and he slipped back into the gentle twilight.

* * * *

After wiping his face with a damp cloth, Meg returned it to the basin. She glanced over at Moira, who was curled up beside him on the counterpane. She had finally surrendered to much needed sleep.

She shifted her gaze back to Richard's face. Propped up against the bolsters, a thick fringe of dark lashes resting against his pale skin, he looked so vulnerable. Shallow lines bracketed his mouth and creased his forehead. She reached out to brush the tangled curls away from his eyes, then quickly snatched back her hand. She had no right to touch him in such a way. He belonged to Moira. She could only pretend he was hers in these stolen moments of the night.

* * * *

Voices. He could hear voices, softly whispering. And there was the fragrant scent of roses, mixed with lavender in the air. He opened his eyes a slit and could just make out the faint orange flicker of the fire in the hearth. He sensed that he had lain there for a long time, wrapped in steaming cloths, which grew cold and were taken away and renewed. He knew that hot drinks had been forced down his throat, sometimes nauseous herbal mixtures, and sometimes strong spirits mixed with hot water. How much time had passed he knew not as he lay and burned and shivered and suffered the horrid stuff they forced down his throat when he was too weak even to vomit it up.

Moira, he tried to say, but his voice was all gone. His throat hurt so bad. He tried to swallow, but there was no moisture there.

And then someone appeared. She had a bowl in her hands. Food, he thought weakly. *Am I hungry?* He tried to ask, but nothing came out.

He felt himself being lifted, propped against his pillows. Somehow, he managed to swallow three spoonfuls before everything blurred away again.

* * * *

The eleventh day was very quiet. The morning passed, and the day wore slowly on. Mary came that evening as was her usual routine, to change the bandages and tend her brother's wounds.

Moira sat in her place by the fire, telling her beads. She crossed herself and kissed the crucifix, closing her eyes, her lips moving silently in the Pater Nosters and Ave Marias. Meg sat nearby. She set aside the spindle she's been working in the fruitless hope of calming herself.

Mary untied the bandages and saw with relief that dry, brownish crusts were forming around the edges of the raw flesh, instead of the pasty green-yellow ooze. The wounds 'angry red had diminished, and the swelling lessened. She felt his forehead and armpits, and they were cool. The fever had departed. Laying a finger aside his wrist, she noted his pulse had slowed. It was a true sign of healing.

"The Holy Blessed Virgin be praised!"

Richard shifted restlessly, awakening from a sticky, clinging slumber, and opened his eyes. His head was thrumming and he could not think, as he squinted up at her with an effort, forcing her shimmering image into focus.

"Mary?"

His voice, unused for so long, came out so hoarse and raspy that he hardly recognized it as his own. He remembered nothing since that first night, only a mingled recollection of what had happened to him, and an overwhelming feeling of weakness and exhaustion. He blinked up at her.

A smile that Mary could not suppress dimpled her face for an instant as she looked down upon his troubled expression. "Aye, it is, ye wee gowk," she said, as she pressed a cloth soaked in a dilution of water and herb thyme to his forehead and wiped his face. " 'Tis about time ye opened yer eyes and joined the living. Are ye yerself again?"

The ghost of a smile touched his lips. "So far as I can tell…I dinna ken. My head swims. Have I been ill?" he asked, his voice cracking. It was an effort to speak, all he could do was whisper. His face was gaunt and shadowed with illness and fatigue, but his eyes were clear.

Moira, roused from her prayers at the sound of his voice, opened her eyes. Her heart raced as she rose from her chair, and pressed her hands against her gown to still their trembling.

"Richard?" she whispered, not daring to believe. She rushed to his side. She looked down on his wan, stubbled face, and saw that the eyes that returned her gaze were awake and aware. Relief engulfed her, and took the strength from her knees. She sank down on to the bed heavily. *Praise the Virgin, indeed! He had survived!* She reached down to lovingly cup his whiskered cheek, and he could see that she had suffered, too. She was shaking, and her face was very pale. Her hair had lost its luster, and her eyes were lifeless and red-rimmed.

"What has happened? How long have I been ill?" *Days, weeks, years, centuries?* he wondered, surprised by the change in her. He reached out a groping hand, wanting to give comfort. "Are ye all right?" he asked her, and the genuine concern in his voice made her smile. She took his hand and squeezed it.

"Aye," she answered. "Ye've been ill for ever so long, mo cridh. I've been so worried for ye."

Meg's heart had leapt with relief and happiness also when she had seen Richard rouse back to life, but she held herself back. As she sat watching them from her chair, she breathed a silent prayer of thanksgiving.

Moira bent close to him, touching her cheek to his, as his eyes slipped shut and he slept again.

After he drifted off to sleep, Moira watched the regular rise and fall of his chest. Her spirit lightened. She leaned forward to touch him. He was warm, but there was no trace of fever. She gently stroked his head, smoothing his rumpled curls. And that night Moira knelt and gave fervent thanks.

He slept for two days, waking only to take a little nourishment. In the days that followed, he progressed back to health and gained strength with amazing rapidity. The red lines of infection that had crept through his body first reversed their direction, then faded, then disappeared, and his wounds healed well.

His quick recovery brought the color back to Moira's cheeks and lips, the sheen to her hair, and a smile lit her eyes once more.

* * * *

A hand on his left shoulder gently shook him awake.

"Sit up, if yer able," he heard his sister say. "I've something for ye."

He slowly pulled himself up, feeling a dragging weight in his body. His muscles seemed to have turned rusty while he had been asleep. With his first effort, he thumped heavily back against his pillows. He managed on the second try, then rubbed a hand over his stubbled face. Feeling as though it would take a good while just to wake up, he slowly opened one eye, and Mary's face floated into view. She grinned at his efforts.

"What are ye laughing at?" he asked her.

Mary poured the ruby liquid she had brought for him into a pewter cup. "Time for yer elixir," she said, handing it to her brother.

"That's what ye have for me?" He grimaced when he took the cup. His arm still hurt when he moved it. "What is it?" he asked.

"Honey, claret, crushed rose hips--I gathered them myself--"

Richard made a face as he peered into the cup. "Ye gathered them yerself?" he asked doubtfully. "Are ye sure they're no' poison? Can ye tell the difference between a toadstool and--"

Ignoring him, Mary turned to Moira. "This must be made on a waxing moon, and I'll teach ye how." She looked back at Richard. "Ye will drink it three times a day. Moira, ye will see to it that the stubborn clot-heid drinks it all. And I'll tell ye another remedy that probably saved yer worthless life," she added, watching his face, "Moldy bread and cheese."

"Moldy--" Richard shuddered. "Was that the rank stuff ye forced down me when I could barely swallow?"

"Aye," she nodded. "I read that it cures fevers, especially those caused by injury. The Arabs always give it on the battlefield. They even plaster it on wounds."

"Faugh!" Richard said in disgust. "Ye most probably enjoyed choking me with it."

"Aye, brother, ye'll never ken just how much I did."

He peered into his cup once again. "Och, well, if I have lived through aught ye've done to me until now, I suppose I will live through this as well," and with that thought, he drained the cup.

* * * *

Dressed in his blue brocade dressing gown, Richard stirred restlessly against his pillows. Rees glanced over at him.

"I believe t'is time to try my legs," Richard told him. "I would like to surprise Moira when she returns from wherever it is my sister has dragged her off to."

"Mary took her to the garden. Ye ken she spends too much time cooped up in here with ye, ye disagreeable auld sod."

"Och, so she leaves me wi 'ye, ye wee gomerel. I might as well be alone, for all the stimulation ye bring me."

He gingerly swung his feet over the side of the bed and sat swaying dizzily for a moment, his head buzzing. He groaned as the movement sent a bolt of lightning from his leg right up through the top of his head. A lancet of pain flashed, and small, flashing lights danced before his eyes. His mind seemed to spin and fragment as faintness washed over him, and he began to sway back and forth. He put out his hands, as if to cling to something, and began to list to one side. Rees grabbed him by his uninjured left arm and eased him back against the pillows.

"I'm not supposed to stimulate ye, ye stubborn ox. I'm supposed to keep an eye on ye, to be sure ye dinna do anything foolish. Lie back now, and rest."

Rees 'image flickered and came apart, and suddenly Richard thought that he seemed to have many more eyes, noses and mouths than he had a moment ago. "I seem to be a wee bit dizzy," he sighed, closing his eyes. "My head is spinning like a top." He put his head down, waiting, willing.

Rees crossed his arms over his chest and leaned back in his chair. "I am certain that Moira would rather see ye safe and sound, biding in yer bed, than stumbling about the room." He glanced at his brother-in-law's bent head. "And yer sister, as well. I'd like to keep my head attached to my shoulders, if ye please."

Richard snorted. The faintness had passed. Slowly he opened one eye. There seemed to be only one Rees again, with the right number of parts, and all in their proper places. "Aye," he said with a grin. "She's a wee hell-kite when she's riled." He pulled himself erect and tried again to rise, only to have the world waver and spin around him.

"Aye, a bonny wee hell-kite, to be sure," Rees agreed. Then he noticed Richard's movements. He stood over him, and sighed with exasperation. "Ye willna do as yer told, I can see. 'Tis stubborn ye are." He studied him with concern, but then gave way to him reluctantly. "Mind, the next time ye see me, if I am without a head, 'tis yerself to blame. Can ye stand without help? Put yer arm on my shoulder."

Richard set his teeth and tried once more, this time more slowly. Holding onto Rees with his left hand, he pulled himself up, tottering gracelessly to his feet. To his surprise, he did not immediately keel over and collapse on the floor. He was up, standing on quivering legs.

He lurched a few steps, walking with the weaving, wavering steps of a drunken man, his balance as unsure as his legs. He frowned in concentration as he hobbled the length of the room unsteadily, leaning on Rees 'shoulder with one hand, grasping at the furniture with the other, to help him along. He walked slowly, with a pronounced limp, and with each step he winced. Then he caught his weight on his injured leg, and a jolt of exquisite pain surged up from his ankle, buckling his legs and making him groan. A sick ache throbbed in his head, and faintness stole over him once again, but he fought against it. Rees quickly got him to a chair and he sat down heavily, his hair falling in his eyes. His chest was heaving as he gasped for breath, his ankle throbbing. The effort had left him pale and sweating. The swirling lights that danced before his eyes slowly began to fade.

"I can do no more just now," he said breathlessly. He ran his hand through his hair to push it from his eyes as a shiver wracked his body and his teeth began to chatter. His head pounded and sweat poured down his face. The miscalculated step and ensuing pain had quickly convinced him that he needed to go more slowly and carefully.

Rees poured a cup from the flagon that Mary had left on the table. It was a cordial of wine, flavored with spices. "Here, drink this. Ye still have the sweats, I see."

Richard took the cup with trembling hands, as Rees wiped his moist forehead. He drank deeply from it, and felt some strength come back into him, and the watery feeling went out of his legs.

"Lie down for a bit."

He reluctantly obeyed, and lay down without protest when Rees turned back the covers. He felt ashamed of the weakness of his body. But his color soon returned, and the ache in his head faded, as he lay gazing up at the embroidered tester. "How long must I lie here like a bedridden auld man?" he grumbled.

A clatter of dishes in the corridor, and a knock upon the door announced dinner.

"Enter," Richard called, and Aggie let herself in.

"Welladay!" she cried, staring. Freshly shaven, dressed in his blue brocade dressing gown, she thought he looked very handsome, indeed. "So brisk and debonair, sir? Ye are indeed a marvel of recovery!"

"I dinna supposed ye've brought me anything solid to eat? Mrs. Campbell's chicken broth and egg yolk custard are tasty, but dinna stay on a man's stomach for long."

"I ken a man's on the mend for certain when he can eat and complain." Wry humor warmed her tart words as she placed the tray beside him "Aye, I've brought a bit of boiled beef, if ye think ye can manage it, and some new tatties mashed with cream."

He flashed her a smile of gratitude and made quick work of the meal. Having a full stomach revived him further. He leaned back with a satisfied sigh.

Rees got up from his chair and wandered over to the window, peering down into the courtyard. He saw Bram down below, strolling toward the stables.

"Now that yer nearly recovered, brother, I've been wondering what ye plan to do about Bram."

Richard frowned, and sat up straight. "Yer sure my cinch was cut, and yer sure it was him?"

"Aye, brother, I ken for sure the leather was cut. I can show you, if ye like. As for Bram, I canna prove it." He turned back and faced Richard, shaking his head. "But I dinna have a doubt that it was indeed him." His eyes rested upon Richard's face. "Is there anything ye wish me to do? I say the man has escaped retribution long enough."

Richard ran a hand through his hair, then rubbed at the back of his neck, though it did nothing to ease the strain. He took a deep breath and let it out slowly, hoping to ease his tension. "Nay, do nothing. I will deal with him myself."

He slumped back, frowning in quiet thoughtfulness. But he was tired, his body ached, and thoughts came with aggravating slowness. The food he had eaten suddenly felt like a stone in his roiling stomach. God in heaven, he did not feel up to confrontation, but he could see no way to avoid it. Something must be done about Bram.

* * * *

That evening, Richard and Moira sat together quietly by the fire in their room. She embroidered on the baby's gown, and he sat in his chair beside her, still dressed in his blue brocade gown with a blanket over his knees. He was watching her contentedly as the fire flickered and crackled, when suddenly he saw her whole stomach shift.

"By the saints, Moira!" he whispered, awestruck. He leaned closer to her. "Did that hurt?" He raised his eyebrow in question.

She smiled back at him and took his hand, laying it high on the mound of her stomach. "Nay, it doesna hurt, but 'tis uncomfortable sometimes."

The child thumped beneath his hand, then rolled. He shifted his hand to follow the baby's movements, until he felt a large, hard bump. He looked up at her.

"What part of the baby d'ye think I am feeling?"

"I canna guess," she answered with a grin. "Sometimes I think I can recognize a hand or a foot. But other times, I'm not sure." She gave a little laugh. "Every so often it feels as if the babe has more arms and legs than it should."

"Could there be more than one?" he asked. The thought had never occurred to him before.

"Yer sister assures me there's but one--and that it bears the proper amount of limbs." She smoothed her hand over the mound of her belly, pausing to stroke her fingers against the tiny protrusion where the baby pressed a foot or elbow hard against her. "Soon, little one, soon we'll be able to touch ye, to hold ye," she whispered. Then she cupped her hand over Richard's and smiled. He glanced up into Moira's face, gilded by firelight and at ease once more, and thought how beautiful she was at this moment. He couldn't have looked away if his life had depended on it.

* * * *

Richard was beginning to chafe at his confinement. He was restless and felt ready to return to his daily activities, he was sure. After all, he was able to walk around his room now without wobbling, and to savor the good meals sent him from the kitchens.

83

And so he greeted Mary one morning with a warm, but determined smile.

"Good day to ye, sister dear," he told her with practiced charm.

She observed his smile and sensed what he wanted. With a smile of her own, she recognized the evidence of his returned health. "Good day to ye, brother," she answered as she walked across the room to open a window. He turned toward her as she brushed by him, his arms outstretched.

"As ye can see, I'm nearly well. 'Tis time that I returned to my duties," he said, glowing with impatience at his inactivity.

She eyed him speculatively and nodded. Although she was not entirely satisfied that he was well enough, she had been expecting him to say something of the sort.

"Let me see ye walk across the room first," she said, frowning and crossing her arms over her breasts.

He smiled back at her sweetly, and gave her a demonstration, as she watched him keenly. Pain still shot through his leg as the nerves continued to mend, but he thought he hid the wince well. He glanced quickly up at her, and noticed that her frown had deepened. He braced himself for instructions to stay put.

However, as though she begrudged the words, she did agree. "Aye, Clot-heid, I suppose ye could go back to work. If ye promise me that ye'll not overdo. Ye'll land yerself back in bed if ye try to do too much."

"Ha!" he said triumphantly, the grin spreading across his face. He grabbed her hand in his and swung her around, twirling her about his room in his arms. "I kent ye'd see things my way!" Still laughing, he pulled her to a stop. She took a swipe at his head.
"I told ye not to overdo!" she warned him, her voice heavy with exasperation.

He cupped both his hands to her face and kissed her forehead. " I dinna believe I've told ye yet. Thank ye, Mary, for saving my life."

"Och, weel," she sniffed, touched by his show of affection. "Sure and I dinna ken what made the Blessed Lord chose to spare yer miserable hide. To be sure, I certainly dinna care a whit."

"Aye," he said with a smile, his thumb gently brushing away the tear that spilled down her cheek. "So ye say."

CHAPTER FORTY

The Rogation Days, the Monday, Tuesday and Wednesday before Ascension, had, in the past, been celebrated in the countryside under the name of Gangdays. The people of the village went "aganging" anyway, in procession led by a bold youth, who took the place of the village priest. He carried the cross, while others carried banners, bells. and lights around the boundaries of the village, "beating its bounds" with willow wands. The procession halted at the customary points, while the youth said the old prayers, which blessed the crops.

Next came Whit Sunday, the third and last of the May time feasts, with another week's holiday. At Whitsun, the peasants began to be less afraid that the frost might nip their tender crops and the work in the fields increased. Sluggards who preferred to stay abed were dealt with as always. The Reverend Edmund Corrie was also one who enjoyed sleeping later and later in the lax religious atmosphere of Ravana.

This particular morning, six young squires made their way up the stairs to his room with a bucket of cold water. Lifting the latch ever so quietly, and stifling their sniggers of anticipation, they roused the peacefully snoring vicar with a dousing of cold water and peals of laughter.

* * * *

June burst into bloom--leaves burst forth on every tree and bush. Daisies, larkspur, meadowsweet, thyme, foxglove, thimbleberry, purple thistle flowers, and yellow whorls of blooming fennel erupted by the road and in the meadow.

After the sheep shearing, Midsummer, the feast of the summer solstice was celebrated. St. John's day, June 24th, was also the traditional time to begin the hay harvest. It was the first day of summer, and the longest day of the year, and was celebrated with bonfires. The boys of the village collected bones and rubbish and burnt them, and carried brands about the fields, to discourage any dragons that might be about, set to join in on the fun. A wheel was set afire and rolled down the hill, to signify that the sin had reached its highest point and was turning back.

As the hay dried in the field, a green bower was erected before nightfall to shelter sleeping fairies, the villagers said, but in the years past it was built as a shrine for the Virgin Mary's statue. The Reverend Edmund Corrie condemned it all as paganism, and determined to strive harder against the intolerable papish idolatry.

* * * *

Meanwhile, letters from Edinburgh continued to pour in, keeping the Laird abreast of the news there. The Lords of the Congregation, unhappy with Mary and Darnley's wedding plans, filled Edinburgh with armed men to frighten the queen out of the marriage. But she proved not to be the malleable girl they had originally thought her to be. Instead, she held the Ceremony for the Revival of the Thistle, and gave Darnley honors. Their banns of marriage were announced openly in the church. Word arrived from Throckmorton that Queen Elizabeth expressly forbade the marriage. But Mary ignored everyone, and in the end, would have her own way.

And it was about this time that Richard returned to his duties as steward of the castle. The morning was spent in his office, closeted with Rees, pouring over the books that Rees had kept for him during his illness, bringing him up to date.

The afternoon found him heading for the stables, and for Bram. As he entered, the pleasant scent of clean straw and horses welcomed him. Jasper and Lackland were laying out clean hay in the stalls by the door.

"Hallo!" Jasper greeted, looking up as his shadow crossed the walkway. "'Tis good to see ye well and hardy, my friend!" He held out his hand and Richard shook it. "What's it been? Two months?"

"Aye," Richard answered. "Two months since the joust." He glanced over at Lackland, who had also stopped his work, and was leaning on his pitchfork. "I'll have a word with ye about that day, if I may."

Lackland nodded. "Aye, sir."

They walked outside into the paddock, and Lackland told him what he knew. He could prove nothing. No one saw who cut the cinch. But Bram never bothered to hide his hatred of Richard, either. He repeated what Bram had said to him during the joust. Richard smiled at him grimly and clapped him on the back.

"I thank ye for yer honesty, Lackland."

Lackland nodded. "I'm verra sorry, sir, for what happened."

"Thank ye. D'ye ken where I might find Bram?" he asked as they walked back inside.

"Aye, sir, I believe he's in the tack room wi' one o' the lads."

Richard nodded and strode up the aisle toward the tack room. Outwardly he had held his temper, but now his anger throbbed through every fiber of his being. He entered the tack room without preamble.

"MacKenzie, I'll have a word with ye *now*." His voice rose, despite his intention to remain calm. He glanced at the boy's shocked expression. "Leave us, Barney."

Seeing the dark scowls on both the men's faces, Barney hastily scrambled out the door.

"What d'ye want, Buchanan?" Bram asked, eyeing him up and down. "I see that ye have quite recovered from yer injuries." He fairly spat the words.

The sentence was barely out of his mouth before Richard fetched him a terrible clip on the jaw. Bram cried out as he reeled backward on his heel, then stumbled and fell to his knees. He slowly raised his head to look at his assailant, his beady eyes blazing. Blood welled from the side of his mouth.

Richard stood over him, his hands balled into fists. "Aye, that I am, and with no thanks to ye!" The outrage in his voice matched the expression on his face. "Get up! I ken I was sabotaged. *Someone* cut my cinch. I'm asking, was it ye?"

Bram suddenly chuckled and shook his head as he rose to his feet. "And what makes ye think that? *I* wouldna do such a thing," he sneered at him, gingerly probing his split lip. "Ye canna prove a thing."

Richard narrowed his eyes at him. His hands itched to hit him again. "No, I canna," he snarled back. "But I dinna trust ye, Bram MacKenzie. Ye and yer family will leave Ravana."

The color drained from Bram's face before his eyes. "What?! Who d'ye think ye are? The Laird? I willna go! I will take this matter up with him!"

"It will make no difference. I will give ye seven days, for the sake of yer wife and son. Then ye will go." His voice was cold as ice.

"Ye canna do this! Ye have no right! Where will we go? We have no other family!"

"That is yer problem. Seven days. Ye should be thankful I dinna throw ye out now."

"I was born here! My father was stable master before me, and his father before him!"

"Aye, and I will make Jasper the new stable master."

With a guttural sound, Bram grabbed a pitchfork from the wall hook and lunged at Richard. Rees called a warning as he stepped out of the shadows, his sword drawn. He shouldered Richard out of the way as he parried the weapon aside, slicing the handle neatly in two.

"Get out of my sight right now," Rees said, his voice hard. "Ye have seven days to move yer family. I would not have been so merciful. Ye'd best stay out of my sight until then. Go now and tell yer wife."

The stable boys' heads peeked around the door to see what the commotion was about. Defeated, Bram threw down the piece of the handle he still held in his hand. He stalked from the room, turning once to shake his fist defiantly. "I will speak to the Laird about this!"

Rees glared after him, thinking him lucky he hadn't suffered worse than the bruise he sported on his cheek.

The boys scattered as Bram stormed away, then came back together, watching Rees and Richard with wide eyes.

"Go back to yer work, lads," Richard told them as Rees sheathed his sword. Reluctantly they shuffled off.

Rees clapped him on the back companionably. "Yer reflexes have slowed, brother. Good thing Lackland came and told me what ye were up to. Ye'll be needing a bit of practice, I'm thinking, and I'm just the one to help ye along."

Richard snorted at him. "Yer a great nuisance to me, y'ken," he said dryly.

"Ye shouldna have confronted him alone."

"Ye should mind yer own business."

"Och, yer a crabbit get. Ye are my business, like it or no'. I risk my life to save yer worthless hide, with nary a word of thanks from ye. Yer sister would never forgive me if he'd run ye through with that pitchfork. Not to mention yer wife."

"It wouldna have happened."

It was Rees' turn to snort. He raised an eyebrow. "Och, aye, to be sure."

"Och, I suppose I should thank ye, ye wee eejit."

Rees grinned back at him. "Aye, ye should. And yer welcome. Come, let's give Jasper the news of his promotion."

He started off, but Richard grabbed his shoulder and pulled him back sharply. Slow or not, his strength was coming back to him.

"I'll no' have ye bragging about this, ye gallus bretherer."

"Och, yer a crabbit get, so ye are."

* * * *

A messenger arrived the next day with an invitation for the Laird of Ravana and his Lady. Mary, Queen of Scots, would be married at Holyrood on Sunday, July 29th, to Henry Stewart, formerly Lord Darnley, now the earl of Ross and Duke of Albany, soon to be the King of Scots.

That same evening, after supper, Moira and Richard passed their time in their room. Richard drew Moira's chair toward the fire in the huge hearth while Moira placed her basket of sewing near at hand. Grabbing onto the chair's arms, she eased herself down into it, hoping to accomplish something on the baby's Christening gown. Richard settled himself nearby and began to read aloud. His voice was soothing as she pulled the needle through the fabric, but for some reason she could not seem to concentrate. She jabbed her finger with the needle yet again, this time drawing blood. She hastily dropped the piece of soft white linen into her lap to keep from staining it.

"Och, fie!" she muttered, shaking her head. "I canna seem to do even the simplest task!" She brought her finger to her mouth.

Richard put down the book. "Let me see." He went down on his knees beside her and took her finger to examine it. "Tis quite a poke," he told her as he quickly reached for an unused piece of fabric to wrap around it to keep it from bleeding. A tide of warmth flooded through her at his gentle ministrations. She savored his closeness. His scent filled her senses and she was tempted to lean closer, to touch the soft curls that gleamed in the firelight as he bent his head to his task.

But she didn't, for she knew that her love always seemed to overwhelm him.

"There," he said, glancing up at her and smiling.

A flush rose to her cheeks. "Thank ye," she said softly, and sought to distract herself by putting her sewing back into her basket. Then she levered herself up out of the chair. Straightening, she rubbed her lower back, the arching movement emphasizing the mound of her belly.

"Moira, does yer back hurt?"

"It's never ached so much," she said. "But it's been a long day." She glanced down at her belly.

"Would it help if I rubbed yer back?"

She nodded her head.

"Come then," Richard said, brushing a kiss across her cheek. "One fond kiss, ye've earned yer rest. To bed with ye."

She didn't move, and an odd expression passed over her face. "I dinna believe I'll be resting for yet a while, my love."

"What d'ye mean?" he asked, though he thought he knew the answer.

"I mean, mo cridh, that our babe is about to be born," she told him, laughing.

"Are ye sure?"

"Aye, a leannan, I'm sure now," she said, grimacing. "The pains are coming on, and there is a dull ache in my back that doesna go away." She took his hand and placed it over her belly. He felt it draw up and tighten into a hard knot.

"All right, I believe ye," he said, concern lacing his voice. He raked his hand through his hair. "I'll get Mary," he said, then headed for the door.

He found his sister in the solar, sewing with the other women.

"Mary," he said. "Please come. 'Tis Moira's time."

She immediately put her sewing aside and stood. "M'lady," she said, turning toward Meg. "D'ye wish to come also?"

"Aye," she answered, excitement tinged with fear fluttering in her stomach. She glanced at Richard and saw the apprehension that etched his features. She returned her sewing to her box and followed them out the door.

When they returned to the chamber, Moira was in the process of spreading an ancient quilt over the bed. She had already changed into an old nightgown.

"Och, let me help ye," Mary offered, hurrying to the other side of the bed to straighten the cover. "Go now and sit in the chair by the window. Never ye mind about this."

She straightened without a word and smiled, and with a dreamy expression in her eyes, did as she was bid.

As Mary finished with the bedding, she told Meg to call down for clean linens and water, and the two busied themselves with the preparations for childbirth.

Richard crossed the room and laid his hand anxiously upon her shoulder. She covered it with her own, smiling up at him in reassurance. He squeezed her shoulder lightly, and leaned down to kiss her cheek.

She sucked her breath in with a hiss then, putting both her hands on her distended abdomen. She moaned as another paroxysm twisted through her.

Richard wrapped her in his arms. "Shhh, mo suirdhe," he whispered in her ear. "I am here with ye." Her belly drew up, tight and round. She bit her lip and breathed heavily digging her fingernails into his arms, but he did not flinch. After a moment she relaxed, and her belly resumed its normal shape.

At first Moira was able to join their conversation, but a lull would find her bending over and holding her stomach, as the contractions became increasingly powerful. She soon lost interest in their chatter, and leaned back in her chair, resting quietly as the pains tightened their grip. Meg grew more nervous as the contractions grew stronger. It was difficult for her to watch her friend suffer, and not be able to do more for her. Though she did seem content to have Richard with her.

Finally, after a pain that almost bent her double, Moira rose to her feet, and made her way to the bed to lie down.

Mary gave her a preliminary examination. Everything normal so far. Aggie had produced a pile of clean sheets for their use, and Mary took one of these, still folded, and pushed it under Moira.

"Have ye decided upon a name yet?" she asked.

"Aye," Richard answered. "Ann."

"Ann?" Mary asked, raising an eyebrow. "Is that all? Are ye so sure, then, 'tis a girl?"

"Aye, that he is," Moira said breathlessly, smiling into her husband's face. The pain washed over her then, filling her and leaving room for little else. She clamped her lips together and breathed heavily, as the full force of the pain came on. Richard smoothed her hair aside and pressed a gentle kiss to her cheek.

"Think on something else, Moira. We'll go someplace else together, in our minds. Peace, enjoyment," he whispered as he slid his hand down to cup her belly, feeling it draw up hard beneath his hand. "Love and pleasure. Think on our life together with this new wee one. She will be our joy and treasure." The warmth and strength that flowed from his touch calmed her fears and eased her pain.

He picked up her hand and laced his fingers with hers as another pain filled her body. "Think on something pleasant, peaceful," he murmured in her ear, and he held her through the seemingly endless pain. Panting, she slumped back once the spasm eased. He rested his forehead against hers when it was over.

Reaching up to smooth her hair away from her face, he told her, "Squeeze my hand as hard as ye need to, mo cridhe. We'll do this together. Wee Annie awaits us at the end of it."

They all settled down to wait. Mary and Meg talked quietly and comfortingly to Moira, while Richard rubbed the small of her back, pressing hard during the contractions. The pains became more frequent.

The pressure in her belly began to build once again. She squeezed Richard's hand. "Here comes another," she whispered, her voice trailing off in a deep, faint groan. He leaned over her, murmuring endearments as they rode out the spasm together.

Weariness vied with anticipation, but with the soft bolsters nestling her in their warmth, along with Richard's soothing embrace, and the hypnotic dance of the flames in the fireplace, Moira's thoughts drifted, even as her eyelids slipped closed.

She slept in between contractions, while Mary and Meg busied themselves with their preparations for the coming baby. Richard stayed near his wife, murmuring softly to her through each pain, wiping her face with a cool cloth while she rested between.

Suddenly her belly dropped down, startling Moira from her drowsy sleep. She lifted herself on her elbow, and water gushed out, soaking the pad beneath her.

"Tis all right, a leannan," Richard soothed, realizing that her water had broken.

Meg quickly helped Mary to exchange the wet sheet for a dry one, and settled Moira once more.

All at once the pains seemed to return full force, coming one on top of the other, until Moira wondered how she would bear them. But Richard gathered her in his arms and held her through each one, sharing his strength, murmuring comfort in her ear.

"I feel like I need to push," Moira groaned.

"Aye, then, push! Bear down with them!" Mary urged her. "Tis time."

Panting and sweating, she bore down with the pain, pushing through the core to the very end. And then suddenly she felt

94

movement. She could actually feel the baby slide into the birth canal and begin to emerge, slippery and wet.

"Make ready!" Mary cried in her excitement. "Make ready!"

Meg rushed over to the foot of the bed with wrapping sheets.

"Tis here! 'Tis here! Oh!" Mary cri ed, as the vigorous, squirming, wonderful aliveness of the baby wriggled into her hands. "*She* is here! Och, 'tis a girl!"

Moira could hear her baby crying, mewling and tremulous-- and an infinite relief washed over her. But…was she whole? Richard stood up, straining to see, his face alight with excitement.

Mary quickly cut the cord. "Our blessed Lord be praised!" she said as she held out the slippery, gleaming baby to Meg, who gently wrapped her in a sheet and carried her to the warmed water for a bath. The baby wailed loudly.

Moira could hear the gentle splashing of the water, and the baby's cries became soft whimperings, as Meg exclaimed over her delightedly. She was perfectly formed, then, she thought with relief. *Thank the blessed Mother!* Richard kissed her face several times, and squeezed her hand, beside himself with joy.

Mary slid clean linens under Moira, wiped her sweat away with warm scented towels, and gave her a fresh gown. A dry pillow was given in place of her soaked one, and then Meg put the wrapped baby into her outstretched arms.

She was beautiful--pink and white, her hair a downy gold. Her tiny puckered rosebud mouth worked and her little eyelids opened, showing bright blue eyes. Tears welled in Moira's eyes and spilled down her cheeks.

Richard leaned over Moira's shoulder and traced his finger across one soft, pink cheek. "Hello, there, wee Annie," he said. "Tis Papa."

The baby stared up at them both with dark blue unfocused eyes, and clenching her tiny fingers into fists, began to howl.

"She's certainly got yer singing voice, brother," Mary said casually, gathering up the dirty linen.

"Aye," he agreed proudly, tucking the blanket up around his daughter's tiny chin. His eyes were suspiciously damp as he met Moira's gaze above the downy head. "She's a bonny one," he murmured. "Ye've done well, mo suiridhe."

Moira put up her hand to trace his loved face.

"I'm sorry it was so bad," he said, kissing her fingers.

"Not that bad. I've forgotten already."

Mary sidled up to her brother and peered at her niece over his shoulder.

"She is a sweet, wee thing," she crooned softly, reaching out to stroke the downy head. "She favors her mother, I think."

The baby's moist pink underlip quivered faintly, the preliminary to another full-fledged wail.

"But she definitely has yer voice, Clot-heid."

Richard grinned, and lacing his fingers with Moira's, brought her hand to his lips. "Ye've given me so much, Moira. Ye've made me the happiest man alive. I swear I'll protect ye and our babe always."

She reached up and stroked her hand through his disordered curls, and held his words in her heart.

Meg made her way back to her own room, feeling hollow and alone. Her empty room greeted her with silence, save for the fire crackling on the grate. The warm family scene she had just left was etched indelibly in her mind, Richard and Moira's head bent together over the downy softness of their babe. She longed for the same for herself, but knew that she would never have it. Not with Kenneth. And she was glad that he had gone into the village after supper, and hoped that he would not come back, to force himself upon her, as was his way.

She walked across the room and knelt beside the chest that she had brought with her from Gladstone. Slowly she opened the lid, then pulled out the linen handkerchief hidden in its secret recesses. Carefully she unwrapped the treasure nestled in its soft folds. The diamonds and sapphire of the brooch twinkled brightly, reflecting the flames from the hearth. Tenderly she kissed it, then quickly wrapped it once again in the linen square, and thrust it back into the chest.

She closed the lid, and saw through the window the gray light of dawn, and was conscious for the first time just how tired she was. It had been nearly twenty-four hours since she had slept. Sighing, she silently readied herself for bed. Laying back the covers, she crawled between the cold sheets and lay shivering, until she finally fell into a troubled sleep.

* * * *

The next morning flew by in a daze for Moira, as she sought to regain her strength and care for wee Annie. Richard had left hours ago. Aggie had brought up her breakfast and cooed over the baby for a moment, and now she was alone.

She laid back against the pillows cuddling her tiny daughter to her breast, listening to the contented smacking sounds, and marveling at the miracle that was her child.

The latch on the door lifted quietly and Richard stepped inside, holding something behind his back.

"What have ye there?" Moira asked, a smile lighting her eyes.

He drew his hand out, holding in it a single red rose. Leaning down, he kissed her forehead. "A rose for ye, a leannan."

She gave a merry laugh, deeply touched by his simple gift.

He laid the flower on the bedside table, then pulled a chair up by the bed. "I canna stay long, but all I could think of was ye and Annie." He smiled and reached out to touch the tiny button nose with one fingertip.

The baby released her mother's breast and Moira looked down at the swaddled bundle she held cradled in her arms.

"D'ye want to hold her?" she asked tentatively.

"Och, aye…" he said, an expression of blissful devotion on his face. With gentle hands he lifted the tiny bundle from Moira's arms and cuddled it against his chest, nudging back the flap of blanket that covered the baby's face. Her eyes were closed, blonde wispy lashes barely visible in the crease of her eyelids, and her small puckered rosebud mouth worked as if she still suckled. He traced a long finger over her flushed, smooth round cheek, astonished at the purity and wonderment of his daughter. A smile crept across her features, passing so quickly that he wondered if he had imagined it. At that moment, he felt that nothing on earth could have brought him more joy.

"Och, she's bonny," he whispered in awe. Here, in his arms he felt the promise, the hopes and dreams of the future.

He could see her pulse beat visibly in the soft spot on the top of her head, and she suddenly seemed disturbingly fragile to him. An overwhelming impulse to protect her surged through him, and he pulled the blanket back up over her head, cupping the small fuzzy skull in the palm of his hand as he lifted her to his shoulder. The tiny body slumped against him, a warm, soft and comforting weight.

* * * *

Bram attempted several times to speak with Kenneth about the matter of his leaving. But Kenneth was too caught up in matters of court to take the time to listen to him. He did not see Bram, but sent word that they would talk when he returned to Ravana, after the wedding.

* * * *

Meg and Kenneth, together with their small retinue of soldiers, left for Edinburgh for the royal wedding on the 25th of July. The trip was uneventful, and they arrived at Kenneth's uncle's manor home late in the afternoon of the next day. Meg felt unusually tired, and rested a few hours before supper. She awoke refreshed, and joined the others in the Great Hall.

The next morning, Lord Patrick, his son William, and Kenneth cloistered themselves together in serious discussion, while Lord Patrick's wife, Lady Jane, did her best to entertain Meg. But as the morning passed for Meggie, she found that none of the diversion Lady Jane engaged in appealed to her. Gradually she realized that part of her restlessness came from a physical discomfort. There were fleeting twinges of nausea. Her nerves were stretched taut, her stomach knotted, making her wish she had skipped eating all together.

Could it be the dinner last night? she wondered. Her head felt light and her stomach queasy. Despite her best efforts to distract her thoughts, a wave of uncertainty assailed her that had her fidgeting and starting at each and every tiny noise. Unable to face supper that evening, she retired to her chamber, where the smell of food wouldn't reach her. She couldn't allow herself to be sick now.

The next night her stomach again rebelled against the sight and smell of food and she remarked to Lady Jane that she seemed unusually high strung.

Lady Jane merely smiled, and waited to see if the sickness would recur the following night. It did.

The next morning, they all gathered at the Palace of Holyrood to watch the queen and Henry, the Duke of Albany, become man and wife. The ceremony was a quiet one, and afterwards they joined in the feasting and dancing. Henry never took his eyes off his beautiful bride, dressed in a gown of scarlet, embroidered with pearls and golden thread, stiff with richness, covered in jewels. Her thick and shining auburn hair spilled down her back behind the pearl encrusted satin cap as he held her in his arms.

Outside, in the streets of Edinburgh, the people were in near riot over the marriage. A royal herald, accompanied by two soldiers and trumpeters, pushed their way toward the Mercat Cross, and mounted its base. The herald unrolled his parchment to a trumpeted fanfare, and read aloud the Queen's Proclamation that her beloved husband Henry, Lord Darnley, Duke of Albany, was from this day forward to be honored as Henry, King of Scotland.

No one cheered.

CHAPTER FORTY-ONE

The morning after they arrived back at Ravana, Kenneth stayed in his rooms, his head pounding. A servant brought his breakfast up to him, but Kenneth did not answer. Instead, he lay in bed moaning and clutching a raging headache. After a short wait, the servant decided that the laird did not wish to be disturbed, and took the tray back down to the kitchen.

* * * *

"Where is Kenneth?" Richard asked, as everyone settled themselves in the Great Hall for the noon time meal.

"I dinna ken," Meg answered. "I havena seen him all morning. One of the servants took breakfast to his chamber, but he brought the food back untouched."

"Strange," Richard mused.

* * * *

Betsy MacCallum moved restlessly about the kitchen from one chore to another, stirring the steaming pots and checking the tray of herbs that lay drying by the fire. She felt anxious and ill at ease as Mary entered.

"Good day to ye, Betsy. How goes it?"

"Och, m'lady, naught goes well this day."

"Is something amiss? Is Rabbie all right?"

"Och, aye, he is fine, the wee rascal. I dinna ken what it is that bothers me. But I fear that something is not right."

"What?" Mary looked at the normally imperturbable woman. She watched her movements as she stirred the steaming pots. Something did seem wrong with her. Betsy's eyes were watery and her face did seem unusually flushed. Of course, it could be caused by the steaming pots, but something in the air did not seem quite right. She glanced around the kitchen. Others seemed out of sorts also. A dread fear crawled up her spine. She decided to have a walk around the castle grounds and see things for herself. She laid a reassuring hand on the woman's shoulder.

"Dinna fash yerself, Betsy. I am certain it will pass."

She crossed the kitchen and stepped outside, turning to glance back with a worried frown. She walked through the herb garden and courtyard, watching and listening with careful attention. She heard Bram's angry voice carry on the breeze from the stable and then an abrupt reply. She could hear many antagonistic and hostile words from every corner, yet some seemed completely unaffected.

She went back into the castle and climbed the stairs to the solar to join the other women.

* * * *

Richard became worried that he had not seen or heard from Kenneth all morning. He had a niggling feeling that something was wrong as he went through the motions of his daily duties. So he decided to see for himself. He headed up the stairs to the laird's room and knocked. There was no answer.

"Ken! Ken, man, are ye in there?" He waited a moment, then lifted the latch and stepped inside. The stench of vomit stung his senses, and he grimaced. The drapes were still closed over the windows, and the dying embers of the fire cast little light into the room.

"Ken?"

A deep groan sounded from the bed. He made his way toward the sound and found the Laird fevered, shivering and listless. There was a revolting stench about him, and he started violently when Richard touched him.

"Holy mother of God," Richard murmured, feeling the swollen lymph nodes in Kenneth's neck and armpits. He bolted out the door and down the stairs.

* * * *

In the solar, the women all seemed cheerful enough, gathered around the fire, sewing, gossiping, and laughing. Mary looked up from her hoop at the animated faces around her. Moira seemed very intent as she pulled the thread through the piece she was working on. She could see that her hand shook.

"Is aught wrong, Moira? Is wee Annie all right?"

"Aye, she is."

"That clot-heided brother of mine hasn't upset ye, has he?"

"Och, nay, Mary. I dinna ken what ails me."

"I have a strange feeling myself," one of the other ladies said, and a buzz went around the room as others admitted to feeling anxious or uneasy.

The warning once again prickled up Mary's spine. She could remember a similar incident many years ago, like déjà vu. But the memory was elusive, like a discordant note in a lingering melody...

Ring around the rosy
Pocket full of posy...

There was a loud banging, and one of the kitchen maids burst through the door, breathing heavily from the long run up the stairs. Mary jumped to her feet, startled from her thoughts by the sudden noise.

"Mistress!" she panted, trying to catch her breath and speak at the same time.

"What is it?"

The girl took in deep gulps of air and continued on. "Ye must come quickly to the kitchen! 'Tis Betsy! Och, I dinna ken what ails her, but 'tis something awful!"

Meg was on her feet, but Mary waved her back. "Nay, m'lady, stay here with the others. I will see what's amiss."

She followed the frightened girl back to the kitchen, where she found Betsy leaning over a bucket, shivering and retching, while the rest of the kitchen help stared at her with wide eyes, standing away from her as far as they could.

Mary took in the scene, and the persistent feeling of déjà vu became reality. The awful memories came swirling back to her. She recalled the previous sickness that had come to Ravana ten years before, when half the population had died, taking with it her beloved parents and the Laird and Lady of the castle.

"Mary!" Richard's voice called. She turned to find him standing in the doorway. "Mary, 'tis Ken. He's..." His voice trailed off when he saw Betsy. "My God...'tis happening again, isn't it?"

Mary nodded. "Has Ken sickened as well?"

"Aye," Richard nodded grimly. "We must do something, and right speedily.'

Hysterical mutterings rose in the air. Mary glanced up and noticed several of the servants making the Sign of the Cross, their lips moving in whispered prayers. She suddenly remembered Father William. She must see to him at once.

"I'll find Rees," Richard said. "We'll have to bring bedding to the Hall. If everyone is in one place, they will be easier to care for."

Mary nodded. "Secure the castle," she told him. "Lock the doors in the curtain wall, raise the drawbridge. We canna risk infecting the village."

"Aye," Richard agreed, then went to find Rees.

Mary went to Betsy, who had stopped vomiting. She was sitting in a chair, her head in her hands. Mary put her arm around her shoulders. "All will be well," she told her comfortingly. Turning to face the kitchen staff, she began to call out orders. "Wat! Bring the barrels of vinegar to the Hall! Duncan, bring braziers so that we may burn lavender and spices to purify the air! Alex, fetch blankets and pallets!"

The sounds of the great chains lifting the drawbridge sounded, and anxiety swept anew through the kitchen. The huge wooden bridge groaned and rumbled, straining into its assemblage with a resounding boom. The distinct chink of the iron tipped portcullis rang out as it dropped onto the rock floor of the gatehouse with an ominous resonance.

Betsy looked up at Mary through watery eyes. "My Rabbie," she rasped. "Please..."

"Dinna mind for him, Betsy, 'tis yerself we must care for now. Rabbie will be removed with the others who have not fallen ill," she told her with a reassuring squeeze of her hand.

She left her then and went through the dark corridor behind the kitchen to check on Father William. She knocked upon his door.

"Father William?" she called. There was no answer. She lifted the latch and stepped inside. The stench that met her was nauseating. She heard his labored breathing from the cot on which he lay. She went to him and found him fully dressed in his black cassock, muttering prayers to himself.

"Father, 'tis Mary. I've come to bring ye into the Hall. Can ye walk?"

"Leave me, my child," he said in a hoarse whisper.

"Nay, Father," she told him, pulling the old man to his feet, and looping an around her neck. He felt thin and frail beneath his cassock.

"I must not leave my room!" he protested. "I willna endanger ye wi' the Laird!"

"I canna care for ye properly in here."

"Then leave me, to live or die as God wills."

"Nay," Mary said firmly.

"I'll not go."

"Aye, ye will."

She half pulled, half carried the old priest as he struggled against her. She shoved open the door with her shoulder and he gasped as she heaved him through, and started down the corridor.

By the time she had reached the Hall, Richard had come to help her. "The priest has sickened as well."

He looked at Father William and nodded, bending to lift the vaguely protesting priest. "Come, the pallets are being readied. We've put Kenneth in the minstrel's gallery."

Already the atmosphere of Ravana was changed. The Great Hall had become a sickroom, full of pallets quickly filling with those falling ill. The braziers filled the room with a cloying smoke, and the casks of vinegar had been tapped, adding to the overpowering odor.

Richard laid the priest down on an empty pallet, and he immediately curled into a knot.

Richard turned to his sister. "We must gather everyone together who hasna become ill, in the wool house perhaps." Apprehension clouded his eyes. "We've dealt with this disease before, Mary, and survived. We can care for the sick ourselves. We must save the others, if we can. I will send those down here to the safety of the courtyard. Ye find Matty, Moira, Annie, and Meg. Get them safely away."

Mary nodded and headed up the stairs, while he turned in the other direction. He noticed Edmund Corrie enter the Hall, glancing around him at the seeming chaos.

"What is happening?" the vicar asked Richard.

"There is sickness here, Reverend. If ye havena had it, I suggest ye get yerself to the wool house, and right quickly."

The vicar blinked at the sick who lay upon the pallets on the floor. He spotted Father William.

"Who is that?" he asked calmly. "A priest?"

"Aye, Reverend," Richard admitted with a sigh. "He is the old priest who was here before ye came. We have hidden him here within the castle walls these last months because I couldna turn him out." He narrowed his eyes at the man, watching his reaction with apprehension.

Reverend Corrie's face twitched into a small grimace of distaste, then settled back into impassivity. He sank down on his knees beside the priest, and turned his head. "I will help ye care for the sick. I have had this sickness before."

Richard gave the man a grim but thankful smile.

* * * *

Upstairs, Mary went first to Eleanor, who was in the nursery, watching the children. They were sitting near the fire, three month old Gwyllyn at her breast, baby Annie sleep in her cradle, Matty held enthralled by the story she was telling him.

Eleanor turned toward the door when she heard it open. She saw the expression on Mary's face and knew that something was wrong. "Mary, what brings ye here? Is aught wrong?"

105

"Aye, Eleanor. Ye must take the children to the wool house and remain there with them. Others will join ye there. There is sickness here."

Eleanor blanched, but did as she was told. "Come, Matty," she said, taking his hand and helping him to his feet.

"I will fetch Moira and Meggie."

She left the nursery and went to the solar, where she found a disheartening sight. The women there were gathered around a prone figure on the floor. The small group parted when Mary entered, and she could see Meg cradling Moira's head in her lap. Meg looked up at her helplessly.

Mary's breath caught in her throat and her heart gave a squeeze. "Sweet savior," she murmured. Suddenly the terrible reality of the situation came home to her, as she saw her sister-in-law, lying flushed and shivering.

Mary took a deep breath. "Everyone who is not feeling ill, hurry to the wool house, now, and stay there."

She went down on her knees beside Moira as the others rushed out of the room. Pressing her hand gently to her forehead, she felt the burning fever.

"She has the sickness, as well," she sighed. "The whole castle is falling ill."

Meg bit her lip. "I believe this sickness came to Gladstone Castle many years ago when I was a child. I recovered."

"Ye have had it then?"

"Aye. It was before Moira came to us."

"Help me. We must get her downstairs to the gallery to tend to her with the others."

Rees was in the gallery when he saw his wife and Meg struggling with their burden. He hurried to them quickly and took Moira in his arms.

"Where is Richard?" Mary asked. "He must be told."

"Downstairs," he said, nodding toward the Hall. He laid Moira on a pallet and Meg pulled the blanket up over her. Moira moaned and rolled her head restlessly, as Meg pressed a cool cloth to her forehead.

In a moment Richard was there. "Och…God, no," he groaned, panic stricken. It was as much a prayer as an exclamation of dread. Meg looked up at him, and the agony of his white face tore at her. He raked his fingers through his hair and went down on his knees beside her.

* * * *

The sick soon filled the Hall and the long gallery above and behind the Hall. Rees and Mary moved among them, caring for them and comforting them. They wrapped them in blankets as their temperatures rose to alarming heights. They forced watered vinegar down their parched throats, but nothing seemed to help. A rash covered their bodies, they vomited and coughed up blood, and then became comatose.

Everyone who was well had been sent to the isolation of the wool house, but were told to bring themselves quickly to the Hall at the first sign of illness. They huddled desperately together at first, praying for the sick and for each other. But the efficient Mrs. Campbell quickly took the situation in hand. She delegated duties to everyone, from fetching water and preparing food, to caring for the children. Soon everyone was busy, the paralyzing fear of what could happen only a nagging worry in the back of their minds.

As the day turned into evening the deaths began. Betsy MacCallum was the first, followed closely by Father William and Tibby.

The rush lights were lit, lending their smoky odor to the spice and lavender filled braziers. The Hall was suffocating with the stench of disease. Reverend Corrie moved about the Hall, giving comfort where he could, easing their parched thirst with watered down vinegar, listening to their dying words. They worried for their relatives in the safety of the wool house. What would become of their children, wife or husband, without them? What if they also became ill? The Reverend did his best to instill a peace in their fevered minds, praying with them, and for them. But still, the dying prayers on many lips were distinctly Catholic.

* * * *

Reverend Corrie came down on his haunches beside Richard. "How is she?" he asked quietly.

Richard raised his eyes to the Reverend's face, then shook his head slowly. "I dinna ken...I dinna ken..." he repeated in a broken voice.

Edmund Corrie put a comforting hand on his shoulder. "Let me pray with ye, Richard."

Richard gave him discerning look. "I am a Catholic, Reverend, not a Protestant."

The reverend gave a dry laugh, a glint of humor momentarily brightening his eyes. "All in good time, my friend," he said with a grin.

Richard shook his head. "Reverend, I dinna think--"

"Come, come, Richard. We all pray to the same God, do we not?" he pointed out. "He hears all prayers said with sincerity. He is a merciful Father to us all."

"Aye," he admitted with a sigh. "I suppose ye are right." He nodded his head. "Aye, then, let us pray together."

They bowed their heads, and Reverend Edmund Corrie asked for God's mercy for Moira and Richard, and all those at Ravana. When he was finished he glanced around, and saw Kenneth. He turned back to Richard.

"So, ye hid the priest within these walls these many months," he nodded toward the laird, "and he never kent it?"
Richard shook his head. "No." He smiled at the Reverend. "Neither did ye. Ye willna tell him, will ye?" He shook his head, thinking what consequences there would be. "There would surely be Hell to pay-- och," he glanced sheepishly at Corrie. "Sorry, Reverend."

Edmund Corrie grinned. "I understand. I've seen enough of his ways to ken that ye are right. I will not tell."

Richard looked at him gratefully. "Thank ye for that. And thank ye for your prayers and yer bit of enlightenment."
* * * *

Rees and Edmund Corrie watched over the Hall, while Mary and Meg cared for the sick in the gallery. They saw to it that they took in enough liquids, bathed their fevered faces with cool cloths, kept them warm through their fits of shivering, and made them as comfortable as possible.

Richard sat beside Moira, refusing to leave her side. He cared for her himself, alternately pleading with and ordering her to get well. Meg saw the heartbreak in his eyes and heard it in his voice, but she could do nothing to ease his pain.

A groan behind her made her turn. It was Kenneth. He lay nearby, alternately shivering and sweating, his fever alarmingly high. She went to him and lifted his head, and offered him the vinegar-water. He drank thirstily. Then she laid his head back down on the pillow and wiped the sweat from his brow.

* * * *

By midnight the deaths had climbed disturbingly. And still the misery wore on. Rees, Corrie, Mary, and Meg continued to make their rounds, doing what they could, but it seemed a hopeless cause as they watched their friends drift away from them into oblivion.

Richard looked up as Meg approached, his face drawn with worry and fatigue. Her heart was wrung as she dropped down beside him. She leaned over to touch Moira's brow. "I think she is less fevered."

A slow smile lit his haggard features. "I kent it so, but I couldna be sure."

She could hear the barely concealed spark of hope in voice.

She smiled up at him. "I believe she will live."

"Och…praise God if it be so." His eyes were damp as he took Moira's hands in his. "Aye," he agreed. "I believe she is less fevered."

Meg stood and rested a comforting hand on Richard's shoulder, as he looked down at Moira tenderly. Then she moved away to see to the other patients. She longed to step outside for a breath of fresh air. It was stifling in the gallery.

The night passed and a new day dawned. Moira began to stir. She opened her eyes and looked up into Richard's ashen face.

"Are ye all right, mo cridh?" she asked him, her voice a mere whisper.

"All right?" he repeated, a relieved gin spreading across his features. "All right? Me? 'Tis ye who have been ill," he said. "How d'ye feel?"

"Strange…Where is Annie? She hasna been ill, has she?" There was panic in her voice as she tried to raise herself. Richard laid a restraining hand on her. "She is safe with Eleanor and the others in the wool house. Rest now."

"Are ye sure?"

"Aye, mo cridhe. All is well, now. Ye must rest." He smiled and raised her hand to his lips.

"Ye look as if ye could do with a bit of rest yerself."

"I am fine. Dinna fash yerself about me." He pulled the blanket up and tucked it under her shoulders. "Sleep. 'Tis an order." He kissed her lightly on the forehead, and she closed her eyes and drifted off to sleep.

* * * *

Night came. The rush lights were once again lit, the eerie light dancing across the Hall and gallery, casting macabre shadows upon the walls.

Kenneth groaned. "Where am I?" came his hoarse whisper.

Richard moved over beside him. "Welcome back," he said with a grin. He pressed a hand to Kenneth's forehead and found him cool to his touch. "Ye've been verra ill. A sickness has come to Ravana. We have lost many."

"Where am I?" Kenneth repeated.

"In the minstrel's gallery. Most are in the Hall. It was easier to care for everyone this way. The others are safe in the wool house."

Richard lifted Kenneth's head and pressed a cup of vinegar-water to his lips. The sharp scent struck him and he turned his head aside.

"Drink," Richard commanded.

"I dinna need the foul stuff," he muttered.

"That ye do," Richard answered him, with a firm authority in his voice. Kenneth lacked the strength to argue, so he opened his mouth and sipped, his head swirling. He felt his body quiver under the strain.

"A bit more now. Aye, that's it," Richard coaxed.

Kenneth turned his head away, as a wave of dizziness washed through him. He sank back against the pillows and closed his eyes.

* * * *

Aching from head to toe with weariness, Meg climbed the stairs that led to the battlements. She stepped out onto the walkway to breathe in the fresh air. She had been suffering from twinges of nausea throughout the day, and gulped in the cool refreshing element, hoping to calm her raw nerves and settle her stomach.

A blue-grey caul of mist lay low in the air, obscuring her view of the village. *Was all well there?* she wondered. She hoped that the sickness had not come to them, as well. She leaned her forehead against the damp coolness of the stone crenel. A sadness lay heavy on her. So many had died. She prayed the village would be spared......and Moira...

She recalled the lost and frightened look in Richard's eyes the last time she had seen him, and she prayed that Moira would live, and that he would be spared such heartbreak.

She heard footsteps behind her and turned toward them. It was Richard. He stood framed in the arch of the stairwell. He must have followed her up the stairs, she thought, tightening her hands on the crenel notch. He looked mentally and physically exhausted as he moved toward her.

"Moira's going to be all right," he told her. "The fever has broken. And Kenneth's, as well."

Overcome with relief, he put his arms around her and rested his chin against her temple. She was aware of his fine whiskers, a gentle roughness, as his warm breath tickled her ear, and she let herself surrender to his embrace for just a moment, before telling herself she must pull free of him.

The delicate scent of lavender drifted up to him from her hair. He was amazed that the scent had stayed with her, after all the dark hours spent with the diseased and astringent smells wafting through the Hall and gallery. It stirred bittersweet, half-forgotten memories.

"Och, well, 'tis good news, indeed!" Meg said, nervously stepping away from him, her heart pounding. *What was his expression?* In the faint light she could not see. But her desire for him was unlike anything she had ever experienced, or was even prepared for. It was a strange mixture of yearning for possession, a physical ache, and yet she felt protective of him. And she knew that she must take her leave of him before he could see it. There was an awkward silence. The mists were creeping higher in the hills, and the moon shone with a fuzzy, shrouded light.

"Ye must be tired. Will ye rest now?"

"Aye," he said, tracing his hand lightly over her cheek. Then he sighed and turned away from her. He stopped as he opened the door. "Fare ye well," he said over his shoulder, then disappeared down the passageway.

"God keep ye," she whispered, feeling her strength departing with him.

* * * *

Richard walked back through the Hall, through the misery and wretchedness he found there. He stood aside as Wat and Lackey heaved yet another body between them, out into the courtyard. He could hear muffled sobbing to his immediate right, and turned toward the sound. It was Leah, kneeling beside the prone figure of Bram, her husband. The breath rattled in his chest, the dark rash of the sickness on his skin. Bram opened his eyes a slit, and raised his hand slowly, as if it were weighted with chains.

"Buchanan," he croaked. It sounded as if a powerful hand had tightened around his throat, squeezing off the flow of words. Richard went down on one knee beside him. Bram curled his fevered fingers around Richard's hand.

"What is it, man?" Richard asked quietly.

"I am dying," Bram wheezed, "and there is something I must tell ye…before I meet my Maker." He coughed, a dry hacking sound.

Leah wiped away the blood, and Richard lifted a cup to Bram's lips and helped him to drink. When he had finished, and caught his breath once again, he continued.

"I've never liked ye, Richard Buchanan, ye've been too well blessed in this life...and...I've wished ye evil for it. It was me who cut yer cinch in the joust...and nearly killed ye."

Richard stiffened and pulled his fingers from Bram's weak grasp. Bram grabbed for him, attempting to rise.

"Nay, nay..." Leah crooned, pushing him gently back down onto his pallet.

"I ask yer forgiveness...before I leave this world...I beg ye, dinna turn my family out when I am gone." Bram closed his eyes, his breath coming in difficult gasps. Leah began to sob again.

Richard swallowed convulsively, watching the scene before him. He suddenly felt detached from it. He saw Bram's pinched face, his ferret eyes opened, pleading in a skull's face, and Leah's bulky form huddled over him, her shoulders shaking. Bram once again lifted his hand toward him in a supplicate gesture.

Richard did not understand the impulse that made him tighten his own hand around Bram's in reassurance. He swallowed again, with difficulty. "Aye, Bram, I forgive ye. Yer family will be spared."

To Bram, Richard's face, and the things around him, began to disappear into deepening folds of grey. His voice seemed to come from a great distance.

Richard felt the tension go out of him, and Bram's hand relaxed, as the comfort flowed from his touch. Bram closed his eyes once again, and lay back against the pillow.

* * * *

The two-day siege of the sickness finally dispersed, leaving more than half the populace of Ravana alive and well. Neither Moira nor Kenneth had succumbed to the disease. The survivors were weakened by their ordeal and some would never be the same. Moira quickly regained her strength and was soon reunited with wee Annie, who was untouched by the disease, as were Eleanor and the children.

Ravana once again opened its gates, drawbridge, and portcullis and the people were allowed to come and go as they pleased. Thankfully, the village had been spared.

Mrs Campbell was back in her kitchen, having found able bodied boys and girls to take over the duties of the ones they had lost. Silently she wondered if Leah would ever be her robust self again after losing Bram. She watched as the poor woman shuffled aimlessly about the kitchen, the spirit seemingly gone out of her.

And with the loss of Betsy...*well, what would become of young Rabbie?*

But Meg had already been thinking about that problem, and believed that she had the perfect solution. She intended to ask her husband if they could take him in, and educate him, and treat him like the son that he was. *Surely the Laird would allow it, since the lad's mother was gone,* she reasoned. She took him from the wool house herself, comforting him the best she could, and installed him in the room next to her own.

Young Tom, the blacksmith's apprentice, was dull witted after his bout with the sickness. It looked as if his mental capacity would not return. Mr. Campbell kindly gave him a permanent position as his helper, and took another boy to train in his place.

Many people from the village joined the Ravana household. Esme became part of the kitchen staff, her husband Rory went to the ale house, and Mrs. Sutherland, Esme's mother, became part of housekeeping. Lackland's family also moved to the castle, where everyone found their own comfortable niche.

* * * *

There was rebellion in Ayr, on the west coast of Scotland. Lord James gathered a band of rebels together, and prepared to take the throne. Mary herself, along with Darnley, and the lords who were still loyal to her, advanced to meet them. But to their surprise, the rebels did not stand to fight them. Instead they attempted to slip by them and take advantage of her absence from Edinburgh. Wheeling her troops around, Mary's forces retraced their own steps, but were stopped by a sudden violent storm.

The rebels entered Edinburgh before the storm hit, but found no sympathy there. The people did not like Darnley, but still felt loyal to their queen. Unable to rally the people to their cause, they went south to Dumfries, where they waited forlornly for English aid. In the end, the rebellion came to nothing, and Lord James and his compatriots fled to England and took sanctuary there.

The fiasco was laughingly referred to as the Chaseabout Raid.

CHAPTER FORTY-TWO

Meg took Rabbie into her own care while Kenneth recovered. She let him take the few treasures and mementos that he wanted to keep from the room he had shared with his mother, and gave him the room next to her own. She held him and rocked him while he cried over the loss of his mother, and comforted him as best she could. She herself cleaned him up, and ordered new clothes to be made for him, and made arrangements for his education. They spent a lot of time together. Slowly, cautiously, he began to trust her, even seeking her out, and timidly slipping his hand into hers. She caught a glimpse of the steel that lay under the boy's surface as he grinned up at her, and she flushed with pleasure at his shy smile.

A letter arrived from Gladstone Castle shortly after the sickness had left Ravana. Things were just beginning to get back to normal. Kenneth was out hawking so the messenger was taken into the kitchen to warm himself by the fire and eat a bit of food. Meg was there, talking over the evening fare with Mrs. Campbell, as he sidled up to the fire.

Meg recognized him t once. "Kit!" she called enthusiastically, and ran to meet him.

"Och, m'lady!" he greeted, a smile spreading across his face. "I dinna think I'd see ye!"

"Have ye a letter for me from my mother?" she asked, anxious for any word from home. "How is she? And Fa? And wee Jamie?" She couldn't contain her joy at seeing a familiar face from home.

"Och, slow down, mistress, slow down," he chuckled. He pulled the missive from under his cloak and handed it over to her.

She broke the seal and quickly read:

July 31, 1565

My Darling,

Yer fa and I have just returned from visiting Sir Thomas and yer cousin, Gilly. They have been blessed with a son and heir to

Hayvenhurst. Sir Thomas is beside himself with joy, and our darling wee Gilly seems happy enough. The child was born last fortnight and thrives. I hope this letter finds ye well and happy, and that yer Laird will allow us to see one another again soon.

Mother

* * * *

After the messenger had gone away, Meg went to Moira to show her the letter. The news of Gilly's baby and apparent health, even though it seemed he was an early baby, did not seem to gladden her heart. She merely hugged wee Annie closer to her and rocked back and forth, saying nothing.

Meg did not understand her reaction, but was not feeling well enough to pursue it. The physical discomfort she had felt in Edinburgh had not gone away. So, she took her leave of Moira, and hurried to her own chambers.

She went to the wash basin behind the screen in her room and washed her face. She felt nauseous, cold and clammy, but the thought of ringing and giving an order for some stomach bitters or peppermint tea seemed a tremendous effort, and she lay down instead.

After a two hour sleep she awoke feeling much better, and very hungry. She called for a servant and ordered a meal to be sent to her room.

Aggie brought up the tray, and set a small table for her, then discreetly departed. But Meg found that after a few mouthfuls her appetite had vanished. The sight and smell of the food revolted her.

She pushed back her chair and rang for a servant. It was Aggie who again answered the bell. "Aye, m'lady?" she said, curtsying. "Did I forget anything? Was there something else ye'd be wanting?"

Meg gestured feebly toward the food. "Take it away, please-- at once!"

Meg sat on her bed, leaned her swimming head against the bedpost and shut her eyes. She could feel her stomach roiling in protest.

Aggie gave her a puzzled look, but obediently began to clear the table. The clatter of dishes hid the sound as Meg slipped from her bed and went to the basin behind the screen.

But then there was another kind of noise, and Aggie turned to see what was happening. Meg was suffering a violent attack of nausea. The maid flung down the tray and rushed to help.

Even through the spasms of retching and vomiting, Meg was aware of the gentle hands that held her head, and the cool cloth pressed to her temples.

"Puir pretty lady," Aggie soothed, "ye'll do fine now. Come, let me help ye to bed. Put yer head on my shoulder."

Leaning against Aggie's sturdy body, she tottered to her bed and lay down, slumped against her pillows. Aggie tucked the coverlet tight around her exhausted body, then stroked her hair back away from her face.

"Thank ye," Meg whispered. "I think the dinner last night was tainted. Was anyone else ill?"

Aggie smiled a knowing smile. "Tis not that, I'll be bound. When was yer last flux?"

Meg mentally counted the days, which had somehow turned into months. She had not realized the passing of the time, what with wee Annie's birth, the queen's wedding and then the sickness that had taken its toll on Ravana. "I canna believe it," she murmured, half to herself.

Aggie laughed out loud. "The Laird will surely be pleased." She brought a cup of water to the bedside table, within her reach. "I'll be leavin' ye to rest now."

"Nay, dinna go, please." Meg held out her hand. "I dinna want to be alone. Stay and talk to me a while."

Aggie looked at the white face on the pillow. The forlorn note in her voice touched her heart. "What shall I talk about?'

Meg cared little. She only wanted companionship while she tried to adjust herself to this startling new concept.

So Aggie stayed with her and talked. And nursed her through two more hours of sickness, until she finally began to feel a little better. Meg lay drained and panting on the bed when it was over. She held her hand out to the girl.

"Please, Aggie, promise me ye willna tell anyone about the baby. I wish to surprise the Laird with the news myself."

"Aye, m'lady," Aggie responded, curtsying. "Whatever ye wish."

* * * *

"Ts all right," Meg murmured to herself. Gazing into her little mirror as Eleanor brushed her hair, she smiled with a confidence she did not feel. She must present her case to Kenneth very carefully.

She planned to ask him about Rabbie tonight.
She had set the stage with a subtlety she had not realized that she possessed. She had ordered an intimate supper of the things he liked best brought to her chamber.

Eleanor had helped her to wash her hair and brush it. It fell down her back in a dark red mantle that rippled down to her slender hips. She had also chosen one of his favorite gowns, a sapphire color that matched her eyes. A rope of pearls decorated the rising mounds of her breasts above the low décolletage.

"Och, m'lady, ye look grand. 'Tis fair as the queen, ye are," Eleanor told her, admiring the results.

She smiled faintly and looked at her little French clock as it chimed upon her desk. "Thank ye, Eleanor, ye may go now. 'Tis almost time."

Eleanor nodded with a reassuring smile and hurried out.

* * * *

She saw in one quick thankful glance that Kenneth had returned from hawking in an excellent humor.

"Mo suiridhe," he greeted her laughingly, bending his head to kiss her. He complemented her on her gown, and his eyes rested for a moment on the swell of her breasts. "Ye look lovely, mo cridhe. And what a fine supper ye have provided!"

They sat and ate, keeping the conversation light. And after they were finished he drew her to the open window of her alcove, which formed almost a private room about them. It was a night of stars, and a frail new moon hung high over the roaring sea. The twinkling darkness reached down and enveloped her, bringing peace. The firelight which danced behind her made an aureole of light of the fine ends of her hair, and the warmth of her body set free the delicate scent of lavender that seemed to float about her. A happy confidence came to her, and her laughter trilled out.

Kenneth looked down upon his wife then, and studied her face. Her soft beauty and gentleness struck a chord in him that he could not help but respond to.

"What amuses ye so?" he asked with solicitous interest.

She looked up into his smiling face and all of her anxieties dwindled to nothing. *Of course, he would be delighted that she was taking such an interest in his son,* she told herself happily.

She was soon disillusioned.

At her first laughing words, "My lord, I've something to confess. Ye see, while ye've been otherwise engaged, I've--" her voice dwindled away as his arm dropped from her waist. He shut the windows and drew the curtains.

"Well, what is it, mo suiridhe?" he asked lightly enough, but his eyes had hardened into cold emeralds.

The reassuring beauty of the night was shut out, and there was no support in the rush lights that burned in their sconces. She forgot her carefully thought out speech and stuttered and stammered. Wildly she searches for the right words. Her promise to Rabbie, and his ecstatic delight flashed in her mind. Her teeth sank into her lower lip, she drew a deep breath, and began again.

" 'Tis yer son, Rabbie. I've put him in the room next to mine. I wish to raise him, educate, and provide for him. He needs warmth, sympathy, companionship, and love. Ye ken what it is to lose a mother."

"Ye mean to say that ye have taken it upon yerself to establish that filthy wee urchin as a son of this house?" he said incredulously.

"His mother is gone. He only has ye. Surely ye must recognize him as yer own and want to provide for him."

Kenneth laughed harshly. "If I were to provide for all my bastards, we'd have to build them a village here at Ravana." He sat down on the plush covered chair by the fire and crossed his legs.

Meg clench her fists. "The child has no one! I made him a promise!" she cried desperately. Then stopped. The anguish in her voice echoed in her ears. She dragged a hand through her hair, and for a moment coherent thought ceased. She must do something to convince him to let her keep Rabbie. She managed to control herself with agonizing effort. She saw his mouth twitch with amusement at her distress. She did not care. The continuance of this new relationship meant too much to both their lonely hearts. She moved toward Kenneth, her arms outstretched in desperation. "Please…"

He laughed. "Och, aye, yer quite lovely, mo cridhe, but all the same, ye'll dismiss yer new acquisition in the morning." There was a hint of mockery in his voice.

She drew a harsh breath, and cast about for another way. There was something else she could use, one last hope. She threw her head back and looked at him. "I havena been feeling well these last days. I've been vomiting. I believe I am going to have a baby."

The sudden change in his expression surprised her. He jumped up and grabbed her arms. "D'ye mean it? Are ye sure?" He searched her eyes and knew it was so.

She nodded. "Aye. Does this at least please ye?"

She saw the triumph on his face. She did not need an answer. "Can I keep Rabbie then?"

He took her hand and raised it to his lips. "Ye may have anything ye desire, be it in heaven or hell, if ye give me a legitimate heir!" There was an exultation in his voice.

Relief flooded through her. She had known that Kenneth, like most men with property and a title to pass on, wanted a legitimate heir. He had made it clear enough to her many times in the past. It was a natural desire. But his attitude, now that his desire was to be fulfilled, was not.

CHAPTER FORTY-THREE

From that night on Kenneth's behavior toward her changed. Without exception, he guarded and protected her from anything that might cause her distress, both mental and physical. Where before he had taken great pleasure in outwitting her plans, frustrating her wishes, and forcing his will upon her, he now gave in to her every whim. He treated her with care and affection, as one cares for the object that will fulfill one's desires.

He surrounded her with the things she loved, allowing her to provide for young Rabbie's education, and on the days she felt well enough, to spend time with the boy. He did whatever he could to amuse her, and even indulged young Rabbie, because it pleased her, buying him sweets when he went into the village, and letting him come on short walks with them through the gardens. But he was always careful to return before there was the possibility of her tiring. He sent her to bed early every night, and constantly ordered dishes that might tempt her fickle palate and stay on her stomach.

For the next weeks, her physical sufferings were too draining to allow room for any other thoughts. The swimming in her head and sudden almost painful salivation led again and again to the inevitable conclusion.

* * * *

One evening as Kenneth and Meg walked alone in the garden after supper admiring the sunset, they heard a rustling in one of the trees. They turned toward the sound, and saw a tiny, featherless baby bird had fallen from its nest. Brown and naked, it struggled on the ground, peeping loudly for its mother. Quick as lightning, one of the cats from the stables jumped down from the tree and snatched the helpless creature up in its jaws, then bounded away with its prize.

Meggie gave a moan and swayed against Kenneth, as nausea rose from the pit of her stomach. She pressed her linen handkerchief against her lips. Kenneth swept her up in his arms and started back toward the castle.

"No, please," she cried faintly.

"Dinna fash yerself, my pet," he said lightly.

He was always like that now, wishing to protect her from every unpleasantness, surrounding her with earnest concern. With kindness and gentleness, he attended to her embarrassing bouts of sickness with a patience that continually surprised her, for he despised illness of any kind. She buried her face against his shoulder as he carried her through the Hall, and up the stairway to her room, where he laid her upon her own bed. Moira, who had followed close behind from the Hall, knew what to do--cold cloths soaked in mint scented water for her forehead, a stick of peppermint to hold in her mouth. These things she kept on the table near her bed.

"She will be all right, m'lord," Moira said, as she tended her mistress.

But Kenneth did not leave. He watched his wife from over Moira's shoulder.

For some time, Meg was too sick to notice, but finally the nausea ebbed, and there would be blessed peace for a while. She opened her eyes and gazed passed Moira, into Kenneth's solicitous face.

Moira stepped back out of the way as he stepped closer to the bed and gazed into his wife's eyes. He studied her face for a moment before drawing breath to speak.

"Feeling better, mo cridhe?"

Meg looked up at him gratefully, smiling weakly. "A bit." This was what she had wanted from him. These last weeks with him had brought her what she had hoped for in her marriage. Moved by the impulse of these feelings, she slipped her hand into his. But his fingers did not respond to her simple gesture. They remained slack, her hand unwelcome.

She withdrew her hand and turned her face away.

"Well, then." He said, convinced that all was well, and threw a glance at Moira.

"Stay with her. See that all her needs are met."

He left the chamber without a backward glance, or another word.

* * * *

Lammas was celebrated with a feast of first fruits and then the harvest time was begun in earnest. The reapers who worked for Ravana during the harvest booms bent to their work and began to bring in the bounty.

* * * *

Richard and Moira had Annie christened by the Reverend Edmund Corrie when she was six weeks old. It was done in the old chapel, and Kenneth, feeling generous, gave them a celebration feast in the great Hall, and everyone was invited.

Meg watched them wistfully, and thought of her own child. Holding wee Annie in her arms, the baby, her own baby, began to seem like more than just a far-off thought. It began to take the shape a living thing to her.

* * * *

The morning after the christening, Meg began to plan her own baby's christening gown. She chose a length of white satin and began to sew. *The collar and tiny sleeves would be trimmed in Italian lace,* she thought, *as well as the hem.* She sketched designs of butterflies and daffodils on long willowy stems, that she would transfer onto the gown and emboss with white silken thread. It would be her best work ever, she knew, because it was so special to her.

* * * *

The sun of late September beat down. The summer was waning, but the still air was warm, and the grass in the meadow was lush, emerald green and very high. It seemed a perfect day for fishing.

Richard gathered poles, his nephew and Rabbie and headed for the moat. He whistled tunelessly as they walked along together, the slope of the long gentle hill of the meadow spread out before them in the golden light of the warm afternoon. The oaks stood strong, their wide, outstretched limbs dotting the green. The trees of the forest beyond stood tall, with their long slender trunks gleaming silver in the sun.

They watched as a graceful family of swans glided by, sharing the simple magic of sunlight and water, dreaming richly in the cradle of summer.

Matty flung himself down on the grass as they settled themselves on the bank. Rabbie tumbled down beside him. They sat in silence, watching Richard as he bent his head, his lean fingers fixing the lures on their lines. Then he cast, the line streaking out low and fast, pulling back on it in a way that made the lure weave lifelike in the water. He glanced down and gave Matty and Rabbie a wink.

"Ye think ye can do it?" he asked with a cheeky grin.

From the grass at Richard's feet, Matty gave a little exclamation and sat up. Doing his best to imitate his uncle, Matty tried it, but he pulled it back too quickly.

His uncle slanted an amused glance at him. "Och, slow down," he said with a laugh. "No fish can swim that fast. Not in this lazy moat. Watch closely, like this."

Flipping his lure close to the bank with a flick of his wrist, Richard felt a fish strike and saw the swirl of the water as he took the bait. His line tugged and veered as he pulled the fish in.

Squinting into the sun, Matty followed the line. His small face split into a grin. "Och!" Matty cried, his eyes goggling at the 18-inch pike. "'Tis the grandest thing in the world!"

Rabbie grinned and rolled over, watching them. Hooting noisily, he jumped to his feet as Richard held up the struggling fish. The pike's elongated body and large, sharp-toothed jaws snapped in his bill-like snout as he fought for air, his silver underside and dark green back sparkling in the sunlight. Rabbie smiled worshipfully up at him, while Matty reach out to touch the fish in wonderment. A breeze, faint but with an edge to it, picked at their legs.

"Come," Richard said with a smile. "Let's take it to Mrs. Campbell to cook for yer supper tonight."

* * * *

Meg had spent most of the day in the solar with the other women, sewing on her baby's christening gown. It was nearing supper time now, and they had stopped their activities and gone back to their rooms to prepare themselves for the evening meal. Meg walked into her room, and lovingly laid the silk and lace across her bed. It was beginning to take shape, she thought wistfully. Someday my own child will wear it. She crossed the floor to her dressing table and sat down. Looking at her reflection in the mirror, she smiled, and imagined herself as a mother, her baby in her arms.

A tentative knock at her door interrupted her musings. She quickly picked up her pearl handled combs and began to run them through her long auburn hair. "Enter," she said.

The door opened and young Rabbie wandered in. He was a well-built lad, if a bit skinny, with large green eyes and an aristocratic little nose, above a wide, sweet mouth. He charmed her with an endearing smile.

"Hello," he told her.

"Hello," Meg said, an answering smile lingering on her face for him. "And what did ye do today?"

"Och, Richard took me and Matty fishing in the moat!" he said with enthusiasm, his eyes alight.

"What an adventure! Did ye catch anything?"

He gave a pleased little wriggle. "We caught a pike, and Richard told Mrs. Campbell to cook it for our supper!" he informed her.

"And did she?"

"Och, she was cross wi' him, but she did. It was 'licious!" he added with relish, rubbing his tummy and smacking his lips. Meg touched his dark silky hair in a gentle caress.

He smiled up at her, then turned and ran to her bed, throwing himself upon it.

"Is this what ye've been doing today?" he asked, looking at the silk on the bed with interest.

"Aye."

"What's it to be?"

"A christening gown for my baby," she told him.

He curled up on her bed and fixed her with a penetrating gaze that reminded her of Kenneth. "Does it hurt?" he asked, his expression suddenly blank.

"Does what hurt?"

"The baby." A look of faint dismay crossed his face.

Meg giggled. "No, mo simplidh, of course it doesna."

A relieved expression transformed his features. " 'Tis good, then," he sighed, but his voice wobbled in a way that wrung her heart. His lower lip jutted out, but his emotions were quickly controlled. She went to him and touched his cheek with a gentle hand.

"What is it, mo cridh?" she asked. She saw the boy's mouth was trembling, as he strove to keep back the tears.

"My mam," he sniffled, as he rubbed his sleeve across his nose. "She told me she was going to have a baby, and then she died." His large eyes swam with tears that threatened to spill over. He gave her a half sob, and flung his arms around her with a hint of desperation.

Meg gathered him into her arms and kissed the top of hid head. So Betsy had been pregnant when she had died. She did not show the signs of it. It must have happened when Richard had been so ill, after the joust, she thought, mentally counting the months. At the time she had paid no heed to anything but Richard's health, and had not been aware of anything that Kenneth had done. Never mind, she thought, as Rabbie burrowed himself closer to her. She hugged him tighter, and her heart ached for him.

"'Tis all right, mo cridh. I am here with ye now."

"Forever?" he demanded. "D'ye promise to stay wi' me forever?"

"Forever is a long time, a leannan. For as long as ye need me."

After a moment he relaxed in her arms, and became more content. He lifted a rapturous little face to her. She saw in the smiling boy's face some of the physical attraction of his father. She kissed his little aristocratic nose.

"Come, mo aingeal, 'tis time for a bath, and then to bed."

He twisted his face up into a scowl. "Canna I stay up wi' ye?" he pleaded.

"Nay, mo cridh."

He sighed. But he was a biddable lad, and he responded well to her firmness.

She called down for a bath, and helped him to wash, as he prattled on about his wonderful day, his fears forgotten for the moment. He submitted to a vigorous towel drying, and then she tucked him into bed.

"My mam used to tuck me in a night," he told her, his voice wobbling ominously.

She leaned down and tucked his hand in hers, afraid to speak in case she said the wrong thing.

Rabbie clung. After a moment, he whispered, "D'ye ken where my mam is now? Is it dark? Is she alone?"

Meg sat down on the bed and pulled him into her arms. "Dear heart," she said, stroking the damp hair off the tragic, bewildered little face. "I'm certain she is not alone, and I'm sure it isna dark where she is. She is happy with God now."

"But why did God take her away? He doesna need her as much as I do. I miss her. Why did God take her away from me?"

"Och, a leannan, we dinna ken why He does some of the things He does. We must just believe that He kens what is best for us. I ken 'tis hard to understand, but the hurting will go away someday, I promise, and ye'll be able to remember her without feeling so sad."

Rabbie pressed his hot little face into Meg's breast, weeping, seeking comfort once again. Her heart ached for him. She leaned her cheek against the soft, baby fine hair and rocked him back and forth. After a while his sobs died away, and he was still for a long time in her arms. Then he sat up, saying drowsily, "I was nearly asleep." His arms wound around Meg's neck and he gave her a swift kiss on the cheek. He sniffed, but was apparently comforted, and slid back into bed, curling up in the blanket that she tucked lovingly around him.

* * * *

As the nights grew longer, it became custom for Richard and Moira to join Mary and Rees in their chambers. They spent many comfortable evenings settled in around the hearth, with Moira rocking Annie by the fire, Richard sitting on the floor, leaning back against the desk, with his knees drawn up, ankles crossed, one hand holding the other wrist. They talked companionably about the events of the day and enjoyed their quiet evenings together after supper.

"Catch me!" Matty shouted, as he launched himself from his mother's lap at his Uncle Richard. Richard laughed as he twisted around and got to his knees. He caught him and brought him down to the floor, rolling him around with his big hands. Matty screamed with delight.

"Och, calm down, will ye!" Mary admonished them, shaking her head. "I'll never get the wee rascal to sleep tonight if ye dinna stop!"

Richard let the lad go, but Matty immediately hopped up on his back, and round they went again.

"Och, ye heard yer mother!" Rees said, jumping up to join the fun. He grabbed his son around his middle, lifting him off Richard's back. "Early to bed this evening. Tomorrow ye can stay up a little later." He placed a foot on Richard's backside and gave him a shove, pushing him into the desk and bumping his head. Richard turned over and sat down on the floor, rubbing his head, and scowling up at Rees.

Mary and Moira burst out laughing, while Richard demanded indignantly, "Now why did ye do that?"

Rees ignored everyone but his son, whose lower lip jutted out.

"But I want to stay up!"

"That's enough."

There was just enough sharpness in the injunction to stop the whining outburst, but not so much as to upset the overtired and over stimulated lad.

"Och, all right," Matty said offhandedly, then flung his arms around his father's neck.

Rees smiled at his son and carried him off to bed.

* * * *

129

As the time passed, Meg spent her evenings with Rabbie, teaching him to read and write. She had noticed his eyes lingering on the letter that she had written to her family at Gladstone, and knew that the time had come.

"D'ye wish to learn to read, Rabbie?" she asked him gently one evening.

He gazed up at her with hopeful eyes. "Aye, I do want to read, and write, too."

Meg spoke with Mary the next day about it, and she lent her some books that she could use. They set to work. Rabbie was avid, and worked very hard, learning quickly. They read together in the evenings after supper, until he began making mistakes.

"'Tis enough for now, mo cridh, yer too tired."

Rabbie protested. "But I want to learn more."

"Yer tired, a leannan. When people get tired, they make mistakes. Too much is as bad as too little, my bonnie wee doormouse. Come, off to bed with ye now. Whist!"

She smoothed away the strands of dark hair from his brow, and he gave her a swift, fervent hug. Then he jumped down and ran to the door that adjoined their rooms.

Ten minutes later, clad in his nightshirt, Rabbie hurled himself into bed. Yawning sleepily, he held up his arms to her. Meg kissed him, and held him for a moment, enjoying the comfort of the warm, sturdy little body.

"Good night, mo cridh," she said softly. "Sleep well. Ye can come to my room in the morning when ye wake up."

A final kiss, and Rabbie settled back against his pillows. His lashes fluttered, and he said her name in a drowsy little voice, then turned over on his side, clearly lost in the fathomless sleep of childhood. Meg stood for a moment, smiling down on the sleeping child, then leaned down to blow out the candle.

* * * *

September ended with the vintage festival of Michaelmas, which marked the end of the harvest, and the beginning of the season when nature sleeps. On the last day of reaping, teams of workers raced each other to see who could first finish the last ridge, but saving the last stand of corn. They all took turns throwing their sickles at it, until at last, it fell. The last sheaf was then decorated and brought into Ravana's barn with music and merriment, and the laird provided a Harvest Home supper for them.

The villagers were then bid to open the hedges and allow their cattle to enter the harvested fields to graze on the remaining stubble, and as plowing and harrowing began on the previously fallow fields, Richard totaled up the accounts.

October turned into November and they all settled in for a peaceful and cozy winter. Christmas came and went uneventfully, so unlike the year before, and the old year slipped quietly into the new.

CHAPTER FORTY-FOUR

As Meg's pregnancy advanced, she began to feel lethargic and suffered from constant bouts of sickness. Kenneth continued to show her patience and indulgence, patiently reading to her, or when she felt well enough, they walked in the gardens, taking Rabbie with them sometimes. And in the evenings, he would play with Rabbie by the fire in her chambers, because that pleased her best. And on Sundays they attended Reverend Edmund Corrie's sermons. It seemed that at last they were a family.

All these things contented and reassured her. The unhappiness of their life before faded. Life was suspended, hushed into a pleasant monotony. There were no outbursts of violence, no rages, or disagreements. She began to bloom. The past and future both melted into the distance.

The outside world became unreal. It was rumored that Lord Patrick was very ill, quite possibly dying. She knew vaguely of the progress at court, that her husband had received several letters from his uncle, and was very displeased by them. Word came that the queen was pregnant, and that there was a conspiracy in the air to do away with Riccio, the hated little Italian secretary. Meg saw a restlessness in him each time a letter arrived, but he did not share the news with her. Instead he would go off into the village and disappear for a day or two, as if to return to his old ways. It seemed that news from Edinburgh was the only thing that stirred him to his darker side.
* * * *

One evening before bed, Meg dropped wearily into her plush chair at her dressing table. Moira stood behind her, loosening her long hair and brushing it with soothing strokes. The cherry wood fire crackled cheerily and gave out a faint fragrance. Meg had been working on the baby's christening gown most of the day, and now her strained eyes closed and she relaxed, letting a peace steal over her.

Suddenly she gave an exclamation of surprise. Her hands flew to her abdomen.

"Moira!" she cried. "What was that?"

Moira paled. "Was it a pain?"

Meg shook her head. "No pain. It dinna hurt. It was a curious fluttering, like butterfly wings."

"Och," Moira cried with relief. "The Blessed Mother be praised! I've been so worried these last weeks. 'Tis life ye feel, m'lady. Yer wee bairn is moving within ye."

Meg smoothed her gown over her stomach and gazed down at herself in amazement. She laughed. "It has never seemed so real before! Och, Moira, why did ye say ye were worried? 'Tis a wondrous feeling!"

The thrill of the miracle of her child came to her then, an expectation so poignant that it erased the last traces of uneasiness that Kenneth had caused her.

"Tis only that it's late ye are feeling it, m'lady, with ye into yer seventh month. I've been watching ye, and waiting for the wee one to make himself known."

Her laughter trilled out once again. "Perhaps he is very fat and content," she mused.

Moira laughed too, but as she tended the fire and helped Meg into bed, tucking the blankets and pulling the coverlet up around her, she silently prayed that the reason was not that the baby was too weak to make himself known.

* * * *

All the castle lay sleeping that night, wrapped in slumbering peacefulness.

But Mary was having a dreadful nightmare. She saw a sword, poised ominously in the air, light glinting from its blade, held ready to strike. A feeling of terror swept through her. She threw her hands up to shield her eyes as the deadly weapon swung down with a surety that sent anguish surging through her whole being. She could hear someone screaming over and over and suddenly realized that it was herself. She came awake, and sat bolt upright in the large bed, looking at the room through her own spread fingers. Rees' arms wrapped around her protectively.

"What is it?" he gasped, roused from a sound sleep by her screams.

Her arms went round him and she clung to him. "A nightmare," she said breathlessly, her body shaking as though with a chill. Her eyes were wide, her nightrail soaked through with perspiration. She shook her head to disperse the lingering echoes of the dream.

"Are ye all right?" he asked softly, taking her wrists gently from his neck and pushing her away from him so that he could study her face in the firelight. She shrugged, and favored him with a thin smile.

"Aye," she answered, nodding briskly, but he heard the undertone of fear in her voice. He did not take his eyes from her as he rose from the bed and went to the table for a cloth and the water jug. He came back to bed and sat down next to her. She drew her knees up and hugged them tightly to herself, rocking back and forth. He could see that she was still trembling and breathing heavily. Swabbing her brow with a gentle hand, he smoothed the heavy wet hair away from her face.

"Mary?"

"I'm all right," she said, smiling up at him. "I'm all right now."

Rees put the cloth down, poured her a cup of water and handed it to her. Her face was still white in the moonlight, but she was breathing more easily, and the trembling had eased.

"What did ye dream about?" Rees asked, settling next to her.

"Death," she whispered. A deep shudder gripped her as she raised the cup to her lips and took a slow sip of water, trying to shake off the chill remnants of the nightmare.

"Lie down with me, Mary," Rees said, and his arm stole around her as he pulled her down beside him. He pulled the blankets up over both of them and held her close. After a while the trembling quieted, and she drifted off to sleep. He leaned down and gently kissed the swell of her breast, and closed his own eyes.

* * * *

134

With a groan, Richard sat straight up in bed, shivering and bathed in sweat, awakened suddenly from a terrifying nightmare. His heart pounded painfully against his ribs, and his lungs heaved and burned as he gasped for breath. In the dream he was fighting fiercely for his life, but he could never see who he was fighting against. He had had the same dream many times of late, and was becoming troubled by it. He ran a hand through his damp hair and shuddered again.

Moira stirred beside him. "What is it, mo cridh?" she asked sleepily.

He looked down at her with a thin smile. "Nothing, my love, just a dream. Go back to sleep," he whispered in a dry voice.

Catching a glimpse of his pale form in the moonlight, she leaned up on one elbow, and reached up to touch his face. "Nothing? Ye look terrible."

He took her hand, brought it to his lips, and kissed her palm. " 'Tis all right, a leannan. It was just a dream, as I said."

He lay back down beside her and pulled her tightly against him to dispel the nightmare. He pressed his face into the warm hollow of her neck, and closed his eyes.

The dream did not return that night.

CHAPTER FORTY-FIVE

Frightened shrieks pierced the air of a cold, late February morning.

Richard and Moira sat up in their bed.

"What is that?" Moira whispered, her eyes wide. She looked to Richard.

"'Tis Meg!"

He threw back the quilt and grabbed his kilt from the chair, hurriedly buckling it at his hip. Moira flew from the bed and pulled her robe around her. Together they ran from their chamber.

They found Meg clinging to her bedpost for support. She had crawled to the edge of the bed and dragged herself to her feet. Her wet nightshift was twisted around her body, and her bed was wet. It was obvious that her water had broken and her labor had begun. She cried out and doubled over as pain twisted through her belly, wrenching the air from her lungs, and causing her legs to crumble beneath her. Strong arms caught her and kept her from falling. Richard swung her up into his arms, cradling her against his bare chest.

"By the Virgin, her time has come early!" he said, his voice urgent. "Quickly, Moira, fetch Mary!"

Meg couldn't reply. She could only wrap her arms about her stomach and try to breathe, as the pain continued to swell. Meg moaned in his arms, and her pale face contorted as another spasm stiffened her entire body, sending a long spill of auburn hair cascading over his arm. Murmuring comfort, Richard brushed her hair away from her face.

Kenneth suddenly stood before them. "She'll be fine," he said gruffly. "Women have babies every day."

Meg opened her eyes, raised her head and tried to speak, but the world went black and she knew no more.

Richard glanced down at her, nestled limply against his chest. He wanted to get her settled comfortably in a dry bed as quickly as possible. He scowled at Kenneth's indifference to her situation. "Get out of my way!" he growled, shouldering Kenneth aside.

Kenneth turned easily toward the door. "Let me know when it is over and my son is here," he called over his shoulder and he strolled from the room.

Mary and Moria met him in the doorway. Moira, red faced and out of breath, hurried ahead to open the chest and pull out fresh sheets. Mary found a dry gown. They set to work, stripping the bed, turning the mattress and making it up again with dry linens. They dressed Meg in a dry shift, while Richard threw more wood onto the fire. He opened the bed curtains wide to let the heat from the fire warm the bed.

Pain filled Meg's body as the two women fussed over her. She curled into a ball and bit back a scream at the severity of the pain, half rising from her chair. Richard scooped her up and eased her against the mound of pillows at the head of the bed. She groaned. "Nay," she whispered, her voice scarcely loud enough to hear, when he would have straightened and stepped away. She clutched at his arm. "Dinna leave me," she pleaded.

He covered her hand with his own, turning it so that she grasped his fingers rather than his sleeve. "M'lady, ye need attention."

Her fingers tightened about his and she moaned, curling into herself.

He gently pulled his hand free and moved back so the women could attend her. Richard hovered near her, as footsteps sounded on the stairs, heralding a small army of servants bearing hot water, a basket of dried peat and a stand of candles.

Mary watched her brother's worried expression from the corner of her eye.

"Go to yer chores, brother, there is nothing ye can do here."

"Richard," Meg called weakly. Ignoring the bustle surrounding her, she held out her hand to him. He bent and took it, cradling it in his own. She squeezed his fingers and slumped back against the pillows, groaning and twisting upon the bed. Mary put her hand on Richard's shoulder and gave him a gentle push.

"Out wi' ye now, and leave the birthing to us."

"But, d'ye ken--"

"Go." Mary glared at him, her arms crossed over her bosom. "Now."

He pressed his lips together tightly, and slid his hand from her grasp. She looked so pale and frightened as he made his move toward the door that pain clutched at his heart. With a last glance over his shoulder at Mary and his wife, he turned and left the room. He could hear Meg's pain filled cries as he headed down the corridor toward his own chamber.

Meg moaned and thrashed. It hurt. It hurt from the very first pang she had felt slice through her. She had been told that it would start easily, but the very first pain was like a sharp knife thrust through her, the pain starting in the middle of her lower back and passing through her sides from her back, to meet in her belly. Nor did she find any respite once they had truly begun.

She had been with Eleanor and Moira at their time, and knew that they had been able to do needlework and converse in the early stages, but she felt as though she were wrestling with an adversary inside herself, one that seemed bent on overpowering and destroying her at any moment. The pain ripped through her, and she felt as if she were being torn in two. Children were born everyday--women did this all the time, did they not? Why, then, did she find it so difficult? She let the hated tears slide down her cheeks.

"Hush, dearling," Moira comforted, wiping the tears away with a cool cloth. "Save yer strength for when it is worse, when ye'll truly need it."

Worse? Meg despaired. They were all she could manage now.

As she lay in the great bed, clinging to the knotted bed sheets, she tried hard not to scream as she writhed through the spine wrenching pain. She did everything they told her to do to ease the suffering--she turned on her side while Mary rubbed the small of her back, pressing hard during the contractions, all the while talking quietly and comfortingly to her; she grasped the bed sheets tightly, until her knuckles turned white; she smelled a handkerchief soaked in lavender water--but nothing helped, and she groaned with the full force of the pain. The pains grew stronger and more intense until she felt the thing inside her was going to split her apart.

"Take my hand!" Mary ordered. "Squeeze it hard!"

She did as she was told, although she did not have the strength to squeeze as hard as she would have liked. Her face and hair were soaked with perspiration, her face red from exertion. Moira wiped her cheeks and brow with the cool lavender scented cloths and spoke soothingly to her, but the next two hours stretched out interminably. The pains increased, but little progress seemed to be made.

What are these pains accomplishing? Mary began to wonder nervously.

Receptive and malleable at first, Meg had become unresponsive, lying panting at the end of each contraction, her face fading from red to white in a matter of seconds. She twisted and moaned in the bed, seemingly unaware of those around her. Mary began to have a vague foreboding. Something wasn't right, she felt, and the fine hairs prickled on the back of her neck.

Meg dozed briefly between contractions. Time had no meaning--indeed, it seemed as though the white-hot knife had seared through her body for an eternity. She started awake when another spasm, more intense than the others, rolled through her body and settled, hot and painful, low in her belly. Catching hold of the knotted bed sheets, she tried to will herself somewhere else in her mind, as Richard had told Moira to do when wee Annie had been born, until the worst of it eased. But there was no wishing this one away, that much was clear. She gritted her teeth and held her breath, and finally, as the pain began to fade, her thoughts began to drift. "Richard..." she murmured.

Mary glanced over at Moira, who sat beside the bed. She knew that she had heard, but Moira merely wrung out the lavender scented cloth, and leaned over her mistress to wipe the cool cloth across her forehead. She too was afraid, and wished for his quiet strength. "Aye," she whispered, barely loud enough for Mary to hear. "Perhaps it is his comfort she needs at this time."

Mary looked over at the hour candle on the bedside table and calculated the time. It had burned through the twelve-hour rings. The flame guttered in the waxy liquid before it expired in a wisp of smoke. Something must be done, and quickly. Meg could not go on like this.

Mary excused herself and hurried down the corridor to find Richard. She knocked lightly at her brother's study, then lifted the latch and stepped inside.

"Richard!" she whispered urgently.

He sat at his desk, his head in his hands. He lifted his pale face to her, a stark look in his eye. She realized suddenly that he had been listening to Meg's pain filled cries throughout the day.

She patted his shoulder. "Please come," she said, her voice compelling as she bent over him. "I fear there's something queer with Meg and the baby."

He pulled himself quickly to his feet. "What is it?" he asked.

"I dinna ken. The contractions are powerful, yet the baby doesna come. Meg seems to have given up. I have a dread feeling."

He rubbed a hand over his stubbled face. "Where is Ken?"

"I dinna ken, Richard," she said impatiently. "Please, just hurry. She asks for ye."

* * * *

He followed his sister to Meg's chamber. He found Moira lingering protectively near the great bed, where Meg lay moaning. Moira turned toward him, relief flooding her face.

As he came alongside the bed he could see how pale Meg was. He rinsed a cloth in the cool water in the basin and wiped the perspiration from her face. A long, shuddering moan escaped her, and she opened her eyes, a question forming in their cloudy depths, as they focused on his face.

"Richard?" she whispered.

"Aye," he answered, smiling. He smoothed back the matted auburn curls from her temples. "Hush now. Dinna ye worry. I'm here with ye now."

From far away she could feel the pain send its first warning tingle. It wound itself around her spine, and spread its tentacles slowly around her body, squeezing, wrestling, grinding her quivering body into submission. She groped blindly for Richard's hand, and as his fingers wrapped tightly around hers in a strong and comforting grip, she felt her first assurance of the night.

The pain eased from her body as the demon withdrew, and she closed her eyes and slept.

"What d'ye think?" Mary asked.

"I dinna ken," he said, shaking his head. "Perhaps it only goes slowly," he added.

She merely pressed her lips into a thin line and said, "I only hope that ye are right."

Meg stirred and moaned again, as the shafts of white-hot pain seared through her. She sought Richard's comforting touch, and he was there, speaking soft, soothing words, his fingers lingering on her cheek.

They continued through the hours to make her as comfortable as possible through the relentless contractions. She was tiring badly. Unable to keep from pushing, she was wearing herself far past the point of exhaustion, her body struggling past the bounds of ordinary strength as she strove to force the child into the world.

At four o'clock of the following morning she was delivered of a son. He was handed over into Eleanor's care. The baby was well formed and handsome, as he could hardly help but be, having come from exceptionally good-looking parents. He had a good deal of dark hair and straight brows like his father, and the delicate features of his mother. His arrival was greeted with wild rejoicing. The church bells clanged welcome, a signal to the tenants that there would be whisky and punch and beer served all day from the kitchens. The servants poured themselves mug after mug, unchecked by any discipline.

Moira crept away to her room to offer a prayer of thanksgiving.

As for Kenneth, he refused to leave the cradle in the nursery where the baby lay nestled in silk and lace, but stood motionless, gazing down at his little face.

It was Richard who stayed with Meg. She was floating in the drowsy peace that follows childbirth. In this state of confused joy, nothing seemed very real, but she was faintly conscious of hurt that Kenneth had not come to her after the ordeal, but more sharply conscious of her gratitude to Richard. He had been the rock to which she had clung through it all, his quiet voice and soothing touch her only comfort. She knew only that she was at peace and happy.

But for him, there was neither happiness nor peace. He had known from the moment in which she had blindly reached for his hand that there would never again be peace in his life.

But this disquieting revelation he pushed aside to be dealt with later. There was a more important fact to be faced right now, and he sat rigid by her bed, trying to determine what to do. His sister's nervous forebodings had, after all, been right.

CHAPTER FORTY-SIX

Richard had known the moment that he saw the child. There was a bluish tinge to the baby's skin, and a clubbing at the tips of the tiny fingers. Before he let Eleanor take the baby away, he had placed his ear to the little chest and found his worst fears confirmed. The heartbeat was weak, a spasmodic flutter. It seemed that each sighing breath the infant drew would be its last.

He could be wrong, he thought grimly. He had been wrong before, and he silently prayed that he was wrong now. But he knew that he was not. The baby's heart was imperfect. He may live an hour, a day, a week, or perhaps even a month, but longer than that was impossible.

He quickly decided not to tell Meg until she was rested, but he thought that he should tell Ken right away.

He walked down the hall to the nursery, and found Kenneth standing beside the cradle. He stood by the door watching him for a moment, thinking how much his own Annie meant to him, and he grieved for Ken, all the past forgotten in the face of this tragedy. He knew all the hopes and dreams that Kenneth placed in this tiny bundle, and he felt that he would rather submit to the rack than to tell Kenneth what he knew. He cleared his throat and took a deep breath, visibly gathering himself as he stepped inside the room.

"I have some bad news for ye, Ken."

The laird of Ravana turned his face slowly toward him. All softness left his features, and his expression became hard and defiant. He fixed his gaze on Richard.

Richard's eyes were compassionate. "Yer son is not well. He has a bad heart."

There was not the slightest change in Kenneth's face or manner. He appeared perfectly unconcerned, as his eyes shifted back to the baby in the cradle. Richard waited and watched him expectantly, but Kenneth did not indicate that he had heard with so much as a flinch. Not a muscle stirred. "Ken, did ye hear me, man?"

The Laird made no response. He just continued to look down upon the sleeping child in the cradle with a stony and steadfast composure.

What's the matter with him? Richard thought. He did not understand the cool contempt of Kenneth's manner toward him. He suddenly wondered if the baby still lived, and peered into the cradle, but the baby still breathed.

So, he persisted, determined to break through the barrier of Kenneth's impenetrable reserve. "I canna tell ye how sorry I am, Ken, but sometimes things like this just happen. At least Meg has come through it all, and--"

Ken raised his head and looked at him, an indescribable expression on his face. His temper smoldered a warning in his emerald eyes. Richard instinctively stepped back. There was a momentary flush in the firm, handsome face, menace in the poised body. His hands twitched, a sure harbinger of a coming outburst of rage. Richard felt a sharp, primitive fear. He knew the violence of which Kenneth was capable.

But even as he watched, Kenneth mastered his rising agitation, and with a smile of grim sarcasm, looked at him as steadily as ever.

"My son is entirely well," he said softly.

A hot anger rose in Richard. He stepped close to Kenneth, a look of fury on his face. "Ye won't believe me, will ye?" he cried roughly. "Ye never believe anything dinna want to believe, do ye?" He clenched his jaw tightly, struggling to control his rage. The baby gave a feeble, gasping cry, pitifully unlike the ordinary cry of a newborn. Richard impulsively leaned over the cradle, sensing as he did so, the protective motion of the other man, as though Kenneth would fend him off.

"Listen," Richard said, his anger gone, dissolved into pity for Kenneth's tenacious guardianship of such a hopeless cause. He put his hand on his shoulder. "Ye've got to face it, Ken," he said softly. "The baby willna live. 'Tis a miracle he wasna stillborn. His heart is defective. No amount of care will help. 'Tis no one's fault. 'Tis just a tragic misfortune." He chose his words carefully, determined to break

144

through the indomitable barrier which loomed between them. He was disheartened to see that he had not made the slightest impression.

Ken shrugged his hand from his shoulder. "Ye seem to have a great confidence in yer opinion," he said with self-possession, disciplined anger expressing itself in the mockery of his tone and manner. "But in this case I have none." He left the cradle and walked to the window.

Silence fell on the room. The only sound was Eleanor's baby, Gwyllyn, as she suckled him at her breast, and the creak of her rocking chair.

"At least I can prepare Meg," Richard said quietly. "Whatever ye may wish to believe, 'tis a wicked cruelty not to tell her."

Kenneth turned from the window and looked at him. "My wife?" he said. "There is no reason to worry her with this nonsense of yers. Good day, Richard."

He was startled into silence. He could not just leave her like that, he thought, to face this tragedy alone. He looked back at Kenneth, and he could see by the set of his jaw that it would be pointless to argue with him. He walked to the door, hesitated, and turned around to look at him again.

Kenneth was back beside the cradle, staring down at his tiny son. His stubborn disregard of the truth drove Richard from the room without another word.

* * * *

He went searching for his wife, sure that he would find her with Meggie. He opened the door to her chamber and poked his head inside. Moira sat beside her sleeping mistress, finishing the embroidery on the baby's white christening gown. She looked up when she heard the door and smiled at her husband. He gestured for her to come out into the corridor. Laying her sewing aside, she rose and joined him, a question in her dark eyes.

He took her hand in his. "Moira," he began, "ye must be strong, for Meg will need it."

As he told her of the baby, her brown eyes filled with tears. "Och, puir Meggie, 'tis a cruel hard thing for her to bear." She shook her head and sniffed, looking into Richard's eyes. "I dinna ken the wee one was acting right from the start."

He kissed her forehead. "Ye'll take care of her, Moira, ye'll help her to bear it."

Moira brushed the curl from his worried brow. "Aye, mo cridh, I will."

* * * *

But there was no need for Moira to prepare Meg. She knew from the first moment that she held her baby in her arms. She had slept in exhaustion for ten hours, and wakened when Eleanor came in to her, carrying the tiny bundle.

"I canna make him suck," she said softly, crossing the room. Moira rose from her chair beside the bed as Eleanor laid the baby beside Meg.

Meg raised herself on her elbow and parted the blankets with her other hand. Moira held her breath as she watched her. She gazed down at the baby for a long time, her expression showing nothing. Then she let her head drop back on the pillow. "Leave me, please," she said to Eleanor.

Eleanor turned sadly and left the room. Meg gathered her infant son to her, slow tears sliding down into the baby's fuzzy hair where his head nestled against his mother's cheek.

"Och, Meggie," cried Moira as she knelt beside her. "He'll be happier in Heaven, ye ken he will. Our Blessed Mother will keep your precious angel safe for ye until ye come."

Meg opened her eyes and looked into Moira's sympathetic face. "He must be baptized at once," she said faintly.

* * * *

It was over the matter of a hurried baptism that she first realized that Kenneth refused to admit that anything was wrong with his son. It was only after she begged him with bitter tears that he grudgingly agreed to give in to her foolish wish.

"Later, in a month or two, it shall be done properly, in a kirk, in a ceremony officiated at by John Knox himself and all the countryside as witnesses," Ken told Meg, but she said nothing.

Her heavy heart was lightened a little when the baby had been baptized, and duly christened "Kenneth William Ruthven." The sympathetic vicar whispered his fears to the servants, who soon spread the sad news throughout the village.

The baby lived for three days, and during that time, and despite Kenneth's angry protests, Meg kept her son with her, allowing no one else to touch him but Moira and Mary. It was from her own breasts that he drew a tiny amount of nourishment. But he had not the strength to suckle properly and on a stormy Sunday night he gave a little cry and ceased finding the strength to breathe. She held the baby close to her and whispered the twenty-third psalm for herself and him, and gradually some measure of acceptance came to her.

For Kenneth there was none. When he walked into the room that Sunday night and saw Meg's face, he uttered a violent oath.

She shook her head, looking at him with tears in her eyes. "God has taken him, m'lord," she whispered.

He flung back the coverlet, staring at the tiny, still figure. His face was contorted with anger. He wheeled on Moira, who stood by the bedpost, weeping quietly. He raked his eyes over her.

" 'Tis ye who've done this, ye dreadful creature!" he shouted, advancing on her. The fury in his eyes was chilling. "Ye've mishandled him! Ye've let him fall!" He approached her slowly, putting aside the folds of his plaid, so that the hilt of his sword was free to his hand.

"Sweet Savior!" Moira whispered, shrinking. Her hands flew to her throat, as she backed away from the murderous face. His eyes were fixed on her, madness in the smoldering emerald depths.

"Stop, Kenneth! Let her be!" Richard yelled from the door. Kenneth hesitated a moment, and Moira drew a rasping, terrified breath as Kenneth slowly turned and faced Richard. Kenneth's eyes glittered with a coldness that should have chilled him to the bone, as his tongue darted out and wetted his lips. His hand tightened on the hilt of his sword. "Or ye...Perhaps it was ye who caused this to happen. Ye were jealous that I had a son, and did something to him at his birth!" His mouth twisted, his voice trembled with passion.

Richard took a few steps into the room, his hand out in a suppliant gesture.

"Ye've had a sorrowful shock, Ken," he said, speaking calmly, soothingly. "D'ye sit now, and--"

He had no chance to finish. Kenneth wasn't listening to him. His deep-set green eyes were fixed on Richard's face as he drew his sword from the sheath at his waist. "I shall slit yer throat," he hissed, and lunged at him.

"No, m'lord, please!" Meg screamed, trying to rise from the bed. Moira drew close and put her arms around her. The two women clung to each other in stunned horror.

Richard twisted quickly aside, narrowly escaping the wide armed sweep of the blade. Kenneth whirled on him again, dropping into a fighter's stance, the cold steel of the sword flashing a warning. He shifted his weight from one foot to the other, as he sought the advantage.

Richard dropped low, his feet apart, mimicking Kenneth's movements, his eyes alert, fixed on the point of the threatening blade. "Put that away, Ken," he said, his voice steady and reassuring. "Yer overwrought. Ye dinna mean what ye are saying."

Kenneth made no reply, but pitched himself forward, closing the distance between them. He thrust his sword toward Richard suddenly, a savage motion, aimed upward. Richard pivoted left, was not quick enough. The blade skidded up his side, slitting his shirt, slashing into his flesh. With a hiss of pain, he jerked back pulling his own sword from its sheath to block another blow, as Kenneth's blade struck down on him once again. Richard moved his blade across his body from one side to the other in a semi-circular motion, to engage the blade, and pushed it so far to the side that Kenneth was not able to strike back.

"Ken, man, I dinna want to fight ye!" he said breathlessly.

But Kenneth was beyond listening to reason. He disengaged his blade with a clockwise movement, and thrust without hesitation in a straight line, as he lunged toward Richard once again. Richard parried and stepped back, out of the room and into the corridor.

Kenneth's blade flashed once more in the light as he leapt after him, the clash of steel against steel sounding again. Their grunts and shuffling footsteps sounded down the passageway, toward the stairs. The staccato sounds of clanging metal faded in the distance.

Moira wrenched herself loose from Meg's clinging arms and ran after them. Hurried footsteps could be heard coming down the hall. Mary was the first to reach the doorway, blocking Moira's way.

"What is it?" she asked, breathing hard. "What has happened?"

" 'Tis Lord Ken! He's gone mad! Let me by!" Moira cried, her voice almost incoherent, as fear clutched at her heart.

Mary moved aside, feeling the first inkling of disaster. She caught a glimpse of Meg's white face as Moira ran out. Mary rushed to her side and pushed her back into bed as she struggled to stand up.

"Mary! Ye must stop Ken! He's going to kill Richard!" Her voice was rising with hysteria. Tears coursed down her cheeks, her face contorted with terror.

The slow, cold fingers of dread crawled up Mary's spine at the expression in her eyes. She had a sudden presentiment, and the shock of disbelief turned to dull certainty. Once again, she knew the sense of impending doom that had clung to her since the dream. *The dream! This, then, was the final meaning of it.* She saw the drops of blood on the floor. "Richard," she whispered with shocked inevitability. Cold fear spread over her whole body.

She whirled on Meg. "Ye must stay here now," she told her, striving to keep the disquiet from her voice, without success. "I will be back." She bounded from the room and down the stairs.

She found Moira clinging to the guilded rail at the minstrel's gallery, her knuckles as white as her face. Mary looked down into the Great Hall where her brother and Kenneth still fought. She could hear Richard's voice, soft and gentle, between the clashes of steel, trying to mollify and appease the Laird's anger. It wasn't working.

By now, Rees and the other soldiers were filling the gallery, rushing down into the Hall. They all watched in silence as Kenneth's blows rained down on Richard. He succeeded in blocking every one, which only enraged Kenneth more.

Fight back, Richard! Mary's mind screamed at him. *Ken's anger will get the better of ye, canna ye see?* she thought desperately. *Fight, Richard! Fight! Fight back!*

As if he could hear Mary's thoughts, Richard suddenly advanced on Ken, attacking him with several swift strokes. Kenneth deflected them all, then lunged forward with a fierce roar and a sharp, quick thrust at Richard's midsection. He retreated and parried, dodging the feint, as Kenneth lifted his sword high and attacked.

Richard quickly raised his blade up to deflect Kenneth's next stroke with the clash of metal, but not fast enough to brace it against the ferocity that sent his sword flying. Moira opened her mouth to scream, to call for them to stop, but the scream froze in her throat, the sound emerging as weak and strangled. She groped wildly, clutching her sister-in-law.

"We must do something!" Moira cried in a frenzy. "We must stop them!"

"Hush, sister, there is nothing we can do," she whispered, holding her.

As they stood there watching, Mary saw Kenneth's face, his expression one of quiet elation, and she knew that he would hear nothing through the blind rage that enveloped him. He would see nothing but his goal, a violent revenge for the death of his son.

Mary froze. Time froze with her. Or so it seemed. Icy fear prickled up her spine, and in her chest her heart beat very slow, but very hard, each pulse like a fist slamming on a drumhead. The scene before them suddenly became slow and certain, the sounds vivid, her dream recurring before her eyes. For one long, agonizing moment the world stood still and she braced for disaster. She saw Kenneth raise his sword again, cold and deadly, the light from the sconces glinting off the steel blade as it arced through the air. She watched as he thrust it downward in an unbearably graceful motion, toward her brother.

The point touched the waist of Richard's shirt, then plunged into him savagely, tearing downward in a ripping, twisting wrench that colored the fabric with a sudden flood of dark red blood. White hot pain seared through him.

Kenneth lifted a booted foot and grunted as he kicked against Richard to free his sword. The force of the effort pushed him back a few steps, but he soon found his balance and stood ready, breathing heavily, the mockery of a smile on his cruel lips, the glitter of delight in gratified vengeance smoldering deep in his eyes.

Richard stumbled backward with faltering steps, and looked down at the blood forming on his shirt. He looked back at Kenneth in silent surprise, his eyes wide and clouded with shock. His hands flew to the wound, and he felt the warm blood on his stomach spread through his fingers, sticky and wet, soaking into his shirt. The world lurched in a slow tumble as his knees buckled under him He pitched forward, shoulders hunched, and crumpled to the floor. Dark spots danced before his eyes, and he could feel the chill of shock on his skin as it moved inward, toward the bone.

Suddenly there was a great commotion, shadows moving swiftly around him. He heard voices shouting, a shuffling of feet as several shadowy figures laid hold of Kenneth and pulled him back, as he cursed and struggled against them.

"How dare ye!" he shrieked above the din of confusion. "How dare ye manhandle me!"

He kicked and fought, bucked and heaved, and all the while roared curses at them, but they disarmed him and dragged him down, finally subduing him.

But Richard was only vaguely aware of what was going on around him, as he fought the darkness that threatened to overtake him. He could feel himself slipping into a deep black pit. They say hearing is the last sense to go. It was the one sensation pulling him back. There was one word that he could hear and understand, the urgent cry of his own name, shouted over and over, as if from a great distance, as Moira and Mary elbowed their way through the chaotic press of bodies.

"Richard! Richard!"

"Moira," he whispered. He closed his eyes and lay motionless, as the maelstrom around him settled to a steadier level. There was a single voice above all others, striving for calmness. Someone had finally arrived who knew what to do. He knew the voice well. It was Mary, his sister. Dear, sweet, capable Mary.

"Ye great clot-heid, ye've made a ballock of it this time, haven't ye?" she scolded, her voice choked with emotion, as she knelt beside him.

Helpful hands lifted him as Moira wrested his head into her lap. His lids sagged, half covering his eyes, dull and void of sparkle, his face drawn and ashen. She cradled his tousled head against her bosom and sobbed.

With trembling fingers Mary peeled back the sticky shirt and examined the torn flesh. Her stomach seethed. Panic seized her, but she steeled herself against it, knowing it would do no good to give into it. She reached beneath her skirts to take hold of her petticoat. With shaking hands, she ripped a length of cloth from it and gently pulled the soaked shirt free. She pressed the thick wad of cloth firmly against the wound to staunch the flow of blood, then wrapped another piece tightly about him to hold it in place. Her probing ministrations penetrated his oblivion and he drew in his breath with a hiss of pain as he twisted in agony.

"I should wring yer wee neck, ye thick-heided slack-wit..." Mary's voice faltered. A great lump rose in her throat as she watched the red stain of blood seep through and quickly saturate her makeshift bandage. Her eyes began to sting, as warm tears rose and fell unbidden down her cheeks. She dashed the tears away angrily with the back of her hand. "Or box yer ears, ye lack-brained ninny..."

His mouth twitched with the effort of a smile. *Dear sister, ever the compassionate one...*

Moira's voice came to him in muffled, frightened sobs as she kissed his face and hair, wetting them with her tears, murmuring words of love against his cheek. She clung to him as if she would never let go.

His eyelids fluttered, and with an effort he opened them, as he raised his hand to caress her cheek. Their eyes met and held for a long moment. Her eyes were frightened, her lips trembling, and her ragged sobs caught in her throat.

It drove a piercing pain through his heart. *What will become of her?* he wondered. *Who would take care of her and Annie?* His fingers reached out to entwine hers in a weak grip. *I have failed,* he thought wretchedly. *I promised to protect them, and I cannot. I promised to protect Meggie, and I have not…*

The tears trembled on Moira's eyelashes. She sobbed softly as she kissed his fingertips. The golden glow of the firelight played over his face, every curve and plane which had become so dear to her.

And then suddenly Rees was there, bending over him, touching his shoulder. He nodded toward Moira. "Dinna worry for her, brother."

"No! No! No!" Moira cried desperately, fiercely gathering Richard to her as tightly as she could. She looked up to Mary for comfort, but saw only on her face a stark expression of unguarded hopelessness.

With a tenuous grasp on consciousness, Richard tried to speak. He willed his mouth to form the words, but nothing intelligible emerged. His hands clenched into fists of frustration.

"Hush, now, mo cridh, my heart," Moira murmured with attempted bravado. She pushed his dark curls from his forehead with trembling fingers, smiling at him with difficulty. She slipped her finger into his tight fist. His skin was cold and clammy to her touch, and the chill spread to her heart. She felt a sick flutter in the pit of her stomach. She knew that he was still fighting, struggling to stay alive. "Dinna try to talk now. Ye must save yer strength for healing." The plaintive note in her voice echoed the fact that she recognized the truth, even as she denied it. Her heart ached with the certainty that it was not to be.

With a final effort, Richard summoned his remaining energy. He squeezed her finger as a single tear dropped from the corner of his eye, and he whispered, "I am sorry, a leannan…Dinna let Annie forget her da."

The effort sapped the last of his waning strength. Gathering fog and icy numbness engulfed him, enticing, luring him away with a siren's song, the promise of peaceful oblivion. He gave up the struggle and slipped into the twilight, then let the darkness take him.

CHAPTER FORTY-SEVEN

"Mary! Moira!" came Meg's frantic cries as she ran down the stairs, her nightgown billowing out behind her. She stopped short halfway down, as the scene below met her eyes. Soldiers were everywhere, holding Kenneth back, as he railed and cursed at them, sweat standing out all over his pale face. A small circle of people gathered near the middle of the room, but she could not see why. Moira's sobs met her ears above Kenneth's shouts, as Mary stepped into Rees' embrace and rested her head against his shoulder.

"Richard!" Meg whispered, her heart pounding. She searched the faces that she could see, but could not find him. Her knees grew weak and she leaned herself against the wall for a moment. Moira's wails told her what she already knew.

"Och...God, no!" she moaned. Overcome with grief, she took a few tentative steps, her feet gained momentum, and she ran the rest of the way down the stairs toward the circle of people. She pushed her way into it, and dropped to her knees beside Moira.

Moira still cradled Richard's head to her breast, her heart-breaking sobs wracking her body. Meg put a hand on her shoulder and looked down at the blood-soaked bandage. A choking lump rose in her throat. There was so much blood. The rushes beneath him were stained red with it. It saturated his clothing and covered his hands, which rested motionless at his sides. Moira was covered in it, too, her cheek, where he had touched her, her hands that had held his as she kissed his fingertips, her own dress.

So much blood, Meg thought...*and he doesn't move...or breathe...breathe, Richard, breathe!* her mind screamed, not wanting to accept the truth. She looked helplessly to Mary, whose expression was as grief stricken as Moira's.

She glanced anxiously about the Hall. The disarray, the blood, was everywhere, it seemed. Suddenly her head began to spin, and the images shimmered around her. Black spots danced before her eyes, and she felt a detachment from all that was around her. *This isn't happening,* she told herself, as the scene around her dissolved and fragmented into a thousand pieces. *It is a dream. In a few moments I shall wake up and everything will be...*

Just then, there were hands grabbing her, lifting her. She felt herself in someone's arms. But she did not have the strength to resist, or even care, as her head lolled against his chest. She felt too weak to move. Her eyes closed, her lashes rested against her cheek. *Oblivion...yes, that was what she wanted. Peaceful oblivion...*

"Come, m'lady," a gruff voiced whispered in her ear. "Ye shouldna even be out of bed."

Aggie ran to the chamber ahead of him and smoothed back the quilts, then covered Meg when she was laid in her bed. Aggie wiped her brow, but it did not rouse her.

The soldier quietly left the room. A loud crack of thunder boomed directly overhead, and Aggie jumped at the sound of it. Then she heard the rain, a torrential downpour, striking the stone walls of the castle, pounding the glass panes of the window.

She looked nervously about the dismal chamber. The cradle beside the bed still contained the pale, tiny infant.

"Puir mite," she whispered. But, she thought, perhaps the child was better off in Heaven, then to grow up in this tainted place. She took a deep breath, smoothing her skirts, as she shivered with a chill. She went to the hearth to light the fire, then sat down in the chair beside it, to keep watch over the mistress of the castle.

* * * *

Meanwhile, in the Great Hall, the commotion had died down. Kenneth quit struggling, his temper pacified. He stopped his flow of curses, and the soldiers loosened their grip on him. He shrugged them off, and they backed away as he glared at them. His eyes still blazing, he threw a harsh glance at the group of mourners.

"Get him out of here," he growled at the stunned onlookers, then bent to pick up his sword. A glint of steel caught his eyes, and he saw Richard's sword where it had fallen. He took it also, and disappeared up the stairs to his own chamber. Once inside, he flung Richard's sword across the room as hard as he could. It hit the opposite wall by the window and bounced to the floor, where it remained untouched.

His head ached. It ached unmercifully, and he put his hands to his temples and moaned. The firelight shot pain through his brain, though he shut his eyes tightly against it. *What is happening to me?* he wondered, as he lurched across the room on unsteady feet. *What has gone wrong? My son has been cruelly taken from me, my steward has betrayed and deserted me. Such things do not happen to me! I am master here, the Laird of Ravana! Everything has always been at my command. Why is it not so now?* He threw himself across his bed, held his head, and groaned with the growing, stabbing pain.

* * * *

Wat had gone to fetch Reverend Corrie, and they hurried together into the Hall. Corrie could feel the grief and shock in the air as he crossed the room. He put a sympathetic hand on Mary's shoulder and gave it a squeeze.

"I am sorry," he said softly. He felt a piercing sorrow for this small group of people, and for himself, for he had lost a friend as well. "I am sorry." There was nothing else to say.

Then he looked down upon Moira. She was quiet now, but had not loosened her hold on Richard. She rocked back and forth, her cheek resting against his head. Edmund Corrie went down on one knee beside her.

"Moira," he said gently.

She did not respond. She just continued to rock back and forth.

He sighed and put his arm around her. She did not acknowledge him.

"Moira, let us take him to the chapel."

"No."

Mary choked back her own tears, to be brave for Moira's sake. She rubbed her fist hard against her lips and drew a long breath to steady her voice. "Aye, sister, we will all go together. We willna leave him."

Rees bent to take Richard from her, but she would not relinquish her hold. He looked to Mary for help. She put her hand on Moira's, and spoke softly to her.

"We must care for him."

Moira quit rocking and focused on Mary's face.

"Ye ken we must," Mary said.

Moira nodded. There was a long silence before she answered. "Aye," she finally said. She loosened her hold and let Rees take him.

He lifted him carefully and they all followed Edmund Corrie to the chapel. There he laid his burden down in the first pew, and rested his hand on the thick brown hair, that still felt so incongruously alive. He didn't move for a moment, and closed his eyes, as though reluctant to face the realities of the night. Then Rees turned and laid a hand on Mary's shoulder, drawing her against him. They shared the strength they had, not speaking. Edmund Corrie lit the candles, and prayed with them, keeping vigil with them through the night.

* * * *

Meg dreamed. She dreamed that her infant son lay sleeping peacefully in his cradle. But when she turned away for a moment, and then looked back, she found the cradle empty. She dreamed that she was locked in a tower, and could see a knight waiting outside to rescue her, but his visor was down and she could not see his face.

She dreamed of Richard, playing on his lute and singing by the fire in the evening, his voice so sweet that she sat upright and awoke.

"I must ask him to play that again," she murmured as she drew her feet over the side of the bed. But then she saw that it was still night, and that Aggie was sleeping in the chair by the fire, and the cradle was not empty, but bore her tiny, still son. And it all came rushing back to her.

"No!" she cried. Her son was gone, and now, so was Richard. But they had been so alive in her dream! She lay back down against her pillows, her grief overwhelming.

Aggie awoke at her cry, and came over to the bed. "Och, m'lady, ye must rest. Pray to our Blessed Mother. She also suffered great loss and will help ye to bear it. She understands, and awaits yer prayers."

Aggie gently pushed Meg's hair away from her face and wiped away her tears. "Where is yer rosary?"

Meggie pointed to the bedside table, and Aggie turned to it and opened the drawer. The beads lay inside. She picked them up and put them in Meg's hand. Then she tucked the quilts around her as if she were a child, and turned back toward the fire.

Meg closed her eyes and began to pray.

Hail Mary, full of grace, the Lord is with thee…"

She heard the soft rustle of Aggie's gown as she crossed the room. She heard her pick up the poker and stir the fire, then settle herself back into the chair again.

Blessed art thou among women, and
Blessed is the fruit of they womb, Jesus…

Meg lay in the darkness, awake and fully alert. Despair filled her, a deep aching she could hardly bear. It threatened to suffocate and crush her. Praying did not help.

The fire in the hearth eventually burned itself to dying embers. Meg could see the outline of Aggie in the chair by the fire, and hear her gentle snores. Now was her moment. She must escape, get away from this suffocating feeling and all the pain it held. She quietly threw back the quilts and crept out of bed. She padded across the room to her closet and knelt before her chest. Opening the lid, she thrust her hand inside, and brought out the linen handkerchief from its recesses. Carefully she unwrapped the brooch Richard had given her, and held it up to the faint red glow of the firelight. The diamonds twinkled brilliantly, the pearls felt smooth and cool to her touch.

She remembered Richard's words when he had given it to her, and heard his voice speak again to her heart. "Be assured that as long as ye have it, we shall be together in the next life, and we shall never be separated again, we were born to love again. I shall remember ye from this life into the next…"

She closed her eyes. *Remember me forever…* she murmured into the darkness. *Please forget me never…*

I will be right here waiting for ye…I'll be here forever… she heard the answering whisper in her ear, the voice soft and familiar. She felt a cool rush of air, and it felt as if a hand went through her hair.

Her heart pounded and her eyes flew open, but she saw no one. A sob rose in her throat and she pressed her fist to her lips. She clasped the brooch tightly in her other hand.

Regaining her composure, she quickly pinned it on her nightgown, casting a sidelong glance at Aggie. She still sat sleeping in the chair.

Without taking her wrapper or slippers, Meg crept barefoot out the door and into the passageway, down the spiral staircase, feeling her way carefully. There were twenty steps winding to the right, and she leaned into the curve of the wall. She would go to the stables, she thought. She would find Foxfire and send him galloping into the night, and the wind and the rain would make her forget the pain…she must find relief from the pain…

Through the minstrel's galley and into the quiet Hall she went. Her stomach lurched as her eyes found the spot where she had last seen Richard. He was gone now. She could see that fresh rushes had been put down on the floor. The Hall looked peaceful, as if nothing out of the ordinary had taken place. As if her whole world had not been ripped apart in the space of a few hours' time. That suffocating feeling squeezed in her chest again, so that she could not draw a breath, and her heart pounded in her throat as if it would strangle her, but she continued on, toward the door.

She opened it. The wind whipped her nightrail, beating like fairie wings against her skin. The rain was like a waterfall, falling in sheets before her. She stepped out into it, and was soaked to her skin in an instant. The modest garment covered her from throat to ankle, but was helpless to shield her from the stinging cold, as it pelted down on her. But she did not feel its bite. Her hair hung about her face and shoulders in disheveled strands, her nightgown clung to her body as she ran toward the stables.

She pulled open the heavy door and entered, and it was warm and dry inside. The wind caught the door and tore it loose from one hinge. It banged loudly against the outside wall. The sound did not startle her as she walked quietly down the aisle. The pleasant odor of horses and clean straw invited her. She quickly found Foxfire's stall, as Dambiana neighed a warning sound.

Jasper came running out of the tack room. "M'lady, is that ye?" he asked, startled at her appearance, and on such a night as this.

"What are ye doing?"

She had opened the stall door and brought Foxfire out, into the walkway. "I am taking Foxfire."

Jasper stood squarely and blocked her way.

"I dinna think it would be wise to ride out into such a storm as this," he said, but a loud crack of thunder drowned out his words.

Meg did not care what he thought. She grabbed a handful of Foxfire's mane, and with a mighty determination hoisted herself up onto his back. Then she kicked his flanks, and Foxfire reared. She leaned into his neck and held on, as Jasper pivoted himself out of the way, against the passage wall. They galloped out of the stables and into the courtyard.

Jasper shouted and ran after them, out into the pouring rain, he shouted for the guards to close the drawbridge, but they could not hear him through the howling wind and rain. Meg and Foxfire galloped across the drawbridge and out into the stormy darkness, as fast as his legs would carry them.

Jasper pulled his hat from his head and threw it on the ground with a curse. Then he ran out into the castle to tell them that Lady Ruthven had just taken Foxfire, and ran out into the storm.
* * * *

Another bright zigzag of lightning flashed before her, and a loud crack of thunder boomed on its heels, as the rain drummed down, battering them with a torrential downpour. The magnificent roan stallion's mane flew in the stormy winds which lashed at her own long hair, whipping in from the open sea. Stinging raindrops beat down on her face and body through the thin white gown she wore. Her heart pounded wildly in her breast with an overwhelming heaviness, and her breath came in short painful gasps. Wrenching sobs ripped her very soul apart and she cared not that the horse stumbled over the craggy rocks in his furious flight from the demons that chased them into the dark oppressive storm. They galloped too near the steep cliffs, too close to the edge. Foxfire's hoof loosened a stone and he stumbled and lost his footing, and then they were falling, the horse tumbling, his terrified shrieks joining the howling wind as both horse and rider careened over the jagged cliffs to the rocks and churning sea below.

* * * *

They found them the next morning, battered and bloody, as a pale mist covered sun rose over the water's edge. When Jasper had alerted Rees of Meg's disappearance, he had gathered together a group of men and they had gone out to search for her. Kenneth had kept to his rooms, to pass the night alone with his own secret demons.

The rain had eased and died by the time they reached them, although the heavy mist was almost as wetting. It entered their nostrils, and lay upon their faces, as they made their way down the rocks to the beach below. They tasted it, rank and sour upon their lips. Flattened by the persistent rain, the atmosphere on the beach was distinctly eerie. The rhythmic hollow boom of the surf crashed at the end of some tunnel it had dug in the friable rock, and the wind keened endlessly. Gulls flew upward in screaming startled packs. The waves crashed, then ran silently up on the wet sand, leaving behind lukewarm seafoam in its wake. The argument of many seabirds rose from the rocks closest to them. Some flew away as the men neared the bodies.

Rees sighed, and looked back up the cliff at Ravana. The castle was a dark, formless bulk, looming mysteriously in the smoky fog above their heads. *Wasn't it ever the way here at Ravana?* he thought, clenching his hand hard about the hilt of his sword. *Crush, wreak havoc, then sap the lifeblood of the people, until they were gone.* But here his world lay, and thinking on it could do nothing to ease the plight of those he loved, nor had it changed one whit the hellish reality of it, he reminded himself.

The men's voices came to him, speaking in low tones, oddly muffled by the mists. He turned from the scene before him, his heart heavy with the grim events of the night, and looked back to the churning sea, allowing its simple power to wash away his thoughts. The pale, half-moon beach faded in the mists before him, the jetty a skeletal edifice where the water smoothed languorously over the sands. Gulls swooped and wheeled above them, glittering silver in the mist. Faster and sleeker, flocks of graceful terns dived to capture their breakfast.

The noise sent the seabirds screeching up from the rocks on which they had perched to watch them, screaming at them, as if in jeering contempt.

They brought Meg's body up to the chapel to rest beside that of her infant son, and Richard.

Mary and Moira were still in the chapel, keeping their sad vigil. They stood when the men carried Meg's bruised and broken body inside, and laid her down beside the others. Her nightrail was torn and dirty, but the brooch was still pinned to what was left of the flimsy fabric. Richard's brooch. Moira recognized it immediately. Mary knew it, as well.

Moira slowly walked over to Meg, reached out her hand and touched the brooch. *Aye, so this was where it had gone all those months ago when Richard claimed it was lost. Lost?* No. She had known the truth all along. Another lump rose in her throat, her eyes filled again with hot, heavy tears. They spilled down her cheeks unbidden. She thought she had cried them all away, but she had been wrong.

She unpinned the brooch from the tattered gown, and held it in her hand for a moment, feeling the weight of it, watching the gems twinkle in the sunlight that slanted in through the windows. Then Mary was beside her. She put her arm about her shoulder, and Moira looked up at her, grateful for her quiet strength.

* * * *

The hallowed, consecrated churchyard lay near the east side of the castle wall. Enclosed by a low stone wall, and surrounded by yew trees, it was entered into through the lynch gate. The burial party rested there while they waited for the Reverend Edmund Corrie to meet the deceased at the church style. The gate contained seats for the bearers, and a coffin stone for their burdens.

The clouds sailed heavily overhead before a strong, steady wind. The pauses in the dull beating of the surf were filled up by the dismal moaning of the trees, and the screech of the seabirds. It was a dreary scene and a dreary hour.

Kenneth was not with them as they laid his wife and tiny son to rest on the south side of the kirk. He had refused to let Richard rest nearby. He banished him to the north side of the Kirk yard, the unconsecrated earth, fit only for the burial of the unbaptised and suicides. There he was buried alone.

CHAPTER FORTY-EIGHT

It was then that the sightings began. One of the guards on the wall saw Richard standing on the far side of the moat the next morning. He called to him and the man looked up, smiled and waved. But when he took a step toward him, he seemed to dissolve, and vanish. The shaken guard ran into the castle to tell the Laird.

Jasper also spotted Richard, this time in the stables, currying his horse. He stood watching a moment, his heart beating a tattoo in his chest. The figure looked solid enough, his movement unmistakably Richard's. Jasper tried to raise his voice in greeting, but his throat became so dry, only a croak emerged. Richard turned toward him at the sound, and smiled. But as Jasper stepped closer, the apparition faded. The hair prickled on the back of his neck, and he hurried away to give word that he had also seen Richard on the grounds.

Others saw him, too, in the garden, or about the castle.

* * * *

After hearing these disturbing bits of news from his servants, Kenneth grabbed a decanter of whiskey and stormed up the stairs to Moira's chamber. He flung open the door without preamble, and found her sitting by the window, Annie in her arms. She looked up at him, startled.

"Where is he?" Kenneth burst out, so shrilly that she recoiled.

"Who?" she asked, her heart pounding.

"Ye ken who!"

He strode across the room to the desk, and with a careless swipe of his hand, everything on it crashed to the floor. Annie began to cry, and Moira bent over her, trying to soothe her, although her own fear was mounting.

Kenneth sat down heavily, the decanter of whiskey before him. He grabbed a glass from a nearby table, filled it, raised it to his lips and drained it.

He looked at her angrily then, and her heart leapt fearfully into her throat. But suddenly his expression changed, and he set the glass down. He could hear a strange sound resonating through the air, and feel a strange energy fill the room. He looked up with an expression of uncertainty, his eyes wide with fright.

"Who's there?" he bellowed.

The answer floated back to him in a whisper. "Ye ken who I am."

"Did ye hear that?" he shouted at Moira, jumping to his feet.

"I heard nothing, m'lord," she answered in a faltering voice.

"I ken ye are here!" he shouted violently to the four walls, his eyes rolling like those of a frightened horse. "But I willna quail in fear of ye! Ha! Ye canna frighten me!"

His voice was shrill now, close to the edge. He bent toward the desk, his hands shaking, and poured himself another glass of whiskey. He held his glass up to the light, saluted into the air, to show that he was not afraid. But as he glanced up, he saw the reflection of a man in a small mirror that sat on the mantle above the fireplace. The vision was solid, dressed in a green jerkin, white linen shirt and the Buchanan tartan, but he couldn't see his face. He was sitting in the chair near the bed, his head in his hands.

The glass of whiskey slipped from Kenneth's hand and shattered upon the floor.

"Richard!" he whispered, jerking his head around to look behind him. The chair was empty. He turned back, but the reflection was still in the mirror.

He filled another glass from the decanter, so awkwardly that he upset it, and spilled whiskey all over the desk.

"My sight seems to be failing me," he muttered to himself, in an odd, muffled voice. He slowly set the glass up again, refilled it and drained it once more in one gulp. Then he cried out with a sudden burst of anger that startled Moira. Turning his back on her, he ran from the room.

She sat staring after him, her heartbeat gradually slowing to its natural rhythm. She hugged Annie closer to her, and closed her eyes. She was afraid, and the aching longing for Richard's comforting touch was almost more than she could bear.

It was then that she felt a rush of air, as if fingers caressed her cheek, and she heard someone whisper her name. Startled, she sat up with a jerk, her eyes flying wide open, and her glance darted about the room. She saw no one, but a warm feeling enveloped her, a comforting and protective presence surrounded her, and she suddenly felt very much at peace.

* * * *

That night while Moira lay sleeping, she was awakened by a shimmering light at her bedside. The scent of lavender filled the room, and she became aware that she and Annie were not alone. As her eyes focused, the light from the full moon through the windows showed a form clearly, and she could see that it was Meg. Although the windows were not open, her auburn hair blew as if there were a breeze, and her white nightgown billowed out around her. She stretched out her hand beseechingly.

"Hansel to me," she implored.

Moira raised herself on her elbows, her heart pounding in her throat so that she could hardly breathe. But the vision slowly faded from sight. Moira glanced over at Annie still sleeping in her cradle. They were alone in the chamber again.

* * * *

The weather was warming, and Mary insisted that Moira walk with her in the garden. She had spent most of her time since Richard's death alone in her room with Annie, and Mary was worried for her. Moira did not want to go, but Mary would not take no for an answer. They left Annie with Eleanor, and soon they were walking down the garden path.

Bird song filled the air, and the rosebuds had begun to bloom. Moira stopped to admire them, remembering the morning after Annie had been born, when Richard had brought a rose to her. She asked the gardener to cut her one, which he did.

"Sister, I would take this to my husband's grave," she told Mary, when it was in her hand. "Please, let us go there now."

Mary nodded reluctantly, not wanting to give herself or Moira any more anguish. But they soon found themselves walking through

167

the lonesome grey stone style of the kirkyard. The sun was shining through the thin white clouds, and the air was still and warm. The peacefulness of the lonely kirkyard was overshadowed and saddened by the sound of the dreary surf as it crashed against the rocks below Ravana. Moira walked straight to Richard's unmarked grave and knelt beside it to lay the rose upon it.

"Och, Richard," she said in a small broken voice. "How I do miss ye." *I'll never see ye again,* she thought sadly, *never please ye again, nor see ye smile.* She reached down and laid her hand on the bare earth and closed her eyes. *I see yer face in the night and feel yer warm, yet lost embrace. To feel ye hold me once again…My love for ye will live on long after I am gone.*

Moira was startled from her reverie when Mary laid a cautious hand upon her shoulder. She looked up and saw Kenneth striding toward them, slashing viciously at the flowers along the path with his riding whip. When he was near enough to see her face, he stopped, struck at his boot with the whip, and burst out laughing so harshly that the birds in the tree by which he stood flew away.

"What brings ye here, to this place?" he asked Moira sharply.

She made no reply, but turned her gaze back to the earth. He turned to Mary.

"She has nothing to say to ye, m'lord," Mary answered stiffly, her heart pounding. "Nor do I." The sight of him recalled that night, and she felt once again the terror and helplessness that had overwhelmed her. She both hated and feared him now.

"I hear that ye and Rees have taken wee Rabbie into yer care. Dinna ye think I give a whit for the wee bastard. He will inherit naught from me."

Mary only glared at him.

He waited a moment, then spoke once more to her. "What have I done to warrant such silence from ye?" He looked down at Moira. "Why d'ye come to this unconsecrated ground? There is naught here, I see no marker…there is nothing," he said, a mocking smile on his face.

Moira stood and faced him, her eyes blazing. His smile faltered. "Ye have cruelly killed the only friend ye ever had, and I hate ye for it! Ye are evil and spiteful! And I wish ye to the devil for it!"

Now his smile was entirely gone. Taken aback by her sudden vehemence, he asked, "What makes ye say such things? D'ye think it yer duty to me to stand there, casting damnation on me to my face? Ye live now under my mercy and protection!" he shouted violently. "But instead of being grateful for that, you have taken yer own wicked view of an innocent, and twisted everything! I have done naught wrong!" He poured out the words fiercely, all in one breath, pacing backwards and forwards, and striking about him in the air with his whip. Then he abruptly turned on his heel, and left her alone with Mary.

They had hardly walked half way toward the lynch gate, when Kenneth, who had already passed through it, suddenly stopped and shouted, "There! Did ye see it?"

"See what?" Mary called back to him. "We saw naught."

"The black dog! The black dog, ye wee fools! It ran into the trees, there! 'Tis enormous!" He pointed a shaking hand toward the yew trees along the fence. "D'ye see it?" His voice rose shrilly. " 'Tis the Moddey Dhu!" Then suddenly his manner changed, and he began to laugh wildly. "Ye'll never have me, ye shaggy beast!"

His manner was so frightening, that they hardly knew what to say in answer. *The Moddey Dhu*, Mary thought, *the large shaggy black ghost dog of Scottish legend, with its burning eyes, who, it was said, prowled the grounds of the wicked, and showed himself only to those about to die...*

She glanced up, but Kenneth had turned away again. Before she could say another word, he was walking rapidly toward the stables.

* * * *

Before midnight, Kenneth's strange temper broke out once again. Mary and Rees, taking turns backwards and forwards along the gallery, as had lately become their custom at night, heard his voice calling out loudly and angrily. Almost all the afternoon and evening

169

he had been walking about the castle and grounds in an unsettled and excitable manner, having in all probability, Mary thought, taken an excessive quantity of whiskey at his solitary dinner. He always ate alone now.

"What ails him?" Rees wondered aloud, watching his strange behavior.

"I believe he is going mad," Mary answered, feeling small consolation to the pain he had caused her.

"I will go down and speak with him," Rees said.

"No!" Mary grabbed his sleeve to hold him. "Keep away from him!"

He looked back at her, his eyes full of compassion, and placed a comforting hand over hers.

" 'Tis all right, mo cridhe. I will return."

He pulled away from her, and took the stairs two at a time.

Rees found Kenneth walking backwards and forwards by himself in the Hall. Mary leaned over the railing to watch them, and she could hear their muffled voices as Rees greeted him.

Suddenly Kenneth stopped his pacing and fell to his knees, looking intently at a particular place on the floor just beneath him. When he rose to his feet again, his hands shook, and his face was white.

"Rees," he said in a whisper. "Rees, come here…D'ye see something there?" he asked, catching him nervously by the shoulder with one hand, and pointing with the other to a spot on the floor. His eyes shone with the fire of insanity.

Rees' heart beat a painful rhythm in his chest and he felt a sharp fear. This was the very place where Richard had died. He swallowed and took a ragged breath. "I see nothing, Ken."

"Nothing?" Kenneth whispered, fastening the other hand suddenly on Rees' collar, and shaking it in his agitation. "Nothing! There is blood there!"

He pushed him away roughly, swearing violently, his voice rising in anger. "I willna stay another moment in such a place as this!" he bellowed with oaths and threats. "I will take myself to the village for a diversion immediately! Rees, see that my horse is made ready!" he roared.

In a quarter of an hour Kenneth had joined Rees in the yard, had jumped onto Zeus, and lashed the horse into a gallop, his face as pale as ashes in the moonlight. Rees heard him shouting and cursing at the guards to get up and lift the portcullis. He heard the hoof beats pound furiously over the wooden drawbridge in the still night, then heard no more.

* * * *

On the road, Kenneth heard the galloping hoof beats of another horse coming up behind him, heard the heavy breathing as the other animal approached. He turned, and saw the billowing white garment that the rider wore, her long auburn hair streaming out behind her as she passed him. The hair along his neck and arms prickled. As he watched, the horse lost his footing, and plunged over the cliff, his shrieks echoing hollowly in the still air.

He lashed his horse unmercifully, out of his mind with fear, the shrill keening sound ringing in his ears.

* * * *

It was a full half hour before Rees returned to Mary. He agreed with her--that Kenneth was quite out of his senses--but not through whiskey, as he had supposed, but through panic, and a frenzy in his mind. He was, quite possibly, going mad.

* * * *

When Kenneth returned to Ravana, he barred his door and took to his bed, tormented with mental agony. The fever in his mind gave way to horror as he fought against his hard, savage heart and the stubbornness of his will. He was in a fearful state of mind, as he closed his eyes and cupped his aching forehead in one cold hand. He wondered how long it would be until he simply snapped like a over wound bowstring. A presentiment of death flashed in his mind and would give him no rest.

"Where is that dog of a priest, Father William!" he finally growled to himself, pulling himself upright in his bed. "Where is he, I say?" he shouted at the walls. He began to mutter to himself.

"Ungrateful villain… But wait, he is gone. I sent him away, did I not? I remember now. The Reverend Edmund Corrie has taken his place." He thought a moment and his voice became light. He stood and paced back and forth by his bed, slamming one fist into the palm of his other hand. "I will call Edmund Corrie to come to me, then, to hear my confession--he is priest of sorts, and may be able to give me absolution."

He paused another thoughtful moment, then sat down heavily upon his bed and shook his head. "But nay, I should as well confess myself to the devil, as to him. I will pray myself. There is no need to bribe the false priest…but I…do I dare?"

"Sir Kenneth Ruthven, laird of Ravana," said a grim and gruff voice close by his bedside. "Say ye there is that which ye dare not?"

With raw, shaken nerves, Kenneth's evil conscience heard the voice of a demon, sent to distract his thoughts away from the meditation of his eternal welfare. He shuddered and drew himself together. Summoning his courage, he exclaimed, "Who is there? What are ye, that dares to echo my words? Come before me, so that I may see ye!"

He heard a rustling near his bed and looked up. He saw a tall figure shrouded in black, his features not visible beneath the dark cowl. "I am yer evil angel, Laird Kenneth," it replied in a rasping voice.

"Let me see ye, then, in yer bodily shape, if ye are indeed a fiend," Kenneth replied. "Dinna think that I will tremble in fear of ye. By the devil, I shall grapple with these horrors that hover around me, as I have done with all mortal dangers!"

"Think ye, instead, on yer sins, Lord Kenneth," said the unearthly voice, "On rebellion, on murder! Who aided yer wicked uncle to stir up the Lords against their generous queen? Who murdered, in cold blood, Riccio, the queen's secretary? And also Richard, yer only friend? Who drove yer wife to her death?"

"Whether ye be fiend, priest, or devil," he spat, "ye lie! It wasna I who stirred the rebellion--not I alone! There were fifty noble lords and barons, the flower of the Midlothian counties--better men never took sword in hand! Must I answer for the fault done by fifty? I defy ye! Leave me, and haunt me no more! Let me die in peace, if ye are mortal. If ye are a demon, yer time is not yet come. "

"In peace ye shall not die," repeated the voice with a shake of his head. "Even in death, ye shall think on yer murders--on the groans with which this castle has echoed--on the blood ingrained in its floors!"

Kenneth forced a ghastly laugh. "Ye canna shake me by yer petty words," he answered. "My unfaithful steward, Richard--it was merit with heaven to deal with him as I did! The wee Italian secretary who was slain, he was the foe of my country and of my liege lord! Ye see? Are ye silenced yet?" he asked, looking around. "Have ye fled?" Hearing and seeing nothing, he heaved a sigh of relief, thinking himself alone again.

"Nay, foul murderer!" replied the voice after a long moment. Kenneth jumped at the sound and turned toward it. "Think on yer steward, think on his death! Think on the Hall, flooded with his blood, and that poured forth by yer own hand!"

"Ha! What do I care?" answered the laird, after a long pause. "Go, leave me, fiend! Go, I say!" He bared his teeth and raised his fist, shaking it in defiance at the apparition.

The demon laughed. "Do not grind yer teeth, nor roll yer eyes--clench not yer hand, nor shake it at me with that gesture of menace! The hand that has done these foul deeds ye now suffer for is rendered powerless against me!"

Kenneth cowered before the apparition. "Vile demon! Detestable fiend!" he cried in misery. "Have ye come to exult over me?"

"Aye, Lord Kenneth, Laird of Ravana, I will dog ye to the very instant of yer death!"

"Nay!" exclaimed Kenneth. "That moment ye shall never witness! Rees! Wat!" he cried. "Seize this damned ghoul, and hurl him from the battlements! Rees! Wat! Where are ye? What takes ye so long?"

"Call them again, valiant laird," said the ghoul, with a smile of grisly mockery in his voice. "Summon yer vassals around ye. There are none so faithful as Richard, whom ye have slain. Doom them that loiter, but mark well these words, mighty laird," it continued, suddenly changing its tone, "that ye shall have neither answer nor aid, nor obedience at their hands." The voice turned sarcastic. "Why d'ye lie there like a worn out dog? What has happened to yer great strength?" The demon gave an evil laugh.

"Gods and fiends!" Kenneth despaired. "I would give all I own just to feel my fingers close around yer neck and throttle ye, choking, to the ground!"

"Think not on that, valiant warrior!" the fiend replied with a laugh. "Ye shall die no brave death, but an ignominious one."

"Hateful apparition! Ye lie!" he exclaimed in anguish, as he dragged himself from his bed and stumbled toward the fire of his open hearth. He grabbed a large piece of kindling and thrust it into the fire, watching the flames leap onto it, the dry wood catching fire. He pulled it from the flames, crackling and popping, and thrust it toward the spirit, laughing wildly.

"By my honor, this fire shall consume ye, and I shall live to hear that ye are gone from this earthly fire, and ken that ye are consumed with the fires of that Hell which never sent forth a fiend so utterly ruthless and cruel-hearted!"

Sparks from the kindling fell upon the rug and chair by the fire as he waved his weapon in the air. The fire caught and quickly began to spread.

"Hold yer belief until proof reaches ye," the demon laughed. "Ye ken, even now, the doom which all yer power and strength is unable to avoid. It is prepared for ye by yer own hand." The apparition gestured around the room. "Mark ye the smoldering and suffocating smoke which already roils through the chamber? Did ye think it was but the darkening of the evening sky? Do yer eyes burn? Is yer breathing labored? No, it is not evening--look about ye! Ye have set fire to yer own belongings! Yer chamber is in flames!" The demon laughed. "And now, farewell! Ye shall find small comfort in the place where yer soul shall spend eternity! Let each stone of this vaulted rock find a tongue to echo yer end into yer ear! I will see ye in Hell!"

Kenneth could hear the crash of a beam as he shouted in agony for help, and fought his way through the thick billows of choking smoke. He coughed and his lungs burned as he struggled to draw a breath. "Rees! Wat! I burn here unaided! Help me! Curse ye! Dinna abandon me here, to perish so miserably!"

But they could not hear him, his voice was lost in the din. In his mad frenzy of despair Kenneth shouted, and uttered curses on himself, his wife and Richard, on the whole of mankind, and on Heaven itself.

The smoke swirled and churned, thicker and thicker, and Kenneth shielded his eyes and choked for breath.

The flames caught upon the floor, suddenly making the inhabitants below aware that Ravana was burning. Rees, and a few of the soldiers who were in the Hall, ran up the stairs toward Kenneth's chambers. They beat upon his barred door, and shouted for him to open it.

"The red fire flashes through the thick smoke!" he exclaimed, hearing their cries. "The demon marches against me! Foul Spirit! I willna go with ye! Ha! Ha! Ha!" And he laughed in his madness until the vaulted ceiling rang out with it. "Who laughed there?" he exclaimed again, as the echoes of his own mad laughter returned to his ear. "Who laughed there? Foul Spirit, was it ye? Speak, demon, for only a fiend of Hell himself could have laughed at such a moment. Begone! Leave me! Go, I say!"

He could hear his men shouting, pounding on the door, trying to save him. But the billowing smoke roiled before him, choking and blinding him. Another beam fell, blocking his way. He shielded his eyes once again with his arms and backed away from the inferno.

The heat from the fire blew out the glass from his window with a loud crash, exploding it into a thousand shards that rained down into the courtyard below. Panic seized him, confusing his sense of direction. The fire roared, and the voices of his would-be rescuers were drowned out. He could not find his way to the door to unbar it.

He put his hands out before him to feel his way, his heavy feet stumbling across the floor. But he could not get his bearings, and the toe of his boot caught against Richard's sword, lodged where he had thrown it. He lost his balance and tumbled out the window, to his death below.

CHAPTER FORTY-NINE

Consciousness slowly floated up towards me, as if I were swimming to the surface of the water after a very deep dive. My lungs burned to breech the top. Pain drummed a compelling rhythm in my head. Every part of my body ached with a deep, pounding persistence. I heard a monitor beeping, and the bubbling noise of the Pleur-evac machine. A prickling sensation in my hand commanded my attention, and I tried to brush it away, but a gentle hand kept me from it.

Yet there was something else. A change in the atmosphere, some electricity in the air, that caused me to lift my heavy lids. Unease rippled through me, making the tiny hairs on my arms stand on end. I turned my head to the side and opened my eyes.

There she stood…or rather, floated, a foot or so off the floor. Meg was watching me…the same girl in my dreams. But this time she looked confused, unsure, frightened.

A hand tenderly touched my arm and I felt someone lean close. The familiar, comforting scent of my mother's perfume filled the air around me.

"Where am I?" I whispered hoarsely.

"What did you say, dear?" my mother's voice came back to me anxiously. "Doctor! I think she's coming around!"

Shadows moved around me, anxious murmurings, and as reality came flooding into focus, I saw the apprehensive faces of my family above me. I was in a hospital bed, a crisp white sheet pulled up around me, blankets neatly folded at the foot.

"Oh, darling!" Mother cried. "We've been so worried!"

A tall man, well over six feet I thought, approached the bed. He bent his blond, curly head and flashed a set of strong white teeth in a grin.

"My name in Dr. Munro," he said in a deep, masculine voice. "I saw your car overturn on the motorway and made the call for assistance. I'm afraid you'll be spending a few days in hospital.

You've some broken ribs, a punctured lung, and a broken ankle, among other things. Unfortunately, you'll be feeling a bit uncomfortable for a while."

"A bit?" I asked, as I raised trembling fingers to explore one cheekbone, wincing at the swelling I found there. Even more carefully, I lifted my hand to investigate my throbbing temple. A small tremor wracked my body.

He reached down and pulled the blankets up over my shoulders. "You've a mild concussion, some bumps and bruises. The pneumothorax seems to be small, but we will continue to monitor you for a couple of days with portable chest x-rays every twelve hours. There's oxygen here by the bed, in case you need it, but so far you're doing quite well without it. You'll be fine," he told me crisply.

A pale attempt at a smile touched my lips. *Brilliant,* I thought sardonically, *just what I need.* A hospital stay and a broken ankle are not exactly included in my plan of escape.

"Whatever made you go out in this kind of weather?" my father asked.

At that moment, a frightened looking young nurse scurried into the room. Jack followed closely on her heels. "Dr. Munro--" she began, but Jack interrupted her before she could finish.

"Where's my wife?" he demanded loudly, as he swayed in the doorway. His eyes glared from the nurse, to the doctor, then to my family. They finally came to rest on me. I felt the color drain from my face as a swift terror grabbed at my heart. "Jack…" I whispered. A sharp, clenching pain in my chest suddenly took my breath away.

"I suppose the car's a total loss, eh?" he growled. "Och! You're nothing but trouble!" he spat. The smell of whiskey permeated the air as he swaggered into the room.

My father jumped up, indignant. "Now see here--"

But Dr. Munro had things in hand. He took a few steps toward Jack and grabbed him by the elbow. "Your wife has been hurt. She needs to rest. Come into my office with me and I'll fill you in on the details," he said with the sharp note of authority in his voice, steering him out into the hall.

Tears slid softly down my cheeks and dropped onto my hospital gown. My mother gently wiped them away and I looked up at her. The fierce pain in my ribs was beginning to fade into a dull ache, but my head throbbed incessantly, and the room began to spin. Dark circles danced in front of my eyes, and a wave of nausea rose from the pit of my stomach. "I'm going to be sick," I groaned.

The nurse was at my side in an instant, emesis basin in hand. She pushed away my hair from my face and crooned softly through my spasms of retching and vomiting. When I finally laid back against my pillows, exhausted and shivering, my mother gently wiped my face with a cool cloth. Pain thrilled through every fiber of my being. The dull ache in my ribs peaked to a distinct, sharp crescendo, and my ankle and foot throbbed with a deep-seated persistence.

"Mr. MacCallum has gone home," a voice spoke incisively from the hall.

I glanced up through my lashes and slowly focused on Dr. Munro, almost filling the doorway. He stepped inside, his blond curls gleaming with copper highlights, as his eyes searched my face. "Right," he said briskly. "I think our patient needs to rest."

"Yes," my mother agreed, and she and my father bent to kiss my cheek.

"Goodnight, darling," they called as they left. "We'll be back tomorrow morning. Rest well."

The nurse soon followed after them, and when she had gone, Dr. Munro came across the room towards me with a lithe grace I would not have expected in so large a man. He stopped by the side of the bed.

"How are you feeling now?" he asked, taking up my wrist and stretching out his other arm to read the second hand of his watch. A flaxen curl fell across his forehead.

"I've been better," I answered self-consciously, feeling suddenly exposed, the lines of my body revealed too clearly for my tastes by the sheet and thin blanket that covered me. Clumsily I dragged them up to my chin with my free hand. He smiled down into my face, his unusual silver-grey eyes compassionate. He released my hand and it dropped down on the bed at my side.

"It's all right, you're safe now," he told me quietly, his voice infinitely comforting. To my dismay, a lump gathered in my throat and tears welled up in my eyes, spilling down my cheeks. I covered my face with my hands and sobbed, embarrassed and humiliated, but unable to regain control.

Then I felt the side of the bed depress, and a firm but gentle arm drew me gingerly into the hollow of his shoulder. Pillowed against his crisp lab coat, I could feel the sleek muscles of his torso hard against my cheek, his heart thumping slow and steady in my ear. The consoling warmth I found there banished my feelings of hopelessness and dread, and soon I succeeded in stopping the flood of tears. His comfort, freely and generously given, without threat, soothed my overwrought emotions and gently calmed me. Instinctively, for reasons beyond my grasp, I felt I could trust him.
"You're exhausted," he said, his voice encouraging as well as sympathetic. "I think you should try to get some rest now. Don't worry about anything. You're safe now, and everything is under control."

I hiccupped and sniffed as I pulled away. He pushed tissues into my hand.

"Thank you," I said, ducking my head to avoid those strange, pewter colored eyes. I blew my nose, then looked around for someplace to put the tissue. He pointed to the small trash bag that hung from the mobile bedside table. I tossed it in, then glanced up to meet his piercing grey eyes. They looked back at me, clear and direct, and I could tell that he had something else to say.

There was a note of irony in his voice when at last he spoke. "I have some more news for you on your condition. I was waiting for your husband to arrive before I gave you the good news, but it seems the time for that has passed. Several routine tests were run on you when you arrived in Casualty. Congratulations, Mrs. MacCallum, you are pregnant."

An odd feeling washed over me at his words, and I suddenly felt nauseated again. I laid back against the pillows and closed my eyes, my lashes flickering against the tender skin of my cheeks. I swallowed back the large lump in my throat that threatened to resurface, as the tiny pinpoints of light danced behind my lids.

I heard the water from the sink running, then felt the cool cloth on my forehead and cheeks. My stomach slowly calmed, and the whirling behind my eyes ceased.

"Don't look so hopeless. It's all right, you know," he said in soothing tones. "I know it all seems a bit overwhelming now, but after a good night's sleep," he paused, knowing how impossible that would be. "Or perhaps you should give it a few days," he suggested gently. "Things will sort themselves out." *He had a voice that could make you believe anything,* I thought. *Smooth, dependable, he exuded a confidence that I envied. It was a quality I had never possessed.*

I smiled ruefully. "Thank you, Doctor."

He put the cloth on the bedside table. "Try to get some sleep." he said gently. "I've scheduled a sonogram for you in the morning so we can see how the baby is. Do you have any idea how far along you are?"

I shook my head. "I've always been irregular," I croaked, embarrassed at revealing such intimate details of my personal life to a stranger, even if he was a doctor.

He watched me with an amused smile. "Well, we'll know tomorrow. Good night, Mrs. MacCallum." He walked through the door and into the hall, leaving me alone to contemplate this new and unexpected bit of news. I laid back against my pillows, closed my eyes and sighed.

* * * *

My heart beat like a trip hammer and the scream caught silently in my throat. Something horrible, unknown in the darkness, was chasing me! I could hear its breath behind me, gasping, panting loudly in my ears! My chest strained as I dragged in agonizing breaths of air and tried to run faster through the trees, but the branches pulled at my clothes and hair, the roots reached up to trip me, as my movements suddenly slowed, like the action of a slow-motion camera, as the thing came closer--closer--

"Wake up!"

A hand on my shoulder, fingers strong and firm, was shaking me. I whimpered, frightened, as the nameless horror grabbed me and wouldn't let go. My hands flailed out at the unknown assailant.

"Mrs. MacCallum! Wake up! It's only a dream!"

A voice, curt and commanding, penetrated the formless terror of my dream, and I began to fight my way through to wakefulness, clutching wildly at the nearest thing to me. My sobs died in my throat, my heart began to slow to its natural rhythm, and I opened my eyes.

The room was dark, illuminated only by the light from the hall coming through the open door. The silhouette of a man loomed over me, and I was clinging desperately to the surgical greens that Dr. Munro wore, as though he were my only hope of salvation. Mortified, I jerked away, desperately trying to control the panic that I felt, and the shudders that wracked me. The sudden movements caused pain in my chest and made me wince.

"Careful of those broken ribs," Dr. Munro said. He pulled up a chair and sat down next to the bed, taking my hand in his, as he would a child's. I found myself relaxing, my breathing returning to normal, lulled by a sense of security that I had not felt in some time. *What was it about this man,* I wondered, *that made me feel safe, unthreatened, protected?*

"Better?" I heard him ask softly, after a moment.

I nodded.

"Do you often have nightmares?"

"Not usually," I whispered, then cleared my throat. "Was I screaming?"

He gave me a sympathetic smile and said quietly, "Aye, you were. I heard you from the hall, and rushed in to see what was the matter." His eyes searched my face.

Self-protection caused me to lower my lashes until they rested against my cheek. "I-I'm all right now, thank you," I stammered.

"You're sure?"

I looked back up at him, thankful for the semidarkness. Stupidly, I could feel myself blush, and was grateful that he could not see it. I sensed, rather than saw, his eyes narrow at me.

"How's your ankle?" His voice was crisp and impersonal again.

"It's stopped throbbing, thank you," I said, my tongue suddenly too big for my mouth. I may be unsophisticated enough to blush under his scrutiny, but I would not let him know it.

He leaned back in the chair and crossed his arms over his chest, still surveying me. "Where were you going tonight in such a hurry?"

"I don't know. Away. I was running away." *Why was I telling him this?*

"I see," he said.

A sharp rap on the door made me jump. It was the nurse.

"I've brought your painkiller and a sleeping pill," she said, setting her tray upon the bedside table, and pouring me a glass of water from the pitcher beside it. I took them without question, then slipped back down against the pillow. Dr. Munro stood.

"Right," he said, with a voice that fairly crackled with authority. "I'll leave you to sleep now. Goodnight, Mrs. MacCallum."

I watched the two of them walk out into the corridor, feeling suddenly bereft and alone. I hoped that I hadn't made a fool of myself, the way I had cried and clung to the doctor. He must think me a complete idiot.

The rain outside had turned to a drizzle, and the wind had eased. Suddenly drained of my last reserves of strength, great surges of weariness rolled over me, and I sank into the oblivion of sleep.

CHAPTER FIFTY

"Good morning, Mrs. MacCallum," called a cheery voice. "Time for breakfast!"

Dazzling sunlight slanted across my eyes as I blinked awake. The smell of something vaguely resembling bacon, accompanied by the nutty smell of oatmeal, filled the room. I opened my eyes a little more, and was greeted by the smiling face of a young woman of thirty or so, with tightly permed red hair, and the freckles that went with it. She bore an air of unquenchable confidence. I wished I felt so sure of myself. Right now I felt a bit groggy and out of place.

I yawned, and stretched gingerly, wriggling my toes. I grimaced a little at the resulting pain, then struggled to sit up.

The woman came across the room and set the tray down on the bedside table. Then she helped me to settle myself comfortably, fluffing the pillows behind me.

"Ankle still hurting?" she asked, as I leaned back against the soft pillows.

"A little, thank you," I sighed, then gave her a diffident smile. "Along with my chest, and I've got a pounding headache."

"Och, well, buck up, and eat your breakfast. Nurse is passing out pain medications now."

She swung the table in front of me, and smiled as I took spoon in hand, suddenly realizing that the pain in my stomach was hunger.

"There's a good girl," she said. "Och, I'd nearly forgotten. Your parents came by earlier, while you were sleeping, and brought your overnight case." She pointed to the chair by the window, where the case had been left.

"You'll be having a portable sonogram this morning. You must be sure to drink all the water that's on your tray, all right?"

I nodded, almost greedily swallowing a spoonful of oatmeal, which was thin and tasty.

"My name is Irene," she said. "I'll be back in ten minutes to help you into the bathroom, so that you can clean up a bit." She inclined her head toward my food. "See that you've got it all inside you by then," she ordered briskly, and disappeared into the corridor.

The nurse brought my pain meds, and true to her word, Irene was back in ten minutes. I washed, and cleaned my teeth, then settled back into bed. Irene brought my overnight case to me, and set it on the bedside table, then left me on my own.

I lifted the lid, and stared, horrified, at my reflection in the mirror. There were scratches and abrasions on my face, a cut above my brow, and the bruise on my cheek now encompassed my eye in shades of black and purple. Pulling a face, I ran my fingers through the riotous tangle that was my hair. It did not have the desired success of smoothing the tresses into some semblance of order. Shrugging, I began searching through the case for my brush. After finding it, I dragged it through my hair, until the locks, at last, were tamed.

A short while later, there was a knock at the door. A pretty lab technician peeked her head into my room.

"Hi, I'm Cathie. I'm here to do your ultrasound."

She entered, pushing a cart with the ultrasound equipment and monitor. She stopped beside my bed, and began to plug in and set up the machine.

"Did you drink plenty of fluids?" she asked, pulling the curtain around my bed.

"Yes, I'm sloshing," I admitted.

She laughed. "Good, because we need a full bladder to help with the sound wave transmissions. Now. I'll need you to lie flat."

She adjusted my pillow under my head and shoulders. "Don't worry," she told me, pushing my covers down, and pulling my gown up to expose my stomach. "This won't hurt a bit." She draped my lower half modestly. "I'm going to apply a cool gel to your abdomen," she explained, squeezing lines from a tube of Vaseline-like gel over me. "This will improve the conduction of sound waves between your skin and the transducer."

Just then, there was a sharp rap on the door, and Dr. Munro peeked his head around the curtain. "Good morning," he said cheerily. "How's our patient this morning?"

"Better," I said.

"Good." He nodded toward Cathie.

"We're just about to start the ultrasound, Doctor. Would you like to stay?"

"Yes, I would," he said with a smile, and stepped inside. "Do you mind?" he asked me, almost as an afterthought. He lifted a brow in my direction.

"No, of course not," I said, but gave a quick, involuntary glance downwards at my exposed belly. Unbidden color flaked across my cheeks, but neither seemed to notice, their attention on the monitor.

Cathie placed the transducer crystal against my skin, and began to guide it across my abdomen with a gentle pressure. The screen flickered, and an image appeared. My heart caught in my throat, for there on the monitor, I could see a tiny being, pulsing with life.

"Is that my baby?" I asked, my voice full of wonder.

"Yes," Dr. Munro answered, pointing. "Do you see that pulsing? That is your baby's heart beating." He smiled down at me.

I stared, unable to believe. It was incredible. I was awestruck. Already, without my being aware of it, another life was stirring inside me. It floated gently back and forth, it's tiny arms and legs moving up and down...my own baby...

Suddenly there was a commotion out in the hall. Dr. Munro pushed the curtain aside, walked across the room and put his hand on the door. But just as he did, it was yanked open, and Jack stood in the doorway, breathing hard.

"Hello, Doctor," he sneered. "I've come to see my wife." He glanced at me through the partially open curtain. "What are you doing to her?" he demanded loudly.

"An ultrasound, Mr. MacCallum," Dr. Munro said dryly. "But this is a hospital. You'll have to keep your voice down." He took him by the arm.

Jack shrugged him off. "You can't tell me what to do!" he shouted. "What's all this for, anyway?" He gestured toward the machine and technician.

"I-I'm going to have a baby, Jack," I stammered, my heart pounding painfully against my ribs.

"What!" He covered the ground between us in three long strides, and grabbed my wrist. "What did you say?"

My chest burned, and I felt as if my air supply had been cut off. I began gasping for air.

"Careful of her ribs!"

Dr. Munro was there in a moment. He pried Jack's hand from my arm and shoved him away from me, as I struggled for breath.

"Her condition doesn't warrant this kind of behavior, Mr. MacCallum. I'll have to ask you to leave." He turned back to me as I coughed and wheezed.

"Is there a problem, Doctor?" someone asked from the hall.

"Yes! Call security! Get him out of here!"

I felt something slip over the end of my finger, and heard one of the monitors begin to beep. The doctor cursed under his breath, and reached for the nasal cannula that hung on the wall behind my bed. My chest ached, and my breath came in short, painful gasps.

Dr. Munro pulled the tubes over my head, and placed the cannula securely. He cupped my head in his hands. "It's all right, Mrs. MacCallum," he whispered soothingly. "Just relax. Breathe slowly. ...Slowly...that's it..."

"Code green," I heard the operator call over the loud speaker. "5100."

"I-I didn't mean to upset her..." Jack stammered. His voice suddenly sounded repentant.

"Get out, Mr. MacCallum," Dr. Munro said, his voice calm. "You've done enough."

Footsteps could be heard in the hall, walking swiftly, as they came through the door. Two security guards grabbed Jack by the arms.

"Come with us, sir. This way."

"I'm not going with you!" he snarled at them, attempting to shrug them off him. Instead, their grip on him tightened.

I opened my eyes a slit as my breathing became easier, the reedy gasps quieting. I could see Jack struggling between the two men, his face purple and contorted with rage, as they dragged him into the corridor. I closed my eyes against the sight, but could still hear his threatening shouts as they took him away.

I turned my head toward the wall, humiliated beyond words. And then I felt a hand close over mine, warm and reassuring.

"It's all right," Dr. Munro said gently. "You're safe now. He can't hurt you here."

Cathie and her equipment were gone. I caught my trembling lower lip between my teeth, and drew in a slow breath, trying to control the flood of tears that burned behind my eyes.

He let go of my hand, and I heard him sit down in the chair beside the bed. After a moment I opened my eyes and looked at him. His long legs were stretched out in front of him, his eyes narrowed as he searched my face. A tiny muscle flicked in the line of his jaw. His elbows were propped up on the arms of the chair, his fingers steepled, and resting against the tight line of his mouth.

I lowered my lashes, not able to meet his steady gaze.

"You know," he said at last, "I should report this to the authorities."

My heart almost stopped, and my eyelids flew open. "What do you mean?" I asked in a panic.

His mouth curved into a reassuring smile, and he leaned forward in the chair, his unusual pewter colored eyes compassionate. "You told me that you were running away. I assume it is because he behaves like this often?"

I bit my lip, averting my gaze to hide from those piercing silver eyes, and my lashes flicked once more against the tender skin of my cheeks.

He resumed gently, but with an inflexible note in his deep tones. "Tell me. I think it would probably do you good."

I shook my head at the whole unfortunate situation. Willing myself to relax, I met the glint in his eyes with resolution. "Yes, he does. And now I am leaving. That is all there is to tell." My ankle was throbbing, and my chest burned, as if to remind me of the setback to my plans. I let out a sigh, and grimaced at the pain. "This bit wasn't exactly part of my intentions." I sucked the inside of my cheek, holding my shoulders stiffly, and stared down at my hands. From the corner of my eye I saw him lean back in the chair and survey my mutinous expression with humorous appreciation.

"No, I suppose not," he said smoothly. "Where will you go when you leave here?"
I moved my shoulder, more a wriggle than a shrug. "Home, I guess." I cast him a quick upward glance through my lashes. I saw the sympathy I'd expected in his eyes, but I also saw more. Approval, support, respect.

"And home is where?"

"My parents, if they'll let me. UntilI can look after myself. Perhaps I'll move back in with my old roommates, my friends at work."

He rose from the chair. "Sounds like a good enough plan. See that you do it, then." With those words, he disappeared into the hall.
* * * *

That evening Jack called. He sounded quieter, more subdued than usual. He was not happy about the baby. His attitude helped me to tell him my own plans.

"Jack," I said, gathering courage with a long, deep breath. "I'm leaving you. I'll raise the baby by myself. No need for you to worry about it. I want a divorce."

"What did you say?" he demanded, incredulous.

"I'm seeing a solicitor when I leave here, Jack. It's over."

"The hell it is!" he shouted. "You belong to me! Don't think for a minute I'll ever let you go!"

"Don't be ridiculous," I said, trying to stop the quavering in my voice. "You don't want me or this baby."

"I'll show you what I want!" he yelled, then slammed the receiver down in my ear.

CHAPTER FIFTY-ONE

"So, you're leaving us today," Irene said, as she brought me my breakfast.

"Yes, I think the doctor is signing the papers now for my release. My mother will be here to pick me up later."

I tried not to act as apprehensive as I felt, as she placed my tray on the bedside table. I was worried about what I saw as a long, hard road ahead of me. I had already spoken with Melanie and Virginia, and they seemed very enthusiastic about my moving in with them after my plaster cast came off. Until then I would stay with my parents. And I would be seeing the solicitor in a day or two to draw up the papers for the Decree Nisi. Jack would have six weeks to respond to them. If not, the Decree Absolute would be filed, and the whole nasty nightmare would all be behind me. Mentally I crossed my fingers. Then I became aware that Irene was chattering away.

"...and of course, you must be sure to bring that wee one by to see us!" she was saying.

I looked up at her and smiled, grateful for her friendliness. "I'll be sure to do that," I told her.

"We'll all be anxious to see how you're getting on, you and the baby."

"Good morning!" Dr. Munro said from the doorway. "You'll be leaving us today."

"That's right."

He stepped into the room and walked to my bed. "You be careful, now, and do what you said you would. Take care of yourself." He pointed to my stomach with a grin. "And the wee one, too."

"Aye, aye, Captain," I smiled back.

"Right. Well, I'd best get back to work. I just wanted to say good-bye. Take care." He patted my hand, then nodded to Irene, and was out the door.

Irene sighed. "Such a nice man," she said. "I wish he worked this floor instead of Casualty."

"Irene! What's that I hear in your voice?" I asked her, teasing.

"Well, he's no' attached, is he? A lass can hope!"

We both had a laugh together, and after I finished eating, Irene cleared the breakfast away, and helped me into the bathroom for my morning ablutions. Then I dressed to leave. The plaster on my leg and the pain in my chest slowed me considerably. The bruises on my face were beginning to fade, although they still looked a nasty color. I carefully applied my makeup and fixed my hair. The end result wasn't too bad. Thank goodness I was finally ready when, shortly before noon, my mother arrived to take me home with her.

Mom, dad, and my brother still lived in my grandmother's old house, that she had left to my father when she died. It had been home to me since I was twelve, and a part of me still yearned for the haven which had been my room for so many years.

Irene brought a wheel chair and helped me into it, and my mother gathered up my things.

"Don't you look grand?" she told me with a smile. "Are you ready to go?"

"Yes," I answered.

"Are you hungry?" my mother asked. "I was thinking of having lunch at the pub across the way."

"The Royal Falconer? Good idea," Irene chimed in, as she steered the chair out into the hall. "The food is very good there. We, all of us, go there for a nosh. You must be very tired of hospital food by now," she said to me.

"Yes, I am," I laughed, nodding eagerly.

Irene wheeled me out to the car and helped me inside. We said good-bye, then my mother drove us over to the pub.

Once inside, we saw a chalkboard sitting in front of a darkened room to our left. The words on the board read: "Do not go in here. This section is closed." I smiled to myself as a waiter directed us to a table. He chose a comfortable seat for us, near the huge hearth that warmed the room.

The common room was cozy, clad in dark oak and illuminated by Tiffany-style chandeliers. Huge wooden columns supported the ceiling from the center of the narrow room. Edinburgh street scenes, cricket bats, and an imposing sculpture of a falcon decorated the walls, but its most distinctive feature was a shimmering copper-topped wooden bar, which at 50 feet in length, could easily seat a couple of rugby teams. French doors opened out into a patio where one could dine al fresco, and the atmosphere was quite pleasant.

The waiter graciously held my chair out for me, and I slid clumsily into it. As I settled my cumbersome plaster cast under the table, he assisted my mother into the chair across from me. Then he handed us our menus.

We ordered Scotch eggs, and he brought us our drinks. As I took a sip, I glanced around the room. I faced the door where I sat, and saw several hospital personnel that I recognized, as they came and went. Dr. Munro, seated at a table in front of the window, nodded to us from across the room.

Our food was served, and we began to eat. The Scotch eggs were fried to a crunchy perfection, and served with a spirited whole grain mustard. The meal was heavy, but extremely satisfying, after days of bland hospital food.

The door opened, and out of the corner of my eye I saw Jack enter. I blanched, then gasped, as he glanced around the room and caught sight of me. I lowered my lashes quickly. With stumbling steps he came across the room, drawing all eyes to him. I heard him coming, and my heart leapt in fear. I could tell that he had been drinking, and was past the point of caution.

He rudely clasped my arm and hauled me out of the chair, while my mother gasped, and screamed for help.

"You bitch!" Jack shouted. "How dare you leave the hospital and not tell me! Just where did you think you were going? I swear to you, Jennifer, I'll never let you leave me!"

Jack brought his fist around, and I tried to brace myself, certain the blow would fall with brutal force. I waited, but it didn't come.

Instead, Dr. Munro shot out of his chair with a flare of rage, and seized Jack by the arm, whirling him around, yanking his wrist in a painfully tight grip.

"Take your hands off me!" Jack bellowed, attempting to gain his freedom. But the strong, broad hand held him fast.

Dr. Munro's voice was calm. "I beg you to consider your actions, Mr. MacCallum," he warned him. "Mrs. MacCallum came here with her mother. You are disturbing the peace, and you insult us all by such a display. Would you like the manager to call the police?"

As if coming out of a fog, Jack became aware of the crowd of diners who watched us from their tables. Red-faced, he hurriedly stuttered an apology, and Dr. Munro released his hold, giving Jack a short, backward thrust as he did so.

Turning, Jack hitched up his jeans, glared about at those who still stared, and walked up to the bar.

With tears of humiliation stinging my eyes, I sat down, conscious of the dull throb of my ankle, and the pain in my chest.

"Thank you," I murmured to Dr. Munro.

"All right?" he asked, his anger gone as quickly as it had come. He put his hand on the back of my chair and leaned down.

"Yes, I think so," I said, taking a slow, deep breath. I looked up at him. An odd, enigmatic smile curved the corners of his mouth. He chuckled, and whispered to me, "I'll admit that I would have enjoyed seeing him sprawled on his arse."

I smiled at the picture it conjured in my imagination, and laughed a little, too.

My mother watched us with an odd expression, then said, "Thank you very much for your help, Dr. Munro."

"My pleasure, ladies," he said, straightening. He glanced over toward the bar where Jack was, his back to us. "I'll leave you to finish your meal. Take care, now," he told me.

* * * *

A few days after being released from the hospital, my mother took me to see the solicitor. The papers were now in motion.

On the drive home I was very quiet. Mom tried several times to draw me into conversation with small talk, but I was worried. I had no idea how Jack would react when he received the divorce papers.

194

I walked into the house, threw my purse on the sofa, and sat down with a dejected plop.

"Jenny, dear, don't worry," my mother told me, sitting down beside me. "Everything will be fine."

I looked up at her. "But I am worried, Mom. I can't help it. Everything is so uncertain now, so different. What will Jack do when he receives those papers? And nothing will ever be quite the same." I gestured toward my stomach. "Everything has changed."

"Mom!" my brother, John, called from upstairs.

"What is it, dear?" she called back.

"The elastic ripped off my underwear. Can you sew it back on?"

Mom turned back to me with a smile. "See, sweetheart, not everything has changed."

I made a small noise in my throat. "I hate to admit it, Mom, but that actually comforts me."

CHAPTER FIFTY-TWO

Six weeks later my cast was removed, and I moved in with Melanie and Virginia. I bought a used Volvo with not too many miles, and my father and brother retrieved my belongings from the flat I shared with Jack.

I settled in quickly. We ordered pizza for dinner that first night, laughing together just like old times. I hadn't heard from Jack again, neither had he responded to the Decree Nisi. It looked as though I had worried for nothing.

The flat had two bedrooms, and since Virginia had the larger of the two, she agreed to share her room with me. We went to bed late that night, and I fell asleep quickly, exhausted by my busy day.

Sometime later something awakened me. I opened my eyes and glanced around the room. The pale light of the moon shone through the window, and everything looked the same as it had when I had gone to sleep. I could hear Virginia softly sighing in her sleep, and was about to close my eyes again when the scent of lavender came to me. I felt the cold then, and turned my eyes reluctantly to the foot of my bed. My teeth began to chatter, my breath puffed out in white clouds before my face, as a shimmering white light began to take form, the image of the Lady Ruthven. My skin prickled as gooseflesh crept up my arms, and my heart pounded in an uncomfortable rhythm.

The apparition seemed to float in the light, her long white gown billowing out around her, long auburn curling hair moving as if stirred by a soft breeze. She held her hand out to me, beseeching, imploring, "Hansel to me." Then she disappeared.

I sat up, shivering, pulling my covers up tightly around me. *Where had she gone? What did she want?* I wondered. *Would I spend the rest of my life trying to answer that question? I sincerely hoped not.*

Virginia stirred in her own bed. "What is it, Jen? Are you OK?"

"I'm all right," I said, laying back against the pillows. "I'm fine. Go back to sleep."

"Okay," I heard her yawn, and before long, I heard her breathing softly again. I was glad that one of us would get some sleep this night.

* * * *

The miraculous radiant pink, windless dawn I could see from my window had only made me shiver. That warm, glowing pink in the sky was false. in reality, it was cold as ice. My night had been awful, endless, and full of half dreams, along with the fancy that I could hear someone calling to me. Maddeningly, I could not for the life of me figure out what the ghost wanted, no matter how hard I wracked my brain. I felt like I had all the clues to the puzzle, but I could not seem to put them together.

Eventually I gave up pondering my enigma and ate my breakfast while I made out a grocery list. Then I set off to the corner market to buy some food. I took a trolley from the front of the store and headed down one of the aisles, checking my list as I went.

Comparing prices, remembering Melanie and Virginia's favorite things, I moved through the supermarket, trying to decide which special something to cook for dinner tonight. Alone in one of the back aisles, lost in my own thoughts, I didn't notice a low, six-wheeled cart, full of boxes, bearing down on me until it was almost too late.

"Stop!" I cried, but the driver took no notice, and kept coming at me. I looked around in a panic, and saw no other way of escape, except through the double doors that led into the back room. I backed through them, and the six-wheeler burst through after me, banging the doors loudly against the walls.

"Stop!" I cried again. I put my arms out and stepped back, twisting my newly healed ankle. With a burst of pain, I fell down against some stacked blue plastic bread racks as the door swung shut. Thankfully, the cart stopped just in front of me.

Jack came around the cart menacingly.

"I received the papers from your solicitor, Jennifer. I tried to call you."

"Get away from me!" I tried to get up, but he pushed me down, bending low over me, and put his face next to mine.

"I told you that I would never let you go, Jennifer. If I can't have you, no one will. You'd best believe me."

Terrified, I struggled to get away. "Somebody, help me!" I screamed.

He jumped away from me then, and grabbed a broom, raising the long handle as a weapon, and swung it down towards me.

"No, Jack! Please! Someone! Help me!"

He brought the broom handle down with his full force, hitting the boxes right next to me, sending empty cartons raining down on me.

The manager of the store, who happened to be moving pallets in the receiving end, heard the commotion and my screams, and came rushing over to me. I was curled up in a ball against the boxes on the floor, crying. He bent down beside me.

"Are you all right, ma'am?" he asked, concern lacing his voice.

I looked up into his sympathetic face, then glanced around. There was no sign of Jack. "Y-yes, I'm okay," I said with a shaking voice. I attempted to raise myself from the floor.

He put out a hand to stop me. "No, no, you mustn't move. I'm afraid we'll have to fill out an accident report, ma'am. I'll have to call an ambulance."

"Nonsense," I said, trying to sound in control of the situation. Embarrassed, I only wanted to leave the store and go home. "I'm fine," I said, as I struggled to gain my feet. I managed to stand, but my ankle twisted painfully when I put my weight on it. Biting back a groan, I winced, and started to go down again. He caught me, easing me back down to the floor.

"Sean!" he barked. "Come here and keep this lady company. I am going to call 999."

I looked down the length of the room then, and saw the boy who had just begun breaking down cardboard and throwing it into the baler. He came toward us, curiosity written all over his face. I wished that I could dissolve into thin air.

* * * *

Perched on the gurney in Casualty at Good Samaritan Hospital once again, I waited reluctantly for the doctor. I gazed distractedly at all the bits and gadgets lying around, comparing them in my mind to instruments from a Medieval torture chamber.

"Well, back again, I see," chirped a cheery voice. "That makes twice in two months. Couldn't stay away, eh? What is it? My magnetic personality?"

I jumped, started from my thoughts, to see Dr. Munro's smiling face looking back at me.

"I-I fell," I stammered.

He glanced down at the chart he held in his hand. "Yes, I see that. Same ankle, hmmm?"

He bent over my leg, his lean, strong fingers gentle as they lingered over the swollen tissue of my ankle. His hand stroked my instep, gently turning my foot, moving the bruised and darkening flesh until I made a small noise.

He raised up. "Not to worry. I'm almost certain there are no broken bones. You've just wrenched it very badly. Nevertheless, we'll have it x-rayed."

I sighed wretchedly.

"Come now, it's not so bad as you think."

I looked up at him, thoroughly disgusted with life and everything else. "How do you know what I think?" I asked him cheekily.

His eyes glinted as he raised an eyebrow at me. "Aren't we a crabbit get today?"

"You, too?" I asked, raising a twin eyebrow at him.

"Ha, ha, that's better. Now let me schedule that x-ray, and we'll have you patched up and out of here in no time." He started to leave, then turned back to me. He was looking at me in a serious, thoughtful way. "Whom shall I call to pick you up?"

I could tell by his sudden change in manner that he was wondering what I had done about Jack. I looked at my watch. Melanie and Virginia would be getting off work in a few minutes. "My friends will be getting home soon. You can call them." I nodded toward the chart in his hand. "The number is in the chart."

"You did move in with your friends from work, then?"

"Yes, like I said I would. No need to worry, Doctor."

He nodded. "I see. Very good." He closed my chart, and left the cubicle.

By the time my ankle had been x-rayed, Melanie was there for me, her face full of concern. "Oh, Sweetie, what happened?"

"Jack happened. He was at the supermarket where I was shopping. He must have followed me. He pushed me into the back room, and I twisted my ankle."

Melanie gasped. Just then Dr. Munro entered the cubicle, my chart in his hand. I was not sure if he heard what I had told Melanie, but if he had, he gave no sign.

"The x-rays show what I thought they would. Nothing is broken. You've just badly wrenched your ankle. Try to stay off it for a few days. Get some rest. I'll prescribe an anti-inflammatory for you."

There was something in his eyes as he looked away from me. I wasn't sure what it meant. He reached into his lab coat pocket, pulled out his tablet, and began to write. By the time he tore it off and handed it to me, the look was gone.

CHAPTER FIFTY-THREE

I was sitting on the sofa a few nights later, my ankle propped on a stool, when the phone began to ring. I reached over and picked it up.

"Hello?"

"Hello," a friendly voice answered. "Am I speaking with Jennifer MacCallum?"

"Yes," I said, as I recognized the voice. My heart gave a pleasantly surprised thump.

"Mrs. MacCallum, you've been chosen by a local restaurant to participate in a brief survey. Which of the following sounds like best to you. A) eating alone, B) having dinner with your family, or C) enjoying a nice evening in a restaurant with a special bloke?"

"Dr. Munro--"

"Yes, that's right. But you can call me Peter. So, does that mean you pick C?" I could hear the smile in his voice.

"Dr. Munro, how did you get this number? And what do you want?"

"It's Peter. Your friend Melanie gave me permission to call you when you were in Casualty the other day, while you were in x-ray. I've waited the customary three days of proper dating etiquette, am I right? And I would like to have dinner with you on Saturday evening at The Oak Trees. All you have to do is say 'yes'."

I glanced toward the kitchen where Melanie was cleaning up the dinner dishes. *So she was in on this, too.* I smiled ruefully. *What did it matter? The doctor had been in my thoughts the last few days--too often. He did possess a particular sort of humorous charm. And I did find him attractive.* "Let me think about it, okay? Can I get back to you, Dr. Munro?"

"It's Peter. Well, just don't wait too long. The Oak Trees is practically impossible to get into on Saturday nights. I have reservations."

I caught my lower lip in my teeth, thinking how strange it felt to be contemplating a date. "So do I..."

"Very funny. Just a friendly night out, I promise. No strings."

"Let me think about it."

"All right. You win. Take all the time you need. I'll wait here by the phone for your call."

"Good-bye, then," I laughed.

"Who was that?" Melanie asked as I rang off.

"Dr. Munro. He asked me to dinner at The Oak Trees on Saturday night."

Her face brightened. "And you said yes?"

"I said I'd think about it."

"So you've thought about it and you're going to call him back and say yes?"

"I'm still thinking."

"Jenny! Thinking is for math! This is a no-think situation! Stop thinking! He asked you to the Oak Trees? Jenny, it's the ritziest place on earth! You will call him back right now and accept his dinner invitation."

She picked up the phone and pushed the button to redial the last incoming call. Then she held the phone out to me.

"I don't believe this. You're forcing me to--"

"It's fate. And you're welcome. Here."

He picked up the phone on the first ring. "Hello?"

Try as I might, I couldn't suppress the surge of warmth that his voice sent spilling through my veins. *Fool!* I chided myself. *It was silly to allow my emotions to overrule my good sense. Hadn't I done that once before? And hadn't it turned out to be a disaster?* I glanced at Melanie's smiling expression, hoping my thoughts didn't show on my face.

"Hello?" the voice said again. "Is anyone there?"

"Dr. Munro?" I managed to find my voice. "Hi--Hello, it's me, Jenny."

"I wish you'd call me Peter."

"Yes, well then, Peter...I, um..."

"You accept my invitation? That's good! I'll pick you up at 6:30 Saturday night. Is that good for you? My reservations are for seven. See you then?"

"Yes, well...all right...bye."

I hung up quickly.

"To the shops!" Melanie said.

"Excuse me?"

"We have to get you glammed up!"

"Why? Did it ever occur to you that he might like me just the way I am, fat and nearly five months pregnant?"

"Yeah, he is weird. Come on."

* * * *

I guess I needed to thank Melanie after all. The look on Dr. Munro...I mean, Peter's...face as I came down the stairs that night for our date was well worth the $100 I had paid for the dress. It hid my rounded stomach well, and looked quite chic.

"You look amazing," he told me. Something about his voice, the promise in his smile, made a shiver tremble along my spine. The brush of his gaze as it swept over me felt as solid and real as the touch of his hand might. It made my breath catch, my heart thump a bit harder, my skin feel more sensitive. I met his smile with a tentative one of my own as he took my hand at the bottom of the stair. I took his firmly, telling myself that I was not the least bit nervous.

"Thank you," I said, surprised at the way my hand had disappeared within his. I rather liked the way he towered above me.

His smile deepened, showing a dimple at the corner of his mouth. "Are you ready?"

I could see Melanie and Virginia beaming at me over his shoulder.

"Yes," I said, grabbing my coat. He took it from me and helped me into it. Once again I saw the approving looks on my roommates' faces.

We said our good-byes, and walked out to Peter's dark blue BMW parked by our block of flats. He opened the door for me, and as I sat down on his hand tooled leather seat, I wondered if he was perhaps a little out of my league.

* * * *

We stepped inside the restaurant, and the delicious smells of roast beef and spices greeted us. It set my stomach growling, fortunately not loud enough to be heard over the diners. The baby chose that moment to start kicking.

I laid my hand over my stomach. "All right, I'll feed you," I whispered.

Peter's laugh brought a flush to my cheeks. "Demanding, is he?" He reached for my free hand and we followed the waiter to our table. Peter pulled out my chair, easing me into it. Then he sat down across from me, and took the menu that the waiter handed us.

"We can't let the poor child go hungry," he said, glancing quickly at the fare. "Especially since there is so much to chose from."

I picked up the menu, but instead of looking at it, I found myself taking in the room. "Wow. This place is gorgeous."

"Yes, it is, now that you're in it."

Taken aback, I stared at him as he nonchalantly gazed at his menu. *Look out for this one,* I warned myself. *He's already laying on the lines. He's the type of man who says flattering thing, but doesn't mean a word of it.* Nervously I stuck my nose in my menu. "Let's order. I need to go home soon."

He cast me a teasing glance. "Then may I suggest the chicken for you?"

"Ha, ha, very funny," I retorted, then looked back at the menu. "Look at these prices! They're-"

He stifled a laugh and I glanced up at him. There was an amused expression on his handsome face. "Jenny, let me explain to you how a date works. The man asks the woman out. They eat, they talk, they laugh. The hours fly by. He pays. She gratefully says thank you. They both go home happy. She's had a nice meal with a great bloke, and he's enjoyed the companionship of a lovely, interesting lady."

"Trust me. I'm not 30 pounds worth of lovely and interesting."

"Let me be the judge of that."

We ate in silence. I felt a nervous wreck. *I had not been out with another man besides Jack in several years and it felt very strange, yet at the same time it was exhilarating. I was very aware of him, and confused by the feelings he stirred within me. It was a little frightening with my track record. He had offered friendship, but could I trust him?* I reached for my coffee cup with a reflective sigh, and as I sipped, I glanced up and found Peter watching me.

I started to look away, but he leaned closer and reached for my hand. His scent filled my senses, and my heart beat a little faster. He drew in a deep breath.

"Jenny, what's wrong?" he asked quietly, fixing his steely blue-grey eyes on my face. "Every time we start to talk, just when I think we'll begin to know each other, it's as if a shutter closes within you, keeping me at arm's length. I can see the struggle inside you revealed on your face, in your eyes. I know that we haven't known each other long, and I know that you're still recovering from some unpleasant experiences, but I wish you would talk to me. You must realize that I would not hurt you. I just want to help you. I want to be your friend." His expression intent, he scanned my face, lingering on my eyes for a moment. "And will you do me the favor of not looking at me with that suspicion in your eyes?" He shook his head. "Perhaps it's still too soon," he added, so quietly I could barely hear him.

A shudder passed through me. *How could I make him understand my reticence, my fears?*

Before I could try, he spoke again. "I just want to get to know you better, if you'll let me."

How did he know all the right things to say, to make me want to trust him? I closed my eyes and turned away. *I should not succumb to the temptation to trust another man.* I shook my head and pulled my hand away. "It's a hard thing to admit to you what a fool I was." Emotion closed my throat so that I could barely speak.

"Wait a minute. Your ex-husband just lost the love and respect of a beautiful and trusting woman. How foolish is that?"

I took a deep breath and gazed down at my hands in my lap. "Most men would avoid getting anywhere near a woman like me. Yet it seems like every time I turn around, there you are."

"What do you mean, a woman like you?"

He leaned closer, then stopped as I glared up at him. "You know," I said in exasperation. Suddenly unwilling to face him, I made pretense of draining my coffee.

He stared at me for a moment, then shook his head. "No, I don't know what you mean. Tell me, Jennifer, what is there about you that should keep me away from you?"

I glanced up at him through my lashes. Genuine curiosity lit his eyes. I put my coffee down and met his questioning gaze. "I'm pregnant, divorced. Who needs a woman with excess baggage?" I said impatiently.

His expression softened. "Jenny," he whispered, reaching out to touch my hair. And I saw in his face understanding and sympathy, and in his eyes a tantalizing glimpse of what could be. I swallowed hard, focusing my gaze on the knot of his tie at the V of his collar.

"All I see is a lovely young woman," he said, his voice low. "Not a woman pregnant with another man's child."

"You're laughing at me now," I said.

He looked thoughtful for a moment, reflective. "I am suddenly reminded of the bedtime stories my mother used to tell me of a beautiful, mysterious woman who could enchant a man with nothing but a glance, or a smile."

I could feel his gaze on me, but I refused to glance up, to meet his eyes. He slid his chair nearer to mine, leaned close and caught my chin in his hand gently forcing me to look up at him. "Lord help me if you do smile at me," he said with a grin. His fingers grazed my cheekbone, sending a shiver of awareness skittering down my spine and startling me into meeting his eyes.

"I--" My voice faded away. *I didn't want to feel this way. I never wanted to feel this way again, or to have another relationship with another man as long as I lived.* But this close I could see the faint flecks of blue in his pewter colored eyes, and I could feel the warmth rising on my skin. His nearness, the scent of him, the feel of his hand…*God help me, was I so easily tempted? A few kind words? A friendly smile?* His hair fell in a soft golden curl over his forehead, tempting my fingers to reach out and smooth it away from his brow.

I fought the urge, though my fingertips tingled with anticipation.

He leaned closer. "I thought that I had strength enough to resist any temptation. I don't think you realize just how lovely and tempting you are. Forgive me," he whispered.

I sat motionless as he brushed his mouth over mine in a feather-light caress. Warmth spread from his touch, and I was so caught up in the myriad of sensations flooding me, I did not notice that Jack had strolled up to our table until he spoke.

"Are you aware that you are kissing my wife?"

I gasped at the sound of his voice and pulled away, catching the edge of the table with one hand so tightly that my knuckles were white with the strain. *How did he get past the matre'd?* It was obvious that he had been drinking. My other hand settled protectively over the mound of my stomach, which moved visibly. *Could the baby feel my tension?*

"And that it is my child she is getting so fat with," he said smugly, pointing to my stomach.

"I think you mean your ex-wife. And yes, I am well aware that she is pregnant."

"Jack," I implored him. "Please don't cause a scene."

He made a sound of disgust and tossed me a black look. I cringed inside. It was a wonder that the hostility in his gaze didn't strike me dead on the spot. He still had the means to recall the old fear in me.

"Shut up, slut!" He spat the words at me, the hatred in his eyes holding me motionless, stunned. He pointed toward Peter. "Have you already replaced me in your bed with him?"

I saw Peter go very white, and a little pulse began to show on his forehead. He pushed the curl back from his forehead and stood.

There was a remoteness in his face, a chill in his eyes that had not been there a moment before. Jack's scowl deepened.

"I believe you owe the lady an apology," Peter said in a cold voice. "Though nothing you could say will make up for your words." His even gaze appeared to weigh Jack's response.

Jack raked a careless hand through his tangled hair, anger etched in every line of his body. He straightened, his stare a challenge. "You've no right to tell me what to do!" he shouted. Amazingly, what appeared to be righteousness lit his eyes.

I glanced surreptitiously around the room to find the other diners staring openly at us. A chill ran through me, and I rubbed my hands over my arms, but the usually soothing motion did not chase the bone-deep cold away. From the corner of my eye, I could see the matre'd coming toward us, a security guard on his heels.

"I'm afraid you'll have to leave, sir."

The guard tugged Jack around and urged him toward the door.

Jack looked indignantly at both men. "But this man is with my wife!" His eyes shifted restlessly to the faces of the other diners, then back to the men. His expression turned uneasy, and he decided to do as they said. He shrugged the guard's hands from him, and walked toward the door with both men on his heels.

My face heated with shame. I sat huddled in my seat, my body shaking, my gaze lowered to the table. I fought back the sob that threatened to fill my chest, feeling that my life was completely out of my control. Peter pulled his chair close and sat down next to me, covering my hand with his. The warmth of his touch was soothing.

"I wish there was some way I could take away the sting of his words." He cradled my hand in his, squeezing my fingers reassuringly.

I looked up and met his gaze, feeling my cheeks still tinged with color. His expression was apologetic. I took a deep breath to calm my quaking stomach, and gave him a weak smile. "He is blunt." My voice shook, and I took another deep breath, hoping to ease the quavering. It made no difference. I laughed shakily. "He was embarrassing. But--"

He reached out with his free hand to smooth an errant strand away from my face, letting his fingers linger against my cheek. "He doesn't treat you like he should," Peter said. "You owe him nothing, as far as I can see."

Despite the color still heating my face, I allowed my gaze to roam over him. My eyes lingered over the breadth of his chest, before stopping, when I encountered his gaze on me. It was not embarrassment that warmed my face now, but an awareness of him. *His height and build made me feel safe, despite my many fears, as though no one, not even Jack, could harm me, or my child. Could it be possible, then, that I could talk to him, reveal myself freely, without worry that he'd see me as weak?* I met his gaze, gathering courage from him. His eyes drew me in, held a warmth and approval, I must surely be imagining. But when he smiled, his expression said the same.

"Thank you," I told him. "It never occurred to me that something like this would happen. I'm sorry."

"Don't fash. It's done with." He raised an eyebrow in question. "Are you all right?"

I drew another calming breath and nodded.

He turned my hand beneath his, and held them palm to palm, letting the warmth of his touch seep into my chilled fingers. "Will you trust me?" he asked, holding me motionless with his eyes, staring deep into my soul. *How could I refuse?*

"I-I will try," I murmured, my mind in a turmoil.

He released my hand then, and broke the spell he'd cast. "Dessert, then?" he asked with an indulgent smile.

I nodded, feeling more lighthearted.

We finished our meal without any further interruptions, then left the restaurant, and walked toward Peter's car.

"Thank you," I said. "That was a wonderful dinner. I get so tired of my own cooking."

"I'm sure you're a wonderful cook," Peter smiled.

I shivered, and he wrapped an arm around me, enveloping me in his nearness, his scent. I looked up at him and smiled, too, but then suddenly my heart froze. I recognized a familiar car slowly pass by the restaurant. It was Jack. I reached out and grasped Peter's arm in a tight grip, pulling him quickly toward his parked car.

"What's the matter? What is it?"

"It's Jack."

"Again? Where?"

"In that car!"

He glanced toward the street, then looked both ways, seeing nothing familiar. "Are you sure?"

"Of course, I'm sure! He follows me everywhere!"

I saw the car make a U-turn down the street and come back. Frustrated, I turned and shouted, "Get away from me! Leave me alone!"

Peter's arm tightened around me sharply. He quickly unlocked the car door and I scrambled inside.

CHAPTER FIFTY-FOUR

"How did it go?" Melanie asked, as I walked in the door.

"Very nicely. Except Jack showed up. But Peter handled it very well. The matre'd had him escorted from the restaurant."

A smile lit Melanie's face. "Jenny, this is perfect!" she exclaimed, clapping her hands together. "He's like a knight in shining armor come to rescue the fair damsel in distress. Why aren't you happy?"

"I don't know," I sighed, throwing my purse on the sofa. "He seems interested in me...but after what happened tonight--"

Melanie gasped, her hand to her mouth. "Ohmygosh! You're right! There could be hand holding, kissing, romance!" She threw her hands up in the air and ran from the room. "Flee, Jenny! Flee! Run for your life! Hide! Hide!"

I rolled my eyes at her retreating figure. "A bit melodramatic, Melanie, but I get the message. Fine, I'll see him again, if he asks. I'll obsess over him, blab endlessly about him, fret 24-7...Am I good enough? Does he like my hair? Will he care next week? Am I too shy, too fat, too plain? in other words, I'll become just like you."

Melanie peeked around the corner, grinning. "Good! It's about time you came around! Now, about your hair--"

The phone began to ring, cutting her off in mid-sentence. I picked it up.

"Hello?"

I felt my face drain of color. Quiet for a moment, I listened to the threatening voice on the other end. My hand tightened around the receiver. Then anger at the years of abuse burst through in a flood of fury so intense it took me a moment to be able to speak, and when I did, it was with a voice that trembled with rage. "How dare you!" I exploded. "I can see anybody I want! I can have a life of my own, and you can't stop me!"

I slammed the receiver down.

The phone began to ring a moment later.

I picked it up and shouted into it, "Leave me alone! Do you hear me? Stop calling me!"

I slammed the receiver down again. A moment later it began to ring again. But this time I did not answer it.

* * * *

Peter did call again, and I did continue to see him. He drew me to him like a magnet with every new facet of his character that I discovered. He was a good man, moral, helpful, courteous and kind. I felt safe and protected when I was with him. And I found myself looking forward to his company.

Christmas season was approaching. A time of cheer and good will toward men. A time for shopping.

It was Saturday. Peter and I had spent the day at the shops buying presents for our families. We burst through the door of my flat, packages in hand, both of us singing t Jingle Bells at the top of our lungs.

"Dashing through the snow
In a one-horse open sleigh,
O'er the fields we go,
Laughing all the waa-aayy!"
"Ha! Ha! Ha!" Peter sang.

Melanie came running into the foyer, a look of panic on her face. "Oh, Jenny! Thank goodness you're home! There's water all over the kitchen!"

She ran back, and I followed her, Peter on my heels. We could hear the sound of running water, and soon enough, we were ankle deep in it. I stopped short as I gazed around the flooded kitchen in despair. Peter rushed by me and grabbed the tap handles, twisting with all his might. They turned freely in his hands, as water continued to gush from the tap, over the sink, and splash down onto the floor. He reached down through the water in the sink and drew out the stopper, then got down on his haunches and pulled open the doors under the sink. Reaching inside, his expression turned to shock.

"Quick! A torchlight!"

I waded through the water, and ran to the hall closet, returning with it in hand. He took it from me and shined the light under the sink, as he peered inside. "The shut off valves are gone to both the hot and cold lines!"

"What?" I asked, not understanding.

The water continued to flow, quickly disappearing down the drain, but was still ankle deep on the floor.

"Do you have a wrench?" Peter asked.

I turned to our "junk drawer" and pulled it open. Pushing various odds and ends aside, I spied a wrench and held it out to him. He grabbed it and ran out the door. A few minutes later the water from the tap ceased to run. I sloshed toward the sink, my shoes most probably ruined. *Who would put the stopper in the sink and turn on the tap, then leave the water running?* I looked around the kitchen and my heart sank. *And what was I going to do about all this water?*

Peter appeared in the doorway.

"What happened?" I asked.

Melanie cleared her throat. In the heat of the crisis, we had both forgotten that she was there. "I just got home a few minutes before you. When I unlocked the door, I heard the water running. The kitchen was already flooded. I panicked."

Peter was looking around, examining the windows, the front door. "Did you notice anything unusual when you arrived home, Melanie?"

She shook her head, looking about her in total desolation at the mess. "Only the water."

Peter walked toward the back garden. I followed him. As he had questioned Melanie, his voice held enough urgency to make me ask, "What are you looking for?"

"Someone's been here, Jenny. Broken into your flat, and deliberately vandalized your kitchen tap. Ah, here it is. See?" he had been examining the latch to the back door as he spoke. Now he stood aside and pointed out to me the gouges and the splintered wood around the hasp. "Look, it's been forced."

I reached out and touched it in disbelief. "Jack," I whispered.

"That would be my guess," Peter agreed. I met his gaze and saw his anger as he clamped his jaw tight.

I glanced anxiously about the room. I believed the cushions had been moved and plumped up too carefully, the rug by the door left slightly askew. *Could it be a suspicion induced by my uneasiness?*

Suddenly we heard a surprised cry. Virginia was home. I could hear Melanie telling her what had happened. I looked back to Peter.

"I think it's time to call the police."

"Yes, I agree," he said. "I'd better get busy, too. I shut off the water to your flat. Now I need to go and buy shut off valves for your sink. Probably washers, too. I can't leave you without water for the night, now can I?" he added with a smile.

I shook my head and we walked back through the flat toward the kitchen. Virginia was already on the phone to the fire department, Melanie told us. They would come and clean up the mess. I felt relieved. Leave it to Virginia, the level headed one.

"We need to call the police, too. It looks as if someone's broken in through the garden door."

Melanie blanched. "Who would do such a thing?"

Peter left for the hardware store, and by the time he arrived back at the flat, the firemen were packing up their gear. The kitchen was dry. Virginia stood aside, talking to one of the firemen. The police were still by the back door, dusting for fingerprints. One of the officers took my statement, then Peter's. When he had finished, he turned back to the other man, who was shaking his head.

"Find anything, Ronnie?"

"No prints at all, Jim. Whoever it was, they were wearing gloves."

"We'll question your neighbors, Ma'am. Find out if they saw or heard anything unusual or suspicious."

Ice ran through my veins. Peter reached for my hand and clasped it tightly. His touch was warm and comforting. His scent drifted to me, surrounding me with a feeling of wellbeing and security. But now I knew that I couldn't allow myself to grow used to it. I had to stand on my own. Because I knew that Jack had done this. And I was afraid that he might do something else. And I wasn't willing to involve Peter, or risk his safety. Already I had come to care for him, far more deeply than I would have believed possible.

The policemen left and I followed Peter into the kitchen. I watched as he shone the torch under the sink. I could hear Melanie in the other room ordering pizza for dinner over the phone.

"Could you hold the torch for me, just there?"

"Yes."

I bent and took it from him, holding the light where he needed it. My eyes wandered back to him while he worked, my thoughts churning. *Never in my life had I been so confused. I knew that I was falling in love with him, but I did not want to involve him in a predicament that could be dangerous for him. What should I do?*

Once again, his scent drifted to me, and I let myself be distracted. I noticed how well his dark green shirt fit him. I found the way the soft material outlined his shoulders and arms all too appealing. It filled me with a tingling warmth. A flush rose to my cheeks. *What kind of woman am I, practically lusting over Peter, and pregnant with another man's child?*

He must have felt my gaze on him, for he looked back at me over his shoulder and smiled.

"Only be keeping the light here, if you please," he said gently, the glint of humor in his eyes tempering his words.

With my heart pounding, I lowered my gaze. *That's enough of that,* I told myself, and forced my attention back to holding the torch.

After a while, Peter gave a final turn of the wrench with a loud grunt. "There, finished." He swiped his sleeve across his eyes as he stood.

"Be right back," he said, brushing a kiss across my cheek, and headed toward the door to turn the water back on. He was back in a moment, to turn on the taps. Water flowed freely. He twisted them again, and they shut off.

Just then, the doorbell rang.

"Dinner's arrived!" I heard Melanie call, as she went to answer the door.

* * * *

All through dinner, while the others laughed and joked, my thoughts roiled within me. My mind was so muddled, in fact, that I wondered if I could make a sensible decision. *I was upset that Peter had been drawn into this coiled mess. I could not allow him to be put in danger, as well. I would never forgive myself if something happened to him. He had been so good to me, treated me with a respect I hadn't known for a very long time. And what had I to offer him in return? Jack, and whatever trouble he might bring? No, I couldn't do that to him. I must distance myself from him. I must be strong, and stand on my own.* I heaved a sigh. *I would tell him that tonight.*

The few bites of pizza that I managed to choke down sat like a brick on my stomach.

The clock on the mantle struck 8:00.

"Well, ladies," Peter said, rising from the meal. "I think it's time I should be going. I've got an early morning call at the hospital." He turned his smile on me.

Well, now's the time, I told myself, standing to walk with him to the door. *Courage, don't fail me now.*

Peter opened the door and a gust of wind whipped through his hair. He turned to brush his fingers across my cheek. The shiver that passed through me owed little to the cold wind, and everything to his touch. I closed both my hands into tight fists to keep myself from reaching for him. He captured my face in his hands as he bent to kiss me. *The feelings he kindled within me rose so quickly, I thought they would tear my heart in two.* Tears filled my eyes as Peter continued to press his mouth to mine.

"Peter," I murmured reluctantly, unable to fight it, and slipped my arms around his neck, my fingers lightly tracing the collar of his shirt. I heard his indrawn breath, and my lips curved into a smile against his, even as a tear slid down my cheek.

He drew back far enough to search my face, frowning as he raised a finger to follow the trail of moisture down my cheek. "What's this?" he asked. "Did I hurt you? What did I do to make you cry?"

"Nothing," I whispered, as I outlined the curve of his jaw with my fingers, savoring the rasp of his whiskers against my skin. Reluctance made me linger, but I eased my hand away and backed away from him.

"What is it, then?" he asked, reaching for my hand. He met my gaze, and searched my face with his eyes, until I wondered if he could read my every thought.

"Please don't kiss me again."

"What?" His face flushed. "I don't understand...I wouldn't force myself on you, if that's what you're afraid of."

"No, no, it's not you." I felt the burning tears fill my eyes once again. *I wasn't afraid of anything he might do. It was what I might do in return, and what could happen to him if he remained close to me. That frightened me. If he only knew how badly I wanted to burrow back into his embrace!*

"Jenny," he murmured, reaching out to brush away the tears on my cheek. "Sweetheart, tell me what's wrong."

I shook my head. *How could I tell him I couldn't see him anymore?* I did not seem to be able to force the words past my lips, not here, not now.

His mouth firmed into a frown as he scanned my face. *It felt as if his eyes could see into my heart, my mind, into the shadows hidden deep within me.* But I did not look away. *Let him look,* I thought. *Perhaps he will see the truth, and I will not have to say it.*
Finally, I couldn't resist him any longer. "I want to be strong enough to stand on my own!" I cried.

His expression softened, and he nodded. "You are strong," he said. He lifted my chin with his finger. "I don't doubt your strength for a moment. You've already withstood a lot, and I know it's far from over."

"Don't," I choked, covering his mouth with my hand, and shaking my head. "Do you think I want to be the cause, if anything should happen to you?" The mere thought made my heart trip and falter. "I don't think we should see each other anymore."

He raked a hand through his hair. "Nothing will happen to me, Jenny," he said firmly.

"You don't know that," I answered stubbornly.

He was frowning deeply.

"And you don't have to feel responsible for me." My voice sounded spikier than I meant it to be. Even as I tried to explain to him, to pull away from him, I waited for him to disagree. Deep inside, I wished that he would. But he didn't. He said nothing. I found his enigmatic expression daunting. *Why doesn't he tell me what he's thinking?* The chilly outside air seemed to invade the room.

He nodded slowly, and a wounded look came into his eyes. "I see. I just want to help you. If you want to reject my help, then good-bye."

He turned away from me, and I couldn't bear the look on his face. I seized his arm. "Peter, please, don't leave like this."

He put back his head and gave a deep, tolerant sigh, then slumped against the wall. "Just how do you want me to leave, then?" He folded his arms across his chest, and drew in a steadying breath. "You must make up your mind, Jennifer. What is it that you want?"

I didn't know what to say. I was suddenly tired and cold. Tears burned behind my eyes. I wanted to end this foolish babble. "I'm afraid--for me, for the baby...for you," I choked.

Peter unfolded his arms and straightened, pulling me closer to him. I pressed my cheek against his shoulder, as much for comfort as to hide my tears. Here in his embrace, feeling his heart beating strong and steady, was a balm to my frazzled nerves. He put his hand on my shoulder, his touch alone giving comfort.

"It's late," he said, casting a glance at the clock on the wall. "I'll leave you to rest now. But we have to sort this out, Jenny. I'm leaving after work tomorrow to spend the holidays with my parents at Hayvenhurst. We can think about this situation while we are apart. But we'll continue this conversation when I get back, I assure you."

He let go of me then, and pushed himself away from the wall. Giving my hand a squeeze, he turned and walked out the door.

An overwhelming sense of loss enveloped me as I watched him disappear into the shadows. *What have I done?*

When I could no longer see his retreating figure, I closed the door and walked back into the living room. I plopped down next to Virginia on the sofa dejectedly.

"I'm fagged," Melanie sighed. "I'm going up to bed."

As I watched her climb the stair, Virginia turned to me and said, "You're a lucky girl. I do believe he's the one. You'd better hang onto him."

I turned toward her, surprised. "What makes you say that?"

"I've seen the way he looks at you. And I've seen the way you look at him."

Her words struck home to me. *If Peter really did leave now, as I was asking him to, and I never saw him again, I would miss him very much.* My heart squeezed painfully in my chest. It was then that I realized that, far from being on the verge of falling in love, I had already passed well over that invisible boundary. *I was in love with Peter.* A great, wracking sob rose within me, and I pressed my hands to my face and burst into tears.

Virginia put her arms about me. "Honey, what's wrong?" she asked.

"I've just told him I don't want to see him anymore!" I wailed.

"You what?" Her voice rose with disbelief. "Whatever made you do such a thing?"

I sobbed against her shoulder for a moment until I was able to speak. "It-it's Jack. You know as well as I do that he broke into our flat! You saw what he did!" My voice wavered. "What if he turns on Peter?" I cried.

I heard her indrawn breath. She had not thought of that. We sat in silence, as I pulled myself together. Eventually, as my emotions were soothed, an overwhelming lethargy enveloped me.

"I'm going up to bed, Virginia," I told her.

As I climbed the stairs toward my bedroom, the strong scent of perfume assailed my senses. *My perfume?* Baffled, I cautiously stepped through the door and glanced about the room. There was no disorder. I sniffed, and sat down at my dressing table, where the scent was the strongest. I opened the drawer, wrinkling my nose at the strong scent. There lay the spilled bottle on its side, the heavy scent seeping out from under the loosened stopper. I knew absolutely that I hadn't spilled it. There was only one explanation. Jack had been here, had looked in this drawer while I was out? Then I noticed that my clock was missing from my dressing table. I looked on the floor, beside the table and behind it. It wasn't there.

The clock had always been special to me, a small souvenir I had brought back from Paris where my parents had taken us on holiday many years before. My heart began to pound uncomfortably. *Had Jack taken it?* He knew how much it meant to me. *Had he taken anything else?* I suddenly panicked. *Not my grandmother's brooch!* I ran to my dresser drawer where I always kept it, and rummaged through it. My fingers closed around the box I kept it in, and drew it out carefully. With shaking hands, I removed the lid, and unfolded the cotton where it rested…and drew a deep sigh of relief. There it lay, safe and sound, the diamonds twinkling up at me, the pearls full of pink luster, the sapphire cross that rested in the golden circle dark and mysterious. I clasped it to my breast for a moment, then wrapped it back up and replaced it in the drawer.

I changed my clothes and got into bed… and lay there, my mind clouded, overwhelmed. And it didn't seem likely that my mind would untangle itself anytime soon. Peter made me feel secure. He seemed genuinely concerned for my well-being. It felt as if a fist closed around my heart. Already I could see that my feelings for him had gone far too deep. And I feared that I would not be able to shut him out of my mind--or my heart--so easily. *Was there nothing in this life but pain and sorrow?* I could scarcely remember when it had held anything else.

The baby stirred beneath my heart, bringing my troubled thoughts to a welcome end. *The past was done and gone. I was strong, I told myself. This baby and I would survive, and go on. We would have a quiet life together, without Peter. Memories of his arms about me, his smile, his lips pressed against mine, would have to suffice. I would do just fine on my own. For my baby's sake, if not my own. After a night's rest everything would seem better, I was sure.*

CHAPTER FIFTY-FIVE

The next day was Christmas Eve. My doctor had scheduled an ultrasound appointment for me that day and my mother went with me. It was exciting to watch my baby's image on the screen, moving and rolling, even sucking "its" thumb. But unfortunately, the baby was uncooperative, so the technician was unable to tell us if "it" was a boy or girl, but he or she was certainly active and healthy!

I was a little disappointed as we got into the car afterwards to go shopping, that we didn't know whether to buy pink or blue booties. My mother reached over to pat my hand reassuringly.

"You'll know soon enough," she told me. "I had to wait until you and your brother were born."

I grinned back at her. "Yes, yes, I know. Back in the Dark Ages," I laughed, and she took a playful swipe at me.

* * * *

After picking up a few miscellaneous unisex items from the shops, we headed back to my mother to bake Christmas cookies. After all, what was Christmas without my mother's famous cookies?

From the kitchen, elbow deep in flour, I could hear my brother, John, coming down the stairs, singing "Rudolph, the Red Nosed Reindeer" at the top of his lungs, his uneven voice mangling the tune. A contented happiness rose up inside me at the familiar family atmosphere of my parents' home. With a satisfied sigh, I continued to press cookie cutters into the dough.

John burst into the kitchen in his own inimitable way.

"Hey, ugly brother," I said, "We didn't say you could come in here."

"I don't remember asking," he retorted flippantly. He peered over my shoulder. "Making Christmas cookies?"

"Yeah, special ones for each member of the family."

"Which is mine?" he asked, interested.

I held up a cookie that looked suspiciously like a bone. "Here, I made this for you, Bone-head."

"Ha, ha. Very funny," he said, as he grabbed it from my hand and took a bite.

Then he picked up a lump of cookie dough. "And this is you, Lumpy."

"All right, kids," Mom said. "That's enough."

John strolled over to her and laid his arm across her shoulders. "Mom, I came down to ask you if you could give me some ideas what to give my girlfriend for Christmas."

She glanced up at him out of the corner of her eye. "Don't you think you've waited a little late to be asking a question like that?"

"How about glasses?" I chimed in.

John made a move toward me and our mother looked up to Heaven with a sigh.

* * * *

I spent the night in my old room, and Christmas Day with my family. It was warm and comfortable, full of family feelings and fond memories. I helped Mom with our traditional Christmas dinner of ham and all the trimmings, but there was a hole in my heart without Peter. I wondered what he was doing with his own family. Was he opening presents now, or sitting down to their own Christmas feast? I missed him terribly.

* * * *

The morning after Boxing Day I stepped out the door of our flat to warm up the car for the drive to the bank. Peter had not called, and there had been no sign of Jack. I was beginning to put the pieces of my life back into order again.

It was my week to drive the three of us into work. But I stopped short in my tracks, and stared at my car in disbelief and horror. My Volvo had been vandalized! Spray painted with obscenities, and the windows smashed!

Shocked, my heart pounding, I walked with stilted steps to survey the damage. There was a folded piece of paper tucked neatly between the wiper blade and my shattered windscreen. I plucked it out with a shaking hand, and unfolded it. Words had been cut from a magazine and glued onto the paper. The note read: "Are you sorry yet?"

"No!" I screamed. My baby began to squirm inside me.

Virginia and Melanie came running down the steps to see what was the matter.

"Oh, no," they repeated when they saw my car. I held out my hands. Melanie took one, Virginia the other. Together we walked back into our flat. My knees were shaking, and I was fighting back the tears as I sat down on the sofa. I held out the wadded note to Virginia to read.

" 'Are you sorry yet?' " she read aloud.

Melanie gasped, bending over me with sympathy. "Och, honey, don't worry now," she said.

Virginia marched straight to the phone and called the police. They were there within a half an hour, but could find no clues as to the identity of the culprit. But the three of us knew who it was.

The policeman told me, "There's not much we can do, Mrs. MacCallum. You're ex-husband's threats are not proof that he commited this crime. We will do what we can, but we need absolute proof. I don't think we'll find what you're looking for."

They left then, with apologies. I felt too shaken to go into work. Both Melanie and Virginia offered to stay home with me, but I refused. So reluctantly, they finally left for the bank.

Left on my own, I went into the kitchen to brew some tea. This completely ordinary task soothed my frazzled nerves and almost made me believe that I was having a normal day. I filled the kettle with water and put it on the stove to boil. Then I got a tea bag, and just as I reached into the cabinet for my cup, the phone began to ring. Startled by the sudden noise, I dropped the cup, and it shattered into a thousand pieces on the floor. Surveying the damage, I whispered a mild oath under my breath, and hurried to catch the phone.

"Hello?" I said into the receiver.

"Hello, Jennifer, it's me," a menacing voice rasped in my ear. "You're looking lovely today in that blue dress. Did you decide not to go into work today after all?"

The phone slipped from my hand and onto the floor, and for a moment I could only stare at it. Then I grabbed it up and slammed it down onto its cradle.

The phone began to ring again, and I began to tremble. But this time I didn't pick it up, the answering machine did. "Hello, Jennifer? It's Jack. Did you need a lift into work today? Pick up, if you're there...och, well, perhaps you've got your car running. Just wanted to help. Cherrio, then. Bye." He rang off.

I looked around the room at the open curtains at the windows. *He was there, I knew it. And he could see me.* I ran to the windows, pulled down the blinds and closed the curtains. Just then the tea kettle began to whistle, and I nearly jumped out of my skin. *This has to stop!* I told myself, attempting to quiet my pounding heart. *I must get hold of myself.*

I took a deep breath and walked into the kitchen to turn off the fire under the kettle, and to make my tea. While it steeped, I cleaned up the broken china cup on the floor. The phone began to ring again. I stood straight and still, waiting for the answering machine to pick up.

"Jennifer, honey, are you there?" It was Jack again. "I called your work, but they said you were ill. Your flat is closed and dark. Are you all right?" He waited a moment, then spoke again. "If you're there, pick up the phone......right.....Well, I'll just call Mrs. Taggert back again."

I began to tremble. *How dare he call my work and ask about me!* I ran to the phone and picked it up. "How dare you--" I started, but the other end clicked off.

Frustrated, I slammed the receiver back down. If this kept up, I might just break the phone before the day was through.

The phone rang again. I picked it up. "Jack, if you don't stop--" The line went dead. He had rung off again.

This time I replaced the receiver slowly and carefully. As soon as I did, it rang again, making me jump. I didn't pick it up this time, though. My heart thumped loudly in my ears. The answering machine clicked on, and soon Jack's voice began to record.

"Jenny, honey, I'm worried about you. Please talk to me."

I wanted to weep with frustration as I curled up in the chair and sat in the darkness. Never had I felt more powerless than I did at this moment.

* * * *

"Honey, what's wrong?" Melanie asked, as she turned on the lights and saw that I had been sitting alone in the darkness.

"He won't leave me alone, Mel! He keeps calling me! He's spying on me!" My voice rose hysterically.

"Shh! Shh!" Virginia said, sitting down beside me as tears began to course down my cheeks. "We're here now. He can't hurt you. He wouldn't dare."

I sniffed and smiled back at her as she handed me a tissue.

The phone rang again, startling us both.

"It's him!" I wailed. "It's him!"

"I'll get it," Virginia said, leaning over me, and picking it up. "Hello?…oh, hello, Peter. Yes, she's here. Just a moment." She held out the receiver to me. "It's for you. It's Peter."

I took it gladly. I needed him right now. I needed to hear his voice, feel his warmth and strength. If only for tonight. "Oh, Peter! I'm so glad it's you! Can you come over, now?" I asked, my voice hopeful.

"What's the matter?" he asked. "Are you all right?"

"Yes, I am, now that you're back! Please say you'll come! I'll tell you about it when you get here.Let me cook dinner for you…oh…I would need to go to the supermarket…and…" my voice trailed off and I bit my lower lip.

"Shall I meet you there? What supermarket?"

"Yes, all right. That would be good. We shop at Sainsburys. It's not far from here."

"I'll see you there in half an hour."

"All right. See you then. Bye."

"Better, now?" Virginia asked, as I rang off.

* * * *

Thirty minutes later I waved good-bye to Virginia in the car park where she had dropped me off, and walked through the doors at Sainburys. I looked around, and not seeing Peter, decided to begin shopping on my own. I was feeling more confident by now, and knew that he would find me.

I took a trolley and started down the first aisle, took what I needed, and continued down the next.

And then I heard it. Footsteps. With each step I took, I heard another footstep behind me, following me. *Was it my imagination?* My heart began to beat harder against my ribs and I panicked, remembering what had happened here before. I started to run blindly down the aisle, away from the sound of the footsteps. And I bumped right into something big and hard. I opened my eyes wide in alarm, but was unable to focus through my fright. Hands on my arms, fingers strong and firm, were shaking me gently. I whimpered and my hands flailed out.

"Jennifer! Jennifer! Stop! It's me, Peter!"

Slowly, my eyes began to focus. Yes, there he stood. Large, solid, his eyebrows raised in question. I flung myself into his arms. "Oh, Peter! It's Jack! He's following me!"
Peter looked over my head. "Jenny, there's no one there. I didn't see anyone else besides you."

"Yes, he was there!" I said, so vehemently that the woman shopping down the aisle stared at us, blinking her pale lashes. I turned my head and looked over my shoulder. "I know he was!" Desperation that he believes me made me catch at his arm. I looked up into Peter's face, my eyes dark, intense. "He won't leave me alone! I don't know what to do. The police won't help me. When I go out, he watches me. When I walk through the door, he calls. He leaves messages on my answering machine, and if I pick up, he hangs up. You know that he broke into our flat. Last night he vandalized my car!"

He put his hands on either side of my face. A wave of shame washed over me when I saw the concern in his eyes. "Easy," he whispered. "Hush, Jenny. It's all right. I'm here."

I threw my arms around him and hugged him tightly, breathing in his masculine scent, feeling his comforting strength as his arms closed about me.

* * * *

Peter, as always, was comforting, taking the drama out of the situation, yet not denying my feelings. He never made me feel foolish, and succeeded in reducing my fears to something bearable.

"It's a pity I didn't arrive a bit earlier," he said, as he bustled about our kitchen making tea.

I took the cup he offered me, my hands visibly unsteady, afraid the cup would rattle against the saucer. It was strong and sweet as I gulped it.

"It's all right," I said. "I should never have gotten you involved in this."

"What do you mean by that?"

"I'm thanking you for everything you've done. But," I shook my head, and drew a deep breath. "I have to be strong, and stand on my own."

"Back to that again, are we?"

"I don't know what Jack will do next. I think we shouldn't see each other anymore."

"You expect me to believe that?"

"Yes," I said, trying to act like I really meant it.

He was frowning deeply. He said nothing. His eyes narrowed, and he met my challenging stare, weighing what I'd said.

"I wish you'd say something," I said testily.

Still watching me, he dragged his fingers through his hair before settling his hands on his hips.

"Well, do you agree with me?" I said impatiently, my voice challenging him.

"What is it you want me to say?" he said crossly. He shook his head, and added wearily, "And will you please do me the favor of not looking at me like that? I've thought about this long and hard. Have you?"

Shame filled me. "Yes, and I thought I knew the answers. Truth is, I missed you very much."

"And I missed you. Let me be strong enough for both of us, Jenny. Let me be there for you. I can take away your pain."

"But what if Jack--"

"Jack doesn't scare me, Jenny. We can do this. It will be all right."

I met his gaze, and looked deep into the warm silver-blue depths, and saw nothing but good in him. "Yes," I agreed.

At that moment Melanie came into the kitchen. In her hand she bore a handful of mail, and she held one out to me.

"Letter for you, Jen."

"Thanks," I said, taking it and glancing at the envelope. My name and address were typed neatly on the face, with no return address. "Hmmm," I mused, "I wonder who this is from."

I opened the flap and took out the piece of paper folded neatly inside. There were words of all shapes and sizes, cut from a magazine, and glued onto the paper. The words read: "I'll never let you go."

My heart thumped painfully, and my breath caught in my chest. The baby, sensing my agitation, chose that moment to kick me hard beneath my ribs, robbing me of any breath I had left. I grimaced, grabbing hold of the table.

"Jenny, what is it?" Peter asked, leaning over me and taking the paper from my shaking hand. He read it quietly, his face revealing nothing of his thoughts.

"It can't be good for the baby when you become so upset," he said, folding the paper and replacing it in the envelope. "This isn't anything we can't handle together."

I looked up at him, comforted by his words, his confident expression. He sat down beside me, taking my hand in his. Tightening his clasp on my fingers, he nudged me with his shoulder, his mouth curling into a smile. "The fool." There was a glint of humor in his eyes.

The answering spark that coursed through me slashed through the dismal murk clouding my mind and kindled a spark of hope within me. Peter was here, he would help me, share whatever the future held, good or bad. I felt my tension ease. I took his hand and placed it atop my belly. The baby kicked again--hard. I drew in my breath when the baby thumped still harder beneath his hand.

A look of awe stole over his face and he smiled slowly, inwardly, as if to himself. He watched my stomach move, then shifted his hand until it held a sharply protruding limb cradled in his palm. "I've felt babies move before, of course," he murmured, his voice full of an animation I hadn't heard before. He seemed pleased. His eyes brightened. "But somehow, I've never felt...such a," he grasped about for the right word. "I know this will sound silly, but...well...a bond...as I do with this one." He glanced up into my face with an expression of wonderment. "He's right there, under my hand."

I laid my hand on top of his, and my lips curved into a smile as I savored the wave of contentment that carried me in its wake. The three of us had formed a connection at that moment.

"Such a strong lad," Peter whispered, as the baby settled down to more gentle movements.

"Or lassie," I countered, imitating his Scots accent.

"Aye, or lassie," he grinned back at me. "Whichever it is, it seems healthy. Very active."

"You sound like a doctor, now," I said, flashing him a teasing smile. "Whichever it is, it's resting now, though, thanks to you," I said, realizing that the baby's movements had ceased for the moment. He reluctantly eased his hand away.

"I believe the baby likes your touch better than mine, the way it quieted when you laid your hand on it."

He smiled at me suddenly, as if the thought brought him a surprising pleasure. He stood then, making me aware of his size, his strength. "I am here for you, Jenny. No matter what you say, I won't ever leave you. We're in this together, and I will protect you and your baby, whatever it takes. We'll get through this together."

Did he have the power to carry us through these troubles with a happy outcome? His words settled over me like a blanket of peace and security. I believed he did.

* * * *

As Peter drove home that evening he was inundated with thoughts and emotions. He could not deny his attraction to Jenny, nor the fact that his respect and admiration for her grew with every passing day. She drew him to her, without any effort on her part. The memory of their kisses swept through him, her taste, the feel of her rounded body against his own...but that was lust. What he felt with Jenny seemed deeper somehow than the mere yearning of the flesh.

But he would never have believed a pregnant woman could be as appealing as he found Jenny. There was something about her... her innocent ways, her desire to protect her baby, even to protect him...he smiled to himself. What would it be like to have that intensity directed at him, for him to be the recipient of her love and caring? If she loved with that passion...

He wanted her. He wanted to make her his. And the child she carried, as well. He wanted to marry Jenny. But he feared for her--her and the baby both--if she didn't let him share the load she carried on her shoulders. Emotion swept through him at the memory of the child moving beneath his hand. If Jack caused them any harm, he would see that he paid dearly for it. He shoved aside that terrifying thought and stared at the road ahead, until his blood cooled. His thoughts spurred him toward a decision to confront Jack. He would have to make him understand that he must leave Jenny alone. That she had a protector now, and that he would stand by her side to his dying day.

He turned the wheel of his car to park in front of his house. The late hour, coupled with all this soul searching had made him maudlin.

CHAPTER FIFTY-SIX

These thoughts haunted him throughout the night, and well into his shift in Casualty in the next. After work he drove straight to the flat where Jack lived, and knocked on the door.

The door opened, and the tall man who stood revealed in it gave him a highly critical and penetrating stare. "Yes, Dr. Munro?" he asked. "Did you have something you want to say to me?" His voice was curt.

"Yes. I came to speak with you about Jennifer."

Jack's face was taut, his green eyes curiously intense. "Come inside then."

Peter followed him into the living room, where Jack flung himself down on the sofa and crossed his legs, gesturing for Peter to do the same. "Sit down," he said.

Peter shook his head. "I'd rather stand."

Jack shrugged, and leaned his arm across the back of the sofa. "What is it you want to say to me?"

"You must stop harassing--"

Jack smirked, and held his hand up to cut him off. "Is she telling you that I'm following her, calling her, that I broke into her flat? Vandalized her car?" he jeered. He watched Peter's reaction, then began to laugh.

"Yes, and I know it's true," Peter answered calmly.

Jack made a sound of disgust, as he glared back at him with hostility. His hand shook as he leaned forward and reached for his drink on the coffee table. "When we were first married, she was a beautiful, loving wife for the first year. Then she started having bouts of depression, following me, accusing me, shrieking, screaming that I was having an affair. She fell apart." He tossed back his drink.

Peter bit back an angry response. He said instead, " You can't stand to see her in the company of another man, can you?"

A nerve twitched in Jack's cheek, his eyes dark and moody. "Are you attracted to her?"

"You know that I am."

Jack took a deep breath, as though preparing to spew out a burst of defiance, then shook his head and shrugged his shoulders. He reached into his shirt pocket and pulled out a pack of cigarettes. "You don't mind if I smoke, do you?" he said, pulling one out and placing it between his lips. He watched Peter over his lighter. The cigarette caught, and he blew a cloud of smoke in the air.

"Some bloody bastards will use any weak slut they can find to give them what they're looking for."

Peter's reaction was swift. The sneer on Jack's face changed to shock as Peter lunged toward him. In one lithe movement, he had stepped across the table and snagged Jack by the front of his shirt with both hands, lifting him off the sofa. "How dare you!" he growled, pushing Jack's shoulders against the walls.

Jack went pale, his manner shifting from arrogance to submissive in a heartbeat. The cigarette hung loosely between his lips, and his mouth moved, but made no sound, as he squirmed. Peter tightened his grip and pressed him more firmly against the wall. Jack stopped when it became clear that his efforts to free himself would accomplish nothing.

"Whatever my wife does is entirely her own business," he mumbled, lowering his eyes.

Peter tightened his grip and raised Jack higher still. "Ex-wife, don't you mean?" he said, in a more temperate voice. With a final shake, he opened his hands and let Jack drop back into his seat with a thump. Jack slumped back on the sofa, a scowl on his face.

Peter straightened, and stepped away from him. "Fine, then you will leave us alone from now on. You can't scare me away, Jack. Do you understand? I intend to stand by her, marry her, if she'll have me."

Abruptly Jack shoved himself from the sofa, color flooding his face. He jumped to his feet and banged his fist on the table. "Get out!" he snarled, raking an unsteady hand through his hair. "And stay away from my wife! You'll stay as far away from her as you can, if you know what's good for you! Do you understand me?" He reinforced the threat with a steady glare.

"Aye, I believe I do," Peter answered in a cold voice. He turned and went out the door.

* * * *

All day long, the idea had returned to me. I would confront Jack, talk to him, make him see things as they were. I fought down a rising sense of excitement, of anticipation on my way home from the bank, as a scheme began to take shape in my mind. Peter and I could face him together, make him back down and leave us alone. Peter would admire my acumen. He would also have to cooperate. If he refused, I supposed I would have to go alone. I was sure there was nothing to be frightened about. But I did prefer to have his company.

Melanie and Virginia chattered away endlessly, and I nodded absently, making my plans.

* * * *

When Peter came by that evening after work, I told him my plan. But instead of being proud of me, he blanched.

"No!" he said, grabbing my arms and holding me with his eyes. "No, you mustn't, Jenny! Stay away from him!"

"Why? I thought it would be good if we could present a united front against him."

"No, you're asking for trouble, and I won't be a part of it. Please, Jenny, forget this nonsense. I don't trust him. Especially where you're concerned. Promise me."

Startled by his reaction, I said nothing. He shifted nervously, and looked into my eyes.

"Jenny," his voice was like a caress. He looked away from me, as though trying to gather his thoughts, then took both my hands in one of his. "I know this is sudden, but I have to talk to you. Come and sit down."

He led me to the sofa, and we sat down side by side. Nervously he dragged his free hand through his hair, and settled his gaze on me. I don't believe I'd ever seen him so flustered, and wondered what he had to say that would frazzle him so. *Had he had enough of Jack, and decided that I was too much bother, after all? Did he want to tell me that we were a mistake, and that it was over? Was he afraid that if he delayed, he might lose his courage to face me with this sudden news?* I wondered, and as I met his eyes, he glanced away. Despite my curiosity, I wasn't sure that I wanted to know what could make him appear so uncertain.

At last his eyes met mine. He took a deep breath. "I love you, Jenny. I want to be with you, to be there for you always. Will you marry me?"

Shock turned to panic as the full impact of his words sunk into my brain. "M-marry you?" I stammered. My heartbeat faltered, then began to thrum so fast I could hardly breathe. His fingers tightened around mine as I stared at him. He looked back at me, his pewter-blue eyes sincere, his expression wavering between hopefulness and uncertainty.

"W-we can't marry," I stammered. "You don't understand. I can't marry ever again."

"Why not?"

"Be-because…because--" I wished he would move away, take his hand away from me. Stop this assault on my senses so that I could think! But he had surrounded me with his heat, his scent, his touch, until I could think of nothing else but him, and the images his offer planted in my mind.

If we were married we could be together. And I knew he would be a good and loving husband, giving me his support, his protection--it was a seduction more tempting than--

No! I gave myself a mental shake. That was far too dangerous a way to think and feel. It could be dangerous for both of us. I laid my hand protectively over my stomach as the baby rolled inside me. It could be dangerous to all of us. Jack's threats hung over us like a dark cloud. For that reason alone, I could not accept.

"I'm sorry, Peter," I said, trying to infuse my voice with strength. I shook my head and fought back the tears.

The baby chose that moment to renew its kicking. Peter shifted his free hand to the child, and it settled.

"You see? I can help you with this--and with so much more--if you'd let me."

Prickly tears filled my eyes, and I dragged his hand away from my stomach and pulled away from him. "Please, don't!" I averted my face and scrambled from the sofa, nearly sliding to the floor.

"Jenny, be careful!" Peter's hand slid under my arm in support before I caught myself and lurched to my feet.

* * * *

I went alone to see Jack, to confront him, despite Peter's warning. When he answered the door, Jack looked very tired, older than his years. *Perhaps he hasn't been sleeping well,* I thought. He was paler than usual, nervous, haggard. There were lines at the corner of his mouth I had never noticed before. He was untidy, and his eyes were pouched and blood-shot.

"Where's your boyfriend?" He glanced around behind me. "He didn't come with you?" He looked at me, smiling, his head to one side.

"I wanted to talk to you about him. About the two of us. I want you to leave us alone."

He gave me that half smile of his, as he gazed down at me. I did not like it. It made my skin crawl. He stepped back. "Come inside," he said.

I took a deep breath, gathering my courage, and stepped inside. He followed me into the living room and sat down on the arm of the sofa, pulling his cigarette packet from his pocket and lighting up. He blew out a cloud of smoke into the air, and leaned back on the arm of the sofa, swinging his leg. He began to whistle the bar of a song, watching me all the while.

"That's the one, isn't it?" he asked. "That's the tune. Do you remember it, Jenny? We danced to it together the night we were married."

I noticed how his neck bulged over his collar, and how low his ears were set on his head. Those good looks of his would not last him very long, already they were beginning to fade. He was out of shape. I went and stood over on the rug by the empty fireplace. "I don't want to be rude, Jack, but I haven't come here to reminiscence. I've come here to make you understand."

He was not smiling anymore. "Well, then, what is it?"

"It's over between us, Jack. We're divorced. It's been final now for three months. It's time you got on with your life and left me alone."

He slid off the arm of the sofa and came towards me, swaying a little. "No, no, no, Jennifer," he said softly, turning the full force of his gaze on me. "You've got it all wrong. I will never leave you alone. Don't you remember what you promised when you said your wedding vows? 'Til death do us part. And didn't the reverend say, 'what God has joined together, let no man put asunder'? Do you know what that means, Jenny? That means 'to separate'. Isn't that just what that bastard you've been seeing is trying to do to us?" He steadied himself and bent towards me. "Are you sleeping with him, Jenny?" His voice grew louder. "Is that it? I always knew you were nothing but a slut." Suspicion colored his tone, his expression. I watched him getting whiter and whiter as he spoke. He bent closer to me still. I tried to ignore the sensation, the threat emanating from his eyes, but I couldn't.

"Did you know," he said slowly, "that he came by to see me the other day? That he threatened me if I didn't stay away from you? He's got quite a temper, Jenny. I think you should stay away from him," he said with a short laugh, never taking his eyes from me. He was taunting me. "You realize, don't you, that I can make things damn unpleasant for you if I choose? Not only unpleasant, but shall I say, dangerous?" He paused, and went on looking at me, a telltale flicker at the corner of his mouth.

"You're crazy--psychopathic, "I said, backing away from him.

He pretended to think about that, then shook his head. "No, I don't believe so," he said. "I loved you very much at one time, Jennifer. Psychopaths don't feel anything. I've read up on them, you see. I feel so much love, so much hate…"

My hand went to my mouth and I stared at him, swallowing hard. He was threatening me. I closed my eyes, and forced myself to remain calm. I did not say anything, but sat down heavily on the chair beside the fireplace. I held the arms of the chair very tight.

"What are the two of you up to, that's what I'd like to know! Did you think that you and he could just sit back quietly and wait for me to disappear? Well, it's not going to happen! Tell me what you think of that?" This last speech of his was very slurred and thick. I wished that I had never come to see him. I should have listened to Peter.

I met his gaze and raised my chin in challenge. He flushed angrily. "You bloody little fool!" He took my arm, hurting me with the grip of his large hand, and pulled me from the chair.

He hit me then, bruising my face and arms. I held my hands up to my eyes to shield them, and backed away from him, his hatred pushing me back.

"You do realize now that I will never let the two of you be together? 'Til death do us part, eh, Jenny?" he said with a great cackle of laughter.

* * * *

I leaned against the wall of my bedroom, resting my cheek on the cool plaster as I sought strength. Guilt nagged at me. *I should have listened to Peter. What will happen now?* After a time, I pushed away from the wall. I knew that there was nothing to be gained by going over it again and again in my mind, but Jack's words still rankled, and I managed to work myself into a mass of nerves as the time crept by.

There was a knock at the front door. I heard it open, and the sound of voices--Melanie's and Peter's--carried up the stairway to me, bringing my useless, maundering thoughts to a blessed end. I tugged at my sweater to straighten it, and realized as I was about to turn and greet him that my cheeks were wet with tears. I'd never cried so much in my life as I had during the last few months! I found it mortifying, and the tears seemed completely out of my control! I reached into my pocket and found an old handkerchief there. I quickly used it to blot my face before they reached me, though it was likely they'd know I'd been crying.

When I finished, I looked up, and he was there, standing at the top of the steps, watching me. Though I wanted to look away from his probing glance, I met his gaze. He closed the distance between us, his eyes focused on me with an uncomfortable intensity.

He came forward and took my arm, the warmth of his touch soothing, lending me strength. He led me to a chair and sat me down. He knelt down in front of me and caught my chin in his hand, gently forcing me to look at him.

"It must be the baby that makes me cry." *A convenient excuse for the fact that I am a sniveling coward,* I thought. "You must think I'm a spineless ninny."

"Not at all," he said, lifting my chin, and examining the bruises on my face. "Tell me what happened."

I pressed my hands to my face, covering my eyes for a moment to shut out the memory. My body shaking, I slid my hands down into my lap, clenched together so tightly the knuckles showed white. He reached out and covered my hand with his, gently holding it captive when I tried to slide it free. So I grasped his hand in a tight grip, and took a deep breath, hoping it would calm me, but it made no difference.

I told Peter everything, my voice quiet, dead, mechanical.

He turned his hand beneath mine and laced our fingers together as I spoke. I looked at him, my eyes bright with tears, but I didn't free myself from his hold.

I could tell that my words had made him angry. His face had gone very white, and the pain in his eyes was clearly visible, as was the rage smoldering within them. He took me in his arms, and I could feel the thunder of his heartbeat against my cheek.

"He'll pay for what he did today," he muttered, disgust making his voice shake. His outrage was clear, although I could barely hear the whispered words.

The power of his reaction frightened me. His arms tightened around me, twisting the blade of fear deeper into my heart.

He pulled away from me then, and began to pace up and down the room, his head bent, glowering. He gazed up at me, his expression apologetic.

"I'm sorry, Jenny. I've got to go. But I'll be back."

"Peter, please don't do anything foolish," I said.

He did not say anything more. He got quickly into his car and drove away.

* * * *

Jack answered the door with a drink in his hand. He wore a taunting grin on his face, and a half-smoked cigarette dangled from his lips. "Well, well, well, I'm honored. Both of you in one day." He raised his glass in salute, then tipped it back and drained it. "Come in, come in."

He led Peter into his flat and banged his empty glass on the table. Belching loudly, he reached for the bottle of whiskey.

"I'm not surprised to see you here. After all, I didn't figure you for a man who'd want a bitch like my ex around for long." Amusement flavored his voice and his lips curled into a faint smile. "Did you come to ask me to take her off your hands?" He laughed, dropping ashes all over the floor.

Peter's limited patience was reaching the end. His body fairly vibrated with rage. How could he talk to this man properly when all he wanted to do was grab the fool and smash him into the wall? He straightened, and drew in a deep breath, crossing his arms over his chest.

"How can you call yourself a man, and hit a woman? A woman pregnant with your child? I came to tell you that you'll be leaving Jennifer alone from this day forward."

"Or what? What will you do?" Jack scoffed. "What do you have to gain by it?" he prompted defiantly. "Do you honestly believe that having her in your bed is worth all this fuss? She can't be of much use to you now, in the shape she's in."

It happened very quickly. Jack staggered and fell against the arm of the sofa, and down onto the floor. Peter stood just beside him, looking down at him.

"You'll stop talking about her as if she were a whore!" he snarled. "Or else you'll be lucky if you can crawl out of here!" Peter backed off a few paces, all his strength focused on not returning to finish him off. He stood very still, breathing heavily. His hands fairly tingled at his sides, itching for more.

Jack got slowly to his feet, watching Peter. There was a dark red patch on his jaw where Peter had hit him. Jack reached up to rub his face, and grinned. "Damn, you've got a temper!" The expression on his face was ugly, calculating, and there was something of triumph too, glittering in his emerald eyes. "I would never have guessed." An ugly smile spread over his lips.

Peter shook his head and looked at him as if he were crazy. "Well, that's your mistake," he said evenly, his eyes cold, his face pale and set. "Seems I'm human enough to want to fight you where you stand, but civilized enough to keep from it. You are no longer married to Jenny. She is not your possession. If you ever forget that again, I swear I'll come back here and finish what I started."

He turned and headed toward the door, without a backward glance.

Jack watched him go, with the same dark light still in his eyes. When Peter was out of sight, he went to his car, hopped in, and headed for the east side of town.

* * * *

When the knock finally sounded, I pressed my hands together to still their trembling, then crossed the room and pulled open the door. He was alone, I noted with relief.

"Come in," I said, holding the door open wide. I closed it behind him. His face revealed nothing of his thoughts, but I could tell something weighed heavily on his mind. I reached out and took his hand in mine. It was very cold. I held my breath as he gazed down at our joined hands. *What had happened?*

"Jack didn't give you any trouble, did he?"

He averted his eyes, and a spasm of expression crossed his face. It seemed as if I waited forever for his response. I tightened my clasp on his fingers.

He winced, but finally returned the pressure. "Nothing I couldn't handle," he said. He pulled his hand from mine.

What does he mean by that? The words gave me no ease, since I doubted there wasn't much he couldn't handle.

He raked a hand through his hair and stared off into the distance. He seemed to be fighting to control himself. Then he looked back at me and said, his voice harsh with emotion, "I hit him, Jenny. God help me, I lost my temper, and I hit him."

* * * *

Jack could barely stagger through the doors of the police station. He was bruised and bloody, his clothes torn.

"Help me," he croaked faintly, as a policeman took his arm and helped him to a chair to sit down.

"Tell me what happened, sir," the man said gently, as another handed him a paper cup filled with water. "Do you need a doctor?"

"No!" Jack exclaimed. "Not a doctor! It was a doctor that did this to me! It was Dr. Peter Munro, from Good Samaritan Hospital! He just showed up at my flat and beat me."

And having said that, he fainted.

CHAPTER FIFTY-SEVEN

At the hospital the next day, I met Peter in the hallway in Casualty.

"Ready for a nosh?" I asked.

He had a chart in his hand, and was headed toward one of the curtained partitions. "This is my last patient. I'll be ready after."

"Okay."

He pushed the curtain aside, and I heard him say, "Well now, me boyo, fallen out of a tree, have ye now?"

I sat down in the nurses' station, and began to talk to one of the nurses. Out of the corner of my eye, I caught sight of two policemen as they entered the waiting room. My heart gave a sharp jump of apprehension.

Lydia, the head nurse, walked over to them and asked if she could help. Whispers were exchanged, and she looked over to the cubicle where Peter was with his patient. Unease rippled up my spine as my heart gave a hard, agitated beat. Lydia nodded, then walked over and pushed the curtain aside.

"Dr. Munro?" I heard her say.

"Yes, what is it?" he answered. His voice had that far away sound of someone intent upon something.

"I'm sorry to bother you, Doctor, but there are two policemen in the waiting room. They want to talk to you."

"What about?" I heard the sharp, aware note in his voice.

"I don't know. But they are quite adamant about it."

He sighed. "Tell them I will be out in a minute."

She left the curtained partition, and nodded toward the policemen, then came back to the nurses' station. She cast a furtive glance in the officer's direction, then caught my eye, and shrugged her shoulders. A sick, expectant feeling began to churn in the pit of my stomach.

"There," Peter said, and I heard the squeal of his stool, as he rolled it backwards. The sound of running water could be heard as he

243

washed his hands, and the murmur of his voice, as he gave the mother instructions for care of the stitches.

He turned to ruffle the boy's hair as he lifted the curtain aside and said, "Don't be falling out of any more trees, my lad. Next time you mightn't be so lucky."

Then he turned his attention to the waiting policemen, and walked out into the corridor. He did not look at me. No reason for my heart to begin its hard thudding of alarm.

"Yes, Officers, can I help you?"

"Dr. Peter Munro?"

"Yes."

"You are under arrest for aggravated assault."

He looked bewildered, as a fine line appeared between his brows. I felt that little pain again in the pit of my stomach.

"Aggravated assault?" he repeated.

"Mr. Jack McCallum has accused you of assaulting him. Hmmpphh. Beating him to a bloody pulp, more like. Turn around, Doctor, and put your hands behind your back."

A vise clamped down on my heart, stifling the breath from me. *Beat him?* My hands began to shake.

"Beat him?" Peter asked, echoing my thoughts. It was then that he looked at me. And in his eyes I read a reluctant surrender. *What happened last night between Peter and Jack?* Peter did not speak, but turned away and did as the officers had bid.

My legs felt boneless as I pulled myself to my feet. Peter did not resist as they quickly cuffed him and hustled him out the main door. I stood quite still, feeling the strength drain out of me with every step they took away from me. My heart felt like a stone, heavy, numb.

But the sound of the doors sliding closed behind them suddenly seemed to awaken every nerve in my body. I hurried to the window and watched as they put him into the squad car, and drove away.

Then I turned back toward the nurses' station. The nurses still stared, open mouthed. My heart was beating too fast. I knew that somehow, I must dig deep within myself for a reserve of strength, or else I'd find myself a spineless mass on the hospital floor.

I swiftly grabbed my purse, and hurried out the door to my car. Flinging my purse and myself inside, I quickly put the key in the ignition, and unceremoniously backed out of my parking space. With a growing sense of dread, I began to consider this sudden turn of events. *I knew that Peter had not beaten Jack to, what was the phrase the officer had used? "A bloody pulp"? No, I knew in my heart that Peter had not done that. So, what was Jack planning to do now? Would he go so far as to ruin Peter's career, to get him out of his way?*

And now I suddenly realized something else. In the back of my mind, I had been toying with the idea of accepting Peter's proposal of marriage all along, wondering if I should give into him. But now things had changed for the worse. The harm that decision could bring to Peter sent a chill through me. Now Peter had truly been threatened. It was no longer just speculation.

Despite my best efforts to distract my thoughts, a wave of uncertainty assailed me. My nerves were stretched taut, and my stomach was knotted. I was very glad that we hadn't eaten yet. The gears ground loudly as I downshifted too soon at a stop light. I stared out my windscreen at the cars ahead of me, lost in thought.

Finally, I pulled into the car park of the city complex, that included the criminal district court, police headquarters and the central lockup. I parked beside a city dumpster, overflowing with fast food remnants and empty soda cans. While locking my car, I gazed up at the grey cinderblock building that housed the jail. *Talk about a perfect example of architectural form following function*, I thought grimly. The structure was so devoid of any ornamentation that it could easily have doubled as the auto body shop where I'd had my car fixed not long ago, after Jack had vandalized it.

Once inside, it was no better. As I looked around, I concluded that the black and white linoleum floor and the orange plastic chairs were the lobby's most attractive features. A window with a large sign that read: BAIL BONDS--PAY HERE beckoned.

I approached the pretty girl in the tight red sweater behind the bail bonds sign, and inquired about the process of getting Dr. Peter Munro out of jail.

She punched a few keys on the keyboard of the computer in front of her. "He's still being processed, ma'am, so it will be a while yet. But his bail will be set at 600 pounds," the clerk replied. "You can pay with cash, traveler's check or money order."

I gasped, as the adrenaline drained straight from my body and out my toes, it seemed. "Right," I said with a sigh. *What had I been thinking? I didn't have that kind of money in my purse.* Discouraged, I walked back over to the chairs and sat down, wondering *what I was going to do now?*

I sat there with my hands in my lap. Five minutes passed. Ten. Nothing happened. *What was I going to do?* The longer I waited, the more I began to worry and fret. The same uncertainty that had me in its grip on the drive over here had me fidgeting and biting my lip nervously. The baby began to kick and squirm inside me. *What if the police kept Peter locked up? What if they wouldn't let me see him? What could I do? Go home and wait? Wait, as I was waiting now?* I willed myself to be calm and consider what I should do, stroking my stomach absently to soothe the baby. I felt hot, much too hot. I could feel my skin prickle with the heat. *Why doesn't someone open a window, and let a breeze in? We will all suffocate if we sit here with the air like this...*

I started as the door creaked open, and someone came inside. He walked confidently up to the window where I had been talking with the clerk. I heard the name "Dr. Peter Munro" and my head jerked up to look at the man. He was tall, and well dressed, with his dark hair combed neatly back, I observed, as he reached into his vest pocket and pulled out his wallet. He counted his money, and handed several notes to the clerk.

He finished his business at the window, then sat down a few seats from me.
I cleared my throat and he looked toward me. "Do you know Dr. Munro?" I ventured.

He smiled. "Yes. As a matter of fact, I'm his solicitor."

I grinned back at him, relieved. "My name is Jenny McCallum," I said, offering my hand. "I'm a friend of his. I'm so glad to meet you!"

"Connor MacKenzie," he said.

Twenty minutes later, Peter emerged through a door that led from the holding cells. He halted at the threshold, a look of pleasure spreading across his features.

"This is brilliant!" he said, striding across the linoleum toward us. "Connor! I see you've met Jenny!" He shook Connor's hand vigorously, then turned to enfold me in a bear hug.

Connor lifted an eyebrow at us, obviously startled by his effusive public display.

"Well, Jailbird," he said, "You owe me 600 pounds." He lowered his voice, and said in a stage whisper, taunting him, "Did they rough you up? Kidney punch, rubber hoses, the lot?"

"Ah," Peter answered solemnly, "I see. You want to know all the barbaric torture methods I endured in here, is that it?"

"Did they hurt you?" I asked with a smile, for I could see from the glint of humor in his silver-blue eyes that nothing untoward had happened to him.

He shook his head. "It was too terrible to discuss in mixed company," he said, ruthlessly suppressing the urge to smile. He took my arm in a firm, gentle grip, leading the way toward the door. "Come on, let's get out of here."

* * * *

The court date was set. It was to be the Tuesday after Easter, at 2:00. We had lunch at half past eleven. Connor came with us. Lunch was a hurried, nervous meal. We didn't talk much. I took a sip of my water, then put the glass back on the table. I was afraid they would notice my hand was shaking.

"If only I could do something," I said nervously. "I hate just sitting here, idle, waiting, with all this time ahead of us."

Peter reached over and laid his hand on top of mine. "There is nothing you can do," he said.

We went on eating in silence. I had that nagging pain again. I did not want anything to eat. I could not swallow. I gazed steadily at my plate. It was a relief when the farce of the meal was over, and we all got up and went out to the cars.

We did not speak. Peter opened the door and helped me inside. Then he came around and got in himself, and started up the car. The sound of the engine steadied me. We drove away from the little restaurant and out onto the road. Connor followed us in his own car. I had my hand on Peter's knee all the way as he drove. I cast a sidelong glance at him. He seemed quite calm. Not nervous in any way. He looked straight in front of him, at the road. We stopped at a crossroads, and he looked to the right and left, and then drove on.

I felt as if I were going with someone to the hospital for an operation. And not knowing how it would turn out, if it would be successful or not. My hands felt very cold. My heart was beating in a funny, jerky way. And all the time, that little nagging pain beneath my heart…

The courthouse was in the city complex, where police headquarters and central lockup were located. Peter parked the car, and Connor eased his car in beside us. We walked together through the courthouse door, and down the hall toward our designated courtroom, Peter's hand beneath my elbow. I wore a harrowed expression as I thought of the ordeal ahead. It was an ordeal, in spite of Peter's calm way of telling me that everything would be all right. Taking a deep breath to calm my quaking stomach, I gave him a weak, rather tremulous smile. He nodded, his hand on the door.

Then he pushed it open, and stood back, so that I could enter the courtroom. I slipped in, keeping my head low, so that I did not have to look at anybody. The room was smaller than I had imagined. It was hot and stuffy. Peter sat me down just by the door.

I glanced surreptitiously around the room. There were people there I did not know, although I did recognize a few of Peter's friends from the hospital. My heart gave a jump suddenly as I saw Jack. He was sitting right at the back. Gone were his rumpled clothes and haggard eyes I remembered from the last time I had seen him. His eyes were on me, and he leered at me sardonically. There was something sickening about it. I could feel all the color drain away from my face. I leaned back on the bench.

The judge pushed open the door to his Chambers, came into the room, and took his place on the Bench. He was a thin, elderly man with fierce dark eyes behind black horn-rimmed glasses, which straddled a strong nose. The court was formally called to order. The old, nagging pain beneath my heart had not left me yet. It was still there. It continued on with greater force when Peter's case was called. We looked at one another as he stood, and then he turned and followed Connor up to the front. Jack followed his solicitor up as well.

I grew suddenly cold. Peter had told me many times that Connor MacKenzie was a brilliant solicitor. I sincerely hoped that he was right.

Connor arose to address the Bench. "Your Honor, the preliminary hearing in this case is for the purpose of determining whether there are reasonable grounds to hold over Dr. Peter Munro on a charge of aggravated assault--to wit, the assault of one Mr. Jack MacCallum. I intend to present knowledge of prior acts of malice perpetuated by said Mr. MacCallum, which include causing his mother to have a skiing accident ten years ago, engaging in various acts of cruelty toward animals, and other instances.

Basically, I seek to show prior bad character, a pre-disposition to commit crime, and to prove a serious case of fraud in this accusation. There is a basic pattern from childhood to adolescence to adulthood that sheds important light on the modus operandi of the prosecution. The evidence isn't of some trivial childhood transgressions, Your Honor. The testimony doesn't involve a few isolated incidents. What the testimony will show is several instances in which Mr. MacCallum has demonstrated a lifelong pattern of terrorizing the people around him.

And what is his method? He attacks in a very specific, yet devious manner. He destroys something that the object of his attack cares about. For example, he destroyed his mother's health, a beloved family pet, he vandalized his ex-wife's car, and flooded her kitchen.

The list goes on. The first incident is fifteen years old. We're talking about a period of several years. There is ample reason to infer that this disposition to commit violent acts is a lifelong pattern. Violence, Your Honor, particularly ugly violence with particularly malicious flavor, recognizable throughout Mr. MacCallum's life. And now he is attempting to destroy my client's career, simply because of jealousy. Committing these acts of malice is his compulsion, Your Honor. "

The Judge nodded, then said, "Mr. O'Hara, how do you respond?"

Mr. O'Hara stood up, his manner all business.

"Mr. MacKenzie's central point is that all the alleged acts fit a certain pattern. And what is this pattern? That he destroys something that the object of his attack cares about. If that is the pattern, I ask counsel, how does it fit here? Let's assume for the moment that my client does demonstrate such a devious pattern. What is he destroying in this case? In the statement that my client gave to the police he is claiming that Dr. Peter Munro came to his house and beat him in a vicious attack upon his person. How is that devious, or fraudulent, as Mr. MacKenzie claims, on his part? The so-called method, or pattern, of malicious acts, even if there was one, doesn't fit, Your Honor! " he turned to face Connor and Peter. "You can ferret out a hundred things any of us did as children, but that doesn't prove that my client perpetrated fraud against your client." He shook his head emphatically. "It's just that the defense doesn't have anything else to work with, Your Honor."

"Proceed with the case," the judge said. "Is the defendant in court?"

"He is."

"Mr. O'Hara, you may call your first witness."

Jack's lawyer approached the Bench.

"The first witness I call on behalf of the prosecution," Mr. O'Hara said, "is Dr. Wallace."

Dr. Wallace came forward, was sworn, and testified that he was on duty in Casualty at Community Hospital the evening of the second of March when Jack had been brought in for treatment by the police. There were bruises and contusions about his face and upper body, and x-rays revealed two broken ribs.

"I show you a photograph," O'Hara said, "merely for the purpose of identification, and ask you if this is a photograph of Jack MacCallum's injuries on the night in question."

"It is."

"We'll connect up the photograph and introduce it later," O'Hara said. "We would now like to have it marked for identification."

His tone indicated plainly that he expected Connor to object, and that he expected the Court to sustain that objection.

"I have no objection in the world," Connor remarked urbanely. "Introduce it into evidence."

He asked several more perfunctory questions, then said to Connor, "You may cross-examine."

Connor rose from his seat, as Jack's lawyer returned to his.

"Dr. Wallace, did you examine my client after the alleged crime was committed?"

"Yes, I did."

"Did you x-ray his hands?"

"Yes."

"And what did you find?"

"The slight injury to his hand was not consistent with the beating that Mr. MacCallum had sustained."

O'Hara's face showed surprise at this line of interrogation.

"Thank you, Doctor. That is all."

Connor returned to his seat, as Dr. Wallace stepped down.

"Call your next witness, Mr. O'Hara."

He stood and called the policemen on duty that night as his next two witnesses. They related how Jack had staggered into the police station, bruised and bloody, his shirt torn and ragged, begging for help. How they had taken him to Casualty at Community Hospital, where his injuries were evaluated and dressed. Then they took him back to the police station, where they had taken his statement.

Connor cross examined the police officers slowly and carefully, stressing that it was only Jack's word against Peter's as to who had truly perpetrated the alleged crime.

O'Hara called other witnesses. He tried everything he could think of to convince the judge of his client's innocence. And every thrust he made, Connor countered.

At ten minutes to three, O'Hara stood up and said, "I have no further testimony to present, You Honor."

The Judge nodded. "You may call your first witness for the defense, Mr. MacKenzie."

Connor stood and approached the Bench. "I call my first witness, Dr. Reilly."

A grey-haired gentleman in his mid-sixties rose and approached the witness stand. He held up his right hand and took the oath, then walked to the witness chair and sat down.

"Dr. Reilly, can you tell the Court what you are a doctor of?"

"I am a Doctor of Psychology."

"Do you recognize the prosecution?"

"Yes, sir."

"And how do you know him?"

"His mother brought him to me about fifteen years ago for treatment."

"Please tell us what you found."

The psychologist took a deep breath, and began. "He could not control his anger. He was aggressive, always pushing things out of his way, smashing things. He had an excuse for everything, his lies, his cruelties, his truancies. His mother told me that he was angry from the start. His brother was the only person he could tolerate, because he looked up to him. He was an aberration, a deviation from the norm, even as a young child. When he entered his teens, his mother took him to several psychologists. He hated them all. Then she brought him to me. I will never forget how he glared at me with those green eyes that held a glint of something frightening in them.

Then their dog died. His mother came to me and said that his brother had told her that Jack had boasted about running over him.

She wanted to believe his denials, wanted to believe that he would come out of it someday. He was her son, and she wanted to protect him.

They went on a family vacation, and something very frightening happened. They were skiing, and his mother had an accident on the mountain. She was seriously injured. And she said that Jack had come up behind her and pushed her into a tree."

"What was your diagnosis at that time, Doctor?"

"My diagnosis of him then was a borderline sociopath."

"Can you explain to the court exactly what that means?"

"A person suffering from psychopathic personality, whose behavior is aggressively antisocial. Psychopathic means a mental disorder. Antisocial means harmful to the welfare of people generally. Aggressive means inclined to starting fights and quarrels, unprovoked attacks, ready and willing to take issue, or engage in direct action."

"I see. And how does that apply to Mr. MacCallum?"

"He boldly and energetically pursues his own ends, with a ruthless desire to dominate. He applies a forwardness of personality that manifests itself in officiousness, which is a pretense of helpfulness, a readiness to serve. He can be obliging, offering unnecessary and unwanted advice or services. Meddlesome in a highhanded or overbearing way, rude. Destructively hostile to others, or to oneself. "

"Did he respond to your treatment?"

"No, he did not. He was not interested."

"What happened?"

"Eventually his mother gave up and quit bringing him to see me."

Thank you, Dr. Reilly. I have no further questions."

Connor nodded and turned toward Jack's lawyer. "Your witness."

O'Hara showed no sign that he had been bested. He fingered the gold ring on his finger and smiled back. Jack fidgeted in his seat, obviously itching to jump up.

"If I may," he began, and attempted to disprove the witness' testimony, without much success. His line of questioning disproved nothing.

"I call Miss Flaherty as my next witness," Connor said.

A small, dark-haired woman rose from her seat and walked toward the witness stand. She was sworn in and sat down in the chair.

"Miss Flaherty, is it true that you were once neighbors with Mr. MacCallum and his family?"

She glanced nervously toward Jack, and nodded. "Yes, it is. We lived next door when we were growing up."

"Can you tell the court what kind of neighbor he was to you and your family?"

"He was a bully. He terrorized me and my younger brother. He poisoned our dog one day because he was distracting him while he was practicing his music."

"Objection!" Mr. O'Hara said. "Calls for speculation from the witness."

The judge heaved a sigh and looked down at the witness. "Miss Flaherty, can you prove it was Mr. MacCallum who poisoned your dog?"

"No, Your Honor, but we always believed--"

"Objection sustained," the judge said, tapping his gavel.

"I withdraw the question, Your Honor," Connor said, but his point had already been made.

"I call Mrs. Lydia Aird to the stand."

The head nurse, who worked with Peter, stood and walked toward the front of the courtroom.

After being sworn in, Connor asked her how long she had known Dr. Peter Munro, and what kind of person she knew him to be.

"I have known Dr. Munro for five years, now, and worked with him for three. He has always conducted himself with the utmost gentlemanly manner in any situation," she testified.

Peter was called. He came forward and was sworn.

"Can you tell us exactly what happened on the night in question?" Connor asked him.

"Yes. Mrs. MacCallum had gone to visit Mr. MacCallum earlier in the day to speak with him about his harassment of her. He hit her. I went later that evening to talk to him about it. I'm afraid that I lost my temper and hit him."

"Did you beat him?"

"No, I did not."

"How many times did you hit him?"

"Only once. Then I left."

"Thank you very much, doctor. You may step down. I call as my next witness Mr. Jack MacCallum."

Jack strolled up to the witness box and a bible was thrust under his right hand.

"Please raise your right hand and repeat after me."

Jack raised his hand, then raised his eyes to the sea of faces in the courtroom. And as his eyes found Peter, a slow, nasty grin spread over his features.

"Do you swear to tell the truth, the whole truth, and nothing but the truth, so help you God?"

"I swear," he repeated with a grin, lowering his hand.

"You may be seated."

He laughed out loud as he took the witness stand, crossing his legs and settling himself comfortably in the chair. His face was very flushed.

Connor walked up to the witness stand. "You have made some very serious accusations against my client. Have you any proof to back these accusations?"

"Proof?" Jack snapped belligerently. "What the hell do you need with proof? Weren't my broken ribs enough? Proof be damned. Of course, Munro did it. Who else would?"

"Edinburgh has a large population, sir," said Connor, glibly testing him. "Why not go from door to door and take a poll? I might have done it myself. You appear to have no more proof against Dr. Munro than you have against me."

The courtroom tittered. The judge pounded with his gavel for silence.

"He threatened me!" he said contemptuously, pointing at Peter.

"You tell a compelling story, Mr. MacCallum. You were known as a bully in school. Did you ever threaten a fellow student?"

"I can't remember," he said in an even monotone. He was not smiling anymore. It was quite clear that he wasn't pleased with the turn of events, and was ill prepared for it.

"Don't worry, Mr. MacCallum. I'm sure that it will come back to you," Connor observed, getting to his feet.

"I refuse to answer."

"Go on, finish it."

He cleared his throat twice, then mumbled, "I refuse to answer upon the grounds that the answer may tend to incriminate me."

Connor smiled affably. "You threatened your ex-wife, followed her, harassed her, vandalized her car, attacked her in the supermarket, hit her. You threatened my client."

Jack shook his head stubbornly. "I don't see it that way."

"Exactly how do you see it, Mr. MacCallum?" He paused, and looked expectantly at him.

Color flooded his face, and excitement made him sweat. There were beads of perspiration on his forehead. He began speaking in a loud, domineering voice. "Look here. There's no sense in beating around the bush. I can't understand why she is afraid of me, and why he feels he must defend her. He's come to my place and started the arguments and threatened me. I am the victim here. Just because her flat was broken into, her kitchen flooded and there were a few things missing, she accuses me. I ask you, is that fair? She asked for it, anyway. She left me. Yes, I've called her names, and shouted obscenities at them both. What's your point? They both deserved it. She keeps calling the police on me, blaming me for everything that happens, when it's really her fault. I thought to turn the tables on them. The reason I'm here is that he beat me!" He turned to me, his eyes like burning coals, and pointed his finger at Peter. "Don't you see what kind of man he is, Jenny?" These last words were shouted.

His manner was not helpful to him, and I could see by the thin line of the judge's mouth, that he had not taken kindly to him.

"My dear fellow," Connor said, "it's not the slightest use, your losing your temper. Very well. Suppose we get to the point. Tell us what really happened."

He looked from one to the other doubtfully. Then he turned his head and looked slowly toward Peter. "You've asked me, and by God, I'll tell you! There he sits with his high-priced solicitor, and that God damned superior smile on his face. He beat me, I tell you! He beat me within an inch of my life! And I'm telling you now, he'd look good behind bars. Don't you think?" His voice grew louder and he looked directly at me once again. "Don't you think so, Jenny?"

And he began to laugh, the laugh of a drunkard, high pitched, forced and foolish.

Thank God for his laugh. Thank God for his pointing finger, his flushed face, his staring eyes. Because it made the judge antagonistic. I could see the disgust on his face, the quick movement of his lips. The judge did not believe him.

Connor's leg-man walked into the court room and leaned over his shoulder, whispering something in his ear. Then he turned and walked back out of the court room.

Connor stood up. "Your Honor, may I approach the Bench?"

The judge nodded, and inclined his head.

"A witness I have been looking for has just been found. At this time, I move that the Court admit a Mr. King as a witness."

"Mr. O'Hara, please come forward."

A fine line appeared between O'Hara's brows, as he stood up, and approached the Bench. He listened to what they had to say. "I object, Your Honor! This man's testimony is not relevant to this case inasmuch as his statements would be clearly inadmissible. The man is a convicted felon."

"But the Court wants to get to the truth," Connor said. "This is a fact-finding hearing. The Court can relax the technical rules in the interest of justice."

"There are good reasons for technical rules, Your Honor," O'Hara interrupted. "Even in the less formal preliminary hearings."

"I am going to allow the testimony," the judge said.

Counsel returned to their seats, and Mr. King was brought into the courtroom. He sat down near the front.

"Didn't you allow this man, even pay this man to beat you senseless, in an act of revenge?"

Jack waved his arms excitedly. "Your Honor, I resent that accusation!" He jumped to his feet. "It's a lie, Your Honor!" he shouted. "A pack of filthy lies! An attack on my character, it is!" Perspiration beaded on his forehead.

The courtroom was tense with silence.

The judge's face clouded. O'Hara jumped to his feet. "Your Honor!" he shouted. "I object. This is absolutely hearsay evidence. This has no bearing…"

The judge pounded with his gavel.

"That will do, Counselor. Sit down. You are out of order."

"But he shouldn't have to answer. He'll get himself into trouble. I advise him not to…"

There was no smile on the judge's face. "You will sit down and keep quiet," he said. "Or you'll be ejected from the courtroom, and fined for Contempt. Which will it be?"

Slowly O'Hara sat down. He was angry, but expressed it with no more than a titanium glint in his eye.

"And you'll remain seated, and you'll remain quiet," the judge ordered, then turned to Jack. "Answer the question."

Connor stared steadily at the Jack. He squirmed uncomfortably in the chair, and avoided his eyes. There was a perceptible period of hesitation, then he said slowly, "I can't say."

Connor stared at him coldly. "You're under oath, remember that."

O'Hara half rose from his chair, then sat back down with an air of dejection.

Jack gulped. He wet his lips, but remained silent.

Connor motioned with his hand urbanely. "I think that is all," he said disgustedly.

"Your witness," he said to O'Hara.

"Mr. MacCallum, did Dr. Munro ever call on you prior to the second of March?"

"Yes, he did. He threatened me then as well."

"What did he say?"

"It wasn't so much what he said. It was his tone of voice. And he put his hands on me."

"How so?"

"He pushed me up against the wall in my own home, and told me to leave them alone."

"Thank you, Mr. MacCallum. That is all."

Jack stepped down and Connor called Mr. King as his next witness.

"I expect to prove without a shadow of doubt, Your Honor, that Jack MacCallum hired this man to beat him, and to make it appear as if my client had done it."

"This is an outrage!" O'Hara said. "This is convicting my client of fraud without even giving him a chance to defend himself."

Despite himself, the judge smiled. "It is rather an ironic situation, Counselor, but there is no question as to its legality. You will sit down and refrain from interrupting these proceedings again. Continue, Mr. MacKenzie."

"Mr. King, can you tell the court what happened on the night in question."

"Yes, sir, I can. That man there," and the witness pointed to Jack, "came to me and offered me money to beat him up." King shrugged. "I said, sure, why not?"

"And did you?"

"Sure, I did. I made him pay me first, though. Then me and my friends had at him."

Over at the counsel table, O'Hara went through an elaborate pantomime as if registering extreme protest, but remembering the judicial admonition, he remained seated and kept silent. He looked hopefully at the Judge, but the judge skillfully avoided his gaze. It was clear which way it was going to go. We all knew. O'Hara had come to the end of his case. His job had been to show probable cause that Peter was the perpetrator in the crime of Jack's beating. He hadn't met that burden. Not that he hadn't tried.

Connor turned and gave Peter a fraternal wink. He returned to the counsel table, sat down in his chair and smiled over at O'Hara.

"That," he said, "is all." He sighed with satisfaction.

Connor looked over at the lined face of the judge, his black rimmed glasses on his nose. "I think the defense raises a compelling argument. Evidence tends to show that Mr. MacCallum seeks to retaliate violently against those who would aggrieve him in some way."

Mr. O'Hara shook his head. He looked unhappy and beaten.

"The Court will now render its decision. The Court finds that there is probable cause to believe that Mr. MacCallum has committed fraud against Dr. Munro, and against this Court."

The charges against Peter were dropped.

Mr. O'Hara turned to Jack. "He's going to bind you over for trial."

"What?"

"We'll set a trial date for next week," the judge said.

Connor stood up and said, "We move that Mr. MacCallum be immediately remanded into custody."

Things were going so well, so fantastically well, and Jack was about to be led away. But at the very last moment, when Jack was about to be safely neutralized, the judge made a mistake.

"I think we'll have to schedule a formal bail hearing," he said.

Connor jumped to his feet. "He's a danger! The Court should remand him into custody immediately!"

"Sit down, Counselor. I'll hear your motion on Monday morning at eight a.m. So, ordered." He wiped his brow.

I sat there, stunned.

Jack stared contemptuously at the judge, his manner vengeful. I could see the click, click, clicking in his eyes as he tried to decide what to do. He looked off to the side, calculating.

"You think I'm a liar?" Jack shouted, shaking his head vigorously. "Oh, no, my fine friend. You may be a magistrate, but that doesn't mean anything to me. I've got the law on my side, I tell you! Fellows with brains in their heads, who understand the meaning of justice! Not an incompetent judge like you. Peter Munro beat me and I'm going to prove it! Oh, I see how it is," said Jack. "You're going to hold his hand through this. He is a rich doctor, the son of aristocracy. You bloody bastard."

"Take care, Mr. MacCallum. Take care."

Spectators stirred restlessly.

His manner was cold and purposeful. "You think you can get the better of me, don't you? You think I've no case. I'll get my proof for you, all right! I tell you, that man beat me!"

There was a long pause. It seemed to me that there was something about that particular moment, while we waited, that frightened me more than anything that had happened.

I dug my nails into my hands. It was then that Jack turned and gave me a chilling look. I dared not look at Peter. *Surely everyone must hear my heart beating and thumping in my breast? Something was going to happen. Something terrible was going to happen.*
And then he smiled. And I saw the cruelty, and the misery, and the corrosive self-pity in him. And I shrank from it.

* * * *

Peter and I walked down the hall together. I hugged him tightly, my head against his chest. The courtroom scene had been even more horrible than I had imagined it would be. But I determined to be brave, and face the future with a newfound resolve.

"Just a moment," I said, as we passed by the women's loo. "I need to freshen up a bit." A splash of cold water on my face would surely do the trick.

I went into the women's loo, and Peter waited outside for me.

While I was at the sink, an eerie apprehension descended over me. Jack was waiting in one of the stalls. He quietly snuck out of the stall and locked the restroom door, then snuck up behind me. I gasped as I saw his reflection in the mirror.

"Jenny, my darling little wife. Though not so little now, I see," he said in a light, teasing tone that wasn't meant to fool me. He scanned me from head to toe, his grin changing to a leer.

It seemed I'd have a chance to test my newfound resolve already--and completely alone. "What are you doing in here?"

"I'd think you'd be more eager to see me, after all our time apart," he said darkly. "But I'm willing to overlook that."

But he put a hand over my mouth before I was able to say anything else.

"What a stroke of luck this has been for you and that doctor of yours. You won't get away with it, though." An unpleasant smile formed on his lips. His breath on my face was nauseating. "I'll never let you be with him, Jen. You should never have tried."

He threw me away from him then. My head hit the wall with a thunk, dazing me for a moment. As I slid to the floor, he covered the ground between us, looming over me menacingly. I could see the hatred burning in his eyes, and a chill skittered down my spine, to lodge, heavy and frightening, in my belly. "You should not do anything foolish, Jack. It could get you into trouble." Desperation unintentionally seeped into my voice. I hoped he would mistake it for sincerity.

"As if you'd care!" he spat.

"Peter!" I screamed.

"Shut up, you cow!" he yelled. Fresh pain exploded in my face, as he slapped me hard. My head reeled back against the wall and my vision blurred, then slowly cleared. I could feel warm blood dripping from my nose. I tasted blood, and wiped my hand under my nose, grimacing at the red glistening on my hand. I raised my chin in defiance. "You can't do this to me," I told him, hoping he couldn't tell how frightened I was. I felt the tension in him as intensely as the emerald scrutiny of his eyes.

"I can do anything I damn well want!" he sneered. "You think you've won, don't you?" he said, pulling a knife from inside his coat. He waved it threateningly in front of my eyes. "I can get you in a different way. I can keep you and your boyfriend apart forever, if I choose to!"

"Jennifer!" I heard Peter's voice calling me. He must have heard the commotion inside. I heard him try the door. It did not open. He pounded on it with his fist. "Are you all right in there?" He shouted, throwing his body against the door. "Jennifer!"

"We'll finish this later."

The noise at the door rose to a crescendo, and I shut my eyes tightly. With a sound of splintering wood, Peter kicked open the door and found me cowering in the corner. Jack was nowhere to be seen.

"Are you all right?" Peter asked me. Reaching down, he put his arms around me and helped me to my feet.

"Jack…" was all I could manage to say.

Peter ran to the open window and looked out, but there was no trace of him.

Charges of assault with intent to commit murder were filed against Jack, but he could not be found. We were told that he would be picked up as soon as he could be located.

CHAPTER FIFTY-EIGHT

"You have to stop cleaning."

"I have to keep busy. It helps calm me."

"Let me do that."

"No! I don't need your help!" I said tartly. "I'm not a helpless idiot! I know I haven't done much to prove otherwise, but I'm usually competent enough to get by without a keeper."

"Nonetheless, you don't have to do everything by yourself."

I wavered on my feet, but managed the chair and sat down with a plop. I leaned forward, my head in my hands. "I'm tired. So tired I can't see, or hear, or think."

Peter came and knelt beside me. He wrapped me in his arms. It felt so good, his warmth and strength surrounding me. I knew I must break away from arms at once. But he refused to release me. Instead, he cradled me to his chest.

"Don't run away from me," he whispered into my hair. "I only want to protect you, Jen. Nothing more than that."

I eased back and looked at him. He smiled, smoothing my hair away from my face, his fingers caressing my cheek. "For tonight, at any rate."

A tide of warmth flooded through me at his words. I remained in his arms for a time, savoring the closeness and giving silent thanks that things had gone well for him in court that day.

He put a hand on mine. "You're coming home with me," he said with a decisive nod.

* * * *

The room was cozy, Peter's large, calm figure reassuring. I sat on the floor in front of the glowing firelight, and tried to think only of the comfort and warmth in this room. Peter sat on the sofa behind me, and I leaned my head against his knee, and felt my tension ebbing away.

I yawned, my eyes drooping with fatigue.

He ran his fingers through my hair. I snuggled deeper into the cocoon of warmth with a contented sigh, enjoying the pleasurable feeling of fingers across my scalp, knuckling my cheek against the soft wool beneath it. I wondered how I could feel so happy when our little world about us seemed so black. It was a strange sort of happiness. Not what I had dreamed about or expected. It was not the sort of happiness I had imagined in lonely hours. There was nothing feverish or urgent about this. It was a quiet, still happiness. I gave a faint, blissful sigh as I drifted off to sleep.

Suddenly, without warning, my peaceful sleep turned dark and ominous. I opened my eyes in terror and found myself in unfamiliar surroundings. I opened my mouth to scream as hands sought to quiet me, and stop my squirming. I heard a voice as I flailed out with my arms, my fist striking something that shifted away a little, while still holding me.

"Hush, Sweetheart. It's me, Peter. You're dreaming."

Awareness returned to me then, as his features swam into view. "Peter?" Tears streamed down my face. "Oh, Peter, thank God it's you!" I burrowed into his arms, my face pressed to his neck.

Peter cupped my head in his palm, and pressed my tear stained cheek to his chest. His touch was beguiling in its simplicity, rife with tenderness. It made no demands, it asked no questions. I looked up and gazed into his blue-grey eyes, and it seemed the most natural act in the world, as he cupped the mound of my belly in one hand, my cheek in the other, and kissed me. He spread a line of kisses over my face until he reached my mouth. Stroking my lips with his tongue, he invites me to join him. I tasted salt and sweetness, his lips soft against mine. His breathe a sigh, he opened his mouth and gently nipped at my lower lip, before I drew back a little.

"Stay with me," he said softly. "Marry me, Jen."

The chilling shadow of Jack sprang up between us, and I pushed myself upright.

"I can't!"

It was all I could do to force the words past the tightness in my throat, when everything inside me cried the opposite. "Can't you see what a danger I am to you? I can't let you put yourself in such jeopardy for my sake. We don't even know where Jack is! The police are still looking for him. He could find us before they find him. Oh, Peter, there's no telling what he could do to you. Next time he might succeed in ruining your career...or worse..." My voice faded away. That thought was enough to freeze the blood in my veins. "I shouldn't even be here with you," I said in a sudden panic. Once again, I felt the intensity in the glare of Jack's eyes. He meant to watch our every move until he had his final revenge.

Peter slipped his hand off my stomach, the warmth of his touch lingering. "That's nonsense, and you know it," he said, in his imperturbable way. Whatever storm was going on in my head, Peter was keeping his customary quiet, honest, good sense. His words helped to calm my fears. He leaned forward earnestly, and cupped my chin in his hand. "What's the fuss, Jen? If you're worried about him finding us and causing trouble, then come with me to my parents' country home for the weekend. I can take some time off work. Why don't you?" he said, his challenging tone matching his expression.

I met his gaze and held it, weighing his words, and made my decision.

CHAPTER FIFTY-NINE

I took a few days leave of my job at the bank, and began to pack for a weekend in the country. A weekend with a country squire and his family, in a manor home that had been in the family for generations, Peter had told me. I was feeling a bit overwhelmed, but Peter had reassured me that his parents were "just regular people", and not to worry. We would have a peaceful and restful weekend, and when it was over, I would feel refreshed enough to conquer the world, or my little part of it, he had laughed. So, thus reassured, I resumed my packing with the usual overnight paraphernalia. As a last thought, I slipped my grandmother's brooch into my bag, just in case we dressed for dinner.

When Peter picked me up, it was raining. The weather had been miserable of late, but off we went, with a feeling of expectation in the air.

As we drove, Peter rambled on excitedly about his ancestral home. His mood was contagious. "You'll love it there. I promise. It's an old manor home, been in the family for hundreds of years. Only two miles further," he said, pointing out ahead. "You see the trees on the brow of the hill, just there? Sloping into the valley? That's Hayvenhurst, in there. Those are the woods."

I smiled apprehensively, with a sudden stab of panic. Gone was my excitement. I felt like a child on my first day at a new school. I suddenly felt as if I did not belong here with him, that I would not know whether to stand or sit, or what spoons and forks to use at dinner.

The rain had stopped, and the sun was out now, shining and bright in a beautiful blue sky. Peter turned the corner when we came to a cross-road, and followed it along the beginning of a high wall.

"Here we are," he said, with a new note of excitement in his voice, and I gripped the leather seat of the car with both my hands.

He looked over at me and raised an eyebrow, a smile quirking at the corners of his mouth. "All right?" he asked, reaching over and covering my hand with his.

I nodded, but didn't answer. I managed a nervous smile. Perhaps he guessed my apprehension, for he took my hand and kissed it, and laughed a little.

"You mustn't be frightened. Just be yourself, and my parents will love you."

I had my doubts. *How would they feel, as their son introduced me, seven months pregnant with another man's child?*

His gaze shifted back to the road as it curved, and before us, on the left, were two high iron gates, open wide to the long drive beyond. An old fashioned, weather-worn lodge stood behind the gates, bearing a brass plaque which read:

HAYVENHURST

Peter turned his car through the open gates and we drove down the drive.

"See those shrubs? It's like a blue wall along here when the hydrangeas are in bloom."

I suddenly envied him, careless and at ease, and the smile on his lips which meant that he was happy to be home. It seemed so remote to me, a time when I could once again smile and feel at ease. I wished it would come quickly. I even wished that I were old now, with grey hair, my grandchild on my knee. Anything, but this frightened, timid foolish girl I felt myself to be.

The gravel drive stretched out before us, broad and spacious. Above our heads was a great colonnade of trees, whose branches nodded and intermingled with one another, making an archway for us, like the roof of a church. I thought that even the midday sun would not be able to penetrate the interlacing of the green leaves of summer. But as it was, with the branches barely coming into bloom, little flickering patches of warm light came in intermittent waves to dapple the drive with gold. It was very silent, very still. These trees had stood here for hundreds of years. I tried to imagine what it must have been like for a new bride back then, perhaps seeing this place for the first time.

As the drive descended into the valley, more trees came into sight, great birches with lovely smooth white trunks, lifting their branches to one another, so close that I could touch them with my hand if I just reached out the window. On we went, over a narrow stream, and suddenly I saw a clearing in the drive ahead. The trees began to thin, and I saw the drive broaden, amidst acres of beautiful, rolling gardens. We rounded the last curve, and so arrived at Hayvenhurst. It was graceful and beautiful, like the grand houses you see in magazines, lovelier than I had ever imagined. It sat like a jewel in the hollow of smooth grasslands and mossy lawns.

Smoke came from one of the chimneys, and the mullioned windows reflected the green lawns and terrace. The terrace sloped to the lawns, and the lawns stretched down to a beautiful lake, a sheet of blue, placid and undisturbed under the sun.

As we drove up to the wide stone steps and stopped before the open door, Peter's parents came down the steps, followed by two cocker spaniels. A man, who could only be the butler, stood behind them, his back straight as an arrow.

Peter put on the brakes with a jerk, and was out of the car in an instant to greet them. "Well, here we are," he said, hugging his mother, and giving his father's hand a shake. "Duncan, it's good to see you, old man!" he added, turning to the other man to shake his hand, too. The dogs pawed at his legs, their long silken ears strained back with affection, their noses nudging his hands, until he bent to rub their heads. "Goldie, Florence, there's my good dogs. It's good to see you, too."

Duncan came down to the car, and opened the door for me. He took my overnight case and turned to Peter, who helped me from the car. The dogs left him then and came to me, sniffing at my heels, a little uncertain, a little suspicious. I gave them my hand to sniff, which they did.

"Mum, Dad, this is Jennifer."

I straightened, and his mother, small and petite, came forward and took my hand. "Welcome, my dear," she said, looking me up and down, as I had expected her to do. His father, tall, with silver-blue eyes, and blond hair that was now turning grey, stretched out his enormous hand to me. I could see that he was very much like Peter about the eyes and jaw.

"It was raining when we left Edinburgh," Peter said, retrieving our luggage from the boot. "You don't seem to have had it here. Everyone well?"

"Yes, darling," his mother said, putting her arm through mine, her bright eyes sparkling genially. "I'm so glad to see you home. Looks like you've been keeping well." And to me, she said, "I do hope you will enjoy your stay with us."

We climbed the steps and entered a great stone hall, a big round vestibule with magnificent staircases going up both sides of the room, leading to the minstrel's gallery and the stone passages beyond. Wide oak doors on either side were flung open to the library on one side of us, the dining room on the other. Expensive portraits hung on the walls all around.

"Peter, why don't you and Duncan take your cases upstairs, then join us in the library for tea."

"I'll go with you, son," Peter's father said and the three of them headed up the stairs, laden with our luggage, as Peter's mother bore me off to the library. The two cocker spaniels followed us. The older one, Goldie, took herself with a grunt to the fireside and laid down, while Florence, the younger one, put her nose in my hand as I sat down, and laid her chin on my knee, her eyes deep and soulful, her tail-end wagging frantically as I stroked her silky ears.

The library was a comfortable room, with hunter-green walls, and leather-bound books lining the walls to the ceiling. Leather chairs stood beside a great open fireplace, and a big oak desk to the other side of it. Long windows looked out upon the lawns, and beyond the lawns, the lake shimmered in the distance.

There was an old, quiet smell about the room, as though the air in it was little changed. It was an ancient smell, but I could also detect a hint of jasmine there as well. It was a room for peace, for meditation.

Duncan came in and offered sherry. I declined, but Mrs. Munro took a glass, then gestured for him to put the tray down. He did, and left the room.

"Peter tells me what a ghastly time the two of you have had of late. I do hope that you will have a restful weekend here, my dear, and enjoy yourself. I've always thought it does one good to get away."

"Yes," I agreed.

"Tomorrow my husband and I have an appointment with the bishop and his wife. You must have Peter show you the grounds while we are out."

"I'd like that very much."

"We're back," Peter's father said as they came into the room. He walked over and threw some more logs on the fire, then turned to us. "I'm hungry. What is keeping tea?"

"It's only just one now, Thomas," his wife chided good-naturedly.

Peter came up behind me, putting his hands on my shoulders, giving me confidence.

"You're looking well, Peter," his mother said, her head to one side, studying him.

"Thank you, Mother. I'm feeling fit." He glanced down at the dog, who had come to lay at his feet, and gave my shoulders a final squeeze. "Unlike Florence, here, who needs some exercise." He stirred the dog with his foot. She rolled, her tongue lolling.

"She's getting much too fat."

"I'm afraid she hasn't had a run-in week," his father chimed in. "I haven't been taking my usual walks to the lodge gates and back."

Peter raised an eyebrow at his father. "Feeling all right, Da?" he asked.

"Och, I'm fine. Just growing a bit lazy with age, son."

"Well, we'll have none of that," Peter told him.

At that moment, the door opened and Duncan entered, bearing our tea on a tray. He placed it upon the vast mahogany sideboard with a stately little performance, then left as quietly as he had come.

I played with my dripping crumpet, crumbled cake into my hand, and swallowed my scalding tea, as Peter and his parents caught up on each others' news. Now and again, he looked over at me and smiled. I leaned back in my chair, glancing about the room, imagining Peter as a boy, sprawled on the sofa with muddy boots, coming back from the lake with a rod in his hand and a fish on his hook, with a frog in his pocket, or a cricket bat slung carelessly over his shoulder.

My vision was disturbed by the opening of the door, when Duncan came in to clear the tea away.

Mrs. Munro asked, "Would you like to see your room, dear?"

"Oh, yes, of course," I answered, getting up slowly, my old nervousness returning. We went out into the hall. *How big it looked, now that it was empty.* Our feet rang on the flagged stones, echoing to the ceiling.

"It's very big, isn't it?" I said, my voice sounding too bright, too forced, even to my own ears.

"Yes," she answered, her tone warm as she took my arm. "Hayvenhurst is a big place. Not so big as some, of course, but big enough. This was the Great Hall, in the old days."

"Oh, really?" I asked, glancing to my right and left, taking in the weapons on the wall, the pictures, touching the carved staircase with my hand.

We went up the stairs together, and turned through the archway of the gallery to the corridor beyond. We went along a broad, carpeted passage, hung with ancient ancestral portraits, and then turned right through an oak door. She stood aside to let me pass, and I came to a little ante-room, furnished with a sofa, chairs and a writing desk, which opened out to a large double bedroom with wide window seats, and a bathroom beyond. I went at once to the window, and looked out. The rose garden lay below, and the eastern part of the terrace.

"What a charming room!" I said, delighted.

"Thank you. I hoped you'd like it."

My things were already unpacked, and my brush lay upon the tray on the dressing table.

"I hope you don't mind. I had Alicia unpack for you."

"Oh, no, not at all. Saves me the trouble," I said with a little laugh. Then a step sounded in the hall, and Peter came into the room.

"How is it?" he asked, crossing the room and taking my hand. "All right? Do you like it?"

"I love it," I said enthusiastically.

"I'll leave you to yourselves," Mrs. Munro said, kissing my cheek, and patting Peter's hand. "Rest yourself, my dear," she said to me with a smile, "and I'll see you downstairs before dinner."

Peter went and leaned out the window. "I've always loved the rose garden," he said. "One of my first memories is toddling along behind my mother while she cut the dead heads from the roses, and tended the garden. She's always had a green thumb." He stuck his head back in again, and looked around the room. "There's something peaceful and happy about this room. It's always been one of my favorites."

He turned back to the window, whistling quietly, under his breath, rocking backwards and forwards on his heels.

"Where is your room?" I asked.

"Down at the end of the corridor on your left. Why? Were you hoping for a midnight liaison?" he teased, quirking his eyebrow at me, his expression hopeful.

"No," I said, picking up one of the decorative pillows from the bed, and flinging it at him.

He caught the pillow and laughed, tossing it back on the bed. "How did you get on with my mother?" he asked.

"She seems very friendly. What did you tell her about me?"

"Only that your ex-husband was giving you some trouble, and that you needed to get away."

"She seems quite understanding, with all that's happened to you, because of Jack. Not only that, but not every mother would be so accepting if their son brought a pregnant woman home to meet them."

"Don't be silly. I told you my parents will love you. Stop worrying."

"Easy for you to say."

273

He came across to me and kissed me on the top of my head.

"Come along," he said. "Let me show you Hayvenhurst."

He put his arm round my shoulder, and we wandered the rooms, finally ending in the minstrel's gallery, where the family ancestral portraits were hung in an impressive line down the curving corridor. In the shadows of the landing above, they looked decorative and colorful. Stately, stylish men and women looked out at us solemnly from gilded frames, spanning hundreds of years, going all the way back to the 15th century. One portrait especially caught my eye. It was of a young man with curling blond hair and piercing grey eyes, dressed in white hose and blue satin doublet, a fashionable ruff at his neck. The corners of his mouth were turned up, as if threatening to laugh out loud at any moment.

"Who's this?" I asked, glancing at Peter. The resemblance was uncanny.

He chuckled at the expression on my face. "That's my great-great-great-great grandfather," he said. "His name was Richard Peter Thomas Munro. It's an old family name, and mine, as well."

"Your given name is Richard?"

"Yes, but my grandfather went by that name. I've always been called Peter."

"I see." I glanced once more at the man in blue, then went on to the next portrait. A beautiful young woman gazed back at me, her blue eyes dancing, her blond hair parted in the middle, a dainty pearl coif upon her head. She sat with a small dog in her lap, her hand poised tenderly upon it's back.

"And that's my great-great-great-great-great grandmother."

"His mother?"

"Yes. Her name was Gillian. And this was her husband, Thomas. Another family name."

A much older man, with graying hair and the pink complexion of a child, looked back at me, his eyes full of kindness. He must have been a very good man, I thought, glancing back at the portraits of his wife and son. They certainly looked happy. Thomas and Gillian must have been very much in love, despite the age difference.

Peter looked at his watch. "Och, it's already time for dinner. Come, there's no time to change. My folks will be waiting for us."

My footsteps no longer sounded foolish to me on the stone flags of the hall as we crossed toward the dining room, for Peter's shoes made far more noise than mine, and the pattering feet of the two dogs added a pleasing note.

I felt comfortable, and conversation was easy now, no longer an effort, as we laughed, and talked together. Peter and his father discussed their cars, la Crosse and football, while Mrs. Munro and I talked of gardening and babies.

* * * *

When I got downstairs the next morning I found Peter standing in the Hall, shrugging into his coat. He looked at me and smiled. "Morning," he greeted brightly. "I'm off for a walk. Want to come?"

It was after nine, and I felt a little flurried at having slept so late, and made an excuse about having stayed too long in the bath.

"Not a bother," he said, pulling his cap onto his head. "My parents have gone to call at the bishop's house, leaving us to ourselves for a few hours. Breakfast is on the sideboard if you're hungry."

I shook my head. "I don't usually eat until I've been up a while. I think I'll walk with you."

"Good. I'll get you a coat." He reached into the closet by the door and pulled one out. He held it up for me and I shrugged into it hurriedly, fumbling with the collar. It belonged to his mother, of course, and did not fit around my swollen stomach, but no matter.

He whistled for the dogs as we went out onto the terrace and walked down onto the smooth, green lawns. Florence suddenly appeared from nowhere, running around us in circles, barking hysterically at the prospect of a walk. Peter bent down and flung a stick across the green. "Fetch it, Flo!" he said to her, and she streaked away, her long, golden ears flopping in the wind.

"Well, what do you think?" he asked me. "Did you rest well last night?"

Shoots of bluebells, soon to blossom, waved in the breeze along the path where we walked. A butterfly flitted past us.

"Yes, I did. It's very pleasant here. No wonder you love it."

"Aye, I do," he said, as we climbed the grassy bank above the lake. Standing there, with the wind whipping my hair about my face, I could almost imagine that nothing else existed in the world but this peace and beauty, spread out like a feast before my eyes.

Nothing else, except the man whose presence I could feel with an awareness that owed nothing to sight or sound--to any sense that I knew of. I could see him standing behind me in my mind's eye, tall and straight, savoring the wind's power to chase away one's cares.

Compelled to see for myself, I turned, my eyes confirming what my mind already knew. He stood just as I had imagined.

Florence returned with the stick, and he bent down, patting her head and stroking her ears. My heart beat faster in reaction to the picture he made--his face awash with pleasure, relaxed, handsome--or maybe it was in response to the eerie sense of rightness that struck me at that moment.

His cap lifted in the wind and he reached up to capture it before it flew off his head. He laughed, and his pleasure was an irresistible lure to me.

We walked together around the edge of the lake. A swan swam slowly among the reeds, its image reflected in the water. The birds chirped in the trees.

"I was wondering, what would you like to do today?" He bent to take the stick from Florence and to pat her head.

"Let's have a picnic," I suggested, going down beside him, patting and stroking the dog along with him. Florence, unaccustomed to such attention, rolled over on her back in ecstasy. "I could make American Southern fried chicken, potato salad and brownies. What do you say to that?"

"I say, when do we eat?"

"Do you think your cook would mind me in her kitchen?"

"Not at all. Come on." He stood, and lent me a hand up, helping me balance my precariously unproportioned weight. Then he whistled over his shoulder. "Come along, Florence," he called to the dog. And to me, he said, "I know just the place for our picnic. A special spot in the garden, and you shall smell the azaleas."

* * * *

We found the big kitchen empty. Peter helped me to find the things I needed, and I set to work, putting potatoes and eggs on to boil, dredging and frying the chicken, and then started on the brownies. Peter sat at the large work table, and helped by peeling the potatoes and eggs, and by dicing the onions and pickles.

When the food was ready, we cleaned up the kitchen together, then packed everything in a big basket, along with a bottle of sparkling cider. Peter carried it, as we walked together, arm in arm, down a little path out to a little walled garden, by the side of a running stream. On either side of the narrow path stood azaleas and rhododendrons, salmon, white and pink, drooping their delicate heads in the breeze. The air was full of their scent, sweet and heady, and there was no sound here but the tumbling of the little stream over the rocks. On the slope at the end of the path, under the birch trees, we stood quite still, not speaking, looking down on the clear white faces of the flowers closest to us. When Peter spoke, his voice was hushed, too, gentle and low, as if he had no wish to break upon the silence.

"This used to be called the Knot Garden."

A bird began to sing then, a song clear and cool above the sound of the running stream. A moment later there was the answering note from another, hidden somewhere in the trees. The sky above us was blue and clear, and the liquid note of the birdsong fell upon us in complete harmony. It was as if nothing could disturb the soft quietude of this magical, enchanted place.

Peter spread the rug over the little mound under the birch trees, and gestured for me to sit.

"This mound is called the Love Knot."

I giggled as he waggled his brows at me. "And what does that mean?"

"It's where lovers used to come in the old days."

"Seems a little too open for my tastes," I said, glancing around.

He laughed and dug into the picnic basket, helping me to spread our fare before us. We made small talk, and enjoyed the peace of the garden together.

"What will you do now?" Peter asked me, as he finished his third piece of chicken. He licked his fingers after taking his last bite, then wiped them on his napkin. As he reached for the bottle of sparkling cider, I retrieved the glasses from the basket. In a thoroughly expert manner, he eased the cork out of the bottle of cider, filed the glasses, and handed one to me.

Sighing heavily, I shook my head as I took the glass, my shoulders slumped. "I don't know. I guess I'll just go on the same as before…except now we don't know where Jack is, or what he's up to. What if he's followed us? There's no telling what he might do."

I looked up at the sky. "There was a time that I thought I loved him very much. I thought that I could give him anything he'd ever need." I swirled the cider in my glass, staring at the sparkling golden liquid. "I guess I thought that one day he'd turn to me and say 'you're the best woman in the world. You give me everything a man could ever want.'" I smiled ruefully, and swirled the cider harder, then stopped and glanced up at Peter. His face was about six inches away. Pierced by his hot gaze, I lowered my eyes again. "I-I guess I was wrong."

"The man is a fool." He leaned down and said no more. His eyes were a beautiful silver-blue, but I couldn't bring myself to look at them. Neither of us moved.

He leaned closer, nuzzling my hair aside, and pressing a gentle kiss to my cheek. Then he gathered me to him and kissed me, slowly and deeply, with a hunger I could not deny. "You taste so sweet," he murmured against my mouth, and swept his tongue across my lips. And I returned his kiss with equal fervor, pressing close to him. I raised my hand and buried it in his hair, his soft curls sifting through my fingers, sending shards of sensation to stoke the heat I felt to a gentle burning.

* * * *

That night as I lay sleeping, I was awakened by a soft glow of light near my bed. *It's her again,* I thought, not wanting to open my eyes to confirm it. I could hear the rustle of her gown as she moved nearer to my bed, her soft footsteps on the floor. But it was not the familiar scent of lavender that filled the air, but jasmine.

I opened my eyes a slit, just to peek, and my eyes flew open in startlement. For this was not my usual nighttime guest, but another. It was the woman from the portrait in the gallery. She was dressed in pink brocade, her long blonde hair caught in a golden fillet over her ears, as she bent over me and smiled.

And then she vanished.

CHAPTER SIXTY

The weather was dark and gloomy, threatening rain, as we said our good-byes to Peter's family and drove away in Peter's car. They had been so kind and friendly to me, I would miss them, and felt a little sorry to be leaving so soon. I sighed, and leaned against Peter's arm. He stroked my hand.

"Did you enjoy yourself?" he asked.

"Yes, your family is wonderful. Hayvenhurst is beautiful." I looked up at him hesitantly. "Has anyone ever seen any ghosts there?" I asked cautiously.

"Ghosts?" he laughed. "Doesn't every old house have a ghost or two?" He glanced down at my expression. "Why do you ask? Did you see one?"

I hesitated again and looked down at my hands. "Well, yes, as a matter of fact, I did. The lady in the portrait. Your great-great-great-great-great grandmother."

He said nothing for a moment, just looked out ahead at the road. I wondered if I had blundered by speaking.

"I've seen her, too," he said finally, very quietly, almost a whisper. "At night mostly, she's awakened me. I've also seen her in other places, in the house, around the grounds. When I was a child, I thought that everyone saw her. But when I was old enough to speak of her, I soon learned differently. I was told that it was my imagination, or that I was dreaming. She never speaks, she only smiles, and then she disappears." He cast me a look of understanding, and smiled.

I felt a kindred spirit, and my mood lifted. Down the twisting road we went, without a word. I was happy in the silence. A great ridge of dark clouds stretched out before us, and the air was cold and clean. I watched the countryside fly by with a feeling of exhilaration, and shut my eyes to make the experience more lasting. When I opened them, we were by a bend in the road, and a large billboard sign loomed ahead of us. As we got closer, my attention was caught by the word RAVANA written upon it in large, bold letters. My heart lurched.

Ravana. Wasn't that the place that my ghost, the Lady Margaret Ruthven, had spoken of to me so often? Another sign. Bed and Breakfast. Tours. Ghosts. And another. Tour the Castle Home of Laird and Lady Ruthven.

My mouth went dry and my heart pounded against my ribs so hard that I could barely breathe. I glanced around me, and the countryside seemed eerily familiar. Yet I knew that I had never been here before. Emotions that I did not understand began to overwhelm me.

The black towers of Ravana loomed ahead of us in the distance, and I felt something stir deep within me. A sadness began to envelope me...and a sense of destiny, of fate, drew me foreword, toward it.

"Jennifer, what is it? Is something wrong?" Peter asked. "You have an odd look on your face. Are you feeling all right?"

"I-I don't know...there's something here..." *I knew without a doubt that there was something here...and I had to find out what it was.* "Stop," I said, as we approached the entrance road to the castle. "I want to see this place."

"What?" Peter asked, confused by my behavior. "Why?" he asked, taking his eyes from the road for a moment to glance my way.

"Please...do it," I pleaded.

It must have been my tone of voice that made him sigh, and turn the car into the road leading to the castle.

The field stretched on for miles it seemed, climbing a gentle slope of land. And there at the top, the massive bulk rose dark and brooding on the horizon, a pillar of stone like a dagger thrust deep into the heart of the earth. It's base was formidable, yet the towers became oddly graceful as they rose and tapered. The stone of which it had been made was not black, as it looked from afar, but soot-colored. Narrow slitted windows marched about them in a rising spiral. The sky arched above was grey, and filled with dark clouds. They flowed above and around the towers in an endless stream.

I could hear the ocean, and see the vine covered walls of the castle. Peter parked the car, and we walked together toward the entrance. Something akin to anticipation sang in my blood, sharp and tantalizing. Peter opened the door and I could see that the lobby was luxuriously decorated. Plaster reliefs adorned the stone walls, and a hammer-beamed ceiling provided an incredible backdrop to the ancient wooden-wheel chandelier, the centerpiece of the room. It must have been thirty feet from floor to ceiling. Stone steps, set into the thickness of the wall, graced the north side of the Great Hall.

As I stepped inside the vestibule, a coldness suddenly came around me. I gasped as I felt a hand sift through my hair.

"Moira!" I heard a voice whisper. "I ken ye'd come back!"

"What was that?" I choked.

"What?" Peter asked.

"A coldness, a whisper…"

He was looking at me strangely.

"You felt nothing? Heard nothing?"

He tilted his head to one side, listening, and then shook his head. "No." He took my elbow and gently led me toward the register desk. "Jennifer, are you sure you're feeling all right?" he asked me softly.

I wasn't sure. I was full of strange, conflicting, bewildering feelings. And besides, it was cold in here. I shivered, and wrapped my arms about me.

Peter was looking above the register desk at the times posted for the tours. He glanced at his watch. "Looks like we've missed today's tours. The next one scheduled is tomorrow morning."

My heart sank. I looked around the Great Hall disappointedly. There was something about this place that was curiously familiar. A niggling sense of recognition. And the name whispered to me as I entered: *Moira*. That name had touched a chord deep inside me, in some long forgotten, long buried memory. I had felt something stir within me, and it held me in thrall.

Peter touched my hand. "Jen? Did you hear me?"

"Yes," I answered, nodding. "I heard you."

"Would you like to stay the night?"

My spirits rose. "Oh, could we?"

"Aye," he said with a smile. "We can."

He turned back to the reception desk and booked us a room. Then a porter went with us to retrieve our luggage.

We followed the porter across the Great Hall and up the stone steps, to the second floor. There was no banister, only a velvet rope, and we hugged the wall on our way up. The porter led us down the corridor and stopped in front of one of the heavy oaken doors. He unlocked it, then flung the door open wide.

We stepped inside. I turned slowly, glazing about the chamber in awe. Once again, a feeling of déjà vu enveloped me. I had been here before, stood gazing about this room in this very manner before.

The room was beautiful, spacious and luxurious, with high ceilings, supported by heavy wooden beams. The walls were hung with dark rose wallpaper, and a huge four poster bed stood against the wall, hung with rose and yellow chintz. A little couch of yellow and pale blue sat at the foot of the bed on a rose-colored carpet. The huge fireplace that stood in the corner of the room was made entirely of rock, from floor to ceiling. A large portion of firewood and kindling had been placed nearby. A length of oaken beam was fastened to the rock above the hearth to serve as a mantle, and a ledge of sorts jutted out a couple of feet from the floor, to make a place to sit and enjoy the fire. To the left was a small sitting room, decorated in shades of rose and pale blue.

"Will that be all?" the porter asked, setting our luggage in the closet.

"Yes," Peter answered, reaching into his pocket for a tip. "Thank you." He handed the money to the porter, and received the key to the room.

"If there's anything else I can do for you, my name is Arthur. The loo is through that door." He nodded toward a door through the sitting room, then left.

Peter looked back at me as I stood, staring at the fireplace. I shuddered visibly, chaffing my hands up and down my arms.

"What is it?" he asked, walking up behind me and putting is arms around my thickened waist. "You're acting very strangely."

"I don't know," I answered truthfully. I did not understand what was happening to me. "There's…something…here…"

"Yes, you've already said that. But what is it?"

"I don't know…I don't know…" I leaned my head back against his shoulder.

"I hope you don't mind that I only booked one room. It was the only one available."

"I'll get over it," I smiled. Still shivering, I said, "It's cold in here."

He wrapped his arms about me tightly, burying his face in the hair at my temple. *What is happening to me?* I asked myself again.

Two casement windows recessed into the wall, fitted with diamond shaped panes caught my eye. Suddenly I had to see what was below. I had a vague inkling of what I would find there, but I had to be sure. I took a deep breath, stepped away from Peter, and went to stand by the window. There it was, changed very little from what I saw in my mind's eye: the courtyard, the stables, the gardens, and…the family burial grounds. I felt a connection to this place, but I did not know what the connection was. I only knew that the images I was seeing, the emotions I was feeling, represented something I needed to understand. It was almost as if these things had a mind of their own. It seemed like a puzzle with pieces that didn't fit together. "Let's take a walk," I said.

* * * *

As we walked through the gardens and around the sprawling castle grounds, the sensation of recognition grew. Fragments of memories began to show themselves in fleeting images and flashes. Little lights of awareness appeared in my mind, teasing me with the tip of a memory that disappeared the minute I began to see it clearly, eluding my recognition and understanding, zipping out of my mind with lightning speed.

I became very aware of my own breathing, the crisp breezes on my face, and the sun's pale grey light falling upon everything, filtering through the leaves, casting a silver glow. I suddenly understood that I was standing on the edge of a great mystery, and I felt a shudder--half terror and half wonder--work right through me.

It's all here. Everything. Everything is still here, I thought. *But how do I know that?*

Head down, I hastened across the courtyard, toward the cemetery. Ornate gate pillars framed the ivied walls. And as I entered through the lynchgate, I could hear the ring of laughter, and the tears of generations past. A chill roamed my spine, not entirely caused by the wind. *This is the place,* I thought. *Oh, yes, this is it.* Hallowed, consecrated, the churchyard was more than a burial ground for those whose lives had been played out in this place. The memorials spoke of the lives and relationships of those who rested beneath the springy turf. They talked of wealth and love and status. They passed to future generations the knowledge of family history, and local disasters, of savage child mortality and of the triumph of long lives well spent. They not only marked the place of burial, but also told the secrets of the centuries. Weathered by time, the old memorials whispered to us of people long gone, of their places in this castle, of their lives and deaths. My eyes wandered across the stones, and I read their names at random: Mary Catherine MacCraigh, Beloved Wife... Rees W. MacCraigh... Matthew Jacob MacCraigh... Rabbie Kenneth MacCallum...*MacCallum? Hmm,* I mused, and continued on. Annie MacNabb, beloved wife of Gwyllyn Andrew Michael MacNabb, 1566-1620... Kenneth William Ruthven, infant son of Lord and Lady Ruthven, 1566... Lady Margaret Isobel Ruthven, 1548-1566, wife of Kenneth William Ruthven, Laird of Ravana, 1541-1566... Moira Elizabeth Buchanan, 1546-1600. *Moira.* The same name I had heard whispered to me as I had entered the castle. A chill swept over me to the very marrow of my bones, and strange ideas teased my brain. I gave a backward glance at Peter, standing patiently behind me, his coat collar hunched up around his ears. He looked cold. His nose and cheeks were pink. But it was reassuring to see him there. I smiled at him and turned back toward the gravestones.

For those who care to look beyond the bounds of Christianity, the churchyard may even whisper of paganism that still finds a place within these holy grounds. Emotions, feelings I did not understand, began to overtake me. A deep love…an overwhelming grief…

And something else. I held a brief vision in my mind of a woman, dressed in white. She held a single rose in her hand. She walked across the yard to a single stone, and bent to place the rose on the ground before it. Then it was gone.

I looked up, toward the north end of the kirkyard… the north side of the churchyard, seen as the domain of the devil, fit only for the burial of the unbaptized, suicides and criminals… a savage juxtaposition of the innocent and the guilty. There a solitary stone stood, partly concealed in the waving grass. I made my way over to it, hesitating once before reaching it. It was a simple stone, with letters carved on it, but they were so eroded that I couldn't make them out. I knelt beside the marker and closed my eyes. I let my fingers trace each letter, like a blind man reading Braille. Each letter formed in the darkness behind my lids until they made the words. I read them aloud: "Richard Peter James Buchanan. Beloved Husband of Moira, father of Anne."

"That's odd," Peter mused.

Yes, I thought, *very strange indeed…*

My gaze wandered back to the gravestone. There, at the base of it, amidst the dull greys and dead browns of a tangle of dead grass, a tiny, red rose trembled forlornly in the breeze. The bush that bore it was small and weak, little more than a short vine with a leaf or two itself. Yet it bore a single blossom that brought its beauty into our midst. I reached down and touched the delicate petals, and for a moment held a vision of a handsome young man with curling brown hair and piercing blue-grey eyes. He leaned down and pulled a red rose from behind his back, a smile on his lips. And I heard a voice say, "A rose for you, a leannan."

Then, as suddenly as it had come, it was gone, dissipated in the chill breeze that swept the kirkyard. I couldn't quite capture the essence of the memory, but it seemed perfectly real to me. It was as if my memory of that moment was like a photograph. I could remember what the day was like--but the picture was flat and powerless. A long wavering sigh slipped from me. My heart felt weighted with lead.

Then Peter leaned down and placed a hand on my arm. "Come away," he said softly, gently taking my arm and helping me to my feet. He put one arm around my shoulders, drawing me against him as if to protect me from the chilly wind. I looked into his eyes, and suddenly a dawning brightness lifted the gloom that held my heart.

The day was ending. Seabirds were swinging low in the sky and a bitter breeze blew. Few of us feel entirely comfortable in this domain of the dead once darkness has fallen. I tucked myself close against Peter's sheltering body.

"Your hands are like small, cold fish," he said. "Let's get indoors as soon as possible."

We stopped in the gift shop on the way back to our room. Peter played with the pens and plastic change purses while I looked through the rack of postcards. He laughed out loud and showed me a tiny torchlight with "Ravana" stamped on it.

"You'll be needing this for your investigation of the Hall of Haunts later," he told me.
I wandered over to the books about Ravana displayed against the far wall of the crowded little shop, and flipped through them. One in particular called out to me, "The History of Ravana". It had many photographs of ancient portraits, and a long chapter on the 16th century, and Lord and Lady Ruthven.

I also looked at the racks of tote bags with silk-screened photos of Ravana stamped on them. I bought the tote bag, the book, and tickets for the first tour the next morning.

We went into the corridor and turned toward the stair. There, on our right, The Hall of Haunts beckoned.

"Let's see it now," I suggested and Peter nodded his agreement.

"Here, I got this for you." He pulled a small bag from his coat pocket, reached his hand inside and came up with the torchlight.

I laughed. "When did you buy this?"

"While you were browsing through the books."

I took it from him, switched it on, and together we walked through the doors. The room was dimly lit. Several glass protected cases were placed at intervals in the room, some against the walls. Track lights shone directly on the contents of the cases, and the many photographs and portraits upon the walls. As my eyes adjusted to the semi-darkness, I could see that the room was hung with red wallpaper, embossed with velvet designs.

We strolled by the cases, reading the dates and information of the history of the castle, and the people who had lived here throughout the centuries.

There were alcoves on either side of the room with a sign above the entrance. One read Tuning Into The Departed, the other Haunted Photographs. We entered the alcove on the left.

Electronic Voice Phenomenon (EVP) read the title on the first case. The case contained many audio gadgets, some old fashioned and some very modern. A voice sounded over our heads, electronically tripped by our movement.

"Messages from other dimensions cannot be heard by the naked ear. Taped messages from the spirit world have been recorded with these instruments. Ghosts respond to familiar activities, historically significant dates, music or songs, images and conversations that they can identify with tend to draw them out, and they try to interact with the living. They want to be a part of it."

Ghostly voices whispered and crackled from overhead. An eerie voice sounded in the distance, as if from the next room. Gooseflesh crept up my arms and made the hair on the back of my neck rise. I looked over at Peter. He pulled a face at me, and I laughed.

We moved on to the next alcove. The same narrative voice began his informative recital.

"Sometimes film seems to capture unusual phenomenon in the form of ghostly images, faint outlines, mists, vapors and orbs. Souls leave behind tremendous amounts of energy that seem to linger in a place of emotionally significant events, as historical imprints in time. Past and present seem to merge. Perhaps these lonely spirits wish us to see them. The photographs on display here were all taken at

Ravana, and have been analyzed by experts and proven to be authentic pieces of evidence of the supernatural. Browse through them at your leisure, and draw your own conclusions."

The voice crackled and was quiet as we walked along and examined the pictures in the glass protected cases.

There was one photograph of a table with a lamp upon it, probably taken in the dining area of Ravana. A ghostly cloud floated above the lamp in no particular shape. There was another spirit photograph of three mediums, taken in 1872, in one of the guest bedrooms. A smoky white blur drifted above their heads, purportedly a spirit caught on film. In 1940, there was a group photo of employees gathered in the Great Hall, and the ghostly image of a woman dressed in medieval clothing appeared with them. Another picture was of a man, taken recently, partially obscured by a light fogging. And another, taken in the library, I guessed, which revealed the vague figure of a man sitting in a chair. But it was the last photograph that made my heart lurch, and took my breath away.

It was the picture of a young woman dressed in white, kneeling beside a single gravestone in the kirkyard. And in her hand, she held a single red rose. I quickly read the caption beneath it.

"Two tourists snapping random photos in the kirkyard shot a picture of a row of graves. A few days later when the film was developed, there was the image of a woman, a translucent figure kneeling in front of a grave, as though in mourning. They didn't remember seeing her there that day, and sent the picture and the negatives back to the Kodak lab where they had been processed. After serious analysis, they decided that the photographs had not been tampered with, nor were they double exposed.
This particular ghost has been reportedly seen by many guests at the castle. They have said that they saw her in the graveyard, and looked away. But when they looked back a few seconds later, she had vanished. She is always seen in the vicinity of the graves, although she has not been seen in recent years."

My throat was dry and I swallowed hard. *That woman is me. I know it. I feel it in my heart, in my soul, as surely as I am standing here*. I shook my head, as if to clear it. *But how can that be?* I could actually feel the agony of grief that woman felt as I gazed at the photograph, and I knew.

A shudder ran up my spine and I grabbed Peter's coat sleeve. "I'm tired. I believe I've seen enough. Let's go back to our room now."

* * * *

During the walk back to our room, I managed to convince myself that I was having delusions about the woman in the graveyard, and banished the bewildering thoughts from my mind. I slung my purse and packages onto the nearest chair, when we entered the door, and plopped down into the other chair with a weary sigh.

"Are you thirsty? Would you like me to call room service?"

I gave a quiet laugh. "Such attention! You'll turn my head for sure! Who knows what I might agree to if you keep this up?"

"Well, in that case…"

He got down on one knee in front of me and took my hand in his. "Will you--" he began, but I leaned forward and covered his mouth with my hand. I shook my head.

"Don't," I told him. I pressed my fingers tighter over his lips when I felt him try to speak. "Please."

I felt him press his lips together in silent resignation, and moved my hand away. Sighing, I leaned back, and smoothed my hand over the mound of my belly. It did feel good to get off my feet and rest my aching back. "A warm drink would be nice," I said.

He rose and went to the telephone at the bedside table and ordered our drinks. Then he went to the large rock fireplace, and began to pile the wood and kindling onto the grate. He reached for the matches on the mantle, and soon a lovely fire sent its crackling fingers of warmth and pleasant smoky odor throughout the room. He turned and snatched cushions from the settle beside the fireplace and tossed them aside.

"What are you doing?" I asked, then gave a little squeak of protest as he scooped me up in his arms and deposited me on the settle he had just cleared. He took two of the pillows and wedged them behind my back, then moved a low stool closer, and knelt to prop my

290

feet upon it. He took off my shoes and examined my ankles, lifting an eyebrow at me.

"They're a bit swollen, I see."

I glanced down at them. "Yes, but that's normal, isn't it?" I had heard of it happening, quite often as a matter of fact.

"Some swelling is usual. But staying on your feet won't help matters any."

Just then there was a knock at the door. Our drinks had arrived. Peter rose to get the door, then was back a moment later. He handed me a cup of steaming hot cocoa, then made a sweeping bow. "What else shall I fetch for you, m'lady?" he asked, his wide smile infectious.

Laughter bubbled through me, along with a tide of warmth for him. "I'm fine," I told him, patting the cushion beside me. "Especially since I can see you plan to cater to me. Do you want to make me helpless?"

Peter sat down beside me, and put his arm around me, his eyes bright with amusement. "I only want to pamper you, my sweet." Then he leaned back against the cushions with a satisfied sigh, and took a sip of his cocoa.

* * * *

That night after I dressed for bed, I came out of the bathroom and glanced furtively at the bed, then at Peter, who knelt at the fireplace. His movements slow and measured, he picked up the poker, gave the fire a last stir, then laid the poker back on the hearth. He turned back to me with a sigh and stood up. He was dressed for bed, in grey sweatpants and a t-shirt.

"What's bothering you?"

"It's just that I feel a little awkward sleeping together in the same bed."

But Peter shrugged it off. He took the throw pillows from the couches and bed and slung back the covers, making a central barricade with all the pillows. It reached from the head to the foot of the bed.

"Voila!" he said, and began tugging his t-shirt over his head. "Now be sure to stay on your side." His voice was muffled by his shirt and then his head emerged, with his blond curls sticking out in every direction.

I laughed and we got into bed, switching off the light, and snuggling down under the covers to sleep. The firelight cast flickering shadows upon the wall, and I closed my eyes with a sigh of contentment.

Sometime later I was awakened by a strange, soft glow. I slowly opened my eyes, and through the pale light, I could see a man bending over the bureau dresser, rummaging through the drawers, looking for something. I propped myself up on my elbows for a better look. He was tall, with curling dark hair that fell over his forehead. He was dressed in a green kilt, with a long-sleeved tunic-style shirt that laced at his neck, a green jerkin, and a green plaid draped over his shoulder. And I could see right through him! The flames danced brightly behind him, and the rock fireplace stood solidly, more solid than he.

As I gaped, open-mouthed, the ghost suddenly looked up at me and whispered, "Where is my brooch?" Then he faded away.

My heart pounded in my chest and I could barely breathe. I felt paralyzed for a moment, until I felt Peter reach for me over the pillows. His hand closed over mine, warm and reassuring.

"All right?" he drawled sleepily.

I blinked. The apparition was gone and everything was as it should be. The dresser drawers were closed, there was no disarray. "Yes," I smiled back at him, not wanting to tell him what I had just seen.

"Good," he answered, patting my hand and settling himself back against the pillows. He closed his eyes, and soon I could hear his soft, even breathing.

It was a long time before I closed my eyes again. The baby gave a kick beneath my ribs, its usual nighttime activity. I stared at the fire in the hearth, letting my mind wander where it would, and hoping the low, dancing flames might lull me once again into slumber. The warmth and comfort relaxed my body. My mind, however, refused to stop thinking about the ghost. My eyes began to dart suspiciously about the room, searching for this new apparition. I recognized him. He was the man in the vision I had seen in the kirkyard. The man with the rose behind his back. I wondered if he had anything to do with the other one, who had plagued me so often in my life. "Who are you?" I whispered into the darkness.

After a while, though, I was lulled by the warmth of the bed and the soft breathing beside me. I closed my eyes.

Just as I dozed off, I was awakened by the feeling of someone bending down next to the bed. I could feel the breath on my cheek, and the air beside me felt cold. I started awake, and my eyes focused on the man who had been ransacking our dresser. He was kneeling beside the bed, his face not more than twelve inches from mine, and this time he looked more solid than before. My blood ran cold, and I drew in a deep breath, fighting to quell the panic sweeping through me. I shivered, and the man smiled down at me, and put his finger to his lips, as if to say, "shhh!"

A scream froze in my throat. But his expression was kind, not threatening. Somehow, I knew that I did not need to fear him. But that did not stop the frantic beating of my heart.

"Where is my brooch, Moira?" he asked me once again. I swallowed with some difficulty, my pulse thudding in my ears. Something deep inside me stirred at his words. Anger? Resentment? A deep sadness…

" 'Tis Richard, Moira. Dinna ye ken me?" He was looking into my eyes, searching my face. My mouth and throat felt dry, as if stuffed with cotton. I tried to speak, but only a squeak emerged. The apparition smiled sadly, and raised his hand to stroke my hair. It felt as if a soft breeze stirred the strands. I couldn't move.

"Moira, mo puir cridhe. I dinna wish to frighten ye."

He stood then, and looked over at Peter, sleeping peacefully beside me. An odd expression lit his features. "Ye are happy with this man?" he asked me gravely. "He is good to ye, and treats ye well?"

I nodded, still unable to speak. Strange questions for a ghost to ask, I thought.

"Then why d'ye barricade yerself against him?"

"W-we aren't married." *Was I really having this conversation?*

A look of surprise crossed his features and his eyes inadvertently glanced over my pregnant belly.

"It's a long story," I added belatedly.

He nodded thoughtfully, then turned his eyes back to me. "Where is my brooch? I have waited a long time."

What was he talking about? What did all these ghosts want from me? A brooch? I certainly didn't have their silly brooch. I only had one brooch, the one my grandmother had given me. The one family heirloom I possessed, handed down from generation to generation to the eldest daughter on my father's side. "M-m-my grandmother's brooch?" I finally managed to croak. My breath puffed out in a white cloud in the frigid air around me.

"Aye," he smiled. "That would be the one."

I lifted a shaking hand and pointed through the door into the sitting room.

"It's-it's in my suitcase…but why?"

He merely smiled back at me and disappeared.

Later, I thought I heard the sound of footsteps, and then the bed began to shake. I awoke to see my ghost, standing at the foot of the bed. He held up the brooch and smiled. Then he turned toward the fireplace and touched one of the rocks that jutted out. The stone moved in his hand. He looked at me over his shoulder, as if to say, "Do this," and placed the brooch behind it. Then his image and light faded away, and the air grew warm again.

I lay quite still in the darkness, feeling the thunder of my heart boom slowly in my ears. The throb of it echoed in the pulse of my neck, soft and heavy, shimmering with each heartbeat. My breath seized tight within my chest, and the baby rolled inside me. Fear had turned me to a puddle of liquid. I closed my eyes, smoothing my hands over my child, and searched deep within myself for a drop of courage. I drew a breath in slowly, listening.

Once my heartbeat slowed and my breathing eased, I could hear the slow, measured breathing beside me. Peter's breath came in long, regular exhilarations. He hadn't wakened. I turned toward him, thankful for his presence. The quilt was off his shoulder, and the skin of his back lay smooth and bare, dark by contrast to the pale sheets. I saw the gooseflesh prickle up his neck, and emotion for him filled my heart, pushing the ghost from my thoughts. I could not leave him exposed to the chilly midnight air like that.

I summoned back my motor capacities, and rolled over onto my side, propping myself on one elbow. Reaching over the barricade of pillows, I gently pulled the quilt up around his ear. He stirred unconsciously, turning toward me, and murmuring something. I stroked his tumbled blond hair and he smiled faintly, half opening his eyelids as if dreaming. His hand groped, skimming the pillows, in search of a resting place. I seized it, and folded it in both my own hands, holding it against my cheek. His hand curled over mine, and I kissed one knuckle. His eyes dropped closed again, and he took a long sighing breath. His hand relaxed, and he fell back into a deep sleep.

"I love you," I whispered, filled with tenderness.

CHAPTER SIXTY-ONE

During the night, a gale blew up. Great, luminous clouds floated over the moon and tendrils of cold air somehow crept through the closed windows, and made the room chilly. I hadn't slept much. There must have been a dog on the grounds, for I had heard his long, mournful bays echoing throughout the night. As the dawn approached, it felt as though the grey mist touched my face with cool, damp fingers.

I got out of bed just after six o'clock and went quietly to sit by the window. There was a foggy dew upon the courtyard below. It looked like frost, and the trees were shrouded in a white mist. A seagull was poised high in the air, silent and alone, his wings spread wide. He swooped down low, beyond the castle walls, and disappeared from sight, toward the sea below.

Peter turned in bed, and stretched, his blond curls sticking up around his head. He rubbed his hand over his whisker shadowed face and yawned.

"Morning, Sunshine," I greeted.

"Morning, yourself. You're up early. Didn't you sleep well?"

"Not so good. You know, the usual ghosts and barking dogs," I told him matter-of-factly.

"Oh, aye, to be sure," he grinned.

"Apparently you can sleep through anything."

"Apparently so," he said, throwing back the covers and putting his feet over the side of the bed. "Brrr! It's cold in here. I'll start a fire."

He went directly to the hearth and set to work placing the wood on the grate, and striking the match to it. Warm flames sprang to life and he chaffed his hands, and held them up to the fire.

"Ah, that's better. I'm starved. How about you?"

"A little."

"Och, I see. Watching that girlish figure."

"Hrumph," I grunted, glancing down at my stomach. "Right, that's it. Watching it grow."

"Well, I'm off to the shower. We have a tour to see today, you ken." He turned toward the bathroom, and I leaned my head against the windowsill. The wind buffeted, and the courtyard below was alive with crazily swirling leaves. The dark, wind-whipped sea beyond looked chillingly cold. A sudden flurry of leaves blew up against the window with a plunk, startling me.

I turned my head back inside the room. It was cozy and bright in here, with the cheery fire. I could hear Peter's smooth baritone singing behind the closed bathroom door, warbling in a fair imitation of Creed. *Dear Peter! You make me feel so good, so happy and content. I love you. I want so desperately to share my life with you...but I don't see how we can ever be together.* My eyes filled with tears.

I sniffed and flung the tears away with the back of my hand. *I can't let him see me like this. I must get hold of myself.*

Distractedly, I got up and went sit by the fire. Running my eyes over the stones, I remembered the hiding place that Richard, the ghost, had shown me last night. The stonework certainly looked solid enough. I began to push at several of the stones to the far left of the hearth, as he had done, searching for the right one. But nothing happened.

I must have been dreaming after all...it's this place...I have ghosts on the brain...

But I continued to search anyway, my hand against the old stones. I couldn't give up now. I felt compelled. Pushing, pulling, tugging, and then with a final gesture of frustration, I hammered on it with both fists...and a stone moved. It jutted out a few inches father that the others. My heart pounded. Slowly, I reached down and took hold. The stone moved in my hand. I swallowed tightly. *Well, what am I going to do now?*

And then I remembered the brooch. I jumped up and ran into the sitting room to check my case for it. It was still there.

I heard the shower water turn off just then. I replaced the brooch in my case and returned to my place by the fire. After a few minutes, the door to the bathroom opened. Peter stood at the threshold with a big fluffy white towel wrapped around his trim waist, rubbing his hair dry.

"I'll just throw on my clothes. Be right out."

He closed the door to the sitting room, leaving me with the image of his near nakedness, the firelight dancing over his lean, muscular form. That memory alone sent heat flowing through my body. I felt increasingly affected by his masculine presence. It seemed to permeate every nook and cranny of this big room. Richard, the loose stone of the fireplace, and the brooch were forgotten.

I have no shame, I thought with a sigh. I smoothed a hand over my burgeoning belly. *I shouldn't be having such thoughts. I should be concentrating a little harder on what my interest in him might mean to his continued safety. I'd better get my feelings for him under control. And the sooner, the better.*

The door opened and he came into the room, dressed in dark blue trousers with a pale blue shirt, smelling of soap and after shave. The red-gold firelight glowed and danced in his hair, in a bedazzlement of light and color.

He smiled at me, as I sat by the fire, staring up at him. Then his expression changed to a mixture of concern and curiosity. "What's this?" he asked, and touched the loose stone.

"A hidey hole, I believe," I said excitedly. "Last night the gh-" I stopped. There was no use going into that story.

Peter cocked his head at me and frowned. "Go on."

"Um, I noticed it last night when I couldn't sleep."

He looked at me through his lashes in a way that made my heart beat a little faster. "I see," he said softly. He turned and took hold of the rock, twisting it in his hand. At last it came loose. There was a hollowed-out place in the area behind it, just big enough to hide a small package.

"Satisfied?" he asked me, as I stared at it in wonder. Then he replaced the stone, lightly pounding it into place with his fist. "Now hurry with your bath," he told me with a smile. "We've got a busy day ahead of us."

"Yes," I answered, aware only of the decidedly warm look he favored me with, and headed toward the bathroom.

* * * *

As I ran my bath, I tried to think how I should act towards Peter the rest of the day, now that I was determined not to let myself become any more attached to him. *Cool?* I wondered, taking my towel from the hot rail where Peter had placed it, and spreading it on the chair. *Polite?* I asked myself, dropping my sponge in the water. *Remote?* I stepped into the bath and lay back, letting the water run over my body, and gave a quiet snort of laughter. As if I could! I'd yet to act like a proper lady in his presence, at any rate.

When I went back into the sitting room and began to dress, I heard Peter call from behind the door.

"Hurry up, Jen. I'm famished. You must be, too. Are you dressed? Should I come in and help you?" I could hear the laughter in his voice.

It brought me back to reality, and the facing of the immediate future. I turned slowly toward the door, using the time to collect myself, to rid my expression of any trace of unsettling thoughts. "No. Thanks anyway," I said, as I finished dressing. "I'll be right out."

* * * *

The first tour of the day was called. We queued up behind the red velvet rope with a dozen other tourists at the entrance to the Great Hall. There was the low buzz of conversation as we waited for our tour guide. I was filled with a sense of anticipation as I looked around at the beautiful stone walls, with their tapestries and hanging armor, the carved chests and ancient wooden chandelier. Two impressive oriel windows stood on either side of the raised dais in front of the massive fireplace.

Suddenly a hush fell over the crowd as the tour guide approached. She was young, about twenty I guessed, with softly curling shoulder length blonde hair, and a misting of freckles across the bridge of her nose. She was dressed in a burgundy colored gown in the style of the late 16th century and she greeted us with a smile and tilt of her head, as she unhooked the velvet rope from the post that held it, and bid us step inside.

"Hello, my name is Rachel Tuttle, and I will be your tour guide this morning as we explore this ancient dwelling. These silent stones stand in mute witness to the passions and intrigues of the generations which they have sheltered, harboring the shades of the past. Along the corridors and battlements of this windswept castle, in the musty gloom and fog shrouded towers, old wrongs, evils and great longings seem not to die, but to cling like mist to the cold stones that saw their origins.

Many of you have probably come today, hoping to see ghosts. Legends of haunted houses are age-old. But are ghosts real, or are they merely human inventions conjured from the miasmic air and foreboding presence of certain dwellings? Some psychic researchers have suggested that ghosts do haunt houses, if only as nebulous after images of particularly strong feelings and portentous events, ghostly representation of some long past tragedy.

The people who lived here long ago are but a faded memory, but I can assure you that Ravana is touched by many ghosts. Their spirits float on the breeze, and wander down the garden paths. Phantom music is frequently heard. Sometimes, if you listen very carefully, you can hear the faint, echoing sound of a lute, playing a melody of love lost long ago. You may even catch a glimpse of something on the darker side while you are here. Many patrons of this castle have reported hearing chilling shrieks and devilish laughter, seeing glowing apparitions and hearing phantom footsteps. Are ghosts real, or just the product of a fertile imagination? You may judge for yourselves.

Our universe harbors many secrets, but one we may never explain is the kinship between these mysteries and the ghostly presences felt here. I have seen all kinds of things, and feel these ghosts to be a tangible sense of history.

Ghosts have an attachment for a particular place and return to it again and again. If they have left the earth in a traumatic fashion and never got to say good-bye to a loved one, or if they have met with an untimely or violent death, the trauma of that long-ago event is locked into the atmosphere, and can bring the spirits back, to replay the scene again and again. Some of you may experience a momentary sensitivity connected to that long forgotten tragic event.

Perhaps it is not surprising, therefore, that stories of highly charged emotions seem to permeate the lore of hauntings. Ghosts purportedly appear as fearsome harbingers of catastrophe, or as specters of those whose passions in life left them unquiet in death-- people with evil lusts or deep remorse, or a thirst for justice, or a need to play out endlessly the tragedy of thwarted love.

Unrequited love can cause a ghost to linger. When a ghost is known to haunt a specific place, it is thought that they went to their death with unfulfilled passions, and feel that as long as they stay in a certain place, there is hope that their passions will be fulfilled. Some part of life was cut short, left unsettled and unfulfilled. They roam restlessly, trying to get where they should have been. You may indeed encounter restless spirits here, tortured spirits, searching for someone or something, returning to find those they vowed to protect. You may feel the supernatural activity as you walk around, you may sense the spirits, sense the history, and the people who lived here, the tribulation and drama experienced within these walls. It seems that the ghosts are more active on dark and gloomy days, when the sun goes behind a cloud, or there are not as many guests as usual. Perhaps today you are in for a treat.

"Ravana is steeped in the fabric of history. Imagine, if you will, a rip, or tear, in the fabric of time. You may see something, but then it is as if a door closes, and it disappears. Do you feel an inexplicable cold draft? A cold pillar of air? Could it be a trap door to a ghostly plane? A portal into the twenty-first century?" She paused meaningfully, then smiled. "Follow me, and step into the past."

She led us into the center of the Hall, and we all gathered around her, under the great wooden chandelier. The atmosphere was hushed, as we strained to hear what she had to say.

"The early estates and titles of Ravana first belonged to the Clan Cameron, and passed to the first Ruthven, pronounced 'R-r-rriven', in marriage to a Cameron heiress. Sir Walter Ruthven was the first to use the name. Sir Walter's second son, Sir William, led thirty men to help Sir William Wallace at the siege of Perth in 1292.

A peerage was bestowed upon the first Lord Ruthven by King James III in 1487, when the nobles, led by the king's brother, and another Sir William Ruthven, led his clan to help put down the rebellion.

In 1566 Patrick, the third generation Lord Ruthven, took a leading part in the murder of David Riccio, the Italian secretary of Mary, Queen of Scots. He was forced to flee to England, where he died soon afterwards.

The forth Lord, William, found favor with young King James, son of Mary and Lord Darnley, and was created the Earl of Gowrie. However, the following year, he and the other Protestant earls, kidnapped the king, in an act referred to as the Raid of Ruthven, and held him prisoner for a year at Stirling Castle, while they ran the country. The king eventually escaped, beheaded the Earl of Gowrie and his co-conspirators, extinguished the peerage, and the name and coat of arms of Ruthven were abolished. In 1641 an Act was passed, making it lawful for the Ruthvens to assume the name again.

The nephew of Lord Patrick was the last laird to live here at Ravana. His name was Lord Kenneth Ruthven, and it is said that he also took part in the murder of Riccio. He went mad shortly afterwards, when his young wife and infant son died.

But we shall touch on this tragic story at the end of our tour. Come with me now, and see Ravana."

She led us up the stone steps and through the bedchambers of the laird and lady of the castle. Everything was eerily familiar to me, as we passed from room to room, and somehow, I always knew what I would see around the next corner. It was little changed, perhaps a touch of color here, or a new piece of furniture there, but for the most part, I simply knew. From the boldly carved white marble fireplace in Lady Ruthven's chambers, to the bright solar, I seemed to see it all, experience it, as if I had once lived within these very walls.

"There is a typical reported occurrence from many of our guests who stay overnight in the laird's bedchamber. One in particular took place towards the end of World War II, when the American soldiers were billeted at the castle. An officer was taking a bath one day, when the bathroom door suddenly opened, and a young woman with long black hair stepped inside. The officer told her to leave, but she stood there, staring at him. Unnerved, he got out of the tub and tried to push her out the door--but his hand passed right through her. The apparition vanished, and the officer ran naked and terrified down the stairs to report his experience.

Another couple, staying in the same room, saw flames licking a wall, but the fire disappeared while they watched.

In the Lady Ruthven's quarters, a little boy with a mop of dark hair and curious green eyes has been sighted. He sits at a table, open books in front of him, and gazes at our guests in friendly fashion.

Other visitors to the castle have often said that they hear a child crying in the night."

We went down the winding staircase single file from the servant's quarters and into the kitchen.

The room was enormous, and at each end stood a huge fireplace. A big, black cauldron hung inside one of them, suspended by a large hook. The wood was stacked beneath it, but no fire burned. The hearth remained cold and silent. A row of brick ovens was built into the wall beside the fireplace, and a long table ran down the center of the room. The wooden top was wiped clean, polished to a high sheen.

"Down through the centuries, the appearance of a woman we call Head Cook has been reported many times. She is thought to herald fires and other disasters. She was seen some years ago, during the last world war, by a mess cook for troops who were then quartered within the castle. He claimed that while stirring the soup he sensed that someone was watching him. Turning around, he saw the misty form of a woman who was dressed in a long brown frock and apron. No catastrophe ensued, although the mess cook was said to faint dead away."

The crowd tittered, then broke into laughter.

With her blue eyes twinkling, our guide led us through another door, and we stepped into the courtyard.

The air was full of pent up electricity, and there was rain behind the dull grey sky, but it did not fall. I could feel it, I could smell it, pent up there, behind the clouds. The wind lashed at us as it whipped around the courtyard from the open sea, forcing us all against the sheltering walls to hold ourselves upright. The thunder of the waves crashing against the rocky cliffs below made it nearly impossible to hear the guide speak, as we enter the kirkyard through the lynch gate. We stopped and huddle together for warmth.

"There are stories of an enormous shaggy black ghost dog with burning eyes, called the 'Moddey Dhu'. some say the dog is helpful and kind, others that he is a sign of the devil, and therefore a harbinger of death. The 'Black Dog' is one of the most common tales of Celtic folklore. Most accounts agree on the dog's general appearance. He is the size of a calf, with shaggy black fur, and either green or red eyes. However, they are undecided as to whether he is good or bad.

In some areas the dog guards' treasure, in others he will leap out and cause mischief. Others show themselves only to a person who will shortly die. Many locals keep clear of the castle at night, for fear of the 'Moddey Dhu', which is said to prowl the grounds after nightfall. Some people even claim to hear the ghost dog's mournful bays, echoing throughout the night."

A change in the howling of the wind caused me to flatten myself against the rough stone wall. Or was it the sudden thundering of my heart, as my breath caught in my chest. Was it the Moddey Dhu, then, I had heard howling throughout the night? Peter saw me shiver and put his arm around my shoulder, drawing me close into his warmth.

"Lord Kenneth Ruthven was said to be a bitter, cruel man, who mistreated everyone on his property. He was a man haunted by his own wickedness. It is said he was so mean, that when he died, the earth would not receive his body. When the funeral wagon entered the kirkyard, the wheels suddenly locked. The horses pulled with all their might, but the wagon wouldn't budge. They strained against a powerful, yet invisible force. Then, for a moment, the earth seemed to stand still. A quiet, deadly silence filled the air. Then suddenly the ground began to rumble, as if it might explode. All eyes were riveted to the wagon.

No one could explain what erupted from the casket that day. Some said it was the black hound from hell. In Scottish folklore, a person cannot be put into the ground until an animal has taken his sins. The laird's soul was so black, they had to be taken by a black hound. At night, his plaintive howl can be heard resounding throughout the valley."

She turned, and we all followed her up the path, and into the chapel. The walls were bare, with no ornamentation. The pews were carved from oak, and highly polished. They looked as if they were brand new.

"This is the chapel where the people of the castle came to worship. In the late sixteenth century…."

A slow buzzing began to fill my ears, and suddenly I felt sick to my stomach. I could see the guide, the other people, and Peter beside me, but the buzzing rose and rose, filling my ears and drowning out all other sound, until there was nothing else. A misty greyness began to cloud my sight, and the walls seemed to throb faintly. My heartbeat seemed to slow, and take on the cadence of the pulsating walls. To my dismay, I felt as if I might faint. I grabbed onto Peter's arm to steady myself.

What's happening to me? I thought frantically.

"Are you all right?" Peter's voice came to me, as if from a distance, filled with concern.

No! I wanted to say. This faint-headed feeling was most definitely not all right. But I could not speak. I was mesmerized by something in the shadows in the front of the church. *Was no one else aware of it?* Candle light guttered, and I could see people…two women, and several men…soldiers, yes, they were soldiers, all milling about the front. But something was wrong. A sense of melancholy, of grief, filled the chapel, filled my heart, engulfed me, until I thought that the feeling would tear me apart. And it drew me, drew me nearer, until I could see the prone figures the others gathered around so solemnly. The soft sounds of muffled sobbing floated in the air.

There was a man. The very man that I had seen last night in my room. His eyes were closed, and his face was very pale. It looked almost white, framed as it was by his dark, curling hair. And I could see that he was dead. And the woman they laid beside him, her white nightgown torn and dirty, her long auburn hair tangled about her face and shoulders...*was she my ghost? The Lady Margaret Ruthven, who came to me in my dreams? ...She also was pale...pale as death...and upon her breast, pinned to what was left of the flimsy fabric of her night rail...was my brooch!*

The vision lingered a moment longer, and then...it simply ... vanished...

"Jennifer!" I heard Peter declare. "You're white as a ghost! Are you all right?"

"I-I think so...I'm all right...I think..."

I was still standing in the same place; the guide was still talking... and Peter was looking at me as if I had just grown another head.

What in the world had just happened?

I put my hand to my temple.

"Come on," Peter said, taking my other hand. "I'm getting you out of this place--"

"No!" I whispered urgently.

He looked back at me, confusion and concern in his eyes.

"Please," I said.

"I don't understand--"

"Shhh!" several of the other tourists hissed in our direction. Peter looked up at them and blinked. I patted his hand.

"It's all right," I whispered more quietly. "I'm all right. Please, let's finished the tour."

He sighed down at me, then nodded reluctantly.

The guide finished her recital of the history of the chapel and we followed her once again through the courtyard and back into the Great Hall.

"There is a feeling of great sorrow in this room, a very sad and lonely feeling. Mayhem is said to echo still in ghostly form. It is rumored that Lord Kenneth, in his madness, killed his steward in this very room, a bloody piece of history trapped in time. You can feel the tremendous amounts of energy released in this room, like the ebb and flow of the tide. It lingers in this place, then dissipates around you. Emotional traces left over on the fabric of time, memories floating, energy remaining, seeking justice, retribution, revenge, to complete some task, or simply to interact with the living. There is a discernable tragedy behind a haunting presence. It is almost as if they do not want to move on. Ghosts can be linked to their last thoughts as they died. If they wanted to do something, their spirit will attempt to complete the task. Their last wish at the moment of transition is said to be extremely powerful. Reports of unexplained occurrences haven't stopped since the end of the sixteenth century, when the laird of Ravana fell to his death from the ramparts, trying to escape a fire which destroyed part of the upper stories.

After his death, King James gave over the castle to one of his court favorites, who rebuilt and maintained it. He kept on the same household, but did not spend a lot of time here. Apparently, he preferred court life to country life.

There is a story of the last Ruthven laird, although the details are lost in time. From what we can gather, Lord Kenneth Ruthven's steward fell in love with the intended Lady Ruthven when he went to settle the final arrangements of the dowry before the marriage. It is certain that they fell in love almost immediately. Ruthven was known to be a cruel man, and would not allow the lady to bring her maid with her to Ravana. The steward married the maid so the women would not be separated, vowing to protect them both. Unfortunately, it proved to be a disastrous liaison. It is believed that Lord Ruthven killed his steward in this very room, and in her grief, the lady ran out into the stormy night, saddled her horse, and drove the horse at such a wild pace in the pouring rain, that he lost his footing on the cliffs, and they tumbled over the edge together, to meet their deaths on the rocks below.

It is said there was a tremendous passion in her, and that she passed on with that passion yet unfulfilled. Perhaps memories of what could have been keep her here. Accidents have been reported along the stretch of road, where the Lady Ruthven is said to have ridden her horse on that fateful night. People have run off the road trying to avoid a woman dressed in a long white flowing gown, riding her horse hell bent for fury. Some people have actually seen the horse and rider careen over the cliffs. Others only hear the haunting screams echoing over the cliffs. Some have claimed to see her gore-dappled ghost, walking the beach area below Ravana. Perhaps in expiation, perhaps searching for her lost love."

By now our little group of tourists had followed our guide nearly to the top of the stone stair. As she paused for breath, I turned toward Peter, who stood behind me on the narrow stone steps.

And my blood ran cold.

For I could see Jack making his way across the Great Hall, toward the stairs. He paused suddenly, and glanced up. His face, pale and grim, became positively glacial when he spotted me. He pushed past the other tourists and climbed the stair toward us silently, his stride powerful and smooth. My heart began to race, and a chill slithered down my spine. I drew a deep breath, and fought to quell the panic sweeping through me. But my breath seized tight within my chest, and the baby shifted restlessly within me. I stepped back and braced my hands against the wall for support. Peter saw the change in my expression and glanced behind him, but not in time to brace himself. With the death lunge of a predator, Jack's hand shot out and shoved Peter hard in the middle of his chest. He stumbled back and lost his balance.

"Peter! No!" I screamed, as he began to fall straight backwards, over the edge of the stone step, taking the velvet rope and post with him. His arms churned the empty air, and a collective gasp went through the crowd of tourists. Someone screamed.

The last thing I saw was the triumphant glitter in Jack's eyes. I closed my own eyes tightly as I heard the clank! ping! of the metal post and caps, as the end of the velvet rope hit the floor almost thirty feet below. Choking back a sob I opened my eyes, and peered over the edge of the step. But Peter was not lying on the stone flags below. His fall had stopped in midair. He hovered at an impossible angle, the toes of his shoes barely touching the stone step. And then, it was as if he was shoved back onto his feet, and planted safely back on the step.

Unbelieving, I threw my arms around his neck, feeling his solid body against my own, and I sobbed with relief. Peter clung to me as tightly as I held him, and I felt a shiver run through him as he buried his face in my hair.

A spiral of twinkling pinpoints of light appeared behind Peter, slowly taking the form of a man. The same man who was in our room last night, the man in my vision in the chapel, the man buried in the north side of the kirkyard. He seemed to float in the air behind Peter, his image shimmering, like heat waves rising from a hot surface. He glared down at Jack, a scowl upon his handsome features. Jack stepped back fearfully.

I swallowed hard, my sobs quieted, the whole group of tourists stared, entranced in silent awe.

Cruel laughter suddenly began to echo throughout the Hall, reverberating off the walls around us. The image disappeared, and there was the sound of many footsteps running, voices shouting, swords clashing...and suddenly an intense fear enveloped, and overwhelmed me.

I began to sense a menacing presence, emanating from below. It grew in intensity, a dark, faceless horror, evil, and vile, waiting and hating, there with us, in the Hall.

It was hot in here. Much too hot. All these people, breathing the same air, so many people. There was no air left in this place, and everyone pressed close...It was hot, so very hot. The guide was calling for everyone to remain calm.

Jack turned and tried to make his way down the stairs, but the others tourists stopped him. I did not look after him. I looked at the floor. The heat was coming up at me from the floor, rising in slow waves. It felt ominously claustrophobic. The heat reached my hands, wet and slippery, it touched my neck, my chin, my face. My pulse thundered in my ears, and black spots danced before my eyes, flickering, stabbing the hazy air.

"I feel so strange," I murmured, oppressed by the unnatural stillness, and dreamlike sensations that assailed me. The walls, which seemed so close a moment ago, were suddenly farther away than I thought, and all the time, the steps were coming up to meet me.

I felt a swirling, a pulling, and out of the queer mists around me, the voice of Mary, my sister by marriage, strong and clear. "Hush, sister, there is nothing we can do."

And a familiar scene began to play itself out once again.

Then I lost consciousness.

* * * *

Peter felt Jenny slump against him, until his arms were the only thing holding her upright. He realized that she had fainted. Gently, he eased her down, and sat down on the step, laying her across his lap. He felt for her pulse, her breathing. Slow, shallow, but steady.

Suddenly there was a cold rush, and a column of frigid air enveloped him. His breath puffed out in little white clouds in front of him, and the scent of roses lingered in the air. It felt as if a gentle hand touched his face. His breath caught in his throat, and his head came up, as the phantom fingers drifted up his cheek. He glanced up and caught sight of two women standing together in the minstrel's gallery, their arms clinging to one another in desperation, their frightened eyes riveted to the scene below.

Down in the center of the Hall, there was shouting, and the clashing of swords sounded. Two men were fighting with broadswords, surrounded by shouting soldiers. One of the men, the one who had appeared behind Peter on the stair, spoke in low, soothing tones, while the other rained down blow after blow upon him, with all his might.

Suddenly Richard's sword went flying from his hands, and the other man stepped in for the kill. Light glinted off the steel of his blade as it arced down in one graceful movement, then plunged savagely into his rival.

Both men staggered back, and the scene slowly faded from sight.

The crowd stirred and mumbled, in a low, hushed buzz. And from off to his right, Peter heard a choking sound. He looked over his shoulder and saw Jack, white faced and desperate, eyes wide, as if he continued to watch the scene below unfold before him. Sweat beaded on his forehead, and he raked both hands through his hair, leaving it sticking up around his head in every direction. Peter reached out a hand to him.

"Jack," he said quietly, all the while thinking, *I must try to calm him before he hurts himself.*

But Jack paid no attention to him, as if he hadn't heard.

Jenny stirred in Peter's arms and sighed. His eyes came back to rest on her face.

* * * *

My eyelids fluttered open, and the blur I saw before me slowly took on the shape of Peter's dear face.

"Jennifer, are you all right?" he asked me softly.

But I could not answer him because I saw Jack, wild-eyed and frantic. I heard the scraping of his shoes against the side of the stone steps, and heard his frightened cry as he tumbled over the edge.

I heard the sickening thud as his body hit the stone flagged floor below. There was a stricken expression on Peter's face, as he gathered me into his arms and pressed his face into my hair.

I could hear our tour guide's voice, calling for everyone to remain where they were, to remain calm. Security guards came running from every direction.

Peter helped me to sit up straight, and I leaned back against the cool stone wall and closed my eyes, smoothing my hands over my squirming child.

Eventually, my heartbeat slowed to its normal rhythm, and my breathing eased. I raised my head up, and looked into Peter's silver-blue eyes. We looked at each other for a long moment.

A voice called from down below, asking if there was a doctor present. Without taking his eyes from mine, Peter answered, "I am a doctor." Reluctantly, he stood.

"I'm going down there with you."

"No, you're not. I don't think you're up to it right now."

"I am." I attempted, with some difficulty, to get to my feet. Peter leaned down and took my arm, helping me to stand. "I think it's a bad idea."

I set my features in a stubborn expression. He merely sighed and took my hand, leading me silently down the steps. The others tourists moved aside quietly as we passed.

Several security guards were crowded around Jack's prone body. Peter reached down and put his hand to Jack's neck. He shook his head. I went down on my knees beside him, and took Jack's hand in mine. It lay flaccid and pale in my own.

When people suffer a great shock, I don't think they feel it at first. I knelt there by Peter's side, and I was aware of no feeling at all, no pain and no fear. There was no horror in my heart. It was as though I was living the life of some other person. It was unlike anything I had ever known. I was surprised by my lack of emotion, and this strange, cold absence of distress. *Little by little the feeling will come back to me,* I told myself. *Little by little I will understand what has just happened, and what it all means, like the pieces of a jigsaw puzzle all tumbling into place. At this moment, I am nothing. I have no heart, no thoughts, no feeling. I am just a wooden thing.* I shut my eyes.

Peter put his arm around me and pulled me very close. "I am sorry," he whispered.

I willed my face into an emotionless mask as I stared at the remains of the man who had once been my husband. The baby chose that moment to kick hard beneath my ribs, a vigorous sign of life in this chamber of death. *May God have mercy on us all,* I thought, placing a soothing hand over my belly. The child stirred once more. Life and death. My hand cupped my stomach protectively.

I struggled up off my knees and tried to get up, but my legs were made of rubber, and would not hold me. Peter's hands came round me then, and took my elbows, bearing my weight, helping me to stand.

CHAPTER SIXTY-TWO

I was sitting in a little bare room, like a waiting room. There was a desk in it. The policemen were there, bending over me, giving me a glass of water, and someone's hand was on my arm. Peter's hand. I sat quiet and still. The floor, the walls, the figures of Peter and the policemen stood solidly before me.

I sat hunched in my chair, deeply shocked, my eyes blank, my face withdrawn. *What had just happened?* The feeling was coming back to me, little by little, as I knew it would. My hands were no longer cold. They were clammy, warm. Realization flooded me then, and my heart jumped in quick, sudden panic. I felt a wave of color come into my face, my throat. My cheeks were burning hot. I remembered the Great Hall of Ravana, where Jack still lay, motionless and silent, all too vivid in my mind. Everything was over. Jack was dead. Peter and I were together now. Jack could not hurt us anymore. He could do no more to us now.

The officers told me there were a great many questions to be answered, even if, as seemed most likely, they said, the cause of death was accidental. The familiar nagging pain was strong beneath my heart. I sat quite still, my hands in my lap. I did not say anything. Peter did not look at me. I wondered if the presence of the policemen was the reason he was so cool, so distant. He was looking very pale, and his mouth was set.

I must have looked as ghastly as I felt, in that horrible, silent little room where they had taken me, for one of the policemen suggested Peter take me for some coffee in the small café by the gift shop.

"It's very sad. Such a shocking experience," he said gently. "Why don't you go? The sergeant could drop by, and bring you back in half an hour or so."

Peter nodded, and put his arm through mine, and helped me to get up. I did not say anything. I held his arm tightly. He walked with me to the door, and along the passage, and down the steps to the café by the gift shop. We did not speak.

At first, I thought the coffee would make me sick. I held the warm liquid in my mouth, determined to swallow it, but slowly. I couldn't be sick in front of Peter, in this nice clean café with its view of the garden. It must be a charming view in the summer, with more color and sunshine, when the water from the fountains sparkled, and the overhanging trees were green. But for now, the fountains reflected the slate grey of the sky. I went on stirring my coffee. My hands felt hot, damp. I heard the first crack of thunder in the air, and shivered violently. The jagged lightning split the sky. Another rumble in the distance. But no rain fell as yet. *And no more the tearful weakling*, I vowed. It was past the time for me to become the person I wanted to be.

I took another valiant swallow of coffee and said, "It's all right, Peter. I'm not going to disgrace you."

"How could you do that?"

At last he touched my hand. I felt his fingers cover my own, taking my hand in his, and holding it in his lap. "Have another cup of coffee," he said briefly. "We have time."

* * * *

Once more back in our room, Peter knelt to light the fire. I sat down on the sofa and leaned my head back, and closed my eyes. Now that we were alone again, and the strain was over, the sensation was one of almost unbearable relief.

The police had asked us not to leave the area for a day or two, until they had gathered any evidence they needed. We had called our jobs, our families and friends and told them.

Peter still did not speak. I opened my eyes as he stood. He began to pace the floor, his hands in his pockets. I watched him silently. Back and forth. Back and forth. At last he crossed over and threw open the windows. He stood there with his back to me, breathing in the cold air. For a long while he gazed out at the dark clouds in the evening sky. There was another burst of thunder. One spot of rain fell against the window pane. One spot. No more. I came up behind him and put my arms around him. I could see the sea beyond the castle walls, like a vast, black lake. Another drop of rain fell on the window, and another crack of thunder sounded. It was getting very dark. Rain began to patter against the windows.

Gently at first, then louder and faster, until it became a driving torrent, falling from a slate sky. We could not see beyond the courtyard; the falling rain came so thick and hard and fast. I heard it sputtering in the gutter pipes above the window, splashing against the stone walls. There was no more thunder. The air smelled clean and cold. We stood together, and said nothing, watching the rain.

At last, he spoke. "Can you tell me exactly what it is that happened here today?"

There was no sound but the steady falling of the rain. It fell without a break, steady, straight and monotonous. I went on standing there, my arms around him, my cheek resting against his back.

"I don't know."

He shrugged me loose, and swung round from the window. He pulled me close to him and searched my eyes. His face was anxious, strange. There was a line, thin as gossamer, between his brows. "I believe you do know well enough."

I stared at him, my heart beating strangely. My hands suddenly went cold. "Yes," I said slowly. "This place…it is familiar to me, although I know I've never been here before," I said. Then, after a moment's hesitation, I added, "Not in this life."

I glanced up at his face, and saw his lips tighten.

"At first, I was curious. Then I began to be afraid, as I began to remember things…and to feel emotions I didn't understand…like puzzle pieces that didn't quite fit together. I thought that my mind was playing tricks on me. That my imagination was working overtime. I felt like I was going crazy. But everything was so real and so vivid, I couldn't deny it."

I stopped suddenly, and reached for his hand, and laid it against my cheek. He did not say anything. He just went on standing there, looking at me. Waiting. Listening. It was very quiet. The only sounds were the patter of the rain, and the crackle of the fire. Then I heard the watch on Peter's wrist, ticking in my ear. The little normal sounds of everyday. I went on watching his face, watching his eyes.

I turned away from him then, and sat down on the sofa. I put my hand to my forehead. Peter came and knelt down on the floor in front of me. He was very still for a moment. Then he took my hand away from my face and looked into my eyes.

"I love you," he whispered. He kissed my face and my hands. "Tell me," he said, and I held his hands very tightly, like a child, hoping to gain confidence.

I sat there, my eyes wide and staring, looking in front of me, seeing nothing. And I went on holding his hands. Disjointed pictures flashed one by one in my mind. I felt memories teetering on the brink, between surfacing, and being swallowed into oblivion forever. It was like when a word is on the tip of your tongue, but you can't seem to spit it out. I shook my head. "I can't..."

"You can. You must. Relax. Let it flow to the surface."

I began to speak in short, jerky sentences. I told him the story of Moira, and of Meg, and of Richard and of Kenneth. And I held his hands very tightly between my own.

I paused for breath. Still he did not speak. My voice sunk low, so low that it was like a whisper. My hands had grown very cold again. I did not look at Peter. I could hear the rain pattering against the window, thin and light, and very fast. My voice was slow now, tired, without expression.

The jigsaw pieces came together piece by piece, as the past took shape before me. They were all fitting into place, those odd, strained shapes that I had tried so hard to piece together within my fumbling fingers, that had never fit before. Suddenly, the jigsaw pieces came tumbling, thick and fast upon me.

And finally, I told him of my dreams and visitations from the Lady Ruthven. I told him of my grandmother's brooch, and that somehow I felt that I must return it to the lost lovers.

I paused then, and waited. I stared in front of me. It seemed to me that it was no longer raining quite so hard. The fury was spent. The rain that fell now had a quieter, softer note. I could hear the sea as it broke against the rocks below Ravana. Then I looked at him, sitting quietly beside me on the floor.

"That's all. There's no more to tell. Except... I think that I saw Richard, here in this room last night."

He looked thoughtful. "I was nearly killed today," he said quietly, "when Jack pushed me from the steps in the Great Hall. I felt a hand on my back, between my shoulders. It caught me, kept me from falling. Then pushed me back up on the step. I believe your Richard saved my life."

I nodded. "Yes," I said, looking into his eyes. "He promised to protect me once, and now he has kept his promise, by protecting you."

I began to feel very tired. I was limp, exhausted. I looked toward the window. The rain had ceased at last. It was hushed and dark and still.

* * * *

The nightmare of the day turned into another nightmare that night, when I tried to sleep. Peter banked the fire, and we climbed into our divided bed. I tossed and turned, watching the firelight shadows flit across the walls in a macabre dance, and listened, as raindrops dripped from the eaves, and from the gutter above the window. The sounds were rhythmic, steady, and the pulse of my mind beat with it. I shut my eyes, and a hundred images came to me. Things seen, things known, things forgotten. They were jumbled together in a senseless pattern. The black, horn rimmed glasses of the judge, the hard, straight-backed chairs in the dining room at Hayvenhurst, the wide windows of our room at Ravana, the period dress that our guide had worn.

I saw Florence chasing butterflies as they flitted across the lawns, and Goldie, scratching her ear, as she lay in her bed by the fire. There was my mother in her salmon colored dress as she waved good-bye to us from the steps, and Peter's mother, asking if we would stay for tea. I could feel the cold comfort of the sheets against my skin, and the gritty dirt of Richard's grave. I could smell the rain, and the wet moss that grew on the castle wall. I fell into a strange, broken sleep, waking now and again to the reality of my room, and Peter, as he lay with his back to me. I moved, and turned, and slept again. I saw the staircase in the great Hall, and dreamed that Jack had come back. He stood at the top, waiting for me to come up to him. As I climbed the stairs, he backed under the archway of the minstrel's gallery, and disappeared. I looked for him, but I could not find him. Then suddenly he lunged at me from out of the shadows, trying to push me down the stone steps.

I cried out, and my skin prickled with horror as I sat straight up in bed. His white face haunted me. My teeth were chattering. I groped for Peter.

"I'm scared," I gasped, although the sound was more like a sob. "Please, hold me."

The bedclothes were thrown back, and his arm pulled me beside him. His body turned to accommodate me, his warmth and scent at once enclosing me, comforting me. He held my face against his breast, his chin pressing into my hair. "Yes," he said. "It's all right. I'm here."

The skin of his chest was smooth and hairless, and his heart beat with a slow, steady thud beneath my cheek. I liked the feeling of it. It was so strong and reassuring. It would go on forever. Gradually I stopped shivering. The fire cast enough light for me to see his face clearly.

I cupped my hand against his cheek. He promptly caught it in his grasp and brought it to his lips, pressing a soft kiss on my palm.

"Peter, I think I love you," I whispered.

He looked pleased as he entwined his fingers in mine. He raised his eyebrows and looked at me inquiringly. "You only think?" he smiled. "Marry me now, Jen. Nothing stands in our way."

Heat suffused my face at the warmth in his voice, the expression in his eyes. It swept through me, to settle in parts of my body I hadn't realized could feel such yearning. My heart thumped wildly.

"You can't still mean it," I said. I shook my head and tried to pull free of his grasp, but he continued to hold me, with his hand and with his gaze.

"Look at me!" I gestured toward my stomach. "I am huge with another man's baby!"

His eyes, so much more obviously tender in the firelight, met mine. "You are beautiful, Jen. The baby even makes you more so." He brought my hand to his lips once again, then loosed his hold. "If you marry me now, I would be proud to call the child my own. Son or daughter, it doesn't matter. It will be our child."

My heart was jumping again, but this time not in alarm, or fear. "No one would believe it."

"It doesn't matter. I would challenge anyone who would tell me differently."

"Your parents? If it's a son, you can't think they'd accept him as heir to Hayvenhurst."

"It doesn't matter to me."

He kept his arms looped loosely around me, and refused to let me go.

I knew Peter to be exceptionally considerate, decent and caring. The best gift I could give my child was a father who would care for and protect him, honor his responsibilities, and honor me. I knew in my mind, my heart, and my soul, that Peter was that man. I loved him for his character, his humor, his quiet strength. He knew my situation, and my past, yet he still wanted to marry me. And I wanted him, too, with a desire that should have shamed me, I thought with a wry smile. I couldn't have found a better man if I had conjured him up myself. I met his gaze, and looked deep into the silver-blue depths, and saw nothing but good in him. A peace came over me, and a certainty filled me. *How could I deny any longer what I knew was right?*

He was staring at my face, watching my expression, my eyes. He gave a sigh of relief. "You will marry me."

I nodded, and his eyes held so much emotion, I could not mistake it.

"I want you, Jen, I want to be married to you--not because of the baby, or Jack, or anything else. Only for you. I love you, Jen."

My heart thundered in my chest as he held me close. I savored his words, his nearness--it was so much more than I'd ever hoped to have in my life. I slid my hand up, running my fingers over his cheek.

"I want to marry you, too. Our lives begin now. The past doesn't exist. Are you sure you want me?" I said with a shy, beaming smile.

He laughed. "You know that I do."

It was strange how the pretty bedroom did not seem so cold and frightening now. It was warm, and alive, and there was a closeness I'd never felt with anyone else before. I was filled with a great sense of contentment, and I rested my head against his shoulder. I felt his arms tuck in about me, and I knew that I stood at the center of his world.

It left me with a deep feeling of peace, and suddenly I felt as though someone briefly embraced us, a soft hand touched my hair. I nestled deeper into the curve of Peter's body, and fell asleep, wrapped in his arms.

* * * *

The sun slanted across my eyes, waking me to the sounds of birdsong. The happenings of the day before seemed remote, unreal to me. Yet yesterday had happened. The past had happened. I had relived it last night. And Peter had listened to my story, and gone there with me, a shadow in my tracks. He, too, had suffered my pain along side of me. I had remembered it all as I sat there on the sofa, unmoved and detached. But now, with the dawning of a new day, and the knowledge that Peter and I could be together, my two selves merged, and became one. I was the self that I had always been, I was not changed. But something new had come upon me that had not been there before. My heart, for all its anxiety and doubt, was light and free. I was no longer afraid.

I was free now to be with Peter, to touch him, to hold him, to love him. We would share our lives together.

But there still remained one last thing I must do before we left this place of remembrances, of beginnings and endings.

* * * *

"You know what I must do," I said to Peter over breakfast.

He took a sip of his coffee, then set the cup on the table. He nodded, and took my hand. "How do you plan to do it?"

"The guide said that Meg had been seen down on the beach, where she died. Perhaps I can find her there."

"Let me go with you."

"No." I smiled at his wounded look. "Not because I don't want you to. She may not come to me if you're there."

He sighed, resigned.

"You can come with me as far as the path that leads from Ravana down to the beach. But no further. All right?"

* * * *

The sky was now sullen and overcast, so changed from early this morning, as we wound our way toward the path that led down to the beach. I held Peter's hand, but we did not speak. Pink and white flowers bordered the walkway, with sodden petals at our feet, bearing their scent upon them still. And there was a richer, older scent as well. The smell of deep moss and bitter earth, of bracken and salty air. The roar of the ocean filled our ears. Soon we came to the end of the walk, and we were standing on the slope of the cliffs overlooking the sea, where the flowers formed an archway above our heads. We bent down, passing underneath, and when we stood straight again, I could hear the waves breaking on the shore below us. I hesitated, looking down from our rock.

"Be careful," he told me, and kissed my cheek.

I scrambled down the rocky path, towards the mouth of the cove, where the waves were breaking upon the shore. Great jagged boulders hid the view, and I slipped and stumbled over the wet rocks, making my way as best I could.

I came up beside the big boulder that had hidden the view, and looked beyond it. And I saw, to my surprise, that I was looking down into another cove, similar to the one on my left, but wider and more rounded. The bay formed a tiny, natural harbor. The seabirds were circling over the sea, where the waves ran lightly onto the sand. I climbed over the rocks to the beach below.

The beach in the cove was white shingle. It was steep, and shelved into the sea. A tangle of seaweed marked the high water, encroaching almost to the rocks themselves.

I looked back over my shoulder at Peter. He looked down on me from above, a solitary figure against the backdrop of the sky. He stood with his hands in his pockets, the collar of his coat turned up around his ears. I saw him nod his head at me.

I turned and looked around me again, and my feet made a crunching noise as I walked across the shingle. My heart began to beat a little faster, and I was beginning to feel a little fearful, a little afraid. I had an odd, uneasy feeling that I might come upon something unawares, that I had no wish to see. Something that might be horrible. It was nonsense, of course. And so I continued across the white beach.

Driftwood floated on the waves, and the tide had turned, and came lapping up into the bay. The small rocks were covered, and the seaweed washed on the stones. Sea spray floated on the breeze, wetting my cheeks. I wiped the hair out of my eyes, and looked anxiously toward the mouth of the cove, where the waves were breaking upon the rocks.

And there she stood. Not a "gore-dappled ghost," as the guide had mentioned on the day before, but a beautiful lady, all bright and light, her long auburn hair floating softly below her shoulders, and across her arms. She was trembling as she came toward me eagerly. "How long I have waited for you!" she said, her expression full of passionate tenderness.

I was drawn to her, my heart overflowing with such a longing to comfort and to help. Deep called unto deep. I reached into the pocket of my coat, my fingers closing around my grandmother's brooch, and drew it out.

The apparition looked at me with the absolute certainty of joy, as I opened my hand and held the brooch out to her. She reached for it, but her fingers passed through mine like a breath of wind.

Her face betrayed a hint of mixed pain and longing, and my heart beat fiercely against my breast. *How would I give her this thing which she desired most from me?* And then I remembered the secret place hidden in the rocks of the hearth back in our room. *Hadn't Richard shown me where to put the brooch after all?* My heart leapt in anticipation.

I looked at the ghost anxiously. "Meggie," I whispered, falling back into the fondness we had once held for each other. "You can be wherever the brooch is, am I right?"

She looked up at me and nodded. "There is a hidden space in the fireplace in Richard's room. I will leave it there, where it will never be disturbed. No one will ever find it there, and it will be safe. And you and Richard can be together."

Her eyes held such thankfulness, as she reached up to touch my face. Again, I felt the wind touch my cheek.

With one last look, I turned back toward the cliffs. I went back across the shingle and saw Peter waiting for me by the rocks. The climb up from the beach was steep, and Peter met me halfway, to lend his hand. My legs ached, after the unaccustomed scramble over the rocks.

"Did you see her?" I asked him breathlessly.

"No," he answered me. "But I know that you did. You still have the brooch?"

"Yes, I couldn't give it to her," I panted, as we stood under the flowery arch overlooking the beach. I could still see Meg standing there, her hand raised to me in a hopeful gesture. "We must leave it here, in the hiding place in the fireplace. No one will ever find it there, and Meg and Richard will finally be together."

* * * *

Back in our room, I wrapped the brooch in Peter's handkerchief, while Peter removed the stone from the fireplace. Together we placed it inside the hole, and sealed it up once more.

Peter held out his arms to me, and I came to him like a child. This part of my life was over now, as well. There will be no more hauntings. And the hurt feelings of the past are no more. Richard and Meg could at last be together, and I had found my love at last.

I put my arms around Peter, and he held me and comforted me.

* * * *

That night they came to me, in my dreams. I saw them, Richard and Meg, standing at the foot of our bed with their arms around each other's waists.

How my heart filled with love for them! And how infinite are the boundaries of our love, twining in and out of hope and memory.

Richard smiled at me, and said, "May your life be blessed with joy and peace, love and pleasure."

"And you, too," I whispered, for these things are the very essence of every man's life and soul.

CHAPTER SIXTY-THREE

Peter and I were married two weeks later in a civil ceremony, with our families and close friends around us. After a brief honeymoon in Cornwall, we returned home to spend a night with my parents, in my grandmother's house.

I don't know what woke me that night. It wasn't a sound, for when I opened my eyes, I heard nothing. The room was dark, but enough moonlight filtered in through the curtains, that I was able to look about. But I saw nothing unusual or different in the room where I had grown up. I turned to Peter, hearing his soft, even breathing beside me. Everything was as it should be, and I snuggled back down into the covers. My eyes began to close again. But in the next moment, I sat upright, clutching the covers close to me.

Standing at the foot of my bed was Meg, dressed as I had seen her last. She looked at me and smiled, a gentle smile.

"Oh no," I groaned. My breath puffed out in front of me. "I had hoped our business was done." I began to shiver from the cold pillar of her presence.

She nodded, then turned away from the bed and walked toward the door. At the door she paused, and motioned for me to follow her. Then she slid through the door and disappeared.

I sat paralyzed where I was. I had no intention of moving. In fact, I thought, I might never leave this bed again.

I was still shaking when she reappeared at the foot of the bed. The smile had left her face, and she looked a bit sad that I had not gone with her. She motioned once again for me to follow her.

I shook my head no. I had had enough of ghosts, and I was not going to go with her. A soft, patient look crossed her features.

"What do you want now?" I managed to ask. "You have the brooch."

Her face took on a pleading look. She held out both her hands and gestured once again for me to come with her.

I shook my head again. "No," I whispered. "I don't want to go with you."

"Follow me," she said simply.

"No!" I whispered urgently. "I will not!"

Suddenly I remembered Peter beside me, and glanced down to see if I had awakened him. He slept peacefully, softly snoring into the pillow.

"What do you want?" I asked the ghost, a bit quieter this time. "Do you want to tell me something?"

At that, Meg looked around the room, as if searching for something.

"Do you want to show me something?"

She nodded, and her face showed relief at my understanding.

I leaned back against my pillows and closed my eyes. *Why me?* I couldn't help thinking. *Why don't these ghosts just leave me alone, and let me get on with my own life?* I opened my eyes, and saw that she was still there, patiently waiting for me. I sighed. It was pointless to agonize over it. For some reason I had been chosen.

Slowly I got out of bed, carefully, so as not to wake Peter. I grabbed my robe and pulled it around me. It was, perhaps, better to know, than not to know.

At last, I turned and looked at Meg, who was still waiting for me. I took a deep breath. "I am ready."

Meg nodded, then slipped through the door. I quietly opened it, then looked out into the hall. My heart was pounding, my knees weak. There was no one about, and the nightlight from the hall bath cast enough light to see my way clearly. I tiptoed out of my room and into the hallway, following the ghostly shape as she floated ahead of me.

At last she stopped, and pointed to the attic door. It was so dark in this part of the house, that I could barely see my foot in front of me. If it had not been for the ghostly glow of the apparition, I could not have followed her.

"You want me to go into the attic?" I asked uneasily.

She nodded. I swallowed, my knees giving way under me. *What if there were rats?* I shuddered. Meg reached out as though to touch me, but her hand slipped right through my arm. She looked annoyed.

"Okay, okay," I sighed. I opened the trapdoor and pulled the ladder down. With one arm in front of the other, I climbed into the attic. Trembling, I stood up and glanced around. It was incredibly dark. I had another unpleasant thought. *What of cobwebs...spiders...was it possible for bats to get into an attic?*

Meg brought an eerie glow into the room, which I welcomed heartily. Everything was quiet, covered with a thick blanket of dust, as I looked around. There were boxes, an old pedal driven sewing machine, a pedestal dress form, discarded toys from my childhood, an old mirror leaning against the wall, and at the far end, was an old, carved cradle. I walked over to it and gently ran my hand over it. I took a deep breath and turned to the ghost. "Is this what you brought me here for?"

The ghost shook her head, although she cast a wistful look toward the cradle. Then she glided toward a little alcove beneath the big, round window. She put out her hand, and I saw an old, battered trunk tucked away into the shadows. I stepped closer. From the look of it, and from the cloud of dust that rose when I touched it, it was obvious that it had been there a very long time. It was small, and would have been easy to overlook. Its battered leather cover seemed to blend into the wall. But when I tried to open it, I found that it was locked.

There were no identifying marks on the trunk, no initials, no name. I played with the lock. Some of the very old leather flaked off. The covering was extremely fragile, but the trunk itself was not.

I turned back to the ghost. "I can't open it."

At that she seemed to panic. She seemed to think for a moment, then went to one of the boxes beside the old sewing machine, and pointed. I went over to it and opened the box. It was filled with yarn, and an assortment of all sizes of knitting needles. I reached in and held up one of the smallest needles.

"You want me to use a knitting needle to pry open the lock on the chest?"

Meg smiled back weakly, and shrugged, as if to say, "It's worth a try."

The smile was so human, that I was touched. I smiled back at her, then went back to the chest, and attempted to pick the lock. I was so intent on what I was doing, that I did not hear the approaching footsteps behind me.

"What, may I ask, are you doing?"

At the sound of Peter's voice, I nearly jumped out of my skin. I turned, my hand to my heart. "You scared me half to death! What do you mean, sneaking up on me like that?"

"Sneaking?" he asked, incredulous. "I woke up and you were gone. I've been out of my mind with worry, looking for you. What are you doing?"

He shined the torchlight that he held in his hand on the trunk.

"I was trying to open this lock," I said.

He looked at me through his lashes again, as if growing used to my strange behavior. He opened his mouth to say something, thought better of it, and closed it. He bent down, took the needle from my hand, and handed me the torchlight. He began to wrestle with the lock.

I took that moment to glance around the attic. My ghost was gone.

The lock suddenly gave way and fell open. The leather was dry and frail, and there were brass nail heads on it, and it was easy to believe that the trunk had been there as long as the house.

I touched the lid, and felt strangely breathless. I had no idea what to expect that I would find: *money, jewels, treasure, papers, maps...a small dried skull...ha, ha...*but my heart was pounding as I lifted the lid. I almost believed that I heard the rustle of my ghost's dress by my side as I did.

A wave of disappointment washed over me. A small, leather bound book lay atop some neatly folded, musty smelling clothes. I picked up the book, and handed the torchlight back to Peter. He sat back on his haunches and watched me curiously. I turned the book over in my hands, examining it. I suspected the leather might once have been red, but it was faded to a dull brown now. I opened it, and glanced inside. On the very first page I read my grandmother's name, with the date 1939. I realized what it was then. Her diary. I turned another page, and my eyes grew wide as I began to read.

"She beckons to me once again. 'Hansel to me,' she implores, as if I understand her meaning. I don't know what to do. No one believes me..." a shiver ran through me.

Yes, I believe you, Grandma, I thought.

Meg had also haunted my grandmother. The brooch, handed down from generation to generation, was the cause. *Had the apparition haunted my whole family? Was this what the ghost had wanted me to find? Perhaps...perhaps not...*

Peter shifted his weight. "Jenny, can't this wait until morning? This place gives me the creeps. I'll carry the trunk downstairs so you can look through it in our room."

I smiled back at him. "Okay," I said. I closed the lid, and Peter handed me the light. He bent and lifted the chest. It was small enough that he carried it with little effort as far as the attic door. Then he slowly let himself down the ladder, balancing it on his shoulder, careful not to drop it, as I shone the light down the steps for him.

It fell with a thud to the floor in the hall when he was down, and then he turned to help me down through the trapdoor.

* * * *

Now the mystery would be solved. There was a box, resting between the layers of clothing. I drew it out and lifted the lid. Whatever lay in its recesses was wrapped carefully in tissue paper. I gently pulled the tissue paper aside. A shiver of excitement ran through me. For there, in the folds of tissue paper lay a carefully preserved baby's gown. The white satin had yellowed with time, but was not brittle to my touch. A tear rolled down my cheek as I tenderly lifted the garment from its resting place, for somehow, I knew exactly what this garment was, and who had made it. Meg had made it with careful, loving stitches for her baby's christening. It was her gift to me, for my child. My heart was beating fast as I lifted it carefully by the tiny shoulders. I gazed at it in awe. I was surprised to find the fabric still soft and luxurious. The tiny collar, sleeves and hem were trimmed in beautiful lace. Butterflies and daffodils on long, willowy stems had been lovingly embossed with white silken thread, with patient, even stitches. It was stunningly beautiful.

I looked up into the empty air and whispered, "Thank you."

EPILOGUE

"Come here, Emily."

Hands outstretched, Peter coaxed our daughter to her feet. He was seated on a blanket in our back garden, as I brought out a tray of cool drinks from the house. I held my breath as she wavered, gifting Peter with a grin that melted my heart.

"Da!"

Her hands waving wildly, she set out toward him, over the smooth grass, managing three steps before her legs gave out, and she landed on her diapered backside.

Her lips quivered. She glanced at Peter, then to me. Evidently, she decided that it wasn't worth the bother to cry, for she gave a trill of laughter, and was off on hands and knees toward her father.

Peter rose up to his knees and scooped her up into his arms, then dropped down on his back, settling her upon his chest.

The grass smelled fresh and sweet as I stepped onto it, and I closed my eyes a moment, and felt the warmth of the sun on my face. The child I carried beneath my heart chose that moment to kick me hard, bringing a smile to my lips, and a hand to my rounded belly. I had reached the blanket, and I knelt down beside them.

"I'm afraid this one definitely has your feet."

Peter shifted and sat up, cradling Emily upon his shoulder. "You think so? Let me see." he asked, gently resting his free hand over the swell of my stomach. There was a strong kick beneath his palm. He nodded, satisfied. "You'll be needing help with this one, too."

"Yes. I need you." I put my hand on his shoulder and drew him close, pressing a soft kiss on his cheek. "Always."

His gentle smile wrapped itself around my heart and sent it soaring. *After years, lifetimes, of darkness, how had I finally found this light, this joy? My present--my past--my future--were all right here beside me. Peter had given me love and contentment, passion and pleasure.* Smiling, I held my joy close to my heart, and savored the life we had made together.

One never knows what we will find at the end of our journey.
The future is unknown to us. But I have learned that every moment is
a precious thing. And I face my future with glad anticipation.

I thought again of Ravana, with the first struggles of the pale sun coming through the mists, and over the walls. The smoke curling from the chimneys, and little by little the mists fading away, and the trees and gardens taking shape. The glimmer of the sea showing with the sun upon it. Ravana is at peace now. There is quietude and grace, and a certain comfort emanates from its ancient walls. Whoever has lived within its walls, whatever troubles and strife they have known, however much uneasiness and pain, no matter what tears were shed, what sorrow borne, the peace of Ravana would not be destroyed. The flowers that died would bloom again yet another year, the same birds would build their nests, the same trees blossom. That old quiet moss smell would linger in the air. The bees would come, and the butterflies would dance their merry jig across the garden flowers. There would be lilac and honeysuckle still, and the white gardenia buds unfolding slow and tight beneath the misty fountains. No one would ever hurt Ravana. It would lie always in its place like an enchanted thing, guarded by the woods, safe and secure, while the sea broke and ran and crashed again, against the rocks below.